F100

"Do You Understand, Huh?"

A POW's Lament, 1941-1945

"Do You Understand, Huh?"

A POW's Lament, 1941-1945

Theodore A. Abraham, Jr.

Sunflower University Press®
1531 Yuma (Box 1009), Manhattan, Kansas 66502-4228, USA

ISBN 0-89745-143-0

Layout by Lori L. Daniel

This book is dedicated to my wife, Jean,
for her loyal support to see this story published.

Contents

Preface

The following story is based on a diary which I kept while a prisoner of war. Even though most of the events that I have written about are true, I have elected to portray them as fiction in order to express my personal views and not embarrass any of the prisoners.

I have taken on the character of Charlie Alexander throughout the story. Other names of prisoners are fictitious.

The story begins with my positions on Wake Island and my activity during the war, which led up to my captivity.

Chapter 1

It was 2 August 1941. I and a small group of construction workers had gathered on the bow of the supply ship USS *Burrows*. With mixed emotion and excitement our eyes searched the horizon for the Wake Island atoll. For most of us, in our early twenties, it was our first time away from home. Our anticipation of what to expect when we would arrive was somewhat sketchy. I had been working in Los Angeles for a year after graduating from Woodbury College. When I notified their placement office that I would be interested in different work, they suggested that I take my vacation and when I returned they would have a new job. It turned out to be work as a medical secretary on Wake Island. "A marvelous opportunity!" they told me. When I asked where Wake Island was, they pointed to a map on a wall. The small speck on the map was barely visible to the naked eye, a tiny island in the Pacific, 5,000 miles from the United States.

We were told to travel light and bring very little summer clothing, as things mildew in the tropical climate. Others had arrived as early as 9 January 1941 to begin the construction of a naval facility.

The small ship pitched up and down and rolled with the ocean swells, making it more difficult to view the tiny atoll. Finally, there was shouting and pointing of fingers as a white dot appeared in the distance. It glistened under a bright morning sun, and grew in size as the ship approached, but it wasn't until the freighter anchored offshore beyond the encircling coral reef that its size was evident. The island barely protruded twenty-one feet above the water at its highest elevation, and any tropical storm could send water rushing over its three and one-half square miles. There were two smaller islands located at either end of Wake. The horseshoe-shaped group, with the coral reefs and pure white sand, created a shallow lagoon whose rich, emerald-green water was beautiful. The depth of the adjacent waters dropped off sharply and became deep dark blue. The three islands had been created by the eruption of a volcano. The shallow lagoon was the crater portion, and the islands were the outer rims. The soil was mostly crushed coral rock.

Several days prior to reaching Wake, blackouts had been ordered aboard ship, indicating perhaps that trouble was imminent.

I gazed down on the men as they stepped into a motor launch to take them ashore. Fresh out of college, I was tall and slender at that time; my colorful short-sleeved shirt rippled in the warm summer breeze. Shading the glare from my eyeglasses with my right hand, I awaited my turn to enter the launch. The tropical climate appealed to me. I had lived in southern California where temperatures were relatively mild, though here, no coconut palm trees or lush green undergrowth could be seen anywhere, only a low growing bramble bush or ironwood scattered across a sandy coral atoll. Its desolate appearance had induced many men to remain aboard ship and return to the mainland.

The motor launch turned into a narrow channel which had been dredged between Wake and Wilkes Islands and headed for a small wooden landing that had been built to receive men and supplies. Several trucks were standing by to transport the men about three miles down a narrow dusty road to the main construction office.

On the dock, waiting to greet us, was the general superintendent, Hugh McGinis, and his secretary, Bob Wilder, both in khaki shirts and pants. McGinis wore a white straw hat, tilted slightly down in front. Bob was bare-headed, revealing a thick crop of straight black hair neatly combed back. A cigar butt was wedged in the corner of his mouth. He was short and stocky, with a dark complexion, in his late twenties.

"Welcome aboard!" shouted McGinis in a loud gravelly sounding voice. A broad smile broke across his suntanned face as he nervously strutted around waving his arms freely. Middle-aged, medium built, handsome, and scholarly in appearance, he directed us to the waiting trucks.

Standing in the back of a pick-up enabled us to get a bird's-eye view of the island because of its very low elevation. Everyone was amazed at its tiny size and desolation. Without a beach or even a single shade tree, it was anything but a tropical paradise.

I arrived at the construction office and was told to report to Dr. Thomas Buford at the hospital, a small wooden building set back about a hundred yards from the pounding surf, but only a short distance from the other buildings. The wind had swept the white sand neatly against the structure's foundation.

The screen door of the hospital flew open, and I watched a figure clad in a long white gown run barefooted over the hot white sand toward the ocean and coral reef. The cool sea breeze filled the gown like a balloon, as it flipped over his head. Running desperately across the loose sand to catch him before he reached the water, a nurse began shouting, "Hey, Travis, wait a minute!"

The louder he shouted, the faster Travis ran, sand flying. As he turned to look back, he fell and slid on his side. The loose gown gathered around his waist, exposing his hairy limbs and knotty knees. He quickly rose and continued toward the surf as the nurse closed in on him. Plunging in head first, he hit Travis around the ankles, sending him crashing to the sand.

"You're okay, you're okay," the nurse repeated, brushing the sand out of his face.

"Leave me go — leave me go!" Travis shouted. He kept striking the nurse with his clenched fist across his back.

"The doc says you're going to be okay. Do you hear me? He says you're going to be okay," continued the nurse.

"Did he say I'd be all right?" stammered Travis, spitting sand from his mouth and brushing the sand from his hair.

"Everything is going to be all right now," the nurse said. His muscles began to relax as he released his grip on Travis, and they rose and walked slowly toward the hospital.

The nurse stopped to catch his breath and saw me. "Hello there. You must be the medical secretary we've been expecting."

"Yes. I'm Charlie Alexander." As I extended my hand, the patient appeared frightened and moved away, clinging to his wrinkled white gown.

"Welcome aboard, Charlie. I'm Sammy Ball, one of the nurses. Come on in and meet Dr. Buford and the staff."

After greeting the entire staff of six male nurses and Dr. Thomas Buford, the doctor took me on a tour of the hospital. There were eight double-bed rooms, which faced a wide screened-in hallway that could accommodate several more patients in an emergency. A small, moderately furnished operating room and combination clinic and dispensary for out-patients were also available. We walked to the doctor's office, which occupied one corner of the building.

In his early thirties, Dr. Buford hailed from San Francisco, where his father was also a physician. He was single, of medium build, with dark thin hair, blue eyes, and a fair complexion — very professional and soft spoken.

As he pointed out my desk, he began to systematically and slowly enumerate the duties of the job — maintain all hospital records and take case-history dictation. He shook my hand, wished me well, and started to leave, then he stopped and turned around, shaking his head.

"There is one other job that you must do. We have to report all industrial accidents to the insurance company. This requires interviewing the patients and filling out the forms in the filing cabinet over there," he said, pointing to one in the far corner of the room. He hesitated a moment as he gazed out the window.

"Oh, yes. We're in the process of doubling the hospital's capacity. In about three months, we should be finished with the building program around November 1st. One other thing — the food situation — you will be eating at the general mess in the main camp. The food for our patients is delivered here. I hope I've covered most things you need to know. Any questions?"

I thought for a moment. "I don't think so, but I'm sure I'll have some later."

The next four months passed quietly, except for a hurricane alert at two in the morning in early October. Everyone was rousted from their barracks and into trucks to be taken to permanent buildings on Peale Island. Fortunately, it passed us by. In mid-November 1941, a small group of some four hundred and fifty U.S. Marines and a handful of Navy personnel arrived on the island. At the same time, Dr. Louis Shay arrived to replace Dr. Buford, who returned to the Hawaiian Islands. Short and stocky, with crew-cut hair and pointed features, Shay had a marvelous personality.

Our living quarters were screened-in, wooden barracks, nothing fancy but livable. Because the only fresh water supply was rain water caught in large open cisterns, it was used sparingly. Consequently, there were salt water showers with a bucket of fresh water for a rinse.

The walk from the barracks to my office was only a short distance. As I approached the hospital a little before 8:00 Monday morning, 8 December 1941, Dr. Shay, Sammy Ball, and Milton DeWitt were standing outside the entrance, looking toward the ocean.

"Good morning. What's the attraction?" I asked. The surf appeared calm, the sky sunny and clear, except for a few scattered clouds.

"The Japs bombed Pearl Harbor," Dr. Shay said, nodding his head as if pointing to it. His face was pale and drawn.

I was stunned. It seemed unbelievable.

"The Japs struck this morning at 7:30, which would be Sunday morning in Honolulu. It seems incredible. We just received official word from Marine headquarters," continued the doctor as he kept staring at the horizon.

"It doesn't seem possible that a small nation like Japan would dare start a war against a nation as large as ours," said Sammy Ball, running his hand through his blond, curly hair. He was dressed in white cotton shorts and a loose-fitting yellow faded T-shirt; he had on low-cut tennis shoes with saggy socks.

"Aren't you from Hawaii, Milton?" I asked.

DeWitt nodded.

"My folks live in Honolulu; I sure hope they're all right." Milton DeWitt's personal appearance was always immaculate; he never wore shorts.

Inside, Dr. Shay ordered all personnel to remain at the hospital in case of attack. Everyone returned to their jobs inside the tiny building, which was full of patients, except for the new unfurnished wing, the X-ray room, and the kitchen. At the time, the civilian population of Wake Island was eleven hundred and fifty.

Things remained normal until 11:55 that morning when a loud explosion was heard. Peering out the office window, I saw huge billows of black smoke and flame rising in the direction of the Marine camp and the airstrip. I ran outside with Dr. Shay and Sammy Ball, and we watched twenty-seven two-engine Japanese bombers come gliding into the island out of a cloud bank at a very low altitude. Their motors had been cut to prevent early detection. We watched for a few moments until one group headed toward us.

"Inside!" shouted Dr. Shay, looking back over his shoulder as he ran for the hospital screen door. The drone of planes drew closer and the hollow popping sound of machine-gun fire ripping into the earth grew louder. It was a frightening, sickening sound.

We all scattered and took cover inside. I ran into the small clinic. On one wall facing the outside window was a wash basin underneath which I tried to stick my head. My immediate thought was to not get struck in the head. I didn't think about the rest of my body. As the roar of the Japanese planes and the loud frightening sound of falling bombs and machine-gun fire began to subside, a single enemy plane circled by the hospital, so low that the Japanese pilot was visible.

The planes left quickly, however, and a stream of wounded men began to pour into the slightly damaged hospital. Some arrived by truck and on foot; others were carried piggy-back. The beds were full of regular patients and rearrangements had to be made at once to accommodate the wounded. Dr. Shay ordered me to take the station wagon over to Peale Island, about two miles away, to pick up as many cots and mattresses as I could find in one of the permanent warehouses. Weaving in and out around the bomb craters, with one eye on the road and the other surveying the damage, I reached the narrow wooden bridge connecting Wake and Peale and sped toward the warehouse. I could see fires around the island, with flames reaching sixty feet; men were moving about in a dazed condition. The birds of the islands were flying recklessly in every direction, screeching violently. The air was heavy with the fragrance of burning fuel.

The large concrete warehouse, one of Peale Island's permanent buildings, was partially damaged. I quickly loaded the station wagon with cots and mattresses. I had made four such trips between the hospital and warehouse when I was confronted by a Marine officer.

"Hey, you can't go in there," he yelled, waving his arms frantically. As he came running toward me, he kept repeating himself.

I stopped and turned. His fiery dark eyes trembled behind a face streaked with sweat and dust.

"Why, I've been in there several times," I said, stepping back, awaiting his explanation.

"There's a dud bomb inside. No one's permitted inside until it's checked out," he stammered as he turned and walked around the building.

As I got back into the station wagon to return to the hospital at 1:30 p.m., the Pan American clipper took off for Honolulu with a full load of passengers, primarily their employees and other officials. It had arrived the day before and was tied up at the pier near the Pan American hotel, which was completely demolished with many casualties. The aircraft, however, had escaped unharmed.

A crew of civilians had helped set up the cots and mattresses in the new unoccupied wing, in the hallways, and in the nearby barracks. Dr. Shay and Dr. Kane immediately went to work operating, trying to save the most urgent cases first. The nurses cared for some of the minor casualties and worked continuously throughout the night without a break until early morning. Those who didn't survive were identified and placed in a refrigeration box at the civilian camp next to the galley, until burial arrangements could be made. The halls and rooms were covered with casualties — more than the staff could attend. The doctors and nurses couldn't possibly give relief to everyone immediately. Throughout the night, the continual roar of the surf was heard above the deep breathing of the wounded, while inside, the odious aroma of burned flesh and blood-soaked clothing was stifling.

Early the next morning, I made my way among the strained faces of the wounded that cluttered the two hallways. Some of the casualties were fortunate enough to lie on cots or mattresses, but others were on the wooden floor. The nurses were moving slowly among the survivors after the long night, everyone hoping the Japanese wouldn't return that day so that they might get an hour or two of rest.

"Good morning. How are you doing?" I asked one of the wounded, as I ran my hand through my uncombed hair. My summer clothing was wrinkled from sleeping in it, off and on, during the night. The multitude of wounded was made up of a mixture of military and civilian personnel.

"I'm okay, I guess," the young man answered. "The doc said I was going to live, for now anyway."

His suntanned face had become drawn as his pale blue eyes kept gazing at the note pad I was carrying.

"My name is Charlie Alexander. I'm here to gather information for the hospital records," I said. As I spoke, I thought he was one of the lucky ones who made it past the operating table.

"Oh, I understand," he whispered. A smile broke across his face.

"What I need to know is your name, status, nature of wound, and location of same." Looking into his beardless round face, I thought this kid couldn't be more than eighteen.

"My name is Robert Childs. My buddies call me Rob. I'm a U.S. Marine. A piece of shrapnel hit me in the top of my right leg. I lost a lot of blood before they could get it sewed up. The doctor gave me some blood and said I could return to my group in a couple weeks." His face seemed to light up with the thought of returning to his buddies. He kept rubbing his dog tag, which hung around his neck.

"That's fine. You take care of yourself and good luck," I said. He smiled and nodded his head as I moved on to the next patient. I hardly had to move; the wounded were packed in so tight.

"Good morning, how you doing?" I asked.

"Not too good. I've got a headache and I'm dying for a smoke." He appeared middle-aged with graying hair and had a thin ashen face and a bandage near the center of his forehead.

"Maybe I can get one from one of the nurses here," I said as I turned around and stopped Sammy Ball who was passing by.

"Thank you," he said, sitting up quickly. He nervously reached for the cigarette and waited patiently for a light.

"I guess you know the information I need from you."

"Yes. I heard you talking to the Marine. My name is William Hawkins, but everyone calls me Willie, and I'm a civilian construction worker. Surveyor by trade. I had taken cover in the warehouse when I was struck in the forehead by a piece of shrapnel or a shell that pierced the building." He hesitated frequently to puff on his cigarette and coughed constantly.

"Did the doctor say there was any damage to the brain?"

"None at all. He said I was lucky — that I will be able to leave in a day or two. He said it would be safer for me elsewhere. What did he mean by that?" His voice had become louder as his head turned slightly to hear my response.

"I think that he was referring to the fact that the Japanese had strafed the hospital."

In fact, several patients had been killed.

"Don't you have a red cross painted on the roof?" he responded, shaken by the thought of being machine-gunned in bed.

"We did, but Dr. Shay ordered it removed. He felt that the Japanese wouldn't honor it. Maybe they'd single it out as a primary target."

"He's probably right. I just need to get the hell out of here." Hawkins nodded his head slightly, put out his cigarette, and turned on his side.

"Good luck, Willie, and get well soon," I said as I moved on. It took most of the forenoon to interview all the patients. Their morale was good under bleak conditions.

The aftermath of the first day of war left a frightening and sickening feeling inside, as I observed the wounded. They were brave. But would they survive to continue to fight the Japanese? They were eager and seemed to realize that their freedom was in jeopardy.

Inside the doctor's office, which had been partially damaged by the attack the day before, Dr. Shay and Dr. Kane were reviewing the results of their all-night surgery. They were exhausted and were discussing still another raid by the Japanese this day. Would it be around noon or later in the afternoon? I entered with note pad in hand, heading for the desk, but stopped short and pointed at Henry Perkins curled up on the floor.

"Is he all right?"

"Yes," said Dr. Kane as he sipped his coffee. "He's just dead tired. He's one of my corpsmen that assisted all night after working in the field during the afternoon."

"Charlie, were you able to contact all the wounded?" asked Dr. Shay, in a voice weak from fatigue.

"Yes."

"How was their morale; did they appear in a lot of pain?"

"I'd say morale was good; some complained of pain, but most were grateful to be alive. I'll be going to the back room in a minute to see if there are any ID tags on the dead pilots and the Chamorro boys from the Pan American hotel." I wasn't looking forward to it.

"Good luck," they both said, as they rose and left the office.

The aroma of fresh coffee caused me to look up; I saw DeWitt standing in the doorway.

"Would you like a cup? That's all I can offer you," he said. We weren't allowed alcoholic beverages on the island.

DeWitt's face was strained and pale from working all night, but he still managed a smile. His dark hair, eyes, and neatly trimmed mustache complemented his Hawaiian olive complexion.

He brought me a steaming hot cup of coffee, which he set before me, then turned around and sat at Dr. Shay's desk.

"Thanks, Milt," I said. "I know alcoholic beverages are off limits here, but I have to tell you about a trip four of us took to Peale Island in late September. One Sunday, we decided to walk over to the Pan American hotel just to see it. When we got there, we browsed around a bit and then sat down at a table. Pretty soon a waiter appeared and asked us if there was something we wanted, and Aubrey Stone spoke up quickly and said we'd like something to drink. Aubrey told the waiter that he was staying at the hotel and we were his guests. We ended up drinking two bottles of Pabst Blue Ribbon beer apiece."

"You got to be kidding," DeWitt said, shaking his head in disbelief.

"No, it really happened. The beer really tasted good. You'd have to meet Aubrey Stone to appreciate why the waiter didn't hesitate to believe he was a guest there. Aubrey's an eccentric old Englishman in his late fifties. What he was doing working on this island, we couldn't understand. He would never discuss his personal life but was very outspoken otherwise."

Aubrey was tall — skinny as a rail, with a shallow thin face, thinning gray hair, and clear blue eyes that sparkled behind wire-rimmed glasses. He was always clean and neat as a pin.

"He must've been a character. I wonder what's become of him?" DeWitt asked.

"I don't know, but I'll bet that he's out there somewhere cussing the hell out of the Japs. By the way, I watched some of the surgery last night; how did it go?" I asked. He looked haggard but I was sure some of it was brought about from worrying about his folks in Honolulu.

"Well, we lost several. The majority of the wounded we saved were taken to the barracks next door to make room for future casualties." He spoke slowly as he slumped backwards in the doctor's swivel chair, having a hard time keeping his eyes open, then he fell asleep.

I got up and headed down the hallway toward the storage room where the bodies of the Marine pilots and the Chamorro boys had been taken. Halfway, nurse John Parsons came dashing out of one of the eight double-bed rooms yelling at me.

"Hey, Charlie, have you heard if the Japs are coming back around noon today or later in the afternoon?"

In his late twenties, he was single, quite large, and had light-brown silky hair, pale blue eyes, and a fair complexion. He was very articulate. He stopped short in front of me nervously waving a thermometer.

"No, I haven't, John, but if I hear anything the next time I call the main office operator, you'll be the first to know," I said.

He nodded and turned to the wounded. Walking toward the back room, I tried to visualize what to expect. As I opened the door, I smelled the stifling odor of human flesh that had been burned and ripped apart by shrapnel and machine-gun bullets. Most of the bodies had been covered by canvas and blankets and had been arranged in neat rows. Bent over examining one of the fliers were two Marine officers.

I greeted them as I walked carefully toward the bodies. "I'm attached to the hospital. I need to get the names, status, and cause of death of these men."

One officer had removed a dog tag from a body, had wiped it off on his sleeve, and then held it up to the light. He read the name as the other officer wrote it down on a pad.

"We're here to identify our fliers that were killed yesterday attempting to get airborne."

I stepped closer to get a good look at their men. Their bodies resembled charred tree stumps. A horrible sight. The only comforting thing was that they never knew what hit them.

"What exactly happened?" I asked.

"After we got the news that the Japs had bombed Pearl Harbor, we went on alert and sent up four of our twelve Grumman fighters to scout around. When the Japs attacked us, our remaining eight pilots attempted to get airborne in the face of the enemy machine-gun fire and low-altitude bombs. It was hopeless. Their planes became fiery infernos. A tremendous loss. The four remaining planes returned, apparently without encountering the enemy."

The Marine officers returned to the difficult and distasteful task of searching for dog tags or any other identification.

Some of the Chamorro boys who worked at the Pan American hotel had various kinds of identification. A total body count was taken, noting those identified. I didn't spend any more time than necessary as the odor was stifling. Walking back to my office desk, I began to be frightened by this ugly business of war.

I had picked up the telephone and was putting in a call to the operator at the main office around 11:30 a.m. when the second raid began. I dropped the receiver, ran into the X-ray room, and dove under an occupied bed. The drone of distant planes and the dull sound of explosives grew louder. A moment later, the hospital took a direct hit and the floor felt like the bottom of a row boat on a rough lake. Before the roar of the engines had passed overhead, smoke, from the adjoining wing, started pouring in the window. The patient in the bed said, "Let's get the hell out of here," and he took off like a scared rabbit. Some three feet away, the floor had been splintered by machine-gun bullets.

The new wing of the hospital was now in flames and Dr. Shay gave orders to extinguish them, then realized that would be futile. We were told to carry all patients and medical supplies outside. The adjoining barracks, which had contained wounded men from the first day, also had burned to the ground. Several of these men, as well as some in the hospital, were killed by machine-gun fire and shrapnel.

While the flames quickly destroyed the hospital, Dr. Shay and Dr. Kane were dividing the patients and medical supplies into two groups. Shay assigned nurses John Parsons and Larry Smith and myself to help Dr. Kane and his corpsman Henry Perkins. Every available vehicle was used to move the surviving patients and supplies down along the beach some two miles, toward Peacock Point. Fifty feet off the road, and surrounded by thick bramble shrub and ironwood, which flourished throughout the island, we set up our new hospital unit — a large, empty munition magazine, cylindrically shaped and partially submerged. It took the better part of the afternoon to get moved into the new location.

At dusk, Perkins, Smith, and I took our panel truck to search for casualties. The island had been attacked around noon, and we felt sure that the Japs wouldn't be back until tomorrow. We didn't waste any time heading in the direction of Camp No. 2, with one of the corpsmen leaning out the window of the truck, searching the sky for possible enemy planes. Arriving at the machine shop, which was a complete shambles, we found our first body. He had sat down and wrapped his legs and arms around an upright pipe. The explosion of the bomb had stripped him of all his clothing except his shoes, and left his body unmarked, except for a rich tan. We stared at the body, then looked at each other, shaking our heads simultaneously.

"Did you ever see anything like that," said Henry Perkins as he crept a little closer and touched the man.

"No, it's incredible. There doesn't seem to be a scratch on his body," I whispered, viewing him from every angle.

"Let's get him off the pipe and get the hell out of here," shouted Smith, who was becoming very nervous as he kept looking for more victims.

Rigor mortis had set in and it took the two of us about five minutes to pull his arms and legs free of the pipe. We were able to locate three other victims in some of the barracks, which had been riddled by machine-gun fire. After depositing the bodies in a large refrigeration box, which was now filled nearly to capacity, we headed back along the deserted beach to our hospital unit. That evening two more casualties died and were taken out to the road, later to be placed in the refrigeration boxes.

Our hospital unit was set up and ready for future casualties when the third attack occurred around 11:00 a.m. on 10 December, targeting the entire island in general. The hospital had a heavy metal door, which was kept slightly open most of the time for fresh air and light. A small generator provided the lighting for operations and night light. A field phone was installed with direct communications to the command post located in the third munition magazine. The windowless cement structure created a fear of being buried alive with every bombing raid. Dr. Kane scheduled the four of us to work in pairs, looking after the patients. The shifts were four hours on and four hours off, around the clock. Food was brought in once a day from the civilian galley, two miles away, when the coast was clear. The munition magazine was roughly 70 feet long, 30 feet wide, and about 12 feet high in the center, which made it impossible to place the cots against the two walls. The operating table was located toward the front, adjacent to the door. All hospital records were kept in my portable typewriter case. The two hospital units were camouflaged with dirt and paint.

In the early morning hours of 11 December, Corpsman Perkins had stepped outside for a breath of fresh air. It wasn't long before he came running back into our hospital shouting, "Ships! Lots of ships on the horizon. There must be at least a dozen!"

Dr. Kane quickly rolled out of his cot and approached Perkins, who had sat down, shaken by what he saw.

"Are you sure?" he asked.

"Yes, Doc, and they don't appear very far away," he said.

"I wonder why we haven't fired at them?" Dr. Kane asked. His face became ashen. "They surely are attempting to put a landing party ashore." He became nervous as he fumbled, getting dressed.

"I don't know what they're waiting for," said Perkins.

The entire hospital was soon aware that the Japanese were about to try a landing on the island. A short time later, the shelling of the Japanese ships and the island began. Between rounds, you could hear a pin drop as we waited for the blasts to continue. We held our breath and prayed when we heard the whistling of the shells and were relieved when they didn't hit the hospital.

During the attack some of the patients asked if the Japanese took prisoners of war. Some said they never had in the past, while others said they wouldn't dare slaughter everyone because of the consequenses they would suffer afterwards. Fear permeated the darkened cement room.

The shelling soon subsided, and Dr. Kane quickly made his way between the rows of cots to the field phone to call Commander Richard Morley at the command post.

"Dick, this is Gus. What in the hell is going on out there? Are the Japs about to invade us?" His voice cracked, and he stroked his hair nervously.

It turned out that the Japanese had attempted a landing. They had several transports, destroyers, and light cruisers, and Commander Morley had given orders not to fire on them until they were well within range. When we opened up on them, we inflicted considerable damage, causing them to turn and run. Our fighter planes pursued, sinking two more ships. It was a great victory.

"But you can be sure that they will return," Morley said.

When Dr. Kane hung up, a smile broke across his face. He seemed relieved by the good news as he passed his telephone conversation on to the rest of us. Everyone shouted with joy. But it was not long before the Japanese planes came back, shortly before noon, at a high altitude and bombed the island again. While this was going on, nurse John Parsons had left the hospital to bathe in the ocean. He came staggering back, short of breath, wearing only his underwear and carrying the rest of this clothes, which he had washed. He did take time to slip on his wet tennis shoes; otherwise, his feet would have been raw from the hot, coarse sand and coral rock.

"I thought I'd never see you all again," he said. His face had become pale.

"What was it like out there without any cover?" Perkins asked half jokingly.

Parsons hesitated momentarily, as he took a deep breath and sat down. "You won't believe it!"

He stopped to collect his thoughts.

"I had just been enjoying the surf, cooling off and relaxing, you know. Then I had just started rinsing out some of my clothes when I thought I heard a bomb explode. Suddenly, there were more bombs exploding followed by the roar of airplane motors. I went under the water so they wouldn't see me. It sounded like they were flying directly over me. One bomb exploded fairly close, and sent a huge funnel of water over me." He stood up to describe his frightening experience during the raid.

By this time everyone had visualized his humorous but serious predicament and began joking with him about it and asking if he would be going bathing again.

"Hell, no! I'm not going outside again until this damn war is over. I hope those Japs got a picture of my nude body, maybe it would help end the war," he shouted, a little irritated with us. He gathered up his wet clothing and headed for his cot.

An early morning air attack took place around 5:15 on the 12th when Japanese patrol bombers came in at a high altitude, causing only slight damage. One four-motor bomber was reported shot down. Immediately after the raid, Commander Morley ordered a dragline operator and bulldozer to an isolated area of the island. A common grave was quickly scooped out and forty-four bodies, which had been stored in a refrigeration unit, were placed in it and covered over by the bulldozer. Several service and civilian personnel stood in silence as civilian lay preacher, Forrest Hill, from Silver Creek, Utah, eulogized the men.

The short religious man hesitated briefly before finishing, as he wiped his moist eyes. He stared at the common grave as everyone nervously squirmed and occasionally gazed at the sky. Finally, he raised his head and spoke slowly.

"Let us bow our heads and remember these fallen comrades in silent prayer."

The ceremony concluded, and we all went to our various positions on the island. Shortly after the service, Commander Morley gave the orders that all future casualties would be buried where found because of dwarf rats and hermit crabs that inhabited the islands.

The next day, the 13th, was quiet as the Japanese stayed away. But the following day they returned around 11:40 a.m.; their objectives were Peale and Wilkes Islands. Very little damage was reported.

The hospital was becoming congested with patients suffering diarrhea caused from eating uncooked canned foods and drinking too many canned juices. We also received our first shell-shock case, a nineteen-year-old Marine.

On that afternoon, Perkins and I drove our station wagon to Camp No. 2 warehouse for some paint to camouflage our hospital entrance.

"I'll drive, Henry; you just keep an eye on the sky just in case they return again today," I said, sliding into the front seat.

"Hell, they won't be back a second time surely. Will they?"

"I sure hope they don't, especially while we're traveling in this wagon."

"You listen for the drone of their motors. If you hear them before I see them, sing out. We'll need to get the hell out of this thing and head for the brush," whispered Perkins as a frightened look appeared on his round fleshy face.

On our return we approached three naval officers squatting on the side of the road.

"What in the hell do you think they're waiting for?" Perkins asked.

They appeared relaxed and engaged in conversation.

"Who knows? They must be waiting for someone to pick them up. Shall I slow down to see if they need a ride?" I asked as the dust from our vehicle blew in their direction.

As we approached, Perkins waved his arm and shouted, but they responded by nodding their heads negatively. We shook our heads in disbelief and returned to our hospital unit.

Besides several civilians participating in the fighting alongside the Marines, there were between four and five hundred civilians working each night moving the three-inch and five-inch guns because the Japanese were coming over daily after each bombing raid, photographing those positions.

On 16 December, the Japanese returned around 2:15 p.m., and the majority of their bombs fell into the lagoon. Our concrete windowless hospital was becoming claustrophobic. The distant drone of enemy planes created complete silence among the mass of frightened faces. You held your breath and prayed until the sound of planes and the exploding of the bombs faded. Then you relaxed until the next raid.

Shortly after the raid, I decided it would be safe to walk down to the other hospital unit to see if the proper records were being kept. The narrow coral road followed along the beach for about a mile. I had lit a cigarette and was nearly halfway there when a loud shout from the bushes stopped me.

"Put that damn cigarette out! The Japs can see it from the air!"

I turned around but wasn't able to see anyone. I put out the cigarette, but wondered how it could be seen during daylight.

Dr. Shay and his staff were glad to see me. Their unit had its share of casualties and only a few empty cots.

"I just stopped by to see if someone was keeping records," I said. Everyone appeared in good spirits under the circumstances.

"Milton is," Dr. Shay replied, a smile breaking across his tired face.

"Do you want to look at them, Charlie?" DeWitt asked, rising from a cot and walking toward me.

"No, that's not necessary."

"Have you got time for a cup of coffee?" Sammy Ball asked.

"Sure. Tell me how are things going," I said. Everyone grouped around the front metal door, which was half open, letting in some daylight.

"We were pretty busy the first two days, but now it's slowed down a bit. But we've had several shrapnel victims, and we're starting to get diarrhea patients." As Dr. Shay spoke, he glanced around his sparsely equipped unit.

"Charlie, what kind of patients are you getting?" asked DeWitt. Because of the lack of shaving equipment, his small neat mustache had become ragged and his face bearded.

"Well, our situation has been pretty much the same as yours. But we've had one nineteen-year-old shell-shock case. And Dr. Kane performed an appendectomy. We lost one patient, who bled to death from a shrapnel wound that ripped out his total bowel area."

Our conversation continued briefly on our immediate predicament until I mentioned that I wanted to walk back before dusk. I shook hands with them, wished them good luck, and left.

On 19 December, we received news that a task force was on its way to relieve us. Needless to say, everyone's spirits were high around the hospital. The Japanese returned around 2:10 p.m. that day, which resulted in a severe shrapnel wound victim for us. The young Marine was laid on a narrow table used for operations, and Dr. Kane injected him with morphine to ease his pain. It took three of us to hold him down. As I clung to both legs, nurses Parsons and Perkins assisted Dr. Kane in the hopeless situation. The exposed intestines were beyond repair.

"There's nothing we can do but sew him back up," said Dr. Kane.

Before they began pushing his intestines back inside, the sight of the young soldier brought back memories. When I was a teenager I used to hunt for rabbits with my father and two brothers. Invariably, when we shot one, its intestines would hang out. The sight of the rabbits then was commonplace; the Marine was tragic and senseless.

The Japanese stayed away on 20 December, and we received friendly visitors, military personnel from Honolulu, who came in a small flying-boat around 3:30 p.m. They were intercepted by our communications officer, Major Ralph Buchanan. The Major had visited our hospital that evening, hopping mad. Dr. Kane opened the heavy solid metal door to let him in.

"What brings you down here this evening?" asked Dr. Kane, looking very puzzled at his appearance.

"Well, you've probably heard that we had some military brass from Honolulu arrive yesterday."

"Yes."

"They came to inspect the island and make a report on the conditions here. The first thing they asked about was the hotel and having a good time. The sons-of-bitches! They couldn't believe how bad the conditions on Wake were." The Major's voice gradually grew louder as he spoke and became upset.

"Where are they now?" asked Dr. Kane.

"I left them with Commander Morley at the command post. He can entertain them. The reason I stopped to see you, Gus, was to get your assessment on the conditions at your hospital." Dr. Kane's report of our current circumstances and future ability to care for the wounded was brief.

Before leaving our hospital Major Buchanan passed among the wounded, wishing them a speedy recovery and praising them for their contribution to the war. He spoke slowly, directly, and sincerely.

"Sir, I understand that you are returning to Honolulu in the morning with the visitors," I said, approaching the Major.

"Yes. I will be reporting the conditions on Wake Island." His response was professional.

"Would you take a message back for me to my parents?" I asked.

His reply was immediate as a smile lit up his worried face.

"I'd be happy to; just write it on a piece of scratch paper with your folks address, and I'll see that they receive it," he said with a slight grin and then proceeded among our patients.

I later learned that my parents did receive my note.

As Major Buchanan was about to leave, someone shouted at him, "Is it true a task force is on the way to relieve us?"

"That is my understanding. But you know that from Honolulu to Wake Island is around twenty-five hundred miles and anything could happen. I hope they make it," he said as he waved goodbye.

The following morning, 21 December, at 8:30, Major Buchanan left for Honolulu. Approximately an hour later the island was attacked by high-flying bombers. Again, at 12:30 p.m., several dive-bombers raided gun positions on the islands from low altitude. At the time, two of our fliers had entered our hospital, Captain John Toliver and Captain Hubert Fielder, who had received a bullet wound in his right shoulder on his last mission. They reported that the last two planes had been destroyed.

During the noon-day raid, Captain Toliver proceeded towards the large metal door, the only way out of the hospital. I sensed his motive and followed him. The moment he pushed the door open a few inches, a Japanese dive-bomber shot by at low altitudes, creating a loud sucking noise that reverberated throughout the hospital. Dr. Kane came unglued.

"Shut that damn door; you want to get us all killed?" Dr. Kane shouted as he came scooting out from under his cot.

Across the way, Captain Fielder with a sober face looked on, as he perched atop the operating table. The door was immediately closed. The Japanese continued to bomb and strafe the island at low altitudes for quite a while.

The next day, 22 December, no one in our unit was optimistic about getting reinforcements after the devastating attacks of the day before. Things were looking pretty gloomy — no more planes. Everyone was expecting an invasion the 23rd. A discussion of a possible invasion brought up the question of prisoners again. Would the Japanese take prisoners? They never had in the past. But practically all of their wars have been with other races. Some seemed to think that the Japanese wouldn't dare kill us wholesale for fear of the consequences they would suffer later. Others were skeptical. Everyone prayed for help soon.

During the early morning of 23 December, except for an occasional grunt and groan, our hospital was quiet. Perkins and I had a large bucket of navy beans cooking for that day. We had just been relieved of our 10:00 p.m. to 2:00 a.m. watch when the fireworks began.

"Here they come," said Perkins. His round face tensed.

"They must be coming ashore," I said as we looked directly at each other, not surprised by their invasion.

By then everyone was sitting up in their cots. For a brief moment, there was complete silence as everyone listened to the exchange of gunfire. Then sporadic conversations began and continued throughout the early morning hours. Everyone anticipated that the Japanese would invade the island after yesterday's thorough bombing and strafing. No one got hysterical, but we were all apprehensive about the future should we surrender. The thought was tossed around that the Japanese could easily annihilate all inhabitants and declare that surrender terms were not offered.

I was spending the early morning hours nervously smoking one cigarette after another, listening to the battle outside, when our telephone rang. Dr. Kane rushed to answer it. The time was 7:43 a.m., 23 December 1941.

"Hello," he shouted, fearful of the call.

"Gus, this is Commander Morley. I have just surrendered the island to the Japanese. To continue fighting a force which greatly outnumbers us in manpower and equipment would result in an unnecessary loss of life. Also, I have taken into consideration the eleven hundred and fifty civilian personnel on the island. Would you please immediately erect a white sheet outside your hospital entrance surrendering your position. Thank you, Gus, and good luck."

Shortly afterwards, a Marine came running into the hospital and jerked the white flag down.

"What's the idea of raising the white flag? We aren't surrendering. The Marines don't believe in surrendering." His face reddened as he continued to shout.

Dr. Kane immediately confronted him. "I just received a phone call from Commander Morley to place a white flag outside our entrance high enough for the Japanese soldiers to see. We are surrendering at this time."

The Marine simply said, "Oh," and turned and walked away disappointed. The flag was replaced, and the hospital door flung wide open.

As we stood by our cots, frightened, awaiting the arrival of the Japanese soldiers, several Americans in the immediate vicinity entered our hospital to surrender. This group included Gunner John Pappas, a thirty-eight-year-old Marine originally from Czechoslovakia, who spoke very broken English. He was a big man, ruddy complexion, light-brown hair, blue eyes — a very strong and rugged individual.

A squad of Japanese soldiers rushed down the concrete ramp to the hospital entrance. The leader thrust his rifle inside and fired, killing one American instantly and wounding two others. I was located near the entrance, an arm's length behind the man who was shot through the forehead; he had keeled over onto a cot. The Japanese who fired the shot appeared very nervous. I remember his bloodshot eyes. Gunner Pappas, located near the entrance, immediately took charge. The Japanese soldier began shouting at him as he swung his rifle freely in the air.

"He wants you to raise your hands above your heads and drop all your weapons," stammered Pappas. He was very emotional as he continued to shout surrender instructions while the soldier growled at him.

The Japanese soldier began pointing and waving at the prisoners to move out. He began shouting in Japanese at Pappas, making him more nervous.

"He wants you to walk out single file with your hands above your heads. Also empty your pockets as you walk out." Pappas appeared slightly relieved as the prisoners began leaving the hospital.

Just prior to the arrival of the Japanese, I had my portable typewriter and hospital records, thinking that I would be able to take them with me. But they changed my mind. We walked up the hospital ramp between two columns of Japanese soldiers with bayonets drawn. On the road we were moved into a straight line. We were immediately ordered to remove all of our clothing and place it before us. At this time it was collected and taken back to our hospital. Then we were bound together, one after the other, around the legs with telephone wire. Shortly afterwards, our hands were secured behind our backs with a loop around each man's neck.

Everyone was ordered to kneel. We remained in this position for three or four hours. Prior to having our hands tied, I removed my glasses thinking that I wouldn't need them anymore. With Japanese machine-guns set up in front of us, I feared they would shoot us and the thought of falling face down with my glasses on bothered me. I never was able to pick them up.

While we were on the road tied up and nude in the hot sun, the Japanese would go around to each individual and with a smile remove watches, rings, and other jewelry. The islands had not completely surrendered until late afternoon due to communications being severed at different places. This necessitated that one of our officers, accompanied by a Japanese officer, give notice of the surrender on foot to the various fighting positions throughout the islands. Major Frank Duprey, the Marine Commandant, was one of those officers who passed by our group in a very dignified and professional manner. While awaiting our uncertain disposition on the road, one of the Japanese dive-bombers passed over one of our gun positions. It opened fire on the plane and caused it to start smoking as it flew out over the ocean toward the Japanese fleet. Everyone feared that if the plane went down, the Japanese would fire on us in revenge. Fortunately for us, it didn't.

After a long period of suspense, facing a Japanese soldier squatting behind a machine-gun about twenty yards away, our bonds were removed and we were paraded back into the hospital. We found our clothing heaped in a huge pile in the middle of the room. It was like a scavenger hunt as everyone scattered the clothing around searching quickly for something that would fit, while a Japanese soldier shouted constantly, "Speedo, speedo." Needless to say, I ended up with a pair of khaki pants speckled with paint that hardly reached my ankles. We were rushed back up onto the road and marched to the airfield about a mile away.

En route we saw two Japanese destroyers beached near Peacock Point with several shell holes torn in their sides. They had been used for landing parties. The Japanese determination to capture the islands was demonstrated by the large fleet capable of blowing the islands out of the water.

All of the prisoners were concentrated on the airfield with groups arriving as late as 2:00 p.m. on 23 December. We spent the night sleeping on the coral-infested ground without any food. Fear took our minds off of hunger. Surrounded by Japanese soldiers, we could not talk.

On the 24th, Christmas Eve day, the early morning sun rose as bright as usual after a cool evening that found the prisoners huddled close together. As the day wore on, we perspired. The Japanese fleet commanding officer came ashore that afternoon and read us a proclamation: "We hate Roosevelt, not the masses and do not intend to harm all of you but only a few of you."

Before he left, he strutted around like a peacock enjoying his newly conquered islands. Our civilian leader, Hugh McGinis, had asked permission of the Japanese to serve us a meal, which our cooks had prepared the previous day, but the reply was negative. Our food that day had thus far consisted of a piece of bread and jam. Some received a piece of cheese; others received nothing. The water was unfit for consumption after having been placed in gasoline drums.

On Christmas Day, we remained on the airfield until early in the evening when we were marched three miles to our barracks. Upon arrival, the view of the Japanese flag flying atop the camp water tower instead of "Old Glory" was a very depressing sight. This was the final feeling of defeat and the beginning of an uncertain future. The barracks had been ransacked and broken glass was scattered everywhere. It was dark when we arrived and there were no lights.

During our three days on the airfield, we had been fed once each day. The Japanese had erected a wire fence around two different areas of the barracks, which were occupied by the civilians and military personnel. Our food was prepared by our cooks and consisted of hot cereal in the morning and creamed tuna, or salmon in most cases, for the other meal. The food tasted good enough, but was not sufficient.

The Japanese immediately organized work parties to repair the damage done to the island, as well as other jobs. Some of the prisoners were smuggling in canned food that they had found on work parties. Occasionally, the Japanese would catch them and take it for themselves. One day we were put to work digging post holes for a barricade which was to extend around the island along the beach. Digging holes in the coral rock was hard work; every time you would stop to rest, there was a Japanese guard shouting over you. This lasted all day, and I nearly passed out a few times.

On another occasion, a detail of fifteen of us were sent to fill in bomb craters in one of the roads. When it was time to return to the barracks in the late afternoon, part of our group was sitting down on the side of the road a short distance away. Our Japanese guard approached me and went through some hand motions indicating that he wanted the others to join us. I shouted and waved at them to move up. After the second try, the Japanese guard gave me a dirty look, a growl, and then started toward me with his bayonet fixed. I moved out of his way quickly. After an approximately thirty-yard sprint, the Jap decided to stop for some unknown reason. During the course of the run, fear took over as warm blood coursed throughout my body. In the meantime, those prisoners squatting on the side of the road had gotten up and moved toward the other prisoners. They hardly breathed.

After that incident I stayed a safe distance away from that guard. I found out later that the American way of waving one's hand for a person to come toward you is interpreted to mean the opposite by the Japanese.

The Japanese had no compassion. A group of prisoners had reported that the Japanese soldiers had ordered them to pour gasoline on the dead and burn them. The prisoner's request to bury the dead was denied.

On the afternoon of 11 January 1942 we were all congregated on the baseball field with what clothing we then possessed. The Japanese had distributed our confiscated clothes among the prisoners. Only the three hundred and fifty civilians, whose names had been read off the day before, would remain on the island.

Several inquiries were made of the Japanese about our destination. All had different answers, except that it would be cold.

On the morning of 12 January 1942 while we were waiting to be taken by truck to the waterfront, I spotted my civilian boss, Dr. Shay, standing in the crowd. As he saw me approaching, a smile brightened his face.

"Well, are you ready to go?" I asked.

"I'm not going, Charlie," he said. His smile softened as he spoke.

"I don't understand. Why are you staying behind?" I was somewhat surprised. He hesitated a moment; his face became sober.

"I was informed by the Japanese that I have to remain behind to care for the wounded unable to travel."

"Would you like me to stay behind to help you?" I asked.

"No, thank you, Charlie, Milt DeWitt has volunteered to stay. I appreciate your offer."

We shook hands, wished each other good luck, and said goodbye. As he walked away, I thought about Dr. Shay and Milt DeWitt — fine human beings. I later learned that they were among a group of ninety-eight civilians shot to death on a lonely Wake Island beach on the night of 7 October 1943.

Just before we boarded the trucks, which were to take us to the waterfront, we were searched for knives, razor blades, matches, and cigarettes and were issued written instructions governing our behavior on the evacuation ship:

Instructions Before Boarding *Nita, Maru*
Commander of the Prisoner Escort
Navy of the Greater Jap Empire
Regulations for Prisoners

(1) The prisoners disobeying the following orders will be punished with immediate death.

a. Those disobeying orders and instructions.
b. Those showing motion of antagonism and raising a sign objection.
c. Those disobeying the regulations by individualism, egoism, thinking only about themself, rushing for their own gains.
d. Those talking without permission and raising loud voices.
e. Those walking and moving without order.
f. Those carrying unnecessary baggage in embarking.
g. Those resisting mutually.
h. Those touching the boats material, wires, electric lights, tools, switches, etc.
i. Those climbing ladder without order.
j. Those showing actions of running away from the room boat.
k. Those trying to take more meal than given to them.
l. Those using more than two blankets.

(2) Since the boat is not well equipped and inside being narrow, food being scarce and poor, you'll feel uncomfortable during the short time [12 days] on the boat. Those losing patience and disobeying the

regulations will be heavily punished for the reason of not being able to escort.

(3) Be sure to finish your "nature's call" evacuate the bowels and urinate before embarking.

(4) Meals will be given twice a day. One plate only to one prisoner. The prisoners called by the guard will give out the meal quick as possible and honestly. The remaining prisoners will stay in their places quietly and wait food plate. Those moving from their places reaching food plate without order will be heavily punished. Same orders will be applied in handling plates after meal.

(5) Toilet will be fixed at the four corners of the room. The buckets and cans will be placed. When filled up a guard will appoint a prisoner. The prisoner called will take the buckets to the center of the room. The buckets will be pulled up by the derrick and be thrown away. Toilet paper will be given. Everyone must cooperate to make the room sanitary. Those being careless will be punished.

(6) Navy of the Greater Japanese Empire will not try to punish you all with death. Those obeying all the rules and regulations and believing the action and purpose of the Japanese Navy, cooperating with Japan in constructing the "New Order of the Greater Asia" which leads to the world's peace, will be well treated.

Chapter 2

A bright warm sun was directly overhead as a motor launch loaded with American prisoners of war was winding through the ocean swells toward the *Nita, Maru* anchored about one mile out from the tiny Wake Island atoll. The cool ocean spray was refreshing as it moistened the worried faces of the men watching the fluttering Japanese flag atop the water tower fade in the distance. As I sat in the boat with a jacket draped over my legs, I wondered how I could have gotten into such a predicament and what was going to happen to us. Would we ever see our families again some five thousand miles away? The other men's faces were silent as they sat, solemnly searching the shoreline of a once peaceful island. With the passing of sixteen days, death and destruction had come to this waterless atoll, whose natural beauty would always remain with those men who were leaving. The coral reef and pure white sand that encircled the island, with its shallow emerald-green lagoon, were soon gone, as were the loud screechings of the awkward gooney birds.

As the Japanese soldiers yelled above the drone of the motors, we huddled closer together clinging to the wet sides of the boat. We turned our backs on the island, where we had known complete freedom, and looked toward the Japanese evacuation ship, which we now approached. Camouflaged for war, the *Nita, Maru* during peacetime was one of Japan's luxury liners. A barge was secured alongside by a heavy cable, which draped across half the ship. The Japs worked feverishly, catching and unloading large mesh sacks as they swung into position. They tried to secure the launch alongside the ship in front of a small opening as the ocean swells tossed the small boat up and down like a tiny cork, whipping it against the huge ship. When we hesitated at jumping into the ship, the excited Japs screamed, "Speedo, speedo," their arms flying in every direction. The ocean swells made it hazardous to board the ship because we had to jump from the rail of the launch into the small doorway.

As each of us boarded the *Nita, Maru* we received a piece of paper with a number on it and hurried down a long narrow passageway. The glistening white hallway was lined on either side with unusually large Jap sailors with sabers drawn and silent, tense faces.

The sound of metal scraping echoed for some time as we descended the hatches to different floor levels. The dimly lit hold of the ship was like a furnace. Occasionally fresh air would drift in from the hatch above. Musty straw littered the partially boarded floor. Packed like sardines in the foremost section of the hold, we could hardly sit down — to lie down was impossible. We removed our light summer clothing to our waists as the sweat poured from our worried faces.

"Someone is coming!" shouted a voice from across the way.

Two Jap soldiers entered the hold laden with three five-gallon cans with long ropes attached to each. They laughed about something when they entered the stuffy room, but as they approached the floor below, their laughter ceased.

"Give attention to what I am about to tell you," blurted one of the Japs waving his flashlight as he spoke. "These buckets — you put them in three corners, do you understand? You must get okay from Japanese soldier when you need to use them. Just say, *'Benjo,'* and he will understand. Also tell Japanese soldier when full, and he will help you take them up. Before leaving I must instruct you that you will be punished if caught talking or moving about. Do you understand, huh?"

There was complete silence for a few minutes as the smug Japs glanced over the heads of our somber group before making their ascent.

The constant roll of the ship had its effect on several men who stumbled over the rest of our bodies to reach the open containers. The putrid stench of the open "heads" filled the over-crowded room. As the shadow of the Jap sentry left the hold, low voices fell across the room. Squirming next to me, trying to find space for all two hundred and forty pounds, was George Sanborn, a farm boy from Texas. After twisting and turning for several minutes, until the sweat was pouring down his suntanned face, he stood up in disgust.

"Say, George, do you think they're taking us to China instead of Japan?" I said, attempting to lie down in a curled up position. Being tall was a problem. We had only been in the hold about three hours. Already I was becoming seasick. To lie down would have provided some relief.

"Charlie, I think our chances of surviving would be better in China. The further we stay away from their homeland, the better we'll fare," Sanborn whispered, as he took a swipe at a large horsefly buzzing around his head. The flies multiplied rapidly in the filthy hold.

The scraping sound of hobnail shoes heard above our heads caught our attention. Two Jap guards brought two metal buckets. Steam rose from one of the buckets, which they set down in the straw.

"We bring you food. You will be fed twice a day, at eight in the morning and three in the afternoon. A Japanese soldier will see that everyone gets same amount of food and that no one starts until all receive food. Do you understand, huh?" stammered the Jap soldiers.

A few moments passed as the two Japs conversed in their native tongue. One removed his tattered cap to scratch his head, revealing his short hair.

"Two of your men will serve the food. Be sure each man gets same amount of food. Do you understand?" screeched the Jap. The veins in his neck swelled as he wrestled with each word.

The curvature of the flooring with its litter of straw and broken boards made it difficult to walk to the center of the room, where the watery rice gruel was dipped up. As each man received his small portion and cup of water, he looked around for a spot to sit. Tiny flakes of dust were illuminated by the overhead floodlight as the men stirred. A cough here and there broke the stillness as we sat waiting for some signal from the Japs to start eating. They stood erect, closely watching us, hoping to catch someone eating before they had given the word.

"Okay! Okay!" shouted one of the Japs, making a forward motion with one of his hands toward his mouth. Then they left the hold immediately.

The bright floodlight, lighting up the foremost hold of the ship, showed our shadows cast on the curved walls of the room. Our figures bent forward simultaneously with the signal to begin eating.

"Could use some salt," I said, but I was not feeling hungry at this point. Fear and uncertainty had a tendency to curb one's appetite. The constant roll of the ship and lack of fresh air began to affect a number of us.

"I don't think salt would improve the taste. What would you call this stuff? Down on the farm we feed our hogs better-looking stuff than this and a hell of a bigger ration," Sanborn said, shaking his head as he spooned the rice gruel, letting it drip back into his bowl.

"You can have my chow starting tomorrow," I said.

"Seasick?"

"Yeah," I said, "it doesn't take too much to make me seasick."

The afternoon meal was soon finished, and the Japs returned shortly afterwards to collect the dishes and empty buckets. They appointed two of our men to take the utensils topside and wash them. They seemed more excited this time as they informed us that the ship would be underway in two or three hours.

The ship left around 6:00 that evening. As time passed, there was no way of telling day from night as the floodlight above burned constantly. As the ship picked up speed, the loud splashing against the hull subsided and seemed more like the passing of a swift river. The men crawled over one another as they made their way to the latrines before settling down for the hot sticky night. Low whispers could be heard across the room as we lay doubled up or sitting up.

"Someone's coming!" a voice whispered.

For a moment we only heard the buzz of flies; then the scraping of hobnailed shoes on the metal ladder echoed above. As the Jap came into the light, we could see he grasped a wooden club about the size of a baseball bat in his right hand and a flashlight in the other. He made his way quickly to the far side of the room, stepping on those of us who were half asleep.

"Stand up! Stand up!" he shouted, shining his flashlight directly into a prisoner's frightened face.

The man rose slowly, which irritated the Jap sentry, and he began grunting and waving the club.

"Why you talk, huh? Why? Why?" the Jap yelled, and struck a heavy blow across the prisoner's back.

The man groaned, gasping for air as he lay helpless at the Jap's feet. The Jap glowered at him for a moment, then grunted something in Japanese before turning and making his way back to the ladder. Halfway up the ladder he stopped and shined his flashlight into the darkened corners of the room. The deep breathing of the prisoners could be heard above the tapping sound of the Jap's club as he dragged it over the metal steps on his way out.

Early the next morning, we were awakened by a loud outburst in Japanese from above as two legs dangled from the hatchway. Three sentries, with rifles strapped to their backs, came scrambling down the ladder screaming at us. Laying their rifles against the hull of the ship, they continued shouting and waving their arms in an upward motion. Those not quick to stand up were kicked. The formation of lines was irregular as we staggered to our feet, our summer clothing wrinkled and damp. Shoving and pushing their way through the group, the Japs stumbled back to where they had laid their rifles. Standing rigid, side by side, with rifles thrust directly in front of them, their heads poised upward, they shouted in unison.

The over-crowded room became quiet and dusty with the prisoners stirring up the straw as they rose to their feet. A young Jap naval officer in full uniform, saber dangling from his side, entered the hold.

"Did you ever hear anyone scream that loud before," I whispered.

"They sound like an elephant calling to its mate. Here comes the inspecting officer. I wonder what he expects. So far we're suppose to sit in silence," Sanborn whispered, crouching behind the fellows in front of him.

The three guards seemed to quiver when the officer returned their salute. The floodlight above shone directly on his round fat face with its flat nose and small ears high on his head, accentuated by the circular-shaped cap he wore. He stood and walked erect, his fat hands clasped behind his back most of the time. There was a constant chatter of Japanese as the officer inspected our ranks.

"Can you see what the hell they are doing, George?" I whispered.

"No, not exactly. I can't hardly see them, they're so damned short. They seem to be moving the men around in the front row. Taking their damn sweet time, I'd say," Sanborn muttered. He ran his hand through his hair, trying to get the straw out of it.

"Let me know when they get near," I said.

"Pretty seasick, huh!"

There was much confusion as the Japs meandered through the mass of men whose tired faces looked straight ahead. Loud shouts from the sentries signaled their departure, and we fell to the musty floor.

"I guess we'll have to expect this twice a day," Sanborn said. He was smoothing out a place to lie down with his right foot. His soiled shirt hung loosely from his huge frame, unbuttoned but tied in a knot at the waistline.

"Yeah, routine I suppose. But if they take much longer during their inspections, a lot of us aren't going to be able to wait to heave," I said, breathing deeply — swallowing saliva to keep from heaving.

Several men stumbled in three directions toward the heads, right hands pressed against their foreheads, shading the bright light above, left hands extended in front of them to break a fall. The air in the hold reeked a nauseating odor as the heads overflowed and spilled onto the filthy deck. The mass of unshaven faces became silent whenever a Jap guard entered the hold. You might see him early in the morning or late at night — his visits were irregular. During his absence, low voices were heard across the room.

There was confusion in one corner as two men shouted at each other, not realizing that they might bring a guard scrambling down the ladder.

"Will you please quit kicking me in the back of the head. You've done it two or three times now," one said, sitting up, rubbing the back of his head. The side of his face that had pressed against the deck was matted with straw.

"What the hell do you want me to do with them, stick them straight up in the air? Besides, your feet are planted right under my nose, and they aren't the sweetest smelling things," the other replied.

"All right! Knock it off, you guys. You want the Jap back down here? If he comes you'll have more than a shoe in the back of your heads!" a voice cried out.

After several days had passed, the hold was no longer hot and sticky as cold air began drifting in. The warm, damp straw was now cold and dry, and the flies were content to cling to the gray hull of the ship. The cold air freshened the hold, making the odor less putrid.

As the hold chilled, a few thin horse blankets were distributed among us. Some stood to wrap up in their blankets before lying down; others merely crawled under them, so only their nose and mouth were exposed. Still others pooled their blankets and huddled close together. Above the blanket-covered bodies, which by the end of the voyage stirred only for inspection, chow, and to go to the head, our breath rose like steam.

After spending twelve long days in the hold of the *Nita, Maru*, the first five of which I was seasick, I sat up and shook Sanborn, who was snoring in a sitting position.

"Listen!" I exclaimed, hesitating for a moment. "I think the ship has stopped."

Across the room heads were popping out from under blankets, staring and listening but not uttering a sound.

"We *have* stopped!" Sanborn shouted and shook his head affirmatively.

The ship rocked up and down as the water swished against its hull. Just about everyone in the room sat up, assuring each other that the ship had stopped. The talking ceased with the ring of footsteps on the metal ladder.

"Get up! Get up!" a voice screeched from the hatchway. Descending halfway down the ladder, the Jap guard stopped and stammered. "You go from ship quickly, do you understand, huh?"

He indicated with his flashlight that he wanted us to line up and spoke loudly in Japanese as we rose, clinging to our shabby blankets, which were draped around our bodies. When the Jap left, we dropped our blankets on the floor and slowly started up the metal ladder. There was a constant rumble of voices as we milled around, waiting to ascend the ladder.

In one far corner, a fellow motioned to some to move out of the way. Then he began to shout, making sure everyone heard him: "Those yellow bastards made me lay next to this stinking latrine damn it; they can clean up the mess!"

Then he booted the five-gallon can whose foul-smelling contents spilled all over.

It felt good to stand and move about, but it didn't take long to realize that lying on your back for several days made you weak. The cross-bars on the metal ladder felt like ice, when I grabbed them, and the cold air seemed to penetrate deep into my lungs.

"Say, George, let me go first. In case I fall, you can catch me," I said, only half joking. As big as he was, he could probably carry me up the two flights of ladders if I stood on his shoulders.

"And who in the hell is going to catch me?" he replied, pulling himself onto the first step of the ladder, then twisting his huge frame around to see who was behind him. There was a warm smile underneath his heavy crop of dark whiskers.

At the top of the hatchway stood a Japanese in civilian clothes — an elderly man, neatly dressed, slight, and soft spoken. He spoke good English.

"You Americans will be going to China. Be sure and take good care of your health," he replied with a smile.

Chapter 3

Gathered on the Woosung dock were newsmen, photographers, Japanese military personnel, and Oriental civilians awaiting the discharge of the American prisoners of war. The sky was overcast and everything was wet from a recent rain as we made our way down a long gangplank and onto the dock. Directly in the middle of the landing stood a Jap with a hand sprayer and tank attachment. In front of him was a small square box, which sat about six inches off the dock.

We began walking single file, stepping into the open box, which contained a shallow amount of a dark liquid. The Jap enthusiastically squirted each of us with his hand sprayer. Photographers' flashbulbs began flashing as laughter filled the chilly air.

"I guess they don't want us taking germs into China," I said.

It was late January 1942, and the damp, cold weather penetrated my light khaki shirt and pants which reached just above my ankles, well above the oxfords I was wearing. During the boat trip, the Japanese confiscated all jackets and coats, adding to the discomfort of the Americans.

"Either we're putting on a show for those people on the dock, or they're feeling just a little superior right now. All you see is mouths full of teeth, mostly fillings," replied Sanborn disgustedly.

A light mist began to fall on us. There was a brief speech by the Japanese naval officer in command of the ship, who commented on our good behavior during the voyage, and we were turned over to the Japanese army. The Japanese army commander was Colonel Yuse, who stood about four-and-a-half feet tall and was wrinkled like a prune. Perched on a chair, looking out over us, he had to tilt his head back to see, as the bill of his cap was pulled down almost over his eyes. His coat collar was buttoned around his short, thin neck. Underneath his pointed nose was a small fish-like mouth, which moved very little when he spoke, making high-pitched sounds that came in spurts. Standing next to him on a chair was the Japanese interpreter, Ishahara, whose tall, slender figure towered over the Colonel. His piercing black eyes burned behind horn-rimmed glasses. After the Colonel finished his brief speech, Ishahara cleared his throat, sized up the multitude of prisoners before him, and blurted out the Colonel's instructions.

"You people will walk several miles now to Japanese military barracks. There will be some of you older men, sick and wounded, who can't walk so far, so stay at the side of roadway with Japanese sentry, and truck will come later and get you. Do you understand, huh?" he stammered, and jerked his head from one side to the other. Before he continued, the Colonel smiled at him and whispered a few words.

"The work you will be doing in China will consist of building a model dwelling. You will receive more instructions when you get to the camp," Ishahara continued, slowly and deliberately.

The Corporal of the Guard came running quickly toward Colonel Yuse as he stepped down off the chair. There was a loud, shrill noise that came from the strained face of the Corporal as he came to attention and saluted the Colonel.

We were soon walking three and four abreast down a narrow, muddy road. The narrowness of the roadway made it impossible for us to bunch up, and we were scattered along its length for two or three miles. A small number of Jap guards kept running up and down alongside our columns, shouting and thrusting their rifle butts at the stragglers. A short distance ahead, a Jap was trying to make Herman Schultz move a little faster. Schultz, in his late fifties and in good shape for his age, could keep pace with any of the younger men. He spoke with a thick accent, which made it difficult to understand him at times. He also swore profusely. Shaking his fist, he shouted at the guard, "Listen, you little yellow bastard. If you hit me with that gun, I'll take it away from you and wrap it around your God damn neck. Do you understand, you son-of-a-bitch?"

The guard, who apparently didn't expect quite that type of a reception, backed off, growled, and ran ahead. It took about another mile for Schultz to cool off.

The walk was beginning to drive the cold out of my slender body as we approached a small Chinese dwelling. The Japs ran ahead, driving the people away from the roadway and into their adobe house.

"Do you suppose all those people live in that one small house, George? It looks like a one-room affair," I said.

There was a peculiar odor about China that was quite noticeable but indescribable as we viewed what appeared to be a desolate, barren land.

"It sure looks like it, Charlie. Did you ever see such poverty? From the number of people, I'd say two or three families live in that one house,"

Sanborn replied shaking his head. He was rubbing his huge hands together to warm them while trying to avoid the puddles from the recent rains.

"Look at that old woman's hair — all matted down. Probably hasn't bathed for some time," I said.

They stood still, staring at us as we passed by without uttering a sound.

"Yeah, could be that it's too cold. I don't imagine too many can afford soap, something we take for granted. Look at those three small kids standing barefoot in the doorway — no sweaters either. Damn poor, huh," Sanborn said.

There was no apparent way of heating the house — no chimney or other sign of heat, no electricity, no running water.

"Yeah, damn poor," I said.

The narrow road began to wind inland away from the muddy Whangpoo River and its clutter of sanpans and small river boats. Dark clouds clinging to the horizon gave the vast countryside a desolate appearance with its few scattered villages. We saw few trees and birds as we traveled alongside a narrow canal whose muddy water flowed slowly. We saw no machinery or animals in the fields, only Chinese men, women, and children scattered about the brown fields, bent over toward the soil, leaning on long slender sticks. A few stopped what they were doing long enough to look our way — others didn't bother.

The sticky clay soil made it difficult to walk. We kept slipping from one side of the road to the other. Some of the older men and wounded were beginning to drop by the wayside in larger numbers now as we moved farther into the interior. The winter crop of rice was barely showing; a faded green patch appeared here and there.

As dusk fell, the damp air became even colder. Except for our constant chatter, there were no other sounds to be heard. Toward the front, some of the men were taking their hands out of their pockets and pointing straight ahead.

"What is it, George? Can you make out what they're pointing at? I'll be damned if I can see anything," I said, stepping off the road into the field to get a better view.

Moving off the slippery roadway onto a slight embankment, Sanborn jumped up and down trying to see over the long column of men.

"There appears to be some barracks not too far away," Sanborn said as he made his way back to the road.

As the buildings came more clearly into view, we could see a web of wire enclosing the entire compound. Two granite pillars at the entrance supported a patched wooden gate, whose hinges had been broken loose and caused the gate to hang at an angle. Dirty brown weeds were tangled among broken timbers. Inside the gate was a large monument, which rose above the ground several feet.

"Pretty fancy monument, huh, George?" I said, feeling tired and glad we finally reached our destination. "Must be important."

"Yeah, but look at the weeds growing all around it. Doesn't look like it's been cared for, for a long time," Sanborn replied, brushing his hair back in place.

Following some shouts in Japanese at the head of the column, the group turned into an open field which faced the row of wooden barracks. As darkness fell, the barracks appeared as only an outline. About an hour passed before Colonel Yuse and Ishahara made their appearance. More loud guttural sounds brought our group to attention. A moment of silence passed as Colonel Yuse and Ishahara climbed onto two chairs. Finally, after looking over our group, Colonel Yuse cleared his throat, tipped his head back, and delivered his instructions. His address was translated in brief exchanges.

"You prisoners will live in those barracks over there and receive the rules and regulations that the Japanese army will issue. Obey them — they are for your own good — and do not try to escape. It is impossible! Do you understand, huh?" Ishahara screamed.

Ishahara waved his hand at one of the Japanese soldiers as he leaned over and whispered something to the Colonel, who nodded in approval. Clearing his voice, Ishahara continued to translate the Colonel's instructions.

"There will be a morning inspection and an evening inspection. A Japanese soldier will blow the coronet before each roll call or what you call inspection. A Japanese soldier will now blow the coronet for you so you can train your ears to hear it. Please listen carefully!" Ishahara shouted.

A soldier took position on a box overlooking us and placed a coronet against his lips. His fat round face swelled as he blurted out a few sounds from his horn. The longer he blew, the worse it sounded.

We were then divided into groups and paraded into the barracks, after being reminded again of the impossibility of escape. It was pitch dark when we started toward the barracks.

Suddenly my legs became stiff, and I found it very difficult to move them without sharp pains running up and down them. Two large lumps had formed in both groins, apparently from the cold, while we had been standing on the damp ground for a couple of hours.

As we made our way toward the barracks, a few lights began to show inside them. We were divided into smaller groups and assigned to different sections. Inside, we found a central hallway running the full length of the barracks, which were divided into eight sections and a small office. The wooden floor squeaked under our weight as we crowded down the narrow hallway and emptied into the small rooms, which were enclosed on three sides and fully open facing the hallway. A round porcelain lamp hung from the rafters on a long knotted cord and lit up a worn-out wooden table and two benches. We entered our section and sat down on a flat wooden platform built about two feet off the floor running the entire length of the room.

Everyone was walking around, jumping up and down and rubbing their hands together in an effort to keep warm as the cold damp air filtered in through the cracks in the building. The shadow of a couple of Jap sentries appeared at the entrance. One handed one of our men a note. Their bayonets glistened in the darkness.

"All right men, we need a detail to go and get some blankets at the Jap warehouse," someone shouted in the darkness. "Let's not all jump at once."

"Come on, let's go, George. At least it will give us a chance to move around and keep warm," I said, anxious to work those damn knots out of my legs.

In the pitch dark, I stumbled and fell into a ditch on our way to the warehouse. When we arrived, each of us was given a bundle of ten blankets covered by a bulky and heavy rice-matting to carry. After stopping and resting several times, in spite of the prodding from the Japs, we finally made it back to the barracks, our arms hanging limp at our sides. Breaking open the rice bundles, we found the blankets damp and mildewed. We were each given two blankets before we prepared to bed down on the wooden platform.

Across the way, Hawkins was having a nicotine fit as he chewed on one fingernail and then another and paced back and forth. He had spent a lot of time in San Francisco, where he drank excessively and smoked constantly. A slight, middle-aged man, he had caught a piece of shrapnel, which left a small shallow hole in the center of his forehead.

"I don't suppose anybody has a butt hidden somewhere? Don't all shout at once," Hawkins smiled as he spoke softly and poked a finger in his right ear.

"I guess you're out of luck, Willie," Schultz whispered, running his thick hand across Hawkins' stooped shoulders. "I'm getting hungry. Are these slant-eyed bastards going to feed us tonight?"

The constant flow of men going and coming to the head, which was located behind the barracks, made the hallway a muddy thoroughfare. It was midnight when someone shouted at the other end of the barracks, "Chow! Chow!"

Several men shuffled down the hall carrying steaming buckets and shouting how good it smelled. Anything warm would have been welcomed by us — even hot water! The food was only a small bowl of cooked rice with a dipper of thick curry-flavored gravy poured over it. The curry was hot, but the chop sticks were difficult to use. A light rain began falling on the tin roof now as we began to bed down for the night.

"What in the hell are you doing, George?" I asked, propping myself up with my elbows on the wooden platform. He was standing in the light, wrapping the thin horse blankets around him.

"Well, that wooden bunk looks mighty hard to me. If I can get a bit of cushion under me I won't be too sore in the morning," he replied, and he stepped up onto the platform and squirmed into position.

The night was long and cold. Some of us draped our blankets around our shoulders and walked up and down the hallway all night trying to keep warm.

Chapter 4

The fractured notes of a bugle in the distance brought the barracks leader storming out of his room with one hand grasped firmly at the front of his pants and the other gathering up his shirt tail.

"All right men, they'll be here in five minutes. Up an' at 'em," shouted Emery Sloane, continuing down the hallway, repeating himself a little more loudly each time.

The men began to rise with their blankets tightly wrapped around them and stood at the foot of their bunks. Except for Schultz, everyone had a heavy beard and a large crop of hair. The soft, fleshy part of his cheeks showed no signs of ever being shaved. A single strand of black hair curled at the point of his jaw, which he nervously pulled.

"How'd ya sleep, Herman?" a voice shouted from across the hall.

"Huh, sleep! How ya gonna sleep when ya can't get warm, for God sakes," Schultz said, pulling the blanket tighter around his body.

Very little morning light came through the narrow windows as the sky was heavy with low, dark clouds. The wind whipped a cold rain against the sides of the barracks, and the damp, chilly air entered through the cracks into the room.

"Stand by!" yelled Sloane. "They're coming across from the next barracks now. And for God sakes, get those damned smelly blankets off ya. Fold 'em and put 'em on the bunk behind ya."

The barracks became silent as the Japs approached. The wooden door flew open, banging against the inside wall as the Jap sentry let out a loud screeching sound that echoed throughout the building. At his heels was a Jap officer and Ishahara, followed by another sentry, who didn't bother to shut the door. Ishahara and the officer wore capes and rubber boots while the sentries wore faded green uniforms, spotted by the rain. After Sloane saluted, they moved toward our section, and Ishahara began to speak.

"You and your men must learn to count in Japanese during the inspections, and also you must learn a few Japanese words. This will make it easier for you here in this camp," Ishahara said, referring to a sheet of paper he carried in his right hand.

Handing the paper to Sloane, he removed his black horn-rimmed glasses and began wiping the water off.

"This paper will show you how to count in Japanese and some of the words you must learn. Do you understand, huh?" he said.

Sloane responded by saying, "Yeah."

"What sorta talk is 'yeah.' Is that some kind American slang?" Ishahara raged. "When you answer to me, you say, 'yes, sir.' Do you understand, huh?"

"Yes, I mean, yes, sir," Sloane said, correctly this time.

"All right, how many men do you have in this section?"

"Thirty-six."

"That's the total on both sides of the hall?"

"Yes, sir."

"Do you have any men sick?"

"No, sir, not in this section. There are several in the other sections. But if we don't get some warm clothing pretty damn quick, there'll be one hell of a lot of sickness," Sloane said, glancing at his men, who stood erect and silent, their only clothing the light summer wear they'd worn the last three weeks.

"In a few days you will receive Japanese soldiers' uniforms," Ishahara said. "So don't worry about that."

The Jap officer walked slowly in front of us, his hands clasped behind his back, glancing at us from head to toe, pausing now and then to look back. He spoke a few words softly and shuffled toward the hall and Ishahara.

"The Japanese officer wants your men to try counting in Japanese, so I will count first and then they must count in the order they are standing," Ishahara said to Sloane as he turned toward the first man in line and approached him. Looking directly into his face, he raised his left arm straight out, shoved him in the chest, and shouted, "*Itchey,*" and proceeded to the next ten prisoners in order before he stopped and turned around.

"Now the first prisoner will begin to count, quickly!" Ishahara ordered.

"*Itchey, nee, son, see, go, hitchey. . . .*"

"No, no, that is not right!" he yelled. "After *go* is *loco,* not *hitchey*. Try it once more and be more careful. Do you understand?"

He moved directly in front of each man as they began to count off.

"*Itchey, nee, son, see, go, loco, hitchey, hotchey. . . .*"

Schultz couldn't remember his number. He kept moving his lips and rubbing his forehead.

"*Coo,*" screamed Ishahara, and he shoved Schultz, almost knocking him down. "What's the matter with you dumb Americans? You can't remember simple words?"

"*Coo,*" yelped Schultz, trembling but looking straight ahead.

His count was quickly followed by Hawkins' high-pitched "*jew.*" Ishahara looked us over quickly again and walked silently toward the Jap officer in the hall. There was a brief exchange in Japanese as two Jap sentries took a fast count of the prisoners, their bayoneted rifles drawn as they made their way around the room.

"*Son-jew-loco!*" the sentry shouted.

"Thirty-six. Is that the number of men you reported?" Ishahara asked.

"Yes, sir," Sloane replied.

The Jap officer nodded approvingly and shuffled down the hallway followed by one of the sentries, running to get ahead of him.

As the Japs left, everyone grabbed their blankets and remained quiet. The front door was still wide open, and the cold morning air rushed in.

"Can't one of you guys reach over there and shut that damn door before we all freeze to death," someone whispered from across the hall.

Sanborn slipped off the edge of the bunk and tiptoed toward the hall, wrapping himself tightly with his blanket. Just as he was about to enter the hall, he stepped on a corner of the blanket causing him to fall forward. Grasping frantically for a wooden post to steady himself, he managed to loop one arm around it, which sent him spinning in a half circle until he hit the inside wall with a loud thump and bounced in the middle of the hall. The heavy sound of hobnailed shoes beating against the wooden floor grew louder as a Jap sentry drew nearer shouting, "*Coorah,*" several times. Sanborn didn't get up and scooted on all fours under his blanket and flopped onto the bunk. The angry sentry blurted out some words in Japanese and shook his fist before returning to the inspecting party.

"Pardon *me,* but you looked as graceful as a cow. Were you trying to do a swan dive?" I said. The wrinkled brown blanket completely covered him except for the outline of his narrow face. His light gray eyes sparkled as he tried to muffle his laughter.

"I think I broke my arm when I hit the wall," Sanborn said, rubbing his left arm. "You should have seen the look on the Jap's face when he turned around and saw me sitting in the middle of the hall. It's a damn good thing they were down at the other end of the barracks."

"The Japs must have left the barracks," I said. "You can hear 'em walking around."

Leaving my musty blankets heaped on the bunk, I proceeded cautiously toward the front door. The bitter cold air hit me directly in the face and went through my light summer clothing. I banged the door shut and ran back to crawl under my covers.

A low rumble of voices grew louder as Sloane moved briskly back up the hall, stopping momentarily at each section before moving on. He wore a dark peajacket with the collar turned up, which covered his small ears and fit him like a glove. His arms didn't move when he walked. Stopping at our section, he yelled, "I need two men to help bring the chow over from the galley."

Sanborn and Schultz were quick to volunteer for the detail. They threw their blankets behind them and moved swiftly toward the hall. As soon as the Jap inspecting party was finished in the last barracks, the two started toward the galley just behind the barracks.

From outside the compound, we heard the occasional crack of a rifle and short burst of machine-gun fire, while from inside we heard the thundering shouts of Jap sentries changing guard. Sloane and the men returned with the steaming buckets of chow. Several men followed close behind with hot tea pots.

"Hot stuff, men," Sloane shouted. "Get your cups out if you want hot tea."

Steam puffed from the spout of the dented brown kettle and curled upward.

"There's more tea when the pot's empty. Just go to the tin shack next to the galley and tell the Jap you want more *ocha,*" he said, pouring the tea into the cups held out at arm's length. He then set the kettle squarely in the center of the table and departed.

"Not too strong, but it's plenty hot," Hawkins whispered, his cup hidden so that the steam appeared to rise out of the palms of his long slender hands.

Everyone was clinging to the warm cups and sipping the slightly colored hot water while they waited for the chow.

"I wonder why it's taking them so damn long to divvy up the food up in there," I said, getting up to pour myself more tea. "Anyone care for another cup?"

"If you don't mind," Hawkins said, tipping his head back to swallow the remainder in his cup before holding it out for some more. The dirty brown blanket was still draped around his small wiry figure, and he continued to cough.

The door to Sloane's room scraped against the floor as it was forced open, releasing a strange odor. We quickly removed our blankets, grasped the two metal bowls and chopsticks, and scooted to the edge of the bunk, our silent faces focused on the two men who were about to dip up the chow.

Sanborn set the short wooden bucket of steaming rice on one of the benches near the table and began loosening it with a small wooden paddle. In his left hand, he held a metal teacup.

"Okay, let's start in this corner and work all the way around. If there's any left over, we'll begin seconds there. Is that okay with everyone?" Sanborn said.

After some nodded and others mumbled their approval, he filled the teacup with rice using the paddle. On the other side of the hall, Schultz set the bucket of soup in the middle of the floor and stirred the contents with a long stick, which had a teacup fastened on the end.

"Don't ask me what the hell it is because I don't know," he said, bending over the bucket lifting the dipper out now and then hoping to see something other than the large leafy greens and thick stems. "The vegetables look like spinach. That's all I can see."

The steam fogged up his heavy lens, which he wiped clean with his shirt tail. His tired, squinting eyes peered over a thick flat nose and wide mouth. His face seemed divided by the part of his brown hair which started in the center of his flat forehead. After wiping them clean, he adjusted his glasses high on the bridge of his nose and squeezed the wires behind his large puffy ears, and he picked up the dipper again.

"Come and get it before I throw it out," he shouted.

The dragging of shoes across the shoddy flooring and the tingling of metal bowls could be heard as we lined up for our dipper of soup. Our low voices gradually grew louder as we shuffled towards the chow.

"I don't think I want any of that slop, Herman. I just lost my appetite," sighed Dawson as he withdrew his bowl, glancing at the dark green leaves hanging over the sides of the cup. His stringy, coarse red hair went in every direction and his red beard was now beginning to curl up at the ends. The floor creaked under his heavy foot as he moved slowly back to the edge of the bunk.

"You'd better take it, Homer," Schultz replied, holding out the dipper of greens to him.

"I'm not that hungry yet!"

"It might be a long time before we eat again. The Japs aren't going to treat us as guests," he continued and dropped the dipper back into the bucket.

"Yeah, I know. I'll have some of that dirty looking rice," he said, smiling.

Sanborn finished issuing rice to the other side of the section and had started with Dawson. His large, thick hands were now pink as he continued fluffing up the warm rice before filling the teacup.

Outside, a light rain began falling, which was whipped and flung in every direction by the bitter wind. Inside, Hawkins had one of his coughing jags. He doubled up and held his head in both hands. His narrow face had become pale and lifeless. Across the room, the rhythmic beat of chopsticks against the sides of the metal bowls echoed.

Hawkins' cough sounded worse than ever, and his coloring was bad. I was sure he had two strikes against him from the start. I guided the ends of the chopsticks around some rice and squeezed them together. Slowly chewing the dirty brown rice and spitting out bits of gravel, I wondered how bacon, eggs, and a hot cup of coffee would taste right now.

"How's your breakfast, Willie?" I asked.

"I'd settle for a cup of coffee and a stateside cigarette," he replied, and turned to Schultz. "How about you?"

"I'd like a stack of pancakes and some nice crisp bacon, and toast and jelly," Schultz answered. "You can have your cigarettes."

"Why in the hell do you keep stirring your soup around?" Hawkins asked Schultz.

"I want to see if there's anything in it besides these damn tasteless greens," Schultz said, staring over the rim of his glasses. "I'm not quite hungry enough yet to eat them."

Sanborn had finished dishing up the rice and sat down on the bunk after leaving the empty bucket in the hall.

"Watch out, Herman. You might find something swimming around in there," Sanborn remarked, smiling and digging into his rice with his hand instead of the chopsticks. He slouched over his small bowl of musty rice as he poked his fingers into his mouth and then licked his heavy fingers clean.

"You can have anything that's alive," Schultz said. He lifted the thick stems and greens out of his bowl and let them slide back.

"No, thank you."

"Well, if you change your mind, they're right here," he said. He placed his bowl of rice on his legs, which were pressed together, and began poking at it with his chopsticks. His head bent halfway to meet the morsels of dirty rice, which fell free when the chopsticks slipped between his fingers.

The floor creaked as we rose one by one from our bunks and meandered down the narrow hallway toward the wash rack outside. Some of us dumped our soup into one of the buckets in the hall as we passed by, shoving the greens out with the chopsticks. The hollow splash of the soup in the wooden bucket quickly deepened.

"How long do you think it'll take before we're hungry enough to eat this garbage, George?" I asked, taking my bowl of greens in both hands, raising it to my lips. It was warm in my mouth as I swished it around and swallowed slowly. There was no salt or seasoning, and it had no taste or flavor.

"Maybe tomorrow I'll feel like eating this slop," Sanborn said. "I hate to think this is going to be a steady diet. After we're here a while, we'll probably wish we had more. I wish they'd give us a spoon instead of these damn chopsticks."

Finishing his rice, he stood up and brushed the small brown grains of rice off his wrinkled clothing.

"I wonder what work our little brown brothers have lined up for us," I said pouring my soup into the half-filled bucket.

"I don't know, Charlie, but I'd hate to go out in this weather," Hawkins quipped. He was standing at the small window, sipping tea and watching the wind-swept rain bouncing off the barracks next door. He hadn't coughed now for some time as the flushness of his face had become pale once more.

"You can bet there'll be work for us as soon as this rain stops," Schultz said, spitting bits of gravel onto the floor as he continued chewing the rice. His mouse-colored blanket was draped around his shoulders.

"I suppose," Hawkins said.

A few feet from the back door was the wash rack — a long, beat-up galvanized tin trough, buckled in the middle and crooked as a dog's hind leg. Faucets wrapped with old rags and ropes around the joints were spaced across it in no apparent order. A tin roof supported by patched timbers covered the long, narrow rack, which was set in a rich, brown clay soil. The muddy path from the back door to the trough was becoming a mire as we washed our dishes and returned to the barracks. A cold, miserable rain met me as I shoved the back door open and took four running steps, landing at the edge of the wash rack. Close behind was Dawson, who shielded the rain from his freckled face by holding up his left arm.

"How in the hell did you make it without falling on your fanny?" Dawson asked as he skidded in the sticky mud, nearly losing his balance.

"What did you say, Homer?"

I turned around to look at him and grasped the metal wash trough with my hand.

"I said, how did you manage to get over there without falling in this mud hole?"

His shoes had sunk deep into the mud under the weight of his body. There was a sucking noise when he jerked his shoes out and moved toward the men gathered around the open wash rack.

"I don't know. I just made a running jump for it and caught the tin trough with my hand," I said.

"What happened to your hand?"

"I ripped it open on this jagged edge of tin," I said pointing at a strip of tin that had torn loose from the wooden framing.

"You'd better let it bleed a while and then just wash around it. I'd be careful about letting any water get in the cut," Dawson warned. When he stooped over to get a closer look at the cut, rain ran across his wrinkled forehead into his deep-set green eyes.

I continued to hold my hand, squeezing around the open cut, forcing the blood to flow faster. The soothing cold rain took the sting out of it and stopped the bleeding quickly. Wrapping my hand with my dirty handkerchief, I dumped my dishes under a faucet, rinsing them as the wind whipped the cold water against the rough tin.

A Jap sentry who had been strolling between the galley and the tea shack began moving toward us. His bayonet-fixed rifle rested at an angle on his right shoulder and towered over his head nestled beneath his turned-up coat collar.

The wind ruffled the bottom of his khaki-colored slicker as he turned his head sideways, shielding his face from the rain. Jumping across a narrow ditch which ran behind the barracks, he ducked under the far end of the roof of the wash rack and stopped. Sliding the long rifle off his shoulder, he leaned it against the rack. He removed his soiled cotton gloves and fingered opened the top of his trench coat enough to slip his hand in and remove a pack of cigarettes. His wet back to the wind, he lit up and stared at us.

"I wonder what tree he fell out of," Dawson said, setting his dishes under a running faucet.

"What did you say?" I asked.

"Did you ever see such a creepy looking character?" he continued.

The men gathered on either side of the wash rack had now stopped to take a good look at him before starting back toward the barracks.

"I'd hate to meet him in the dark," I said.

He was bowlegged and had long arms. His unshaven face was scaly and looked like it hadn't been washed for weeks! He continued to stare, throwing his small dark head back with each puff. The smoke drifted toward us.

"Just our luck to have someone like that to look after us," Dawson whispered.

He began picking up his dishes one at a time, flipping them free of water.

"They're not like the Jap sailors on the boat coming over. They were sure big for Japs, clean looking and well dressed," I said.

The air was thick with tobacco smoke as the wind carried it through the open wash rack.

We hesitated under the edge of the roof waiting for the rain to let up before making a dash back to the barracks. The steady drip of rainwater from the roof beat into the soil, leaving a small crooked trench the length of the shed.

"Doesn't look like it's going to let up," I said to Dawson, who jumped up and down on the damp ground to keep warm. The chill seemed to penetrate deep into my lungs with each breath of cold air.

"Guess we'll have to get wet again," Dawson said.

Taking running leaps, he nearly lost his balance, crashing into the barracks door. I quickly waded through the sticky mud, almost losing my oxfords before reaching the open door.

"Shut the door!" someone shouted, and I reached for the loosely hung broken doorknob.

Chapter 5

This was China's rainy season. The rich, brown soil had become saturated and puddles dotted the fields. Patches of weeds, which had grown against the barracks, were now brown and rotted. The men flocked outside whenever the sun would shine, but not for long as the cold, damp air sent them back inside and under their blankets. Time stood still the first week. Everyone tried to keep warm, staying in bed, rising only for inspections and chow time. Some days there were only two meals due to the shortage of wood, or perhaps because the water pump had broken down. The Japs placed small wood stoves in the barracks only to remove them the same day. No fuel, they said. Hours seemed like days and days like weeks that first week while we waited for the Japs to put us to work.

The dragging of hobnailed shoes across the wooden floors could be heard day and night as Jap sentries constantly made their rounds. It was midmorning when one Jap sentry entered our barracks. His khaki uniform was streaked with rain and his wet round face was shiny. Mud covered the soles of his shoes and was splattered on his leggings, which stopped just below the knee. Water beaded on his rifle and was dripping off the point of the glistening bayonet which he angled toward the muddy floor. His face was motionless except for his dark eyes, which moved swiftly about the room.

"Suppose he's got a cigarette?" Hawkins whispered, lying stretched out on the bunk, only his head showing from beneath the blankets.

"Go ahead, ask him. Hell, don't be afraid," Schultz said, looking squarely at the Jap.

"Why don't you ask him?" Hawkins said, biting his fingernails nervously.

"Why should I ask him? I don't smoke," Schultz said smiling.

The Jap sentry stood still until his eye caught the knotted light cord, which hung from the ceiling and stopped a few feet above the long narrow table. Dragging his shoes across the wooden floor, he moved toward the cord to examine it. Tilting his head sideways, he studied the metal lamp thoroughly, flipping the light switch off and on.

"Tobacco, you have tobacco?" Hawkins shouted when the Jap started to leave the room.

"I don't think he heard you," Schultz said.

"Hey, you got tobacco?" Hawkins shouted again, going through the motions of smoking with his hands.

The Jap stopped and turned toward Hawkins. Hawkins' face became pale when his eyes nervously met the Jap's fiery dark eyes now focused on him. Hawkins coughed sharply, interrupting the silence, and slowly lay back down on his bunk.

"*Coorah!*" screamed the Jap, his mouth open just long enough to reveal several gold teeth.

Clenching the stalk of his rifle, he turned toward the hall and left the barracks growling.

"Not a friendly cuss, huh, Willie?" remarked Schultz.

There was a rumble of voices throughout the barracks as the men trudged in and out, tugging at their skimpy clothing and trying to keep warm. The bright morning sun poured through the narrow window, making a ribbon of light that divided the dark room.

Dawson was beginning to move off his bunk toward the floor, grunting and groaning with every movement of his large, bony frame.

"Who's for going out for a walk?" he asked as he rose to his feet and started toward the door.

"Just a minute and I'll join you," I replied.

I slipped on my shoes, and we were soon outside walking briskly on the narrow, muddy road.

"Did you ever see such a desolate looking place?" Dawson exclaimed.

His stringy, red hair flopped from one side to the other as he nodded his head from side to side.

"Doesn't look like there's ever been any life around this mud flat," he continued. We stopped to look around in every direction before continuing. "Except for a small clump of trees outside the village, I'd say those are about all the trees to be seen in any direction."

Directly in front of the row of barracks was a large field cluttered with old cans, broken bottles, and weeds. The odor of stagnant water came from the direction of an open ditch that ran the entire length of the field. As we stood there, we saw other men filing out of the different barracks.

"It looks like this road circles all the barracks," Dawson said. "We just as well make the entire tour. What do you say?"

"It's okay with me," I said. "But let's get moving. I'm starting to get cold all over."

The dampness seemed to creep right up my legs.

The narrow, muddy road had already been marred by the Jap sentries' hobnailed shoes as they made their rounds. Electric wire enclosed the camp, and at each of the four corners there were wooden guard towers manned with machine guns. At the far end of the field were two long open sheds and a barn which had housed horses. As we approached the back side of the barracks, there were several different-sized wooden shacks.

I pointed toward a water tank elevated above the building by timbers, which looked like they would collapse any minute.

"That must be our water supply," I said to Dawson.

"From the sound of that noise coming out of that shack next to it, an electric pump must be pumping it into the tank," he said.

"That tank must be full of holes. Water is leaking out of it from all sides," I observed.

The tank itself had a wooden frame. Patches of moss had formed where the water flowed down its sides.

"A damn shame — so much water going to waste," Dawson said.

As we started to move on, a Jap sentry coming in the opposite direction motioned with his hands for us to stop.

"*Coorah, coorah!*" he screamed, and he slapped the sides of our arms.

"What the hell's bothering him?" I asked.

"Damned if I know," replied Dawson.

"Hey, you guys playing games with your little brown brother?" someone shouted from the barracks.

The Jap sentry was becoming angry. He grabbed one of my arms firmly and jerked it out of my pocket. I quickly took the other out, and Dawson did the same. Apparently satisfied, the Jap slowly moved on, talking to himself.

"Those little yellow bastards are going to make it as uncomfortable as they can," Dawson said, turning away from the sentry as he spoke.

"Kinda looks that way, doesn't it?" I said.

We continued on toward the main entrance to the camp. Smoke could be seen rolling out of the chimneys of the galley and the small tea shack.

The Jap office barracks and living quarters were located just inside the entrance. Two Jap sentries had left their barracks and were heading toward the Jap office in a jovial manner when they met one of their officers. They came to attention and screeched in unison as they saluted.

"What a sound! You'd think they were being tortured from the noise they make," I said, rubbing my hands together to rid them of the cold.

"It must be their military training — learning to yell like that. I'll bet the people in Shanghai four miles away heard them," Dawson said.

Some of the men, standing around the wash rack and coming out of the head, stared in that direction.

"They look like they're scared to death the way their saluting arm is shaking," I said.

"It sure does."

"Looks like they're taking hot tea to the barracks," I said.

"You mean *hot water!*"

"Anyway, what do you say we go inside where it's warm and have a cup," I continued.

The men carrying the hot tea to the different barracks were now shouting, "Come and get it."

"*Warm!*" Dawson exclaimed sarcastically. "If you set a stove in every damn section you still couldn't warm these barracks because on a windy day the wind would come through the cracks and put them out."

"The *kind* Japanese will surely furnish us with wood stoves," I laughingly remarked as we made our way into the rear of the barracks.

Inside, some of the men continued walking up and down the hallway with blankets draped around their shoulders, trying to keep warm. Others lay or squatted on their bunks under blankets. The barracks were noisy with talking and laughter. As we reached our section, Emery Sloane, our barracks leader, stepped out of his room and made his way down the hallway when several men shouted at him, "When we going to get some heat in these son-of-a-bitchin' barracks? They going to furnish any clothing? How about cigarettes? Those little bastards going to issue any?"

The men lying under their blankets on the bunks quickly moved toward the hallway with their blankets draped around their shoulders.

"Now just a minute. Quiet down for a moment and I'll try and answer your questions," Sloane shouted as he stood, waiting for the others to gather around him.

"Here's what they told me yesterday. They would place wood stoves in the barracks."

He hesitated a moment as he ran his right hand gently across his thin gray hair.

"When?" shouted Hawkins.

"I asked them that and the answer they gave was don't worry about it. So your guess is as good as mine."

"When they get damn good and ready," Schultz yelled, standing on the edge of his bunk with his blanket tightly drawn around him.

"Yeah!" someone else exclaimed.

"As far as the clothing goes, they said about a week and that could be any day now," Sloane continued. "They said the clothing they'd issue would be old Japanese military uniforms."

"How about cigarettes?" Hawkins asked.

"There will be a small issue of either Chinese or Japanese cigarettes tomorrow or the next day. Now would be a good time for all you smokers to stop. You know you won't ever get enough to satisfy your habit." Sloane's voice grew louder as the prisoners became noiser. It was easy for him to make that remark because he was a nonsmoker.

"Has anything been said about work yet?" someone asked.

"Oh, yeah. They have something in mind this afternoon. So stick around the barracks." He was interrupted by a Jap guard who entered the back door. Sloane's right arm worked simultaneously with his mouth as he instructed the men to make an opening for the Jap to walk through.

"What kind of work?"

"Your guess is as good as mine. I can't imagine what in hell we could do outside as wet as it is," Sloane continued as he turned and slowly moved towards his quarters.

An hour went by, then two. Suddenly, the front door crashed opened and a Jap sentry came thundering in. He pushed Sloane's door in just as Sloane jerked it open from the other side. The Jap went flying, landing on the floor. After a few grunts from the sentry, Sloane came out shouting as the Jap departed.

"All right you guys. Everybody outside! They want everyone to line up in front of the barracks," Sloane repeated, walking through the quarters. Loud groans and bitching followed, and we filed slowly out the front door.

Outside dark clouds gathered as we sloshed through the mud and assembled in front of the barracks. Cautiously making his way through the group, Sloane stopped and turned toward Hawkins.

"What in the hell do you think you're doing with that blanket wrapped around you?" shouted Sloane, glowering at Hawkins.

"I'm trying to keep warm," Hawkins replied, shivering, clinging to his blanket.

"Knock it off Hawkins. You know better than to drag a blanket outside!"

"Look who's talking. You've got a heavy overcoat to keep you warm," Hawkins fumed.

"Just take the damn thing off and be quick about it. Hurry up before the Japs get here," Sloane said, the anger apparent in his voice.

"Listen Emery and listen good!" Hawkins snapped back. "We're all in this mess together. And it's up to each one of us to take care of our health. That's exactly what I intend to do. Now, if you want to come over here and try and take it off, then you just come ahead!"

Hawkins' face flushed and his body trembled. Sloane slowly turned around and continued through the group, grumbling to himself.

Running ahead of Ishahara, like watch dogs on a leash, were the Jap guards. Stepping around mud puddles, he walked briskly toward the group, puffing a cigarette and striking the side of his boot with his riding crop. He was tall and slender for a Japanese. He quickly singled out Sloane who was shouting and waving at his men.

"All right you guys, let's close up those ranks!" Sloane shouted.

"What the hell are we suppose to do, stand in the mud puddles?" one of the men retorted.

"Nobody's asking you to do that, just bunch up a bit," Sloane continued, the anger showing in his eyes.

"Say, Willie, it looks like we're the only barracks being called out. I wonder how come. What's the deal?" Dawson said. He was having difficulty fastening his collar because his thick fingers kept slipping off the button.

"I don't know. Maybe they think we have web feet," Hawkins said, half smiling, maintaining a firm grip on his blanket.

The Jap guards circled the group, prodding them closer together, while Ishahara talked to Sloane.

"Sloane, I want your men to work in front of the barracks and between them filling up the water holes. Do you understand, huh?" Ishahara said curtly.

"Yes, sir!"

"Two Japanese soldiers will show you where shovels are, so send some of your men now to get them," Ishahara continued, pointing his riding crop in the direction of a small shed.

"Okay, I need about fifteen men to get shovels. Murphy, Humphreys — the rest of you guys in the last two columns. Fall out and follow these two Jap guards," Sloane barked.

As the men moved out, Ishahara glanced about the group tapping his riding crop against the side of his boot.

"Sloane, are these all the men from your barracks?" Ishahara asked. His small stubby cap, laced in the back, and large, round, black horn-rimmed glasses accentuated his square jaws.

"No, sir! There are five or six that are sick in bed and another four over sixty years old inside."

"Who tells these men to stay in barracks when a Japanese officer orders everybody outside to work? Who? Who does not obey Japanese instructions?" he screamed, shaking a clenched fist.

"Sir! I felt these men were either too sick or too old to be out in this weather. I'm sure . . . ."

His reply was cut short by a blow across his cheek that sent him reeling backwards.

"We, the Japanese, will decide who is too sick or too old to work. Everybody must work. No work, no food. Now go quickly and send your men outside. In the future, get permission from the Japanese office to excuse anyone from work. Do you understand, huh?" Ishahara shouted.

He stood still for a moment staring at Sloane, flexing the muscles in his jaws.

The unexpected blow across the face left a long swollen red mark, which Sloane gently ran his fingers over. The mark became more noticeable as his face became pale. His large eyes protruded more than ever now as he pivoted his short stocky frame around and started shouting.

"All right, Herman! Run in and tell all those fellows to get out here on the double."

Everyone watched as Ishahara brandished his riding crop at the men, who were jumping up and down trying to keep warm. Men from the adjoining barracks could be seen peering out the windows. The changing of the guard and the distant rattle of machine guns could be heard frequently. Slowly returning on the muddy road were men with shovels, one Jap guard walking in front, the other behind, both screaming violently for them to move faster. Slipping and kicking mud from side to side, they finally reached the group and dropped the shovels in a pile.

"All right, you men step up and grab a shovel. Then spread out and go to work!" Sloane shouted.

"What are we suppose to do? Dig a hole to fill one?" one of us asked.

"No, not exactly. Just spread a little dirt here and there. Then go back and kinda level it off."

We formed small groups with the Jap guard close by to see that we did not remain idle. Dawson kept pulling at his pants and balancing his shovel against his thick chest.

"Having trouble, Dawson?" I asked.

"Yeah, I guess you might call it that."

"How much weight you lost?"

"Fifty pounds."

"Since we were captured, two months ago?"

"Yeah."

"At least you have it to lose," Hawkins joined in.

"I don't think we'll ever get a full belly here," Dawson whispered as he jabbed his shovel into the mud.

"A week ago I ate the ration of rice and dumped the boiled greens back in the bucket. Now I eat both and I'm just as hungry after eating as I was before I started," interrupted Schultz, who had been gesturing and shouting at the Jap guard to see if he understood any English.

"You're not alone, Herman."

"I guess not. It'll get better fellows," Hawkins said trying to console us, his blanket still hanging about his shoulders.

"How's that, Willie?" I asked.

"Your stomachs are going to shrink after you're here a while."

"So I suppose there won't be as much to fill."

"That's the idea."

"Well, if we miss any more meals like we did this week on account of the water pump breaking down or a shortage of wood, our stomachs are still going to be growling."

"I don't know why I ever left San Francisco. What I couldn't do for a thick steak and trimmings," Hawkins said, smacking his lips, gently running his hand over his unshaven face.

"If I get out of this mess, I'm going to open a swank restaurant somewhere in the Midwest," Sanborn said. "I'll specialize in steaks smothered with mushrooms, baked potato, and green salad."

"Okay fellas, let's knock it off," Sloane warned. "You're only making yourselves hungry. Here comes a guard."

"*Coorah!*"

The guard shouted the low guttural sound used frequently by Jap guards and officers who couldn't speak any English. Its meaning depended on the situation and it invariably demanded immediate attention.

The Jap continued to growl and shove us. His short stocky figure moved quickly, his hobnailed shoes scooping up mud, flinging it everywhere.

"What's bothering him?" Hawkins asked.

"Search me," Sanborn said.

"Doesn't seem too happy about something," Hawkins said.

"Hell, he doesn't have to take it out on us — the squint-eyed bastard!"

"Say, Red, wouldn't you like to grab him by the neck and knock the livin' hell out of him," Schultz whispered half smiling, and he shoveled a chunk of mud into a puddle splashing water freely.

"Yeah. He sure acts brave with a gun," Sanborn said.

Each hour passed marked by the shrill shouts of the Jap sentries changing guard. The cold winds whistled between the barracks, rippling the muddy water, and all we could do was cling to our skimpy clothing. Some of us were fortunate enough to have hats to protect us from the frequent showers, while others had only their thick growth of hair and heavy, scraggly beards. All afternoon, we listened to each other coughing and blowing our noses. When the sticky mud became a mire, the Japs decided to stop the work detail.

"Sloane," Ishahara called. His tall slender figure moved quickly between us toward Sloane, who was trying to persuade Hawkins to remove his blanket.

"Yes, sir!"

"Have your men bring the shovels over to road and put them in a bunch. I mean pile."

"Yes, sir! All right, let's take the shovels over to the road and put them in a pile," Sloane shouted and made his way swiftly toward the narrow road.

Two Jap guards collected the shovels, mumbling to themselves. Ishahara stood silently looking on. As the guards finished, they turned toward

Ishahara. "*Hotchey-jew-coo! Hotchey-jew-coo!*" they screamed.

"*Hotchey-jew-coo! Coo-jew! Ah so!*" exclaimed Ishahara and he continued speaking to the sentries.

"Sloane, Japanese soldiers count only eighty-nine shovels. There should be ninety. How come? Your men hiding a shovel maybe?" questioned Ishahara.

"I don't think so, sir."

"Well, then you tell me where it is."

"We'll look for it, sir."

As Sloane turned to tell his men, the guards quickly sprinted among the prisoners, shouting and grunting. With one hand firmly gripping their bayonet-fixed rifles, the other was free to push and jerk the men around. They were short and stocky. Their smooth faces were the color of the muddy clay soil, and their faded khaki uniforms had buttons missing.

"Okay men, they say there's a shovel missing. Let's see if we can find it," Sloane shouted.

"Hell, where do we look?" someone asked.

"Around the barracks. Maybe someone carried one inside."

After searching for an hour, Ishahara approached Sloane again. The smoke from his cigarette, which all of us craved, filled the chilly air with its aroma.

"Have you found the shovel yet?" Ishahara said, striking the side of his boot with his riding crop.

"No, sir."

"Why you haven't found it! Why!" Ishahara screamed.

"Sir, we've looked everywhere," Sloane tried to say calmly. "I don't know. . . ."

He was unable to finish as Ishahara moved within inches of him.

"You and your men will stay out here all night until you find the shovel," Ishahara growled, and turned away.

At the other end of the barracks, some of the men were beginning to bring the open buckets of chow from the galley. Soft curls of white steam rose from the buckets.

"Looks like we're going to miss another meal, Willie," Dawson said, stroking his silky red beard and biting his lower lip.

"Yeah, it does if we don't find that damn shovel."

"Have any of you seen Murphy?" Sloane asked.

"I think I saw him go inside that barracks over there," Dawson said.

"Okay, go get him."

"What's up, Emery?" I asked.

"Well, he helped collect the shovels. I wonder if the Japs made a miscount," Sloane said, pondering the circumstance.

"Loud Mouth" Murphy, as he was frequently called, was short and wiry, dark complexioned, and always bumming a drag from someone else's cigarette. Stepping out of the barracks into the soft mud, he slipped both hands into a snug-fitting leather jacket and headed towards Sloane.

"What did you want, Emery?"

"Did you help check the shovels out?"

"Yeah."

"Do you remember how many you checked out?"

"Not exactly."

"What do you mean, not exactly?" Emery shouted.

I could tell he was becoming more nervous with each minute that passed without the shovel being found.

"Dammit! They were counting in Japanese," Murphy snapped back. "All I remember is they kept repeating *hotchey* something."

"Well, they say there's suppose to be ninety shovels. Now one is missing.

"When we went to pick the shovels up, there was one that had a broken handle."

"What did they do about it?"

"Took it back into the shed."

"That's the shovel we're short," Sloane said with a sigh of relief.

Relieved for the moment, Sloane swiftly headed in the direction of Ishahara. It was getting late. We could hear the shouting and the Jap sentries changing guard at the far end of the camp. As the sun sank lower on the horizon, the air became colder and colder.

"Mr. Ishahara," Sloane called. He proceeded cautiously toward him, finally stopping at a safe distance.

"What do you want? Did you find the shovel?" Ishahara said impatiently, again striking the side of his boot with his riding crop.

"That's what I want to speak to you about, sir," Sloane said nervously.

I could tell that Sloane now realized his predicament.

"What is there to talk about? Until you people find the shovel, you do not eat and you do not sleep. You spend all night looking for it. Do you understand, huh?" Ishahara said, edging closer to Sloane.

"Yes, sir, but. . . ."

"But, but, but what! You damn Americans! Always making excuses for something. You must learn to take care of Japanese property. You will be severely punished for losing or breaking any Japanese property by the authorities, so be careful. Do you understand, huh?" Ishahara continued.

We began to gather around, showing our support for Sloane.

"One of my men told me that when they went after the shovels, one was broken, and a Japanese guard picked it up and returned it to the tool shed," Sloane tried to explain.

He kept shifting his balance from one foot to the other.

Ishahara spoke to the Japanese sentry standing next to him. The conversation lasted about ten minutes. Their faces were stern. Then Ishahara said "*ah so*" to the sentry and turned to Sloane.

"The Japanese soldier says he forgot about the broken shovel that was returned to the tool shed," Ishahara said without an apology. "However, I must remind you again to take good care of the Japanese property. Do not lose or break it. Do you understand, huh?"

We all sighed with relief as the crisis was apparently resolved.

"Yes, sir!" said Sloane, the tension no longer apparent in his voice.

"Sloane, quickly line your men up so they can be checked out and excused," Ishahara snapped, slipping his long slender fingers into his vest pocket and removing a pack of cigarettes.

"On the double! Let's get lined up and accounted for so we can get the hell out of this cold, miserable wind," Sloane ordered us, and he cupped his hands around his mouth, blowing into them to warm them.

The men moved quickly into position as Sloane began counting each group. As he reached the last one Ishahara approached him.

"Are all you men here?"

"Two are missing in this last group," Sloane said with frustration.

I could see he was becoming weary from the chain of events.

"Where are they?"

"I don't know, unless they're in the barracks."

"What they doing in the barracks when they suppose to be outside working?" Ishahara shouted at Sloane. I was beginning to think Ishahara was enjoying this.

"I don't know, sir, but I'll have one of my men go after them," he replied, and turned toward us.

"Okay, does anyone know who they are?"

"It's Murphy and Willie," someone shouted.

"All right, someone run in and get them out on the double," Sloane shouted. He appeared exhausted.

Ishahara stood motionless, his boots firmly planted in the mud as his eyes followed the men into the barracks.

When they returned with Murphy and Hawkins, the two stood erect before Ishahara. There was silence for a moment except for the distant sound of machine-gun fire. Then without any warning, Ishahara lashed out with his riding crop, striking Murphy across the cheek and sending him reeling backwards into the crowd. With lips tightly sealed, Ishahara quickly regained his balance as he struck Hawkins, who threw his left arm up in self-defense, partially blocking the blow, enraging Ishahara.

"What the hell's wrong with you dumb Americans that you cannot obey simple rules, huh?" he screamed at Hawkins, pummeling him in a tantrum with his clenched fists.

Chapter 6

The winter rains seemed to cleanse the air temporarily until the sun broke through the clouds, warming the air and drying up the muddy soil. Then the putrid odor of human fertilizer, which we called "nite soil," would drift into the camp. A tidal canal ran along the outside of the camp, and invariably the Chinese "nite soil" merchants would stop their wooden boats and with long wooden ladles would unload their fertilizer into large urns on the canal bank.

Other frequent visitors to the camp were the "honey dippers." They were the Chinese coolies who came and cleaned out the latrines. They used wooden ladles to dip the waste out into two wooden buckets. These buckets, when filled, were suspended by ropes on either end of a long thick stick. The coolie would crouch down underneath the stick and center it on his right shoulder and extend his right arm the length of the stick. When he straightened up, the two buckets rose above the ground about five inches. The coolies' skimpy clothing revealed thin muscular bodies that quivered under the strain of the heavy loads as they trotted out of the camp with buckets bouncing up and down in rhythm to their chanting.

The first few months of captivity were the most difficult. It took several months for our stomachs to shrink to accommodate the lack of food. The amount of work we had to do made hunger our constant companion. Our lives were no longer ours but belonged to the enemy, who used us as they wished. From morning till night we might be expected to do almost anything.

One of the more interesting early work details we went on was near the Woosung docks. Shortly after our morning breakfast of rice and watery greens, the front door of the barracks crashed opened revealing the tall slender figure of Ishahara, riding crop in hand. He made his way toward Sloane's office. He then left the barracks as quickly as he arrived, leaving behind the aroma of cigarette smoke, which drove the smokers among us crazy.

"All right, everybody outside," Sloane shouted.

He continued shouting as he quickly made his way down the narrow hallway toward the end of the barracks. His fear of the Japanese, especially Ishahara, was apparent in his eyes. The expression on his face was strained, and he appeared nervous. As we filed out of the barracks, the Japanese sentries shouted and ran about in every direction trying to line us up in groups. The ground was damp from a recent rain and the chilly air had us jumping up and down and swinging our arms in every direction trying to keep warm. With dismay, at the far end of the camp, we saw smoke rising from the chimneys of the Japanese barracks.

Upon receiving instructions from Ishahara, our group of approximately fifty men soon departed through the camp gate. The muddy condition of the narrow road made walking very difficult, and chunks of mud flew in every direction. Groups of Japanese soldiers on maneuvers and Chinese farmers tilling the soil were visible in the distance as we approached the Whangpoo River. The wooden bridge that spanned the muddy water had been patched in so many places where it had been cracked and broken through that it swayed from one side to the other with the movement of the people. Japanese sentries in shelter boxes were posted on either side of the bridge, checking civilians in and out of Woosung. As we entered the small village, our Japanese escort turned down a narrow street lined on both sides with white-clay stores. The open store fronts displayed unrefrigerated chunks of fresh pork and beef hanging on hooks along with fruit, nuts, candy, rice, and cakes that made our mouths water and stomachs growl.

On the edge of the village was the railroad station. We waited our turn to board the double-decked, spoke-wheeled coaches, then found ourselves packed in like sardines along with Chinese men and women. The lower deck contained seats and windows, while the upper deck was only for standing, with a few windows. Our presence didn't create too much commotion as the Chinese stared straight ahead or out a window. Both men and women wore their customary long split skirts with the exception of a very few who were dressed Western style. After about a half-hour ride, we arrived at our destination.

We promptly got off the coaches and assembled in two groups so we could be counted. Ishahara, flanked by two Japanese guards, made his way toward the center of the group, where Sloane stood.

"I wish to give instructions to your men now as to what the Imperial Japanese Army expects," Ishahara exclaimed, standing face to face with Emery.

"Yes sir," Sloane responded quickly, and requested our attention.

Ishahara took his time before addressing us. He looked us over for several minutes, flexing his jaws and adjusting his round horn-rimmed glasses.

"You prisoners will be given shovels to work with. Be careful not to break or lose them. If you do, you will be punished. Do you understand, huh? You will be working in that ditch over there," he shouted, and turned around, pointing in the opposite direction.

"You must clean the sides and bottom of the ditch. Put dirt on top of bank. You must be sympathetic toward the Japanese cause and be sincere in your work. Now go work in earnest," he said and quickly turned to the Japanese guards to give them their instructions.

"Okay fellows, everyone grab a shovel," Sloane shouted and led us toward the pile.

We followed him slowly, but the Japanese came running and screaming and soon we were in the large ditch, shoveling dirt. From the top, we could see the mouth of the Whangpoo River cluttered with sanpans and small ships. Japanese guards with their bayonet-fixed rifles that glistened in the bright morning sun were perched up along either side of the ditch. As the morning wore on, the work became very tiring. Our meager breakfast had ceased to supply us with energy to do the job.

At the far end of the ditch, we saw two Jap sentries running down toward two prisoners who had stopped to rest a minute. The sentries approached them yelling and then striking them with their rifle butts, knocking them to the ground. The men slowly rose to their feet and began shoveling dirt, as the guards quickly returned to the top of the ditch growling to one another.

Our noon meal that day was a small bowl of cooked rice and a small loaf of bread. A short distance away, a long line of Chinese men and women formed behind a large steaming kettle. As they received a ladle of the contents in a bowl, they wandered about the open field chattering.

Except for the constant prodding by the Japanese guards to see that we did not stop to rest, the work detail was uneventful. But as we returned to the camp, we encountered four Japanese soldiers who were torturing a Chinaman. They had removed all his clothing and had tied him to a post with his feet stuck in a bucket and a broken bottle hung around his neck to prevent him from dropping his head. The Japs threw buckets of water at him, and sometimes, if they didn't have any water in the bucket, would merely make passes at the man to make him scream. This brought bursts of laughter from the Japanese soldiers as they gathered around an open fire.

It was dusk when we arrived back in camp, and we entered the chilly barracks tired. This evening's inspection would be entirely different from the previous ones. Some twenty Jap guards accompanied the regular inspection party along with Ishahara, whose very appearance brought unrest. Sloane was at the front door to greet them. After placing two or three Jap guards in each section of the barracks, Ishahara and the Jap Officer of the Day turned to Sloane.

"You will be given instructions from Japanese soldiers on the proper way to salute," Ishahara said. "Pay close attention and be sincere. Also you will be instructed on the proper way to bow. This is very important in the Japanese way of life. Also prisoners must wear a hat if they have one when learning to salute."

Ishahara turned to the Japanese Officer of the Day for further instructions. The regular evening inspection was quickly over and the prisoners scrambled behind their beds for a hat.

The array of head gear we had during the early period of our internment was something to behold. Worn-out straw hats and felt caps were in fashion as well as paper and cloth hats we made by hand. To say we were the neatest looking group would be stretching the truth a little, especially as we had neither bathed nor shaved for nearly two months and had only one change of summer clothing. Each barracks section was arranged so that eight or nine of us stood in front of our beds facing another group, approximately fifteen feet apart. As the Jap guards began instructing one group with their backs to the other, we would go through all sorts of motions to distract the opposite group. Improper saluting by the one group brought smiles and laughter to the other, which created much confusion and anger among the Jap sentries. The constant correcting by the Japanese of the position of our arms while saluting infuriated and frustrated our Japanese instructors. When the Jap sentries turned toward our group, Hawkins began making all sorts of funny signs, which caused me to start laughing. After being warned twice by the sentry to stop laughing, I was struck across the side of my face, which knocked me flat on my back. I picked up the glasses I had been given as a prisoner, and stood face to face with the Jap as he glowered at me and firmly grasped his rifle. His eyes searched mine briefly and his jaws quivered. As he moved on, the only noise that could be heard was the scraping sound of his hobnailed boots scuffling across the wooden floor. When the inspecting party soon departed and made its way toward the adjoining barracks, I breathed a sigh of relief.

Bedding down for the evening required that nine of us lie side by side on straw-filled canvas bags for mattresses placed on a wooden platform built approximately two feet off the floor. The straw shifted frequently and after sleeping on the bags a few hours, we felt like we were lying on only the platform. The Chinese cavalry barracks that we occupied were in dire need of repair and subject to drafts of cold wind. The two thin horse blankets that were issued to each of us were hardly enough to keep us warm, and everyone slept in their clothing. There was a constant stream of men going to the head all night because of the watery diet and cold, damp weather.

The winter nights were long and cold, and they provided the time to ponder the past, present, and hopefully the future. Our hunger was always on our minds; we talked mostly about food and survival and surprisingly little about women. The barracks were never quiet at night as men paraded up and down the hallway with their blankets draped around their shoulders, and Jap guards were constantly walking through at all hours.

Suddenly, on this evening, there was a loud commotion across the hall.

"What in the hell is going on over there?" shouted Hawkins, which brought our entire section out from under our blankets.

A Jap guard had caught one of the prisoners smoking in bed. He had him standing at attention as he continued to yell and strike him on one side of the face and then the other. The loud disturbance brought Sloane sprinting out of his office with one hand grasping his pants and the other brushing the hair out of his eyes. It was 3:00 in the morning, and half asleep and lost for words, he began waving his arms to get the Jap's attention.

"*Coorah!*" the Jap shouted as he took a final swing at the prisoner, who ducked his head to one side, causing the Jap to miss and fall. This infuriated the Jap further, who continued shouting, this time at Sloane.

"No smoko, no smoko," he yelled over and over, pointing to the prisoner he caught smoking in bed. He stomped up and down, followed by a burst in Japanese. Then he struck the butt of his rifle on the floor several times in a final note of anger.

"Okay, okay," yelled Sloane, who slowly backed away from the angry Jap. Sloane moved cautiously to avoid being struck himself, and after a brief exchange of "no smokos" and "okay," the Jap guard slowly shuffled out of the barracks growling to himself. Sloane went over to check on the prisoner, and seeing that he was all right, merely shaken up, Sloane started back to his room shaking his head.

"Say, Emery, you're lucky that Jap's gun didn't go off, the way he was banging it on the floor," Hawkins shouted, standing at the foot of his bed with his blanket draped around him.

"Yeah," Sloane replied, continuing toward his room.

The early morning inspection by the Japanese authorities seemed to quickly follow that night's skirmish with the Jap guard. Fortunately, it was Sunday, a day of rest, so we all did just that in order to make it through the coming week. This particular Sunday was special. We were going to be able to take our first bath in two months. No change of clothes, just a bath. The bathing facility, located in an old dilapidated wooden building, was a large vat filled with water heated by a wood fire. Needless to say, by the time our barracks section arrived at the bathhouse shortly after noon, the water was barely lukewarm. Some soap was provided, but we had to be lucky to get it. Dipping the water out of the vat and pouring it over our heads and splashing it over our entire bodies was refreshing. But the thought of putting on those filthy clothes was depressing.

In the early stages of our captivity, we had heard only bad news, since everything seemed to be going in favor of the Japanese. They were quick to let us know about their victories. And hardly two months had passed before we had our first death in camp. A young civilian literally gave up — didn't care to live! He refused to eat and died of starvation. There was in addition much sickness in camp and no hospital or medical care. We were sure there would be many more deaths.

On 13 March 1942, also after less than two months in camp, the first prison escape occurred. Shortly after the 8:00 evening inspection, two American officers, one British officer, one American executive, and one Chinese civilian tunneled under the outer electric fence and headed toward Shanghai.

During the early morning hours, a heavy fog set in, causing them to lose their direction. Unable to find their contact, they walked along the bank of a river hoping to catch a friendly ride on one of the sanpans. They came upon a Chinese farmer who told them, through their Chinese interpreter, that he could hide them in his barn until arrangements could be made for their safe passage out. The prisoners were elated. They showered him with money and gifts and with promises of more if he was successful.

The Chinese farmer smiled and bowed politely at them inside the barn as he shut the door and locked it. With the locking of the door, there were mixed emotions among the group. Some felt he did it for their own protection, while others thought this was the end of their brief freedom. Several hours passed as they anxiously awaited the farmer's return with help. Shortly before midday, he arrived with a squad of Japanese soldicrs. They immediately took the men into custody.

The Japanese had become aware of the prison escape during the following morning roll call. The five men were reported missing, and all prisoners were confined to their barracks as the Japanese began a search. There was much confusion while the Japanese authorities scoured the outer perimeter of the camp looking for the escape route. As soon as they found the spot where the men had tunneled under the fence, they began taking pictures and measurements. Several bloodhounds were brought into the camp. They were taken to the escape area, where the scent was picked up, and they began yelping as they took off across the open field with the Japs in hot pursuit.

The noon meal was hardly over when a Jap guard appeared at Sloane's door, hitting it twice with his fist. When Sloane opened the door, he was handed a slip of paper. After reading it, he nodded his head and gave it back to the Jap guard, who turned and left.

"What do they want now, Emery?" asked Hawkins, who was seated at the wooden table in the center of the room sipping his tea.

"They want everyone to line up outside in the field within a half hour," Sloane said.

He started to walk down the hallway when Hawkins shouted at him, "What for?"

"Your guess is as good as mine," Sloane said continuing on his way through the barracks, shouting to each section that in one-half hour their presence was requested on the field by the Japanese.

The entire camp gathered, waiting for the arrival of Colonel Yuse and Ishahara. They were rarely prompt, as it seemed they enjoyed watching us stand at attention for them — especially when it was raining. An hour passed before the two arrived. They stepped up and stood on chairs, which had been placed there for them. Ishahara towered over the Colonel and had to bend over to speak to him. Turning toward us, Ishahara began.

"You have been asked to come here today because Colonel Yuse has something very important to say to you. So please pay close attention and then I will interpret his message to you afterwards."

Clearing his voice and twisting his small body sideways, the Colonel began his speech. He blurted out the high-pitched sounds in short spurts. We soon became restless as we awaited Ishahara's interpretation. Finally, he finished and Ishahara began.

"It saddens me to think that some of you prisoners must try to escape," Ishahara said. "It is impossible! The Japanese authorities have provided you with a safe place to live, away from the fighting front. You should be grateful to us for this reason.

"Last night, five prisoners escaped. Today, they have been captured by our Japanese soldiers. Later this afternoon, they will be brought into camp in separate cars and paraded through the barracks. You will see for yourselves then that we, the Japanese authorities, do not lie.

"We have decided after much thought that these five men escaped for selfish reasons only. Therefore, this time the camp will not be punished for their personal actions. This concludes my speech for today. You may return to your barracks. Thank you."

Ishahara quickly stepped down off his chair and extended his hand to the aging Colonel Yuse to help him from his chair. As they slowly walked back to the Japanese office, several Jap soldiers stopped to salute them.

The five prisoners were brought into the camp and paraded through the barracks for our benefit. The Japs wanted to impress upon us that escape was impossible. Aside from appearing very disappointed, the escapees looked good, but they were promptly removed from our camp and taken to Shanghai for sentencing. The military men received ten years each while the two civilians were sentenced to two years in a stockade in Shanghai. After the two years, the American executive was returned to our camp in very poor health.

The camp returned to normal the next two days as the Japanese began to take measures to insure against any future escapes. First, they insisted that the entire camp sign a blank piece of paper. This request by the Japanese was firmly protested by both the American and British sections of the camp. Our leaders demanded to know what we were signing, which infuriated Colonel Yuse and Ishahara. They threatened the whole camp with more work, less food, and no more Sundays off. Two days passed and the following petition was presented to us for signing:

a. That we obey and live up to all the rules and regulations set forth by the Japanese.
b. That we do not destroy Japanese property.
c. That we do not attempt to escape.

Except for the British Governor-General of Hong Kong, the entire camp signed the petition and group pictures were taken afterwards. Sir Anthony John, the tall elderly statesman, had earlier requested of the Japanese authorities that Ishahara be removed from the camp because of his inhumane treatment of the prisoners. However, his request was denied by Colonel Yuse.

The following day, Major Charles McGuire accompanied Ishahara and Morisako to Sir Anthony John's quarters. Upon entering his room, Ishahara immediately drew his sword and threatened to cut off his head if he did not sign the petition. Sir Anthony John stubbornly refused for a while, and then angrily complied.

Ishahara repeatedly boasted of his victory in humbling the Governor-General. He also remarked that Colonel Yuse assisted him in his victory and concluded by saying that even if Sir Anthony John were King of England, he would be required to sign the petition. All prisoners are treated alike according to the Japanese.

For the next two weeks, the British Governor-General of Hong Kong was confined to his quarters. After that, we would see him taking his regular early morning walks around the compound. The following month, the Japanese removed him from our camp.

Chapter 7

We usually ended our evenings by going to bed shortly after our late meal. Everyone was bone tired and our beds afforded, besides rest, a place to curl up on our rice-straw-filled mats and forget for a moment where we were. We felt in a small way secluded from the Japanese. This particular night was interrupted by the appearance of Mark Smith from the next barracks, with whom I had become acquainted while working on Wake Island.

"How would you like to come and work with me in the Japanese interpreter's office?" he asked, half smiling.

"Sure, why not," I replied, quite surprised.

"I'll tell Emery you'll be with me in the morning," he continued. "I'll see you then," he said and excused himself.

As I settled down for the evening, I began thinking about the next day. What was it going to be like working in the same office with Ishahara? We had given him many nicknames as a result of his actions and hatred toward Americans. There had to have been a bad experience in his past to account for the violence he exhibited toward us. His catlike quickness in striking out at prisoners was a constant source of provocation. It seemed he hoped we would retaliate so he could mete out a severe punishment. Why would one human being take such an unfair advantage of another? Why wasn't he abiding by the laws set down by the Geneva Convention for the treatment of prisoners of war? Perhaps I would be able to find out what caused him to behave as he did. Surely, observing him up close might reveal his obsessions. In spite of being anxious about the following day and in spite of the loud shouting of the Jap sentries changing guard, I soon fell asleep.

Morning inspection was uneventful, but mess call didn't go quite as smoothly. After Schultz dished up the watery greens, Murphy insisted loudly that seconds start with him. Schultz called him a damn liar and said seconds ended with him yesterday. As Schultz continued serving the rest of us, Murphy swore profusely and became very violent. Setting the empty bucket in the hallway, Schultz advanced toward his bunk. He gently picked up his bowl of watery greens and started toward Murphy, who was sitting on the edge of his bunk. Stopping directly in front of Murphy, he dumped the entire contents into his lap. This immediately brought Murphy to his feet, swinging at Schultz, who fought back. Fists flew in every direction as the fight turned into the kind of brawl one might expect to see in a bar. The brief scuffle ended up on the floor with both men totally exhausted. Murphy received a bloody nose and Schultz a bruised forehead.

Shortly after the morning's entertainment, Smith arrived and we left for the Japanese office. The air was nippy and patches of snow were visible everywhere. The narrow walk that led to the office a short distance away was very slippery. As we approached the rectangular-shaped building, I noticed that it had a hallway running the entire length on the outside with a smaller structure attached midway.

"What's inside the smaller building, Smitty?" I asked pointing towards the attached structure.

"That's the Japs' restroom. It's connected to that hallway so they don't have to go outside," he explained.

Smith's face became tense as we approached the office steps. Ascending the short steep stairway, we proceeded down the narrow hallway to the office door. I followed him inside. The small room was warmed by a potbelly stove in the far corner that was beginning to glow red. The office was sparsely furnished. There were four wooden desks, five straight-back chairs, and a clothes rack. The walls were bare, and two porcelain lamps hanging from a high ceiling provided the only light. Ishahara was slumped over his desk reading a letter, ignoring our presence. Morisako had been standing with a cup of coffee in his hands and looking out the window when we entered. He slowly turned halfway around and greeted us with a "good morning."

"Mr. Morisako, this is Charlie," Smith introduced me. "He's going to help me make the monthly payroll for the camp and with the other office work."

Ishahara continued to peruse the letter as he turned his chair away from the stove. Our American officers had repeatedly complained to the Japanese authorities about working prisoners and not paying them, insisting that they were violating the rules of the Geneva Convention. Apparently they were having second thoughts.

"Hello," Morisako said, studying me closely.

He was very short and thin. His uniform hung loosely and the sleeves nearly covered his small narrow hands. His head was rather large for the size of his body. He had a massive jaw line that protruded forward and was bridged by enormous buckteeth.

"Smitty, I want this official order typed up and one copy delivered to each barracks adjutant today," he demanded as he handed him the sheet of paper.

"Yes, sir. . . ," Smith replied.

Before Smith could say another word, Morisako continued to explain the official order.

"You prisoners of war will commence a new work project that will last about two years," he said. "It will involve building a large firing range three or four miles from camp. All prisoners must work, except military officers, men over sixty years old, and those who are sick. Those that report sick must have an excuse from the Japanese doctor. . . ."

Ishahara abruptly interrupted.

"Smitty, how many prisoners in camp now?"

"There should be about one thousand, sir," Smith said.

"Oh, is that so!" Ishahara said, quickly picking up a pencil and scribbling on a piece of paper.

The room became very quiet as we waited for Ishahara to continue speaking.

"Then maybe eight hundred prisoners should be going to work on special project, huh!" he yelled at Smith, who hesitated before answering. "What do you say, Smitty?"

"I really don't know, sir."

There was a brief silence as Ishahara glanced down at the paper in front of him, tapping it several times with his pencil before turning to Morisako. The two spoke to each other in Japanese a good half hour, while in the meantime Smith showed me the desk that I would be working at. I slowly took my place behind it and sat down in the straight-back chair. Pulling out the narrow drawer, I counted three pencils which had been sharpened with a knife, five paper clips, and a worn-out eraser. Smith sat down at his desk and read the official order that Morisako had given him.

"Do they have a typewriter around here for you to use?" I asked.

Looking up, my eye caught the sight of a Jap airplane pulling a target as it passed by the office window. Shortly after it disappeared from view of the window, three Jap fighter planes appeared chasing it.

"Yes, it's next door," Smith replied, looking up and turning around, pointing toward the door behind him, which opened into the general offices of the Japanese.

Soon thereafter, Morisako went into the other office and returned with the typewriter. It was an old standard Royal machine — an antique! He also brought some plain white paper and carbon paper. Smith quickly typed the necessary copies and handed them to me to distribute.

As I made my way toward the barracks, I read the contents of the official order. It demanded that each barracks adjutant have lined up in front of his barracks the following Monday morning at 6:00 every able-bodied man for work. The adjutant was instructed to make arrangements for the galley to cook each man an extra ration of rice to take to work.

After delivering all the new work orders, I made my way through the mire, stopping on the office steps to remove the mud that had collected in my loose-fitting Japanese issue shoes.

The Japanese had declared that Sundays would be a day of rest; however, our single change of clothing had to be washed. This was accomplished without soap, and we hung our things on a clothesline to dry, which became a problem because theft among prisoners did occur occasionally and survival of the fittest prevailed. Sometimes we got a haircut and shave at the camp barbershop. Long, narrow, wooden benches propped up at one end and wooden barrels were the furniture used by our three men who did shaving. Stumps and boxes were used by two men that cut hair. As compensation, the barbers usually received one cigarette for a shave and two or more for a haircut. Sometimes they received nothing.

Nearly a year had passed and numerous deaths had occurred because of the poor water, which had to be boiled before using, and the inadequate food, clothing, and shelter. The primary causes of death were dysentery, diarrhea, tuberculosis, starvation, dropsy, electrocution, and rifle shots. Even though there had been several work details in and out of camp, this new one proposed by the Japanese, taking nearly everyone away from the barracks, sounded like slave labor. A little work under these confined conditions would have been beneficial to our health, but a lot of work would be detrimental physically and mentally.

On the first day of the new work detail I had not gone with Smith, but had joined the men to work on the firing range. As we filed out of the barracks, the Japanese guards surrounded us and prodded us into formation. Shortly after Ishahara gave his instructions to each barracks adjutant, we were marching three and four abreast out of camp. The width of the column of prisoners varied with the width of the narrow, winding roadway. The column strung out for nearly two miles as guards kept running back and forth on either side. For the previous two days, the weather had been beautiful, clear, and warm without snow, but with lots of sticky mud.

The outline of our camp soon disappeared from sight and we neared a small Chinese village surrounded by cottonwoods, bamboo, and small trees. Our route took us through the village, which was almost completely encircled by a muddy stream. A few ducks floated on the quiet, dirty water. The adobe brick buildings were all attached, opening into a courtyard in the middle. As family members had married, rooms had been added on. The tile-roofed buildings were riddled with bullet holes. We saw chickens and three goats around and inside the houses, and long strips of bamboo hanging from the eaves and from tree limbs were used as clotheslines.

A few Chinese women and children noted our passing from their doorways. A putrid odor emanated from these doors. Inside, the dirt floors were littered with dried grass and trash. As we left the village, we saw a Chinaman making rice flour by bouncing up and down on a wooden platform which had a round peg weighted down by a heavy stone on the other end. The stone went up and down, striking the rice in a stone bowl. Glancing back at the trees and the muddy stream that encircled the village, I thought how beautiful a picture it would make, but I also thought about how deceiving such a picture would be. As we moved out into open countryside again, the Jap guards began shouting at us and prodding us to walk faster. The narrow road seemed to be headed inland, and we were soon walking alongside a canal. Except for a few Chinese working in the fields, there were no other signs of life.

When we approached the new work site, we saw Ishahara and two Japanese officers walking around inspecting a recently completed mess hall. The open framed facility contained five iron pots for cooking, with benches and tables to eat at. It had been constructed by some of our own prisoners two weeks earlier. We were immediately assembled in front of the mess hall by barracks. After a quick roll call, which revealed a count of seven hundred and eighty men, Ishahara swiftly stepped up on a bench, where he could look over our entire group. A few minutes passed as he awaited the arrival of a detail of ten men pulling two wooden carts with the unprepared food.

"Please give me your close attention to what I am about to say," he shouted, slowly jerking his head from side to side. "You will be working here building a large firing range. The main firing wall will be two hundred and twenty meters long, fifty-five meters wide, and twenty meters high. It will be built in the shape of a pyramid with a slope of about seventy-five degrees. There will also be three smaller pyramids running vertical to provide wind breaks. The dirt you will get from behind the large firing wall which eventually will be a lake. . . ."

One of the Japanese officers standing beside Ishahara interrupted him and they spoke briefly.

"The firing range will be constructed just on the other side of the road," he continued, pointing his riding crop in that direction. "You will notice wooden stakes in the ground. They mark the outline of the main mountain and also the lake. Do not destroy them or you will be punished. Do you understand, huh? You will be moving the dirt by small mining cars mounted on narrow gauge tracks. So, today we will begin by putting all the tracks and cars in position and get started. I will give the instructions to each barracks leader after I have finished speaking."

He stopped to remove some of the mud that had splashed on his boots before continuing.

"You prisoners are walking too slow. You took one hour and fifteen minutes to get here. That is too much time. In the future you should not take more than fifty minutes," he shouted, and his high-pitched voice began to crack.

Suddenly, he leaped from the bench with cat-like quickness and struck a young Marine in the front row.

"Why you smile when I talk serious? Why! Why!" Ishahara screamed as he struck him twice more across the face.

Ishahara was furious as he turned toward the group of barracks adjutants to give them their work instructions. The young Marine took the unnecessay beating without a whimper. Blood began to trickle down his pale cheeks from the open swollen marks made by the riding crop. The unfortunate thing about this incident was that the Marine had not been smiling at all, but his natural facial expression made it appear as though he were smiling all the time.

Our large, shabby group began to wander toward the work site carrying shovels, yo-yo poles on which loads were carried, and rice-mat bags. Except for two or three Chinese graves rising above the ground and a small pond, the terrain was perfectly flat. Several small mining cars were scattered in the field, and piles of iron rails glistened in the morning sun. Numerous small crews began carrying the long rails on their shoulders and setting them in place while others were pushing the cars next to the tracks. While all the tracks were being laid to move the dirt by car, our group began moving dirt by yo-yo poles and rice bags. A long bamboo pole was rested on two prisoners' shoulders and a rice bag suspended in the center. A third prisoner shoveled dirt into it. The amount of dirt depended on whether Ishahara or a Jap guard were near.

Hawkins was looking closely at a bamboo pole as he elevated it up and down. Middle-aged and suffering from poor health, his cheek bones had become prominent as the fleshy parts of his face had disappeared.

"What are you going to do with that pole, Willie?" asked Schultz. They had both turned to look at Ishahara, who was standing on top of a Chinese grave, where he could see the entire project.

"Well, would you really like to know?"

"Yeah."

"I'd like to take and shove it up his rear end, the yellow bastard," he exclaimed as he jabbed one end into the damp soil, making a short furrow.

The remainder of the day was spent yo-yoing dirt to the outer perimeter of the mountain under the watchful eye of Ishahara. All the tracks running toward the mountain had been completed with two tracks working.

At dusk, we quickly assembled at the mess hall. After roll call was taken, our weary bunch headed back to camp. There was little conversation as everyone was tired. However, we had a name for the new project — "Mt. Fugi!"

Chapter 8

During the warm summer evenings, we gathered outside our hot, stuffy barracks hoping to get a breath of fresh air while we waited for the Japanese inspecting party. With the over-crowded conditions inside the barracks, it became difficult to breathe at times, especially for the older prisoners. The galvanized tin roofs made the barracks hotter in the summer and colder in the winter!

During the evening inspection of 8 July 1942, Ishahara decided to tag along. His appearances with the inspecting party were irregular and invariably resulted in trouble for the men. When they reached Marine Gunnery Sergeant Wayne Kettering's section, Ishahara immediately began searching the room for something out of place. His eyes stopped at some things scattered on the table. Ishahara waited nervously until the Jap Officer of the Day completed his check of Sergeant Kettering's section. Then Ishahara confronted the Sergeant who stood at attention in front of his men.

"What is the meaning of these things laying on top of that table?" he screamed violently, pointing a finger toward the wooden table in the center of the room. He kept edging closer to the Sergeant.

Kettering remained silent, standing at attention as the inspecting party departed from the barracks.

"Why do you not do your duty proper way?" Ishahara said, continuing to harass the Sergeant.

"That is the men's duty. I am not responsible for that," Kettering said, looking directly at Ishahara.

"As long as you are a section leader you are responsible for your men," Ishahara yelled, striking him without warning across the face with his fist.

Kettering quickly retaliated by striking Ishahara back with his fist. This infuriated Ishahara, who drew his saber and began striking the Sergeant, first with the cutting edge and then with the flat side three times. The tension mounted in the room as we watched helplessly, the strain and fear showing on our faces.

Ishahara acted like a madman. He holstered his saber and struck the Sergeant with his fists repeatedly while a Jap soldier stood behind him. The Sergeant tried to avoid some of the blows, moving his head and arms, trying not to cause Ishahara to become more hysterical. Without explanation, Ishahara turned suddenly and went outside, the Jap guard trailing him. Outside, he told the Japanese officer about the Sergeant's defiance.

Inside the barracks, Kettering and his men discussed his situation and physical condition. His men tried to clean his bleeding face and bruises, but foremost they tried to convince him to control himself from striking back at Ishahara. This is what he wants the prisoners to do, his men explained. Attack him and you give him an excuse to shoot you, they told him.

Ishahara immediately returned to the barracks and began shouting and beating Kettering again.

"You must go now to the guardhouse," he screamed as he continued to beat him with his fists about the head. The Jap guard stood behind him with bayonet poised at his back. The Sergeant proceeded to follow Ishahara outside with the guard trailing behind. There was relief among the Marines inside, but serious concern for their battered leader.

After witnessing the treatment of Kettering, my thoughts turned to Ishahara's recent vicious beating of Lieutenant Richard Hastings. Hastings had been put in charge of recreation for the camp and had been given permission by the Japanese authorities to construct a baseball diamond. He had gone to the carpenter's shop to obtain a board to use as a backstop, not thinking that he needed additional permission. Corporal Tujioka, who was in charge of the carpenter shop, reported the incident to Ishahara, for disciplinary action, instead of to the Camp Commanding Officer. Ishahara immediately went to the carpenter's shop.

When Ishahara and Corporal Tujioka arrived, they stationed one sentry at the back door and two directly behind Hastings with bayonets pointed at his back. Both had wooden clubs in hand, Ishahara's the size of a baseball bat. He ordered the carpenters to line up as witnesses and commenced screaming degrading remarks at the Lieutenant, saying that he had no honor, should be dead, should have died at the front, and even offered his sword for him to kill himself.

Then, his body trembling with anger, he began striking Hastings about the head and shoulders with the wooden club. He continued striking him until Hastings fell to the floor unconscious. Ishahara then kicked him repeatedly in the stomach. Hastings had to be carried to the camp hospital for treatment by one of our doctors. His face was lacerated and his lips were bleeding, and one tooth was knocked loose and later removed.

A formal complaint was made to the Japanese authorities by both American and British senior officers, but their only comment was that they were sorry it had happened. Nevertheless, Ishahara continued to mistreat the prisoners wantonly while the Japanese camp officials looked the other way.

Sergeant Kettering's trek to the guardhouse this night was made in nearly total darkness. The warm sultry evening added to Kettering's discomfort, making it difficult to breath as he wiped the flow of blood from his nose. Until they arrived at the guardhouse, things were uneventful and quiet.

A single light bulb loosely fastened above the guardhouse door faintly lit the entrance. Four Jap sentries stood under the light laughing and smoking when Ishahara approached them. He surprised them at first, and they quickly came to attention and saluted him. Once he became more visible in the light and they realized that he was not an officer, they quickly withdrew their salute and treated him like an ordinary soldier. But even though he was a civilian interpreter attached to the Japanese army, he felt that his superior intelligence entitled him to an officer's status. When the ordinary Japanese soldier didn't recognize him, it infuriated him. As he exceeded his authority as camp interpreter and assumed the role of camp manager, his resentment grew toward the Japanese officers, who were his superiors. He became an egocentric loner.

After a brief exchange in Japanese, Kettering was positioned in front of the guardhouse while one of the sentries held a bayonet against his abdomen. Beads of perspiration began forming on the forehead of the thirty-four-year-old Virginia farm boy, as he braced himself for another beating. Darkness made it difficult for the Sergeant to see many of the punches that were thrown by Ishahara and the guards.

Shining his flashlight directly into the Sergeant's face and blinding him momentarily, Ishahara began shouting violently.

"Maybe now you learn not to resist Japanese authority."

Then he struck him twice across the face with the flashlight, drawing more blood.

As this was going on, we could hear shrill screaming of Japanese sentries changing guard duty in the distance.

"You white American son-of-a-bitch," Ishahara stammered. "All you Americans think you are so superior to us Japanese."

And then he spit into the Sergeant's face.

After being knocked to the ground and kicked in the testicles twice, Kettering was placed in the guardhouse where he remained for four days, during which he was fed only twice.

Three weeks after the brutal beating, Kettering appeared at the interpreter's office requesting to be removed as section leader, but Ishahara refused.

Chapter 9

There were many work details sent out of camp to do various jobs. One of the most unusual involved about fifty men who went to the Kiangwan Racetrack near Shanghai. The group left early each morning with a Japanese escort and didn't arrive back in camp until dusk.

Loud outbursts of laughter coming from the direction of the main gate one evening brought us streaming out of our barracks. The Kiangwan work party was taking much longer than usual to be checked in before being released to the barracks. The Japanese sentries were screaming as they sprinted around the group trying to get the men to stand in one position. Finally, the group broke ranks and staggered slowly toward the barracks, shouting and singing.

As the men passed by some of the British prisoners, one of them shouted, "The bloody blokes are drunk!"

Several fellows from our barracks had made the trip to the racetrack. Orval Plunkett was one of them. Plunkett was from the backwoods of Kentucky. His copper red hair fell freely about his boyish face. Normally very quiet and shy, he, too, was singing, "They'll be coming around the mountain when they come," as he stumbled through the barracks door waving his arms erratically. Schultz followed him to his bunk, where he flopped down on his rice-filled mattress, laughing.

"What in the hell have you guys been doing today? Where did you get the liquor?" Schultz asked.

At first Plunkett just grinned. Finally, he started to speak.

"Well, first of all, the Japs put us on a truck and took us in towards Shanghai to a racetrack," Plunkett explained. "They had us burying fifty-gallon drums of petrol. As it turned out, all those drums weren't filled with gasoline — some had alcohol."

His head kept drooping, and he had to jerk it up repeatedly. He stopped for a moment to brush his hair away from his face and took a deep breath before continuing.

"Everyone was taking a drink whenever the Japs were looking the other way. We dug holes and buried a lot of drums, but there sure are one hell of a lot more scattered around that horse track."

While he was talking, he kept trying to find the end of his shoelaces to untie them, but just couldn't locate them as his eyes seemed unable to focus on anything. Finally, Schultz untied them for him.

"Are you fellas going back tomorrow?" Schultz asked.

"Yeah. We're suppose to be ready at the same time. But tomorrow everyone is going to take empty bottles or whatever containers they can find to bring some of that booze back. Do any of you guys have any empty bottles?"

"I have a couple of small bottles," Schultz said. "I'll ask some of the other fellows if they have any."

Dropping his shoes off the edge of the bunk, Plunkett curled up on his mat and began snoring within five minutes.

By the end of the third day of the detail, a large quantity of alcohol had been brought back to the barracks. Many of us became very drunk and obnoxious. A few fist fights occurred in some barracks, and the smell of alcohol became strong. However, for a while, most prisoners forgot all about their hardships and were jubilant. Another fellow and I were able to trade some cigarettes for a pint of alcohol. We had a few dried prunes left from a recent Red Cross parcel, which we pooled together and placed in a jar of alcohol. The prunes remained in the alcohol for two days and nights, then were removed and placed in another container, leaving a beautiful fawn-colored liquor. We each took a bite of a prune, which tasted good, but immediately our mouths felt like they were on fire. We quickly went for a cup of water. A small sip of the liquor tasted good and was very smooth, but when it reached the pit of your stomach, it felt like someone had fueled a furnace inside you. We saved the liquor for bedtime and were able to stay warm all night. What ill effects the alcohol had on our stomachs, only time would tell.

On the fourth day of the racetrack detail, all other work parties had returned to the barracks except that group. Two hours passed. Still no detail! The evening chow was held up while we waited for their arrival. Darkness fell and the barracks lights began to flicker on one by one. Outside, the screeching sounds of Jap sentries changing guard duty could be heard. Then there was silence.

Suddenly, an uproar of laughter and singing erupted at the main gate. One porcelain lamp extending from a splintered pole at the main gate and another protruding from the Jap guardhouse provided the only lighting at the camp entrance. The back end of the Jap truck was lit up enough so that we could see the men stumble out and fall to the ground. They were very slow to get up, which infuriated the Japs. After much frustration, the Japs finally had the men standing, then began searching them for liquor, which they confiscated. Those caught with the alcohol were immediately jerked out of the group and taken to the guardhouse. Before the detail was released to the barracks, over half the party had been jailed! The Japs stopped that work detail at once.

While I was in the office the next day, a Jap guard brought Plunkett in for interrogation. Ishahara asked the guard to step outside while he questioned him.

"Come here!" Ishahara shouted. He pointed to the exact spot where he wanted Plunkett to stand. Plunkett moved cautiously to the location, stopped, and looked straight ahead. His body seemed to sway back and forth slightly. Ishahara took a long time staring at him before he began his interrogation.

"Why you steal Japanese property when you know it is forbidden by the Japanese authorities?" Ishahara's loud voice was beginning to crack as he moved forward in his chair.

"Well, sir, you see I . . . ," Plunkett stammered, fumbling for the right word to say but taking longer than Ishahara thought he should.

"Did you steal it to drink," Ishahara continued and began clenching both his fists, striking the edge of his desk with one.

"No, sir. I used the alcohol to rub on both my legs. I have arthritis," Plunkett said, trying to improvise a satisfactory explanation.

His boyish face showed no emotions at all.

"You lie! You Americans all lie!" Ishahara shouted.

He rose from his chair and approached Plunkett, shaking a clenched fist. For a prisoner to steal, break, or destroy Japanese property became very personal with Ishahara and often made him behave like a madman.

"I can smell alcohol on you even now," Ishahara continued, sniffing and shoving Plunkett toward the corner of the room. While this was going on Morisako, Smith, and I sat quietly at our desks. Any interference would have further enraged Ishahara. Even Morisako was fearful.

"No, sir, I didn't drink it, sir. . . . I rubbed it on my legs. That's what you smell, sir." Plunkett's face had become ashen with fear.

"We, the Japanese, do not tolerate people who lie!" Ishahara screamed, and struck Plunkett across the side of his face with a clenched fist, which knocked him against the wall.

"You will spend the next twenty days in the jail house. Maybe you will have time to think about never stealing Japanese property again," Ishahara concluded, his body still trembling with anger as he called for the Japanese guard to remove Plunkett from the office.

After the guard and Plunkett left, Ishahara sat down at his desk and nervously lit a cigarette. For the next hour, the only noise we heard was the sound of his footsteps from inside his door.

Later that afternoon, shortly after 4:00, Ishahara stood up and made his way toward the clothes rack to pick up his cap. All the Japanese had very short hair cuts which changed their appearance when hatless. This was especially true for Ishahara. But his disposition didn't change; it was mean all the time. Saying a few words in Japanese to Morisako, he stomped out of the office. The tension was cut in half whenever Ishahara was out of the office at the Mt. Fugi project!

Sliding his chair back slowly, and causing a dull scraping noise, Morisako rose and walked to the window. He clasped a bowl of tea in both hands and sipped it, making loud sucking sounds, while he stared out the window. Suddenly, he turned around and said, "Smitty, starting tomorrow only one of you will work in the office except when making out the camp payroll and when we need both of you. Do you understand? You may take turns going on the outside work details if you wish. So, you decide and I will see one of you in the morning. Okay."

"Okay, Mr. Morisako. We will work out something between us," Smith replied, nodding his head in acknowledgment.

Morisako slowly made his way to the door, dragging his shoes noisily across the wooden floor. Standing in the doorway, he kept glancing up and down the hallway before finally shutting the door quietly.

Smith placed his forefinger across his lips and whispered to me to be quiet. After a few minutes he got up and gently opened the door halfway, sticking his head out and looking in both directions. Pulling the door shut, he let out a sigh of relief as he scratched the side of his head.

"You're going to have to watch out for him. He's very tricky. He'll pretend he's leaving and be standing outside the door listening. So be on your guard when he's around," Smith said, walking to the window, where he leaned forward to peek outside.

"What if he had been standing outside when you opened the door now?" I asked.

"That already happened to me once. I just continued walking down the hallway to the head. Let's wait ten more minutes before we put things away. Then we'll get the hell out of here," Smith said as he went back to his desk.

A small work detail was being checked in at the main gate as we passed through to the barracks, which were enclosed by several strands of electrical wire. Suddenly, we heard a dog yelping loudly from the far corner of the field near one of the guard towers. The dog had apparently gotten under the electric fence. Four or five Jap guards had cornered it and were clubbing it to death.

"Why are they beating it to death?" I asked Smith.

The sight was making me sick to my stomach.

"They're probably going to eat it," Smith replied, shaking his head.

Several men from the barracks had come outside to see what was going on. The whimpering sounds of the dog gradually subsided before stopping altogether.

As we continued toward the barracks, Smith turned and said, "Since they're not going to let both of us work in the office all the time, why don't we alternate and work three days out and three in. Is that fair with you?"

"Sounds okay. I'll go first on the outside work detail tomorrow," I responded.

He nodded his head in agreement and ran to the entrance of his barracks.

The hour hike to Mt. Fugi and back to camp would have been ample exercise for the amount of food we were receiving. However, Ishahara was going to work our flesh right down to the bone.

Shortly after we arrived at Mt. Fugi, we saw Ishahara pedaling his bicycle on the narrow roadway. The weather that day was typical of a beautiful spring day — blue sky with a few scattered white clouds. There was one thing wrong, however; the air smelled putrid from the sprinkling of "nite soil" on the nearby fields.

As we waited for Ishahara to arrive with the work instructions, a Chinaman, who was yo-yoing a couple of bundles of dry grass, was reluctant to move off the road. A Jap guard quickly ran up to him and booted him in the shins, spilling his load, and made passes at him with his bayonet. The Chinaman took off running across the field, while the Jap guard laughed.

An outline of Mt. Fugi was beginning to form in the distance, as piles of dirt made up the base of the mountain. The network of narrow-gauge tracks, laid on the backside of the mountain reaching up over the top, looked like tentacles from an octopus. Empty cars rested on the tracks, where they were left the day before.

Turning his bicycle in front of the group, Ishahara headed toward the open mess hall. He dismounted before coming to a complete stop and nearly fell to the ground as he stumbled forward. After leaning his bicycle up against a post, he made his way to a box in front of the group. Several minutes passed while he stood on the box, looking us over. There was complete silence as everyone awaited his instructions.

"Mr. Morisako and I have read several of your letters and they all complain of the monotonous life here," Ishahara began. "This is monotonous for me also. As prisoners you must do your best whether you are combatant or noncombatant. I am tired of being camp interpreter, and I would like to go to the front, but my duty has placed me here. Also the guards would like to go to the front, but their duty is here. You must do your best today and remember that your brothers and friends are dying for their country. So today will be 'Front Day' and the mountain tracks will make five more trips than yesterday and the track next to the canal will make seven more trips. You must do these trips even if you do not rest. If you think you cannot make your trips by resting when the bugle blows, you must work."

Ishahara quickly stepped down from the box and struck out toward the mountain. His favorite position was atop one of the Chinese graves which rose several feet above the ground. From there he had a bird's-eye view of all the tracks. From above, the continuous movement of the mining cars on the tracks transporting the dirt to the mountain must have resembled an army of ants building an ant hill.

The bugle sounded around 10:00 signaling a short rest period. Stretched out on the ground, taking advantage of the ten-minute rest, we could see Ishahara coming off the top of the mountain and heading toward us. Our foreman rose to meet him. After a short conversation, there was a loud outburst from Ishahara directed at us.

"Why you no make more trips than thirteen when on the mountain they make thirteen trips and it is much harder? Why?" Ishahara screamed. "You must work harder! You must not take rest if you are not working as hard as those men on mountain. Do you understand, huh?"

He then pointed his riding crop in the direction of the men on the ground.

"Yes, sir," the foreman replied quickly stepping back toward the men. "Okay, fellows, you heard what he said. There won't be any breaks until we make our quota."

Ishahara waited until we started shoveling dirt into the cars before moving on. Before leaving, he gave one of our Jap guards further instructions. The moment Ishahara was out of sight, we stopped shoveling for a minute. The Jap guards quickly descended on us, shouting and striking with their rifle butts those who didn't move fast enough. For fear that their loud yelling would bring Ishahara back down, we slowly started shoveling dirt again.

With still an hour to go before quitting time, one of the track crews had put out their quota and started walking toward the mess hall. For an instant, several hundred men had stopped working to watch the men walking off the mountain.

Suddenly our foreman turned around and said, "Those guys are just going to make it harder on everyone by finishing before quitting time. The yellow bastard, Ishahara, is going to figure if one track crew can put out thirty loads, an hour earlier, so can the rest."

Clenching a fist full of dirt, he threw it against the side of one of the cars, shouting, "Fools!"

The sun had begun to set when we started toward the mess hall. Our movement was slow and leisurely. Some of us rested our shovels on our shoulders while others dragged them. Our tired, thin faces were silent — too exhausted to talk. We ignored the constant prodding by the Japanese guards to walk faster. We couldn't move faster even if we wanted to. A quick roll call was followed by a brief address by Ishahara who thanked us for our work. He was soon riding his bicycle down the road, smiling.

Chapter 10

The warm summer months brought hordes of mosquitos and flies. A few mosquito nets with holes were provided to sleep under, but most of the time we were exposed. Cases of malaria, dysentery, and diarrhea were numerous. For a while, the Japanese were offering one cigarette for ten flies or one hundred mosquitos. We were allowed to catch them only when we were not working.

Except for the discomfort caused by the insects, the warm weather was better. We could cool ourselves with water, whereas during the cold and rainy winter we didn't have enough clothing and fuel to ever get warm! Our appetites diminished to a certain degree with the warmer weather. Hunger was a constant companion but not as intimate on hot days.

Summer rains in China occurred occasionally, which cooled the air temporarily, but made it muggy afterwards. Following a two-day rain, the barracks were invaded by "Tiny Tim" and another Japanese officer and several Japanese guards around 3:00 in the morning. Tiny Tim was a young, energetic Japanese officer and soon earned the reputation for being a "super sleuth." One night he announced his visit by slamming the front door open against the inside wall. The thunderous sound echoed throughout the entire barracks, bringing everyone scooting out of their bunks. Tiny Tim immediately hammered on the adjutant's door. Sloane quickly opened it and found himself looking into a dull flashlight.

"Yes, what is it? What do you want?" Sloane asked, turning his head and shading his eyes from Tiny Tim's flashlight.

"I wish to examine your men now. Have them line up in front of their bunks," Tiny Tim said, flashing the light up and down Sloane's body.

Sloane started down the hallway, yelling for the men to line up in front of their bunks for some sort of inspection. A little more light was added to the dimly lit barracks when each section turned on their porcelain lamp, which hung from the ceiling, illuminating a small wooden table. The inspecting party waited at the door for Sloane to return before beginning the surprise examination. The rain striking the tin roof had stopped, but the smell of wet clothes filled the air.

Suddenly, we heard Schultz's raspy voice coming from one of the corners. He was talking to Hawkins, who stood next to him.

"What in the hell do you think those bastards are looking for this time of night for gosh sakes?" Schultz asked.

One of the older men in the barracks, Schultz was also one of the more rugged. He had spent all his life outdoors in construction work. He had a hide as tough as an alligator's. While working near the outer electric fence a week before, he had grabbed hold of it to see if it was hot. It was! Knocked to the ground, he lay there frightened to death but suffered only hand burns. Two months earlier, a young American sailor accidently backed into the same fence while playing catch with another prisoner. He was given artificial respiration for several hours before he died. These electric wire fences were not supposed to have been turned on during daylight hours.

"Maybe they're looking for their leader," Hawkins said. "I wish they would hurry up and get it over with so I can go back to sleep."

Some of the fellows standing nearby were trying to shut them up when Sloane returned. As he approached them, Tiny Tim turned his flashlight on him. The other Japanese officer was carrying a candle an arm's length in front of him. The small amount of light revealed that Tiny Tim was wearing a large sun helmet.

"What are you looking for? Did someone escape?" Sloane asked.

"No one has escaped. That is impossible!" Tiny Tim reprimanded Sloane. "But it has been told to us that one of your prisoners was seen stealing tomatoes from the officers' garden."

He had struggled with his English, and each word had been spoken at a different pitch. Moving toward the first section, Tiny Tim asked that each of us put our shoes in front of him. The Jap guards sprinted around the room checking to see that all the shoes were properly placed. Sloane trailed quietly behind the group as they carefully picked up and examined each pair of muddy shoes by candlelight. The inspecting party proceeded through the barracks at a snail's pace. Weak laughter followed as they finally left out the back door. The super sleuth didn't catch the tomato culprit by way of muddy shoes, but we were sure he would find a way.

The two days of heavy rain was accompanied by strong, gusty winds which ripped off strips of tin roofing, sending them flying through the air. Two outhouses had been completely blown over. The electricity coming into the camp had been knocked out, causing a loss of our water supply, which was being pumped from a well by electric motors. We received only two daily meals on these two days, as water had to be taken from the bathhouse to make the soup. The Japanese carried out their evening inspections by candlelight after much confusion, which was a source of great entertainment for us.

As soon as the summer rains stopped, the hot sun quickly dried up the sticky clay soil. While the warm summer air was refreshing, the putrid smell of "nite soil" intensified in the warm weather. Shortly after morning chow, our barracks received orders that we would not have to polish artillery shells. Instead the barracks next to us would. Our senior officer had repeatedly protested to the Japanese that cleaning these large projectiles was contrary to the rules of the Geneva Convention. Nevertheless, the Japanese continued to ignore his request. A little later, orders came through that we all had to polish shells. Ten minutes later, orders were changed, and everyone had to go to Mt. Fugi.

After the noon rice was issued, orders came that there would be no mountain detail, and we were to straighten up our shelves and get ready for an inspection by the general troops. Everyone was milling around in front of their bunks when Ishahara burst through the front door. His screaming voice echoed down the hallway, demanding that we stand by for an immediate inspection, which brought Sloane hot-footing it out of his office.

Trailing Ishahara was Captain Endo. He was short and dumpy. His head was round and balding, and he had a big mouth and slightly protruding teeth. This was one of the rare occasions when he wasn't smoking a cigarette and dangling his camera at this side — unusual because he was always taking pictures of the prisoners. The inspection caught some of us unprepared. We were immediately ordered to throw all the mattresses back, which revealed books, dirty clothes, and newspapers. Captain Endo grunted a few times and continued through the barracks. The next officer that came through started from the other end of the barracks and that kept up for about one hour with Japanese officers coming through one by one from different directions. The Japs shook down the officers' barracks and found hot plates, toasters, and written literature. In one of the barracks, they found a hand grenade and a clip of shells.

Shortly after the Japanese finished their shakedown, Captain Endo gave instructions to Ishahara. The room became very quiet the moment their conversation stopped. Turning toward us, Ishahara began his speech.

"I am sure you are wondering why we searched your barracks today and confiscated several things. Well, someone broke into our go-down and stole some jam. So until the thieves are caught and the jam returned, there will be no food for the prisoners. Also, you must order all cooks back to their barracks, where they will remain until the thieves are caught. Do you understand, huh?"

"Yes, sir." Our response was spontaneous.

"So go now quickly to your barracks and find the one who stole the jam," snapped Ishahara, whose fingers pressed so hard against a desk that they were turning pale.

During the speech, Captain Endo had turned away from the group and was looking out the window, puffing on a cigarette. He always used a curved cigarette holder, which tilted upwards.

Everyone was confined to the barracks. There was no evening meal. The next day seemed very long because we were so weak and hungry. Around 4:00 that afternoon, two prisoners went to the Japanese office and confessed. They were immediately placed in the jail house for thirty days on a short ration of rice and water. Our cooks were ordered back to the galley, and around 7:00 that evening we received half our regular meal.

The long summer days meant hot dusty hikes to Mt. Fugi. The Jap guards that continually ran up and down the drawn-out column of prisoners had increased their prodding, trying to make us walk faster. But after nearly a year and a half of strenuous work on this small diet, our bodies felt almost lifeless. We were constantly tired and were actually dragging ourselves along. Up till now, our bodies seemed to be surviving, to a large extent, on the care we received prior to our being captured by the Japanese. Those of us that didn't eat properly and those afflicted with some illness suffered the most. Ishahara ran the Mt. Fugi project. He showed absolutely no mercy to anyone. If you could stand up, you could work!

While walking to Mt. Fugi one morning, we encountered a small group of Chinese, who quickly moved off the roadway as we approached. Two Jap guards chased them into the green fields of rice as they scattered in different directions shouting at the Japs. The Chinese had built alongside the road a rice-straw hut, which they had been occupying the past few days. Stretched across the canal, which ran parallel to the roadway, was a large net, which was supported on either side of the bank by huge bamboo poles. The Chinese had dammed up a portion of the canal to make it deeper, and the net was raised regularly bearing its catch of fish.

The early morning air was very still. Consequently, dust rose straight up from the column and hung over our heads. In the distance, the outline of Mt. Fugi appeared on the horizon. The base of the mountain rose out of the good earth and flattened across the top. Perched on top was Ishahara, scanning the surroundings while waiting for his workers.

After a quick roll call, Ishahara assigned the number of dirt loads each track had to put out this day. Instead of the usual grumbling and bitching that occurred after receiving the track quotas, there were utterances of suprise.

"I don't believe what I just heard," shouted Dawson. "He didn't raise the quota on any of the tracks. I guess we can probably expect another Front Day tomorrow."

The strenuous work and skimpy diet hit large, heavy men like Dawson hardest. Their flesh seemed to disappear the quickest, their clothing hanging loosely on their boney frames which began to make them resemble scarecrows.

"You can bet he's cranking something up in that twisted mind of his. No speech this morning and he's too anxious to get back to Fugi," Schultz said.

We began moving across the roadway into the open field toward the mountain. Schultz and ten other older fellows his age had been placed on a sod detail. Their job was to place square chunks of grass, which had been delivered by the Chinese, on the sides of the mountain.

A small pond approximately one hundred yards in front of Mt. Fugi had to be drained and filled in with dirt. The Japanese had acquired a small treadmill-type pump from the Chinese to remove the water, and I and a few other men were sent to pump it out. Cleo Gates was in charge of that group. He was tall and slender, dark complexioned, with high cheek bones and deep-set eyes. Otherwise quiet most of the time, Gates became excited whenever he was gambling. The only two items that he had to wager were clothing and food, which he could not afford to lose. Not too many fellows liked him because he was such a pessimist, constantly telling us that we would never get out of this stinking place.

The men took turns walking on the wooden treadles that rotated the wheel, which caused them to scoop up the water. Each time they stopped to rest, a Jap guard rushed over and struck them with the butt of his rifle, grunting at the same time. In the meantime, the guard was nervously checking on the workings of the water pump. He was bending over at the water's edge when Gates shouted at Murphy standing next to him, "Hey, Murphy, I'll give you my month's ration of cigarettes if you bump him into the pond."

His shouting was followed by laughter. And Murphy looked over at Gates smiling and then at the Jap. He made a pass at him with his foot.

Shortly after lunch, Ishahara made his way toward the pond and Gates. Standing on the bank for a moment, he gazed at a measuring stick on the opposite side.

"How many inches the water go down?" Ishahara asked Gates.

"Three inches, Mr. Ishahara."

"Three inches!" His excited response and frown indicated some doubt.

"Well, maybe about two and one-half inches," Gates replied, stepping back a little in case Ishahara decided to strike him with his riding crop.

"Now, how many inches you say before I look at measuring stick?"

Before Gates could answer his question, Ishahara started toward the measuring stick on the other side of the pond. The men on the pump stopped working, waiting for Ishahara's reading of the stick. The Jap sentry trailed him like a watchdog.

"It's only one and one-half inches, so I should believe only one-half what you Americans say, yes!" he yelled across the pond.

Everyone started pumping the water as he came back around the pond toward our foreman Gates.

"How many fish you catch?" Ishahara asked Gates, as he glanced about the grassy bank.

"None."

"You haven't taken even one fish out?" Ishahara continued.

"No, sir, not even one," Gates replied.

Ishahara now turned to talk to the Jap guard, who also shook his head, indicating that no fish had been taken.

"Okay. Take your time pumping, but when you get almost water all out, pump fast so that we can get fish or the Chinese will get the fish first!" Ishahara then burst out laughing.

Then suddenly he stopped laughing and became very serious.

"After you get the fish out, maybe you go home," he said, his departing remarks finalized by nodding his head a couple times. He promptly proceeded toward Mt. Fugi, and a short time later we saw him pedaling his bicycle back to camp.

Chapter 11

In early August 1943, upon arriving at the Japanese interpreter's office, we were promptly told to start working on a list of skilled men who would be going to Japan. In addition to the detailed list of five hundred and twenty men, a special payroll for them had to be prepared for the first ten days of the month of August.

There was much excitement at the Japanese office as the men scrambled in and out, shouting and waving papers feverishly. Any signs of organization in the preparation for this group of men leaving camp was nonexistent. Ishahara was seated at his desk while Morisako stood beside him. Stooped over with hands in his pockets, Morisako listened intently as they discussed the work schedule and other matters. Their one-sided conversation was soon over as Morisako gathered up the papers and walked around his desk toward us. Scratching the side of his head, he stopped and hesitated before speaking.

"Smitty, this work I discussed with you earlier must be done right away," he said softly.

Our work instructions always came from Morisako, seldom directly from Ishahara, who seemed to want to avoid any contact with us and rarely looked directly at us.

"What do you mean by right away, Mr. Morisako?" Smith asked.

"This group of men will be leaving the camp in no more than a week's time. So all this personal information must be ready to go along with them to Japan. Also, a copy must be made for this office. Do you understand, huh?" he said, his voice gradually rising.

"We're going to need help to do all this work," Smith replied.

Morisako had in the meantime sat down at his desk, while Ishahara puffed on a cigarette, scribbling on some papers, completely ignoring everyone.

"How many men you need?" Morisako asked.

"Three or four at least to start, I think."

"Okay. Tomorrow you bring them. But today you must start on payroll and work as fast as you can," he said and quickly gathered up the papers on his desk and left the room.

As Morisako walked out, a bespectacled, middle-aged Japanese soldier appeared in the doorway. He hesitated at the entrance, standing silently, looking directly at Ishahara. After a few minutes, he stepped forward and entered, leaving the door open. Ishahara sprung up out of his chair and motioned to the Japanese soldier to approach. Then Ishahara immediately began emptying his pants pockets on his desk and took them off. As he handed them to the soldier, he poked his forefinger through the center of the seat and burst out laughing as the Japanese soldier grinned. The seat of his trousers had been stitched several times and appeared threadbare. A brief glance at Ishahara as he stood in his shorts revealed a spindly pair of bird legs! He sat at his desk the next two hours in his shorts until his pants were returned to him.

After a week of working as late as 9:00 some nights and with as many as nine men crowded into the small office and spilling out into the hall, we finally completed all the paperwork.

The group of prisoners were ordered to assemble in the open field in front of the barracks on Sunday, for they would be leaving our camp that day. Their few personal effects were inspected by the Japanese the day before on the field and taken to the boat. Before departing, they received the following speech from Colonel Yuse, which was interpreted by Morisako.

"Since coming to this camp you have been so obedient to the orders issued by the camp authorities that the reputation of the Shanghai War Prisoners Camp has been raised in one year and a half. However, you are going to leave this, your dear old camp, to transfer to another camp for certain reasons issued by military authorities. In reluctance to parting with each other, now I am going to instruct you as follows:

"(1) On the trip you must obey exactly the orders issued by the officials in charge, and you must not do anything to hurt the feelings of the Japanese authorities and people. As you know, it is wartime and you have to reconcile yourself to insufficiencies and inconveniences. Especially you have to take care of your health condition regarding drinking and eating.

"(2) In every camp, camp authorities are unified according to the fundamental rule. Although we cannot get rid of some different details of regulations in view of this fundamental rule, you must endeavor to understand the regulations and rules of the camp as soon as you can.

"(3) I think that in most of your jobs in the new camp you will utilize your special ability, but some of you will have jobs different from your talents. However, I believe that you will soon become skilled laborers by earnest practice of the work assigned you by the authorities and because you have advanced knowledge and character for technical work. Don't forget that it is an unpleasant life for you to live if you work dishonestly and negatively, even though you have much ability.

"(4) Shortly after you reach your new camp in Japan, the refreshing autumn season will arrive. Moreover, the scenery in Japan is unparalleled in the world. There you are going to work with people who like cleanliness in human beings. I hope you will take everything in good spirit because you cannot understand Japanese. You had better say 'okay' and 'thank you' so that everything will be done without trouble.

"I desire and wish you to go to Japan to live a pleasant life and with great hope. This concludes the instructions of farewell. I admire the honesty and industry of your actions during your stay in this camp. I wish you good health.

"May you live long and prosper. Goodbye, so long."

Departing British war prisoners who had wives residing in Shanghai were granted permission to see them that afternoon for ten minutes, at which time only family matters were to be discussed. No mention was to be made of them leaving for Japan or anything pertaining to the war. They were taken into the Japanese reception room, where they were permitted to see their wives in groups of two. Present at the time the wives spoke to their husbands were Colonel Yuse, Dr. Shindo, Jap interpreter Morisako, and Chinese and Japanese representatives of their consuls. They were instructed to speak loud in order that the Japanese interpreter could hear and take notes on what they discussed. There were three small children besides the wives, who numbered nine. All but the one Britisher's wife were free in Shanghai, and she was interned in a British camp.

The men were taken out of camp in two contingents. As the trucks carrying the first group slowly pulled away from the field toward the camp entrance, the remaining prisoners gathered along the inner electric fence. Everyone waved and wished them well. The trucks returned for the second group in about an hour and a half. Those remaining behind expressed a sigh of relief, knowing they were not going to Japan. Most of us felt our chances of surviving were better the farther we remained from the mainland.

Prior to leaving the camp, the Japanese authorities had issued the following written instructions to the departing prisoners.

REGULATIONS COVERING TRANSFER OF PRISONERS

(1) Any disobedience of orders issued by Japanese authorities during this transfer will result in strict punishment.

(2) Prisoners must keep as quiet as possible and engage in conversations only when absolutely necessary.

(3) In case of unexpected accident, prisoners must follow orders

given by those in charge as quickly and quietly as possible. Anyone disobeying at this time will be shot.

(4) Company Leaders and Section Leaders will be in complete charge under the Japanese and must be obeyed without hesitation.

(5) Prisoners must salute all Japanese military men.

REGULATIONS ON BOARDING

(1) Prisoners must not go outside of assigned areas.

(2) Prisoners must smoke only at assigned places and not walk around with lighted cigarettes in their mouths or hands.

(3) Prisoners are not allowed to touch fixtures or any devices without permission.

(4) Prisoners will go on deck only at specified times and then to specified places.

(5) Company Leaders and Section Leaders are responsible for the cleanliness of rooms which are to be kept clean at all times.

(6) Company Leaders must report any case of sickness or accident to the authorities as soon as possible.

(7) Do not waste water at any time and do not drink water other than that issued for drinking purposes.

(8) Men in each section will be appointed to handle food and clean all dishes.

The chaos that surrounded the Japanese office the previous week had finally subsided. However, whenever Ishahara spent the day in the office instead of out at Mt. Fugi, the tension in the room intensified. As he sat at his desk this day, he appeared nervous, constantly squirming and glancing up at the door. The room remained quiet until 10:00 when there was a knock.

Clearing his voice Ishahara shouted, "Come in."

Opening the door and cautiously stepping in and moving toward Ishahara was Major Charles O. McGuire. He was general spokesman and liaison officer for the camp. Short and stocky, he had been stationed in the Orient with the diplomatic corps for many years. He stopped a safe distance from Ishahara.

"Good morning, Mr. Ishahara," he said.

"What's good about it?"

"Well. . . ." Before Major McGuire could complete his reply, Ishahara interrupted him.

"I understand that you have complained to Dr. Shindo about one of our Japanese sergeants slapping three of your men. Is that so?" he snapped.

"Yes, sir, I did complain to Dr. Shindo about three of our men being slapped. I told him the men couldn't understand. . . ," he said and was again interrupted rudely.

"We, the Japanese authorities, don't want to hear about these kind of complaints. In the Japanese army, that is part of the Japanese discipline; even officers are struck. In your army, you do not do this, and that is why you are losing the war. Your men are not strong; they do not obey army rules."

Ishahara picked up his smoldering cigarette and snuffed it out. Major McGuire remained calm as Ishahara rose to his feet to inform him that he ran this prisoner-of-war camp.

"Major, you are getting too strong, physically and spiritually!"

Suddenly, Ishahara drew his sword out, which sent Morisako scooting out of his chair and out the door with us following right behind him. Major McGuire's face became pale as he stepped back, grasping the corner of a desk to steady himself.

"I'm only carrying out the orders of my superior officer, Colonel Avery Burnside. I always discuss these matters with him before. . . ."

And he was interrupted again by Ishahara, who, admiring the long thin shiny blade, handed it to the Major. There was a sigh of relief as the Major accepted it. He started to touch the blade with his fingers when Ishahara snapped at him, "Don't touch the blade. Now go ahead and use it on me."

He dared him to use it on him.

"I probably could take your head off with it," the Major said, resolutely and calmly. "But I prefer to live a little longer."

He quickly handed the sword back to him, commenting on its elegance. Ishahara turned and put it away reluctantly. Before resuming their conversation, he offered the Major a cigarette, which he accepted.

"Mr. Ishahara, as I tried to explain several times before, any complaints brought to the camp authorities by the war prisoners were not to start trouble, but to find out why misunderstandings arise and to see that there won't be further recurrences," the Major said, looking directly at Ishahara whose arms hung motionless at the sides of his body.

"Never mind reporting these minor incidents," Ishahara continued as he grabbed the back of his chair and jerked it back and sat down.

He was furious. He stared out the window, puffing on his cigarette, while Major McGuire stood still, waiting for Ishahara's permission to leave.

"Will that be all, sir?" asked the Major.

"Yes," Ishahara shouted angrily as he continued to gaze out the window.

McGuire turned quickly and left the room. As he passed us in the hallway, he smiled slightly and tipped his head gently, expressing a sigh of relief. We returned to our desks, where we spent a very cautious day!

Chapter 12

The hot summer months around Shanghai were comparable to those in southern California except for the odor of the "nite soil." The sky appeared higher here and the flat terrain surrounding the work project, Mt. Fugi, seemed uninhabited for miles in every direction.

On our way to Mt. Fugi one morning, however, we did notice a tall, middle-aged Chinaman strolling on the opposite bank of the canal. He was dressed in rags that had been patched and sewed together in the form of a two-piece pants suit. The tight-fitting pants tapered down to his ankles. He was wearing a weatherbeaten straw hat whose brim was bent in different directions. His feet were shod with wooden sandals. He had a bamboo pole about four inches in diameter and twelve feet long with a small rope tied on the end. This was thrown over one shoulder, while in his hand he carried a twig with a string of five or six minnows on it. He seemed not to notice us as he walked nonchalantly along the bank.

As the weeks and months passed, the work at Mt. Fugi became more difficult. As the mountain grew bigger, the slopes became steeper, making it harder to push the mining cars full of dirt up the sides to the top.

We had arrived at the mountain ahead of Ishahara one particular morning, and had lined up in groups in front of the mess hall. Over seven hundred of us waited for him to arrive. Some of us were standing, others squatting, others milling around conversing when someone suddenly shouted, "Here comes that yellow bastard!"

Everyone turned around and looked back toward the narrow roadway. Ishahara was pedaling his bicycle, puffing on a cigarette, and gripping his riding crop. He rode erect except for a slight curvature in his back.

After he gave us our instructions for the day and had assigned the number of loads for each track, we slowly began our journey toward the mountain.

Generally four men shoveled dirt into a car and pushed it up the side of the mountain and emptied it by tipping it over. All tracks had six or more cars on them. Our track had eight. We had a quota of nineteen trips to make for the day. Dawson was one of the four working on our car along with Murphy, Plunkett, and me. Dawson was big enough to do the work of three men.

As we started shoveling dirt into the mining car, Ishahara could be seen crossing the mountain top, carefully searching for his footing in the soft dirt.

"He walks like his pants are full of shit," Dawson said as he rested against his shovel stuck into the ground.

"He walks like that all the time . . . the yellow bastard!" Murphy shouted.

When it came to the Japanese a stream of profanities flowed from Murphy's loud mouth. If this wasn't bad enough, his refusal to work threatened additional hardships on us.

After tossing a few half shovelfuls of dirt into the car, Plunkett stopped to brush his hair back out of his eyes. The young boy from the back hills of Kentucky looked across the car straight at Dawson as he slowly began to speak.

"How much dirt will this car hold?" he asked in his slow drawl, requiring Dawson to wait patiently while he completed his sentence.

"I'd guess a good yard of dirt," Dawson said.

He stepped closer noting the dimensions of the square wooden box that was mounted on the flat bed of the car.

"What do ya mean, a yard of dirt?" Plunkett asked, puzzled by what a "yard of dirt" meant.

"Well, a yard of dirt is a yard wide, a yard long, and a yard deep," Dawson explained, demonstrating with his hands. "Do you understand?"

"I still don't understand what a yard is," Plunkett said.

"A yard is three feet," Dawson said with an uncommon patience and understanding for the uneducated hillbilly.

"Oh, I see. Thank ya."

He thought about it for a moment as he slowly shook his head before starting to shovel dirt into the car.

Several Japanese guards were scattered all around the work project while Ishahara was perched atop the mountain, scanning the prisoners with a pair of binoculars. The lack of a proper diet and the tremendous amount of work demanded by the Japanese was really taking its toll on us. In the warm weather, many of us stripped down to our shorts. Our frail bodies bent over pushing the heavy cars up the mountain resembled tree limbs peeled of their bark, revealing knotty joints.

Halfway through the morning, Murphy sat down to empty the dirt out of his shoe. No sooner had he removed his shoe to shake the dirt out when a Jap guard appeared from the opposite side of the car screaming at him.

"Speedo, speedo!" he screeched.

"Speedo your ass, you yellow bastard! Dirto, dirto in shoe-o!" Murphy shouted back, waving his shoe in the air.

The Jap approached him and struck him with the butt end of his rifle, knocking him flat on his back. Murphy quickly scrambled to put on his shoe and rose to his feet. The Jap growled at him as he slowly turned and walked away.

"They're just not going to let us rest even for a minute," Dawson said as he continued shoveling dirt into the car.

The bugle echoed in the distance signaling 12:00 and lunch. We dropped our tools where we stood and trudged over to the mess hall. Sweat poured down our faces, and we used our shirts to wipe ourselves dry. Smoke poured out of the mess hall, where our cooks were preparing rice in five large iron pots and the usual watered-down greens. Everyone sat in groups according to barracks and was fed accordingly. No one ate until everyone was seated and the Japanese gave the order.

Hawkins was yelling and waving his teacup as hot tea was being poured. He was now beginning to cough spasmodically, and his face became pale and his eyes moist.

"Sit down, Willie. They'll get around to us pretty soon," said Sloane motioning with his hand for him to be seated.

"Hell, they always start serving tea over there and we end up getting our tea last," Hawkins complained.

"Okay, I'll see what I can do about it," Sloane said, turning away.

"Yeah, why don't you do something for a change," Hawkins snapped.

Sloane's face reddened and his lips became tightly drawn. He was speechless. He just stood still for a few moments and then walked away. It got extremely quiet until Sloane reached the far side of the mess hall.

"Hey, Willie, I think if I were you, I'd be a bit careful how I talked to Emery," Sanborn said. "He could report you to the Japanese and make it rough."

But Hawkins shunned Sanborn's seriously considered advice saying, "He wouldn't dare."

Steam rose from the wooden buckets that contained the cooked rice and watery greens. The clanging sound of tin echoed throughout the open mess hall as we removed our metal bowls, cup, and spoon from our draw-string cloth bags.

"Hot stuff," shouted the man with the bucket of brownish colored rice, setting it on the ground at the end of our long table. "Come and get it before I throw it out!"

As we filed past, each of us received a packed cup of rice. Shortly afterwards, we received a teacup full of the greens. Everyone returned to the table and waited patiently until all seven hundred of us had been served and the Japanese gave the signal to eat.

When the signal was given, some of us attacked our small ration of food quickly, devouring it within minutes. Others ate more slowly, chewing their rice leisurely and spitting out the bits of gravel now and then. Eating slowly meant we could eat longer and we wouldn't think so much about being hungry. However, when we finished, we were just as hungry as when we started. Our appetites, though, did lessen a little during the hot weather.

Some of us, who had finished eating, stretched out on the ground while others propped themselves up against a post to rest. A few of us were lucky enough to be able to curl up on top of a table or bench. Sloane had walked over to our table and sat down next to Gates.

"Say, Emery, I haven't seen that Estonian around for the past two weeks. Has anything happened to him?" Gates asked.

There was a middle-aged Estonian who had been living in Shanghai as a civilian prior to the outbreak of war and the Japanese had picked him up and interned him in our camp.

"Last Sunday the Japs turned him loose," Sloane said, shaking his head in disgust.

"You mean after keeping him here for nearly two years they decided he doesn't belong here," Gates exclaimed.

"That's right."

"I wonder why they held him so long," Gates said.

"I can't figure out the Japanese mind. Maybe someone in the Japanese office decided he wasn't an enemy of theirs. Who knows?" Sloane said.

"Did they take him into Shanghai and release him?" Gates asked.

"Are you kidding? They took him to the main gate and gave him his walking papers," Sloane said.

The noon meal and brief rest period was abruptly interrupted by loud shouting from the Japanese soldiers. They quickly rousted us out of the mess hall into formation to be counted before returning to work. Soon we scattered in different directions heading back to Mt. Fugi, yelled at and prodded by the Japanese guards.

"Have you ever heard anyone scream like these bastards?" Schultz said, removing his wire-framed glasses and cleaning the dust from them with his shirttail. "They must have a damn mule's lung."

"It kinda gets to you after awhile doesn't it?" Hawkins said, whose cough was aggravated by the dust stirred up in the warm summer breeze.

"You're damn right it does!" Schultz replied.

The breeze swept across the flat terrain and over the top of Mt. Fugi, swirling the loose dirt up into air. The wind blew in from the China Sea, bringing us slight relief from the stifling heat. Perched on top of the mountain,

Ishahara gazed down at us through his binoculars as we slowly made our way to the tracks. When we began working, we saw Ishahara start toward one of the Marine tracks. Then he bolted down the side of the mountain, nearly falling when his riding boots sank into the soft dirt. We all stopped shoveling dirt and turned to see what he was up to.

"Someone said at the mess hall that Ishahara gave them twenty-four trips to make today," Dawson commented. "Hell, they've got the steepest track on the mountain, and they'll have a tough time getting that many loads before the end of the day."

Dawson dug his shovel into the ground using his foot and then grasped the top of the handle with both hands and gently leaned against it.

"He really wants to get those Marines for the Japanese soldiers they killed on Wake," Gates said, working on the car next to us.

"It seems like it," Dawson said. "It looks like he has their leader cornered and is giving the Sergeant Major hell."

Ishahara towered over Sergeant Major Silas Barnes, the short Marine Drill Sergeant. He shook his riding crop at Barnes threateningly and shouted at the top of his lungs. The movement of the cars on the network of tracks came to a halt as we stopped to see what Ishahara was up to.

"Maybe he doesn't like the idea of them riding back down the hill in the empty cars," Plunkett said with a mischievous grin.

"I bet that yellow son-of-a-bitch is telling them not to take any rest break," Murphy snapped, shaking a clenched fist. "I'll bet the bastard has told them they'll be there all night if it takes that long to finish the twenty-four trips!"

The rest of the afternoon Ishahara constantly harassed the Marines, and the Japanese guards screamed whenever someone tried to rest. Later that afternoon, a small group of Japanese soldiers caught a Chinaman at the far end of the mess hall and turned him upside down against a post. They placed a rubber hose in his nose, down which they poured buckets of water. Then they beat him across his back with a club while he screamed mercilessly. The Japs tried to get him to confess to stealing one of their bicycles. The punishment, known by us as the "water cure," lasted quite awhile.

The long-awaited sound of the bugle halted the work on the mountain, but not for the Marines from Wake. As we waited in the mess hall for them to finish, an hour passed, then two. Finally, shortly before dusk, they began straggling off Mt. Fugi with Ishahara trailing behind. He lengthened his stride as he began yelling and waving his riding crop at their Sergeant Major, who had stopped and turned toward Ishahara to wait for him. His men continued walking back to the mess hall.

"Sergeant Barnes, I want you to assemble your men in front of the mess hall. Do you understand, huh?" Ishahara shouted, striking his riding crop against his boot.

"Yes, sir," Barnes replied and saluted, and he quickly turned to join his men.

It was a very tired, quiet bunch of men that began forming in front of the mess hall. Nevertheless, obeying the curt, loud commands of their Sergeant Major, they snapped to attention quickly, eyes fixed straight ahead. After five minutes of drill practice, Barnes shouted, "At ease!" Their performance made us shiver and also made us extremely proud of our Marines.

A Jap guard came running with a wooden box to place in front of Ishahara. Nodding to the guard, he stepped up onto it cautiously. He studied the Marines carefully, and then he cleared his throat before beginning to speak.

"Is this the way American soldiers line up? Straighten up your lines! If your leader cannot line you up correctly, I will assign you another leader," Ishahara shouted at them, his voice cracking when he became violent and emotional.

His body trembled with rage, and he paused momentarily to regain control of himself before continuing his speech.

"Now today I gave you twenty-four loads to do. But you do not finish them on time. How come? I tell you why. You do not work in earnest. You are not sincere in your work. You are what you Americans call lazy." He spoke slowly and deliberately this time as he turned to look at Barnes, who was standing beside him.

The Sergeant Major stood rigidly, facing his men. His weather-beaten face reflected the years of service to his country. He was strict, quiet, and proud, and his Marines respected him highly. He seemed unaware that Ishahara was staring down at him.

"Tomorrow I am going to give you the same amount of loads to do," Ishahara continued. "And if you do not do them on time, I am going to find other means to punish you. Do you understand, huh?"

When he concluded his speech, he waved his riding crop excitedly in the air. As he stepped down off the box, he nearly fell to the ground, having misjudged the distance, and the Japanese Corporal of the Guard began screaming for his soldiers, who came sprinting from different directions with their rifles swinging freely. They gathered in front of the Marines as if they were herding cattle. Their lines were irregular, their posture sloppy, and their rifles were carried unevenly. Standing beside the Marines, the Japanese soldiers, though dressed in neat, complete uniforms, contrasted starkly with the prisoners, who were attired mostly in ragged shorts and faded shirts draped around their waists, but stood uniformly. The prisoners' thin, haggard faces were streaked with dirt, their skinny arms hung limp at their sides, and their spindly legs barely seemed able to hold them up. Some wore hats while those who didn't had their hair scattered in every direction by the afternoon wind. They stood in dusty, worn-out shoes with socks that fell loosely over the tops of them, but they stood quietly, and remained sober-faced and disciplined while watching the Japanese soldiers perform.

The day at Mt. Fugi ended shortly after the inspiring Marine drill performance as Ishahara led on his bicycle down the narrow, winding roadway toward camp.

Chapter 13

At the Japanese office, Smith and I found Morisako alone at his desk. A crumpled canvas mailbag rested on the floor next to him, and there were small neat bundles of letters spread on top of his desk. He was reading one of the letters when we entered.

"Good morning," we both said in unison as we headed for our desks.

"Good morning," he replied. He hardly looked up from the letter he was reading. He continued to study its contents for several minutes. Finally, Smith broke the silence.

"Did the prisoners receive mail from home?" he asked, turning to Morisako, who kept frowning at the letter.

This appeared to be a much larger quantity of mail received for the prisoners than in the past — perhaps between one and two hundred pieces of mail. Because the Japanese censors performed their duties so slowly, it would take a good month before all our mail reached us.

"Yes, much mail today," Morisako said, pointing to the bundles stacked on his desk. "This should make some prisoners happy. Maybe you two will be one of the lucky ones."

Then he quickly turned back to the letter that he had been studying. There was something in the letter that bothered him. Slowly, he turned around toward us to speak again.

"I don't understand the meaning of part of this letter. Maybe you can explain it to me?" he asked.

I said we'd try.

"It says the New York Yankees defeated the Boston Red Sox by a score of twelve to one at Langley Field. Midway through the game, the Yankee pitcher scored twelve strikeouts and walked one. There were many spectators from both sides. What does this mean?" He seemed reluctant to ask for our interpretation.

"Well, the New York Yankees played the Boston Red Sox a baseball game at Langley Field and beat them by a score of twelve to one," I explained. "The first half of the game, the Yankee pitcher had struck out every batter that came to the plate except one or two. Walking only one batter, he had to be red-hot the first four or five innings of the game."

Finally, after having further thoughts about the letter, Morisako slowly folded it up and slipped it back into the envelope. He tossed it into a small wire basket on top of his desk, which contained a few letters that had already been censored. He suddenly remembered that he had forgotten to place the official censor stamp on the letter. His very small body made it impossible to reach the wire basket from a sitting position. Reluctantly, he squirmed out of his chair and stood leaning against his desk as he reached into the basket for the letter. Slumped over it, he leisurely applied the red oval-shaped mark and casually tossed it back into the wire basket before picking up another to read.

The small room became quiet as we began working on the camp payroll for the previous month. However, there was occasional laughter next door from the main Japanese office and loud, slurping noises the Japs made when drinking tea. In addition, the continuous sound of hobnailed shoes dragging along the outside hallway to the head was another reminder that you were never alone.

But the small, sparsely furnished room wasn't quiet for very long. Morisako rarely laughed, but something in the letter he was reading was extremely amusing to him. He was looking at a photograph that came with the letter.

"Is she pretty?" Smith asked, smiling.

"Well, I don't know about that," Morisako said, admiring the photo. "But maybe she is what you call built, huh?"

Finally, he handed it to Smith.

"Look and see what you think," he said.

Smith began laughing immediately, which roused me from my seat to look.

"Wow!" Smith shouted, as he continued to stare at the picture. "I would say she is endowed with a nice pair of boobs."

The young lady was dressed in shorts with a loose fitting halter. She was bending over in her garden picking tomatoes while facing the camera exposing two large, fully developed breasts.

"What does endowed mean?" he asked.

"Well, you might say 'equipped' or 'blessed with' I guess," Smith said, continuing to laugh as he returned the picture to Morisako.

"I understand," he said, slowly rising from his chair and reaching up over his head to jerk a string which turned a light on so he could have a better look. His eyes remained fixed on the photo fully for several minutes before he slipped it back into the envelope. For a moment, he seemed to forget his position as he turned around in his chair toward us and clasped his hands behind his neck, sliding down in his chair slightly while crossing his boots.

"Do all American women look like that?" he asked.

There was a moment of silence while Smith and I looked at each other.

"Well, do they?" he asked again. He was smiling now as he slumped in his chair and appeared relaxed. His eyes moved to Smith, then to me, and back again to see which one of us would answer. Finally, Smith turned to him and smiled.

"Well, Mr. Morisako, that's a hard question for us to answer properly," Smith said. "You see we really haven't had the opportunity to give that much attention to the young ladies these past two years. You might say we've forgotten what American women look like."

Smith smiled while he waited for Morisako's response.

"According to our file, you've both been to college, so you've both been around a little bit. Surely you've observed the young ladies from time to time," he said.

"That's true, but that seems so long ago," I said.

Morisako had risen from his chair, shoved both hands into his pants pockets and walked to the window. He no longer smiled, silently staring out the large glass window. A few minutes passed before he removed a pack of cigarettes from his jacket pocket and lit one.

I looked at Smith, puzzled by Morisako's behavior, and he shrugged his shoulders. We turned to the work on our desks as Morisako stood quietly smoking at the window. After fifteen or twenty minutes, he was summoned next door.

"What in the hell was that all about?" I asked.

"Who knows? He's a moody guy. Talkative and smiling one moment, morose the next. You never know what he's thinking about — if he's ever mad at something you said. Don't try to figure him out; it's impossible," Smith said.

He had been working in the interpreter's office longer than I and seemed more familiar with the habits of the Japanese.

"Do you suppose he'll continue the conversation later?" I asked.

"I doubt it," Smith said. "He'll probably never bring it up again. To hell with the little creep. Don't let him bother you."

The occasional burst of machine-gun fire in the distance and the frequent screeches of Japanese sentries changing guard or meeting an officer were the only sounds we heard the rest of the afternoon. It was getting late in the day when the door to the main Japanese office slowly opened. Poking his round head cautiously through the door was Dr. Shindo. He smiled and tipped his head gently.

"Hello," he said as he stepped inside and tossed a paper airplane, which he had in his right hand. The plane floated slowly across the room and struck the wall, falling to the floor. He quickly proceeded to retrieve it. He threw it again, and this time it circled the room and landed in a wastepaper basket. He appeared delighted by the plane's flight.

"That's a good place for it maybe," he said.

His English was soft-spoken, and he took his time to enunciate each word carefully. He moved toward Ishahara's desk and sat down on it, straddling one corner. He was quite tall for a Japanese and handsome. He was very humane. His approval of medical care by our doctors and work releases for the sick prisoners, however, was constantly watched by the Japanese Commandant. Nevertheless, he showed concern for the health of numerous prisoners, preventing many deaths.

"Yes, maybe so," I said. "Did you make it?"

His unexpected visit left us speechless for the moment. We all felt that here was one human being who didn't go out of his way to harass the prisoners. A shy and quiet man, he never took advantage of his position as did the others.

"What part of the States are you from?" he asked, smiling.

"I'm from California and Smitty is from Montana," I said. "Where is your home?"

Dr. Shindo ran his left hand over the top of his short-cut hair as his eyes fixed on us. He hesitated for a moment before answering.

"Well, when I left Japan, it was in Tokyo. Maybe it won't be there when war is over," he replied.

He was no longer smiling, and his face became calm. His tall, slender body bent forward slightly with outspread hands resting gently on his legs. He appeared very humble as he stared directly at us.

"I'm sure your home and family will be all right, Dr. Shindo," Smith said. "Are you married?"

"Yes."

"Any children?" Smith continued asking.

"No." He seemed more relaxed and interested in talking to us as he remained sitting on the corner of the desk. He spoke slowly but clearly.

"Have you ever visited the United States?" Smith wanted to know.

His eyes immediately lit up as he stood and looked out the window.

"Yes," he said. "In the spring of 1937, I visited Washington, D.C., and attended a medical convention. The cherry trees were in full bloom, which made me very homesick. The Americans that I met were very friendly and courteous to me. I shall always remember that visit. I am very sorry that we are at war with each other. Maybe the war will end soon, I hope."

He had turned away from the window and looked straight at us as he spoke. Then we were interrupted when the door behind us opened, scraping across the shoddy woody floor as Morisako entered. Dr. Shindo quickly acknowledged him with a soft-spoken Japanese word and brisk bow and left the room.

Morisako stood behind his chair, staring at the bundles of mail strewn across his desk. Suddenly, he shoved the chair into the desk and started walking toward the door.

"You fellows may go now to your barracks; it's 5:00," he said, walking back out the door and into the hallway.

He stood outside the door for several minutes before we heard him leave. We both looked at each other, then at the bundles of mail.

"Check the hallway, Smitty, and I'll look out the window to see if he's gone," I said.

As soon as Smitty gave the all-clear signal, I began untying each bundle and thumbing through them to see if we had received any mail.

"Here's one for you from Billings, Montana."

"That's from my mother," Smith said.

Before I untied another bundle, I stopped and looked out the window while Smitty continued to stand in the doorway, looking up and down the hallway.

"Hey, I hit the jackpot. I've got two from home," I said, quickly placing the bundles back in their exact positions.

As I started to move away from his desk, I inadvertently opened one of the desk drawers, and I discovered inside several letters for the prisoners.

"Hurry up, let's get the hell out of here," Smith whispered as he pulled the door shut.

"Here's a letter for Joe Kaiser in this bottom drawer. I'll bet they don't want him to have it, huh."

"No. Put it in your pocket and let's get out."

While walking back to the barracks, we noticed Colonel Yuse in front of the guardhouse instructing a group of Japanese soldiers on the proper way to wear and shape their caps. Tottering in front of them with his stick in hand, he would remove his cap and show them how it should be shaped. The small, wrinkled old man had to roll his head back and look up at them. He used his walking stick to point at each while giving instructions. The soldiers stood rigidly and appeared frightened by him. They shouted each time they received his approval. Their shrill screeches echoed throughout the barren camp.

The front door to the barracks had been pushed open halfway to let in the fresh air. With thirty-six men lying back to back in a section and with eight sections to a barrack, the need for fresh air was imperative. Needless to say, we didn't need competition from the Chinese "nite soil" peddlers, who invariably stopped outside the camp on warm breezy days like this one.

Inside the barracks, Sloane and Steve Springer were engaged in a heated argument. Each man was about the same size, and they were exchanging verbal blasts face to face. Both were becoming red in their necks and in their strained faces. They were like two roosters ready to pounce upon each other.

"What's going on?" I asked them.

"We received some more things from the Red Cross. An assortment of clothing and as usual not enough to go around. So he wants to draw numbers again like before. I don't think it's fair," Springer said, his voice crackling with anger.

"Everyone agrees that is the only way to do it," Sloane retorted.

"Bullshit!" Springer shouted. "Some guys get more than others. Several have jackets and sweaters and others nothing."

"I don't believe that," Sloane said, the calm beginning to return to his voice. "If they do, someone has given them one or they bought or stole it. If someone receives a jacket or whatever, he is eliminated from drawing."

"What did we get from the Red Cross today?" I asked.

Sloane stepped inside his office and returned with the list of items.

"Each section will receive two pairs of woolen pants, two underdrawers, several blue shirts, skivvy shirts, heavy undershirts, four pair of shoes — thirty-one articles for thirty-six men," Sloane said. "Right after chow this evening, we'll draw numbers for them."

"I still think we need to find a better way to distribute this Red Cross material," Springer said, also calming down.

"That's okay with me," Sloane said. "But for now this is the one we'll use."

"Have the Japanese said when we'd receive another Red Cross food parcel?" Springer asked.

After a year's internment, the Japanese authorities permitted the Red Cross to deliver nine-pound food boxes to the camp.

"They said it would be four or five months," Sloane said.

"Why so long? The last ones were only three months apart," I said, sitting down on my bunk.

"They said they were afraid some of the prisoners might store the food for escape plans," Sloane said, and he removed his comb from his rear pocket and began combing his graying hair.

"You gotta be kidding," I said.

"No, that's it," Sloane said.

"Hell, only two groups have tried it and they got caught," I said. "Some of the Chinese in camp might stand a chance but a white man trying to escape in this country would stick out like a sore thumb."

"I know, but the Japanese have a mind of their own," Sloane said, shaking his head in digust, returning to his room.

Springer puffed on a cigarette extended from a handmade holder and walked down the hall, grumbling to himself.

Chapter 14

Sunday, 10 October 1943, was a Chinese holiday, what the Chinese call the tenth day of the tenth month or the Double Ten. Since the Japanese occupation of their country, many celebrations of their holidays had been curtailed. Nevertheless, the Japanese were enjoying their own victory this day, the internment of two hundred and one Italians.

Shortly after noon, they were escorted into camp by Japanese soldiers straggling along either side of the long, strung-out column of prisoners. They wore summer clothing and carried no personal effects. They were immediately assembled in front of the Japanese office, where Dr. Shindo addressed them with the standard instructions, except that they were ordered not to converse with the other prisoners. They were given rice mattresses, blankets, eating utensils, and assigned to an empty barracks. There was a constant chatter as they slowly made their way to the barracks, several waving their arms spontaneously.

"Hey, Giuseppe! What are you doing here in this camp?" shouted an American prisoner, whose loud voice got the attention of several Italians, who then turned and waved to him.

No one seemed to understand the Japanese motive of interning their allies. But then the Japanese were never consistent in what they did. Later in the day, an order was issued from our senior American officer, Colonel Burnside, that we weren't to associate with the Italian prisoners since they were our enemy!

During the course of the next few days, some of the American prisoners obtained the following information from them. They were Italian seamen off the repatriation ship *Conte Verde,* which had been transporting civilian nationals from Shanghai to Lourenco Marques, Africa, a dispersing center. It was on a return trip to the port of Shanghai that they were seized for reasons known only to the Japanese. One hundred of the crew who were in Shanghai at the time were not interned. Most of those aboard ship had no time to gather any of their personal belongings when the vessel was scuttled. They merely jumped over the side and swam ashore into the waiting arms of the Japanese. They told us the Japanese liner *Nita, Maru,* which had brought us to China from Wake Island, had been sunk some time ago as well as other large ships.

During their brief internment they received the same treatment as the other prisoners, including sharing in the same work. Their lot was a happy one as their barracks resounded with song and laughter much of the time. They had their own Catholic priest, whom we frequently saw strolling up and down the sidewalk in front of his barracks. He was dressed very poorly and was unshaven. It took the Japanese officials two months to decide that the Italians were allies and not their prisoners of war, and they were marched out of camp one morning toward Shanghai.

Upon arriving at the Japanese interpreter's office the day before the Italians left, we were personally greeted at the door by Morisako. He seemed very excited.

"You must begin to work at once," he shouted.

He appeared worried about something as he shuffled back to his desk. The small, dimly lit room was cold and drafty. His slender fingers were wrapped around a round bowl of steaming tea.

"What do you want us to do?" Smith asked, staring directly at him.

Morisako had sat down at his desk and was sorting through some papers. He didn't respond to Smith's query.

Ishahara sat quietly at his own desk next to the small potbelly stove and reeked of sake. Feverishly scribbling on a long, narrow pad with head bobbing up and down, he was oblivious to anything else happening in the room. Suddenly, he rose from his straight-back chair and staggered out the door without saying a word.

I sat at my desk and watched Morisako separate the sheets of paper into two stacks. The moment Ishahara left, there was a relaxed feeling in the room. Morisako immediately lit a cigarette.

"Is Mr. Ishahara coming back soon?" I asked.

"No. He won't be back today," Morisako responded quickly and began stamping his feet to keep them warm.

"Would it be okay to start a fire in the stove?" Smith asked, rising slowly out of his chair, something he never would have asked if Ishahara were in the room.

"Go ahead," Morisako said, shaking his arms back and forth, trying to warm himself.

Smith got up and walked over to the small potbelly stove. It soon started belching flames out the front and top, and as the belly of the stove became cherry red, the small room became very comfortable.

"What I want you fellows to do is make up payroll for the two hundred Italians, who will be leaving tomorrow morning," Morisako ordered. "It will be necessary for you to finish today even if it takes all night to do it. Do you understand, huh?"

"Yes sir," we replied in unison.

"So, you must begin at once to figure each man's time of work and then how much money he has coming for the month," he said, placing each stack of time sheets on our desk, and then he stepped into the main Japanese office.

"I find it hard to believe that these bastards didn't know before today that they were going to release these Italians," Smith whispered to me, checking the door behind him.

"During two months, they had to have found out that the Italians were their allies," I said. "It's just another case of mass confusion on their part. No organization."

The morning was very quiet, except for Morisako checking up on us frequently. He was still moody that afternoon as he shuffled back and forth between the main office and ours. However, when we completed the payroll around 10:00 that night, his spirits seemed elevated considerably. He immediately became friendly and talkative, and he brought each of us a bowl of hot Japanese stew. We were surprised at this gesture on his part because in the past he was never concerned about eating in front of us. A strange aroma rose from the vegetable and meat mixture. It was dark in color and thick. I watched Smith slowly taste it.

"Go ahead and eat it," Morisako said, smiling. "Well, do you like it?"

"It tastes sweet for a stew," Smith said, frowning and puzzled by the strange flavor. "Our stews aren't sweet at all."

"Well, you must remember that our customs and diet are different from yours," Morisako said. "We have different tastes than you. Being a poorer people, we don't have the variety of foods to eat like you. So we must prepare our small amount of foods according to our ancient traditions. There have been changes in the preparations in past years, but the ingredients remain much the same."

He had become more serious, but he still seemed relaxed as he settled back in his chair and lit up a cigarette.

"It doesn't taste like any stew that I've ever eaten before," I said.

As I ate a small chunk of meat, I began to wonder if some of the sweet taste could have been the type of meat they used. I had heard that the Japanese used horse meat or even dog meat. This thought lessened my appetite for this stew. Still, not wanting to offend him, I struggled through the small portion.

Morisako began to speak but was halted by a coughing jag that prompted him to put out his cigarette. He rose from his chair and walked toward the window as he continued coughing. Finally, he turned to us and spoke.

"How much the total payroll for the Italians?" he asked, rubbing his moist eyes.

"We haven't run a total yet," Smith said.

"What is the average pay per man? Can you tell me that?" Morisako asked curtly.

"Somewhere around forty to forty-five dollars per month," I said and Smith nodded in agreement. This paper currency was drawn on the Central Reserve Bank of China. Once a month after payday, the Japanese opened up a canteen for the prisoners to spend their monthly pay. The canteen prices were high. A pound of peanut butter cost $500. Ten Chinese cigarettes cost $35. And a one-pound box of salt cost $144.

"They can spend their money in Shanghai," said Morisako, sipping his bowl of tea. The small room was becoming chilly as the fire in the potbelly stove had nearly gone out.

"I would imagine they will be able to buy much more with their money in Shanghai than we can at your canteen. Isn't that so, Mr. Morisako?" Smith asked.

"Yes, that is so. Quite a bit more."

"Why have the Japanese authorities put such high prices on the articles in the canteen?" I asked, looking directly at him.

He had to think about the question for a moment before answering.

"The Japanese authorities want the prisoners to spend that money for food, and we also must recover the money somehow. So you see it is for your benefit. Don't you think?" he said, answering my question as he clasped both hands behind his neck.

"Mr. Morisako, for most of the prisoners in this camp it would take several months' pay to buy nothing in your canteen except perhaps ten Chinese cigarettes," Smith said.

"I don't know about that," he responded evasively.

"You must not be selling much merchandise," I said.

He began squirming around in his chair, a bit uneasy with the questions being asked. He slowly rose and shuffled towards the window.

The dimly lit office became very quiet as Morisako continued to stare out the window. After several minutes of complete silence, he turned around and began speaking again.

"We sell lots of merchandise every month," he said. As he spoke he was unable to look directly at us but glanced beyond us.

"Who can afford to buy your merchandise?" Smith asked.

"The North China marines had lots of money when they were captured, and also some of your officers in camp have money," he replied. "They are able to buy many things."

"Really, Mr. Morisako, the canteen was opened merely to take the money away from the few who had it. Isn't that so?" Smith's question caused him to become uncomfortable again, but there were no signs of him becoming angry yet.

"I don't know about that. Japanese authorities decide how much to sell merchandise, not me," he said, finally, not bothering to look up from his desk.

It was quite obvious that he didn't care to discuss the matter any further.

"I'll bet you're glad the Italians are leaving," I said.

We began putting the payroll together and giving it to Morisako.

"Yes, they have been nothing but trouble for us," Morisako agreed. "We will be glad to get rid of them. Very strange-acting people these Italians."

* * * * *

On 30 November 1943 another group of Italians arrived in camp. They were twenty-nine marines in full uniform wearing green overcoats and carrying seabags. Japanese soldiers quickly moved them in front of the Japanese office, where they stood for an hour awaiting the Camp Commandant's speech.

At the conclusion of this speech, Morisako grasped his written interpretation in both hands and cleared his throat.

"Please listen closely to what I am about to say." He hesitated momentarily before continuing.

"You Italians took part with the Badaglio Government, the betrayer of the Triple Alliance at the time of the collapse of Italy. And because you behaved as our enemy, you are going to be interned here in this camp and treated as prisoners by Japanese Military authorities.

"I request you to comply with the regulations of the military authorities and the orders which are issued by the members of this camp until the restoration of peace.

"Japanese Empire has been noted for the humanistic treatment to the prisoners. However, punishment for prisoners who violate the regulations is very strict.

"I wish that nobody has the misfortune of the slightest misunderstanding. Learn the regulations and habits of this camp as soon as possible and carry them out with fidelity."

This small group of Italians kept to themselves, rarely mingling with the other prisoners. However, their attitude toward the American and British prisoners was polite. Whenever possible, they would gather outside in the sunshine.

Also joining us was another small group of prisoners who were British. They were the crew off the gunboat *Petrel* that had plied the Yangtze River prior to being captured by the Japanese. Their lot was similar to the Italians. They, too, seldom associated with the other prisoners. However, one of them approached me and asked if I would teach him shorthand. I agreed. So twice a week after the evening chow, I would go to his barracks and give him lessons. His eagerness to learn made him a good pupil. His name was Bungie Harrison, and he was married to a White Russian who was interned in Shanghai with their two small children. He was in his early thirties and very quiet. Only on one occasion did he ever discuss his family, when he told me despondingly, "My God, only a distance of nine miles separates us. I feel like I'm almost close enough to reach out to them but can't. What a hell of a predicament to be in!"

One particular evening I entered the British barracks amidst much laughter and music. I asked Harrison what all the sudden joy was about, thinking maybe they heard good news about the war ending.

"One of the bloody blokes received a letter from his wife telling him she had triplets," Harrison said. "Hell, they'll be carrying on like that the rest of the evening. I'm afraid it's going to be difficult for you to teach tonight."

In contrast to our barracks, family pictures dotted their walls as well as other mementos, which they had been able to keep when captured. Their shelves were stocked with clothing and some tins of food supplied by their British Relief Society, which was solely for British subjects.

I went away thinking of the different personalities in the prison camp, their different mannerisms and styles. Ishahara and Morisako were two of the most colorful. Some of the prisoners called Morisako "Mortimer Snerd." His khaki uniform hung loosely on his small, stoop-shouldered frame and the sleeves of his jacket nearly covered his hands. He constantly dragged his shoes when he walked, and he was slovenly. Working as number two interpreter behind Ishahara, whom he feared, made him nervous and insecure, and he was very conscious of his large mouth and protruding buckteeth. He was moody, and his behavior would change rapidly during the day. When Ishahara was in the office, he became withdrawn. He never discussed his personal life or family, only educational and political matters. His spying on us outside the door was frequent. When we received American cigarettes and chocolate candy occasionally from the Red Cross, Morisako would beg for some.

Ishahara, on the other hand, never asked for anything; he rarely spoke to us. The prisoners had a variety of names for Ishahara. Everyone feared him. He was a sinister, mean man, who often struck prisoners across the face for no apparent reason. He seldom looked directly at us in the office. He always communicated to us through Morisako. He wore large, round, horn-rimmed glasses that seemed to magnify his fiery dark eyes. He sometimes lost control, especially when he had to discuss camp complaints brought in by our officers, and especially with Major Charles McGuire, whom he particularly hated. He became obsessed with his hatred toward the Americans. And even though Colonel Yuse was Commandant of the Camp, Ishahara assumed responsibilities beyond his role as interpreter by taking it upon himself to enforce the rules and regulations and considerably more!

Chapter 15

Another winter was approaching, the third, and the death toll among the prisoners increased. Each winter brought the hope that this would be the last. Newspapers, which earlier in the war were circulated in the camp by the Japanese, had been stopped. The only outside news was received from fliers shot down and interned in our camp. And then they were isolated for two or three weeks. Some prisoners were beginning to express fear of never leaving China alive!

Dark clouds were beginning to gather as I stepped out of the dull gray barracks and walked toward the Japanese interpreter's office. Other prisoners slowly poured out of the different barracks to line up for work details. Smith was standing in front of his, waiting for me.

"It looks like the fellows working outside today might get rained on," he said.

"The sky is getting darker by the minute," I acknowledged.

Proceeding in the direction of the Japanese office, we watched the clouds move swiftly in the distance, clinging to the horizon. The ground was still damp from previous rains.

Arriving at the office, we found it empty and cold. Smith reached up over his head and jerked the cord, but the small bulb shed little light as it swung gently back and forth, making a glow and then shadows alternately on the walls.

"Let's get the stove fired up," Smith said. "This room feels like the inside of an ice box."

He was jumping up and down and swinging his arms around trying to keep warm.

"Do you know where they keep the matches?" I asked.

"Look in Morisako's top drawer," Smith said.

Smith began poking in small pieces of wood that had been neatly stacked beside the potbelly stove. Fire soon flamed out of the top, the sides began to glow, and the small room became comfortable, when Morisako arrived carrying a raincoat under his arm.

"Good morning," he said. "Looks like rain, huh."

Hanging his raincoat and cap on a hook, he walked over to the stove. He stood near it with hands extended over the top and slowly glanced around the room and out the window, before returning to the bundles of letters stacked on his desk.

"Yes, it looks like it could pour any minute," Smith said.

"What this means, pour?" he asked.

"It means rain hard," I explained.

"You Americans use too many slang expressions." He seemed disturbed because he didn't understand the use of the word. Lighting up a cigarette, he turned his attention back to censoring the mail for the prisoners.

A light rain began to fall around mid-morning. The small office had been quiet up till then, except for one of us getting up and fueling the potbelly stove. Suddenly without any warning, the door opened with much force; Ishahara stumbled into the room wearing a plastic cape beaded with rain. Trying desperately to control his balance, he reached out to steady himself by touching the walls. Somber-faced, he tottered to his desk, stopping only to hang up his rain cape and cap. As he sat down, he spoke to Morisako briefly, who responded by nodding. Ishahara again reeked of sake.

He fumbled with his large, black horn-rimmed glasses for several minutes, before they finally fell into his lap. Sliding his chair back and dropping his head down, he gathered them with both hands and set them on the desk. He proceeded to wipe the rain from them as his round head bobbed up and down like an apple in rough water. He had a hard time focusing his eyes, and they opened and closed irregularly.

Ishahara sat quietly, swaying back and forth, jerking his head up frequently. The heat from the stove was beginning to bother him as he wrestled with his collar button to unfasten it. After several feeble attempts, he finally succeeded, loosening the collar around his neck. For a short time, the only sound we heard was the occasional ringing of the telephone next door. Outside, the light rain began again. Inside, the aroma of sake saturated the room. Ishahara finally spoke to Morisako. There was a brief exchange of Japanese, after which Ishahara slowly rose from his chair and stumbled past the stove to the window. Pushing the window wide open, he stood in front of it as the cold air quickly filled the room. The stove ultimately burned out, and the office soon became as cold as an icebox once again.

Shortly before noon, a Japanese soldier entered the office, bowed, and spoke to Ishahara. He left immediately, at which time Larry Gibson, the camp baker, entered. He approached Ishahara, who was sitting at his desk censoring mail. He stood patiently waiting to be recognized while Ishahara deliberately ignored him, continuing to censor the mail. Finally, he came a little closer and spoke up.

"Mr. Ishahara."

"Yes. What do you want?" Ishahara shouted, dropping the letter he was reading, turning to Gibson.

"Well, sir. I work in the galley as the baker and I wish to be reassigned to work on the regular work details," Gibson said. He stood erect, eyes firmly fixed on Ishahara.

Ishahara slowly uncoiled in his chair and stood to face Gibson.

"Who are you to tell the Imperial Japanese authorities what you want to do, huh? Why you do not want to work in galley when we tell you to work there?" As he raised his voice, his speech became increasingly slurred.

"Sir, I work twenty-four hours when we bake and then I'm off the next day to rest," Gibson said. "But I'm being made to work the days I'm not baking."

Gibson moved back as Ishahara edged closer to him. Morisako observed the scene, peering nervously over the letter he was reading while we sat helplessly concerned.

"Never mind that. You do what Japanese authorities tell you to do. Do you understand, huh?" Ishahara snapped back, and he staggered closer to Gibson as he became enraged, shaking a clenched fist at him.

Gibson slowly retreated until his back was against the wall.

"But, Mr. Isha . . ."

Gibson's reply was cut short when Ishahara unexpectedly lashed out, striking him high on the cheek bone with his fist. He repeatedly struck him several times in the face, causing his nose to bleed profusely and his face to become badly bruised. Ishahara began to rave, losing control of himself, and Morisako appeared frightened and as helpless as we were.

Ishahara stopped striking Gibson when he finally fell, slumped against the wall from exhaustion. Breathing deeply, Ishahara stood glowering down at Gibson, who tried to stop the flow of blood from his nose with a finger. His pale face was splattered with blood, and his eyes were nearly swollen shut. He had received a severe beating. As Ishahara began to breathe easier, Gibson straightened up against the wall, his body trembling.

The soothing sound of the gentle rain striking the tin roof seemed to have no effect on the happenings inside the room. Moving away from Gibson, Ishahara raised his arm and pointed his finger violently at him.

"You get out of this office immediately and don't you ever come here again," Ishahara commanded. "And go back to kitchen and work. The Imperial Japanese authorities will tell you where to work in future. Do you understand, huh?"

"Yes, sir," Gibson said and turned quickly to leave the room.

Ishahara staggered back to his desk and slumped into his chair in a stupor. He sat motionless for nearly twenty minutes before picking up the letter that he had been reading. Morisako continued to censor the mail and never uttered a sound until noon when he said, "It is time for you to go to your barracks for chow. Go now."

We quickly slipped out of the room and down the hallway and headed back to our barracks in the light rain shower. We walked swiftly, avoiding the puddles. Trails of smoke could be seen rising from the galley. The electric wire fence that enclosed the barracks was beaded with moisture. Inside the compound, we passed the men carrying metal and wooden buckets of chow from the galley to the barracks.

"Did you ever see anyone take such a senseless beating in your life?" I asked.

"There was absolutely no excuse for it," Smith said, stopping in front of his barracks. "He seems to go out of his way to do it."

When I entered my barracks, I found Schultz and Hawkins seated at the wooden table in the center of the room playing cribbage. Each had both elbows upright on the table with hands resting against their cheeks as they studied the board.

"Don't you fellows ever get tired of playing that game?" I asked before stretching out on my bunk.

"It keeps us from going crazy," Hawkins said. "Besides, I get a kick out of beating this mean old bastard once in awhile."

Hawkins smiled and winked at me.

"The only time he wins is when he cheats, the son-of-a-bitch," Schultz retorted. "I think he's going crazy like the guy in barracks one."

"Someone else blow his cork?" I asked, sitting up.

"Yeah, a fellow in barracks number one," Schultz said.

The buckets of chow had arrived in our section, and Schultz and Hawkins got up and walked back to their bunks.

"That makes three or four in camp who have lost their minds, doesn't it?" I said.

"Four," Schultz said.

"What did this one do?" I asked.

"He just walked out the main gate past the guardhouse, waving and smiling at the Jap guards," Schultz said. "The guards sprinted after him yelling and waving their rifles. They spun him around and headed him back into the camp. All the time, he tried to convince them that he didn't belong in here."

The small ration of rice and watery greens didn't take long to consume and left us nearly as hungry after as before eating. The damp, cool, wintery weather sharpened our appetite as well as chilled our bodies to the bone. We talked constantly among ourselves about the inhumane treatment we received from the Japanese. Then we rested ten or fifteen minutes before returning to work.

"How come barracks number three had their ration of cigarettes stopped for a month?" I asked Hawkins.

The Japanese had been issuing six Japanese cigarettes twice a week to each prisoner on an irregular basis.

"One of the fellows got caught by a Jap guard cutting up his Japanese issue of underwear," Hawkins explained. "He got worked over by the guard in the barracks and taken to the Japanese office. They made him stand at attention all afternoon in front of his barracks with both arms extended above his head. In one hand he held the cut up underwear and in the other a sign which read, 'I destroyed Japanese property, underwear made me guilty.' He also spent the night in the guardhouse."

When Hawkins finished explaining, he nervously fumbled through his pockets searching for a cigarette. Finally, he glanced at Schultz sitting next to him.

"Don't look at me. I don't have any," Schultz said, half smiling.

"What did you do with yours?" Hawkins asked.

"I traded them for a cup of rice yesterday," Schultz quickly answered.

Schultz was one of the few nonsmokers who exchanged cigarettes for food. Many of the prisoners sold their food for cigarettes, usually their seconds. Strange as it may seem, the Japanese punished those caught gambling and selling their food or clothing.

"Why didn't you give them to me?" Hawkins asked.

"The hell with you. If I can get an extra cup of rice for my ration of cigarettes, I'm going to do it. Nobody is looking after me but myself." Schultz's cheeks became swollen and red, and his voice cracked when he shouted violently at Hawkins.

"How about the guys you're taking food away from?" countered Hawkins.

Most of the time Hawkins had a cigarette even if it meant standing a night watch for someone or trading off his food. The Japanese made each barracks have a nightwatch in case of fire, even though their own guards passed through them hourly.

"Hell, nobody is forcing them to sell their rice," Schultz said, pointing his finger at him. "You'd better stop smoking and start eating your rice or you won't be able to do either one. You already look like death warmed over."

Their heated discussion was interrupted by the entrance of a hostile appearing Jap guard. He quickly stepped into our section, screaming and motioning with his bayoneted rifle for us to get up.

"*Coorah, coorah,*" he yelled as he ran around, rousting everyone up and out to work.

"*Coorah,* yourself, you little yellow bastard," Schultz shouted back as the screeching guard left the section and headed down the hallway.

"You'd better be careful what you say to them, Herman. Some of them understand a little English," Hawkins said.

"I don't care. I'm not afraid of the little bastard," Schultz continued as we filed out of the barracks.

The rain had stopped momentarily, but heavy clouds still darkened the sky. The ever-present odor of "nite soil" had been partially washed away by the rain.

I stopped at Smith's barracks, but he had already left. On my way to the Japanese office, I met Dr. Shindo coming down the outside hallway. He tipped his head slightly and said, "Good afternoon."

"Good afternoon," I replied.

He smiled a little as he passed me in the hallway. Tall and slender, he took large strides, walking with his head looking down at the floor. With Colonel Yuse gone to Japan, Dr. Shindo had been made the temporary Commandant of the Camp.

I pushed the door open to let myself into the office, and found that the room was still cold. Seated at their desks were Smith, who was wearing a sweater and stocking cap, and Morisako, who was wearing a loose-fitting, faded olive-green military jacket and a snug-fitting cap. Both moved their legs up and down under the desks, trying to keep warm. The tiny room no longer reeked with sake. In Ishahara's absence, the cold air from the open window had cleared the odor from the room.

"Mr. Morisako, can we shut those windows?" I asked.

"Oh, yes." He looked up from the letter he was studying as he spoke.

Folding his arms close to his frail body, he continued to stomp his feet and shrug his shoulders intermittently to keep warm.

Smith quickly shut the windows and turned toward Morisako again, asking, "Is Mr. Ishahara coming back this afternoon?"

"I don't know," he answered softly.

"Would it be all right to build a fire in the. . . ," Smith started to ask, but was answered before he could finish his question.

"No," Morisako said curtly, raising his voice, before Smith could finish speaking, his lifeless face suddenly showing fear.

As Smith walked back to his desk, Morisako rose from his chair and walked to the window. He appeared nervous as he searched his pockets for his cigarettes. He stood staring out the rain-streaked windows, puffing constantly on the cigarette lolling from his lips. The smoke mushroomed and settled over his large head, causing him to cough and wave his arms wildly. In desperation, he left the room, and we quickly opened the windows to let the smoke out.

The door behind us from the main Japanese office opened gently partway.

Expecting someone to enter, we turned and looked at each other and waited. Finally, Morisako entered, pushing the door open with his back and kicking it closed with his left foot. With head slightly bent down, he clasped a small bowl of steaming tea, which was barely visible in his cupped hands. He quietly shuffled to his desk and sat down. Suddenly as though nothing had happened, he turned to us and spoke.

"This letter here for one of the prisoners is from Peru. It is written in Spanish. Can one of you translate it into English?" he asked, his speech a little slurred, partly because of a speech impediment and partly because of laziness. He was, after all, a graduate of the University of Tokyo. Morisako handed the letter to Smith, who immediately handed it to me as I knew some Spanish.

The three-page letter was neatly written on both sides in longhand, with pen and ink. The words were very legible, though some were foreign to me, but I knew enough of others to piece the sentences together. The letter was from the prisoner's mother and brought the sad news of his father's death. It went into great length, describing the funeral and hardships facing the family. I typed my translation of the letter and handed it to Morisako. He took it calmly, showing no emotion. Glancing at it rather casually while slurping his tea and making loud sucking noises, he turned to Smith and said in a low voice, "Go and bring Mr. José Martinez here."

While Smith went to get José, he continued to study my translation, showing little emotion except for an occasional frown. It was late afternoon now as some of the smaller work details could be heard checking in at the guardhouse inside the main gate. The loud screeching sounds of the Jap guards almost drowned out the shouts of the prisoners being checked in. The sun was beginning to set. Smith returned quickly with Martinez and introduced him to Morisako.

"You are José Martinez and your parents live in Peru?" Morisako looked up briefly at Martinez only to return quickly to the letter. Rarely would Morisako look directly at someone he was talking to for more than a moment.

"Yes, sir." Martinez stood erect, eyes fixed firmly on Morisako and the letter in front of him.

"I have a letter here for you from your mother but it is written in Spanish," Morisako said. "However, it has been translated into English. I want you to read the letter to me in English. Do you understand, huh?"

Morisako handed Martinez his letter from home while picking up the translation and waited for Martinez to read his interpretation in English.

Martinez cleared his throat as he took the letter in both hands and moved directly underneath the light that hung from the high ceiling. He began reading in broken English, stopping frequently to gain his composure as tears began to fill his eyes. He was middle-aged, short, and dark; his thin face showed the depth of his sadness. He hadn't read two paragraphs when

Morisako interrupted him rudely.

"Stop!" Morisako ordered. "My copy of the letter doesn't read the same as what you are speaking."

He became very upset when Martinez's interpretation of the letter in English didn't match mine word for word. His face flushed with anger as he turned to me for an explanation.

"Mr. Morisako, I have translated the letter as best I could word for word," I told him. "However, there were some words that I didn't know the meaning of, and I had to guess them based on the others which I knew. The overall meaning of my translation is the same as José's."

He turned back to the letter and studied it further before asking Martinez to continue reading.

After several interruptions by Morisako and further explanations of my interpretation, he finally said Martinez could return to his barracks with his letter. Morisako then withdrew from us and clammed up. The smallness of his body was accentuated by the large size of his head as he slumped over his desk, scribbling erratically on a piece of paper. His suspicious nature seemed childish to us at times.

Guam, 1945. Author, back row, third from left.

Inscription on rock made by 98 American civilian POWs in May 1943 who were later mass murdered in October 1943 on the shores of Wake Island.

Hospital bunker where author served under military doctor and was captured 23 December 1941.

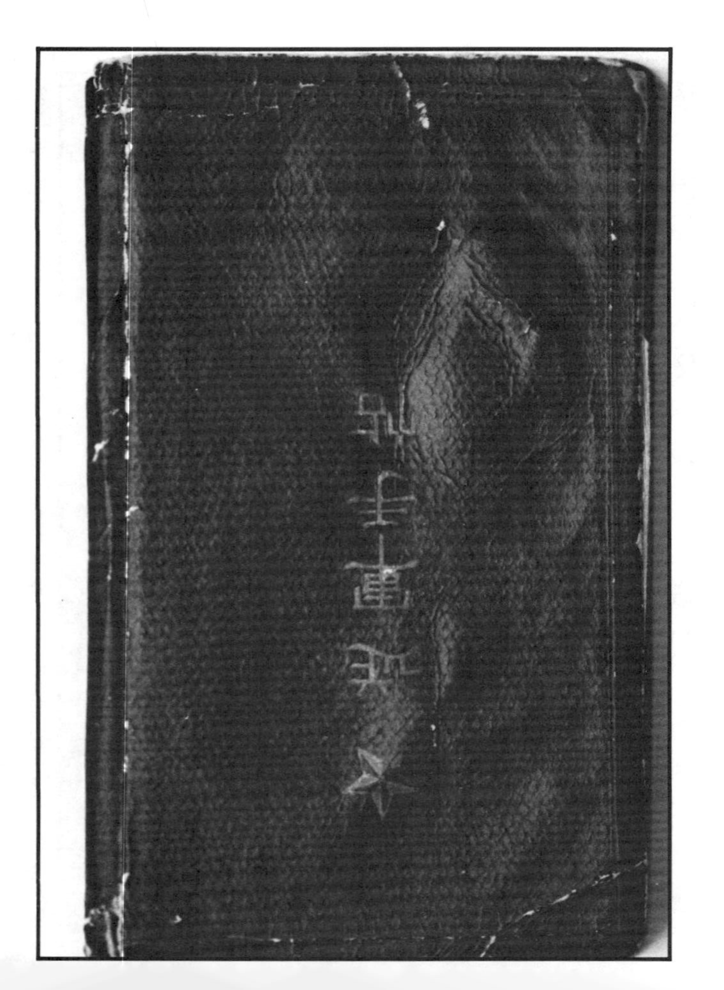

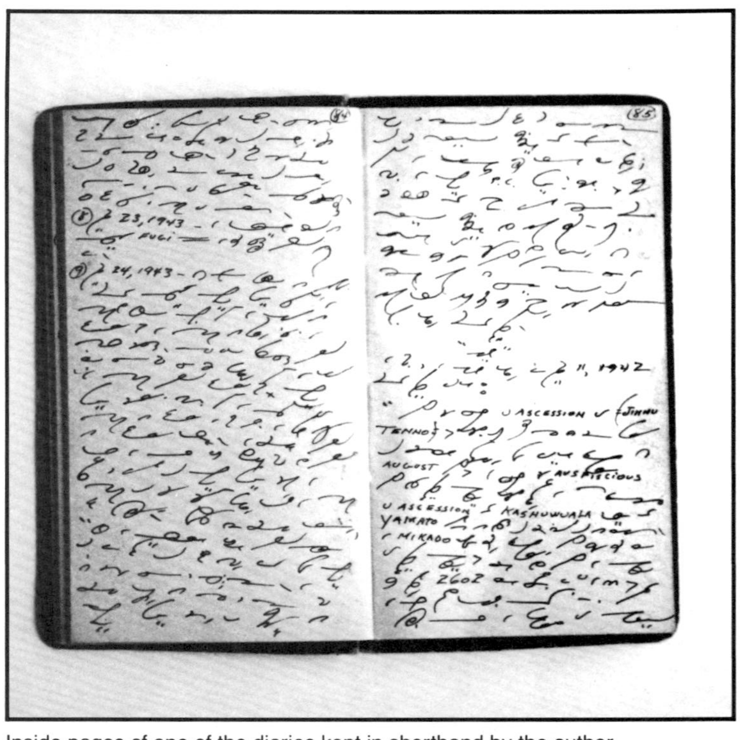

Inside pages of one of the diaries kept in shorthand by the author.

Left: One of four books that contained the author's diaries.

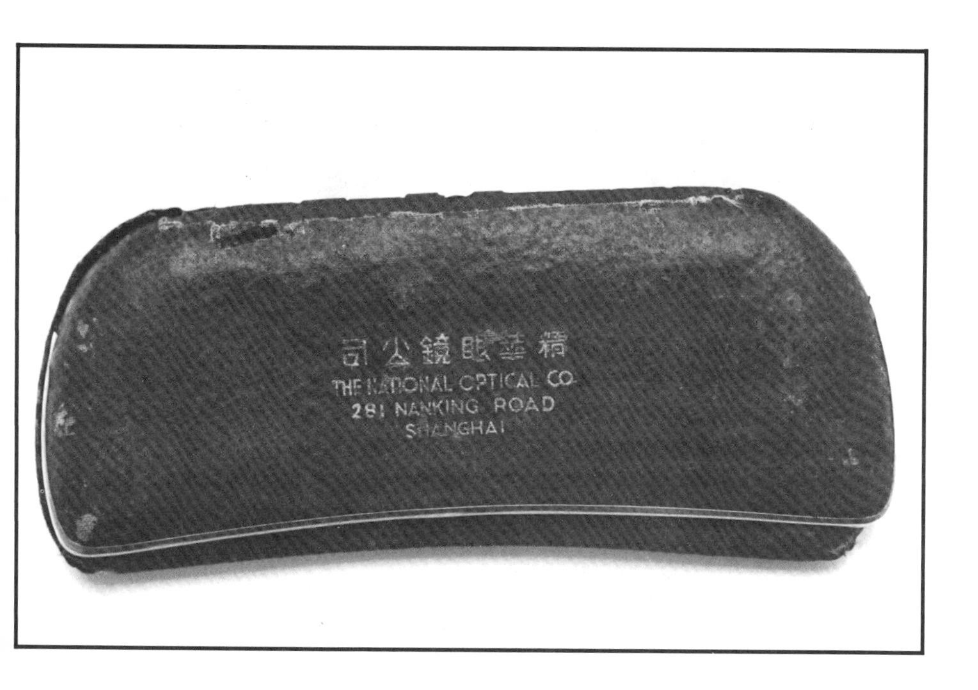

Above and below: Eyeglasses and case received in prison camp in 1942, after the author lost his glasses at time of capture.

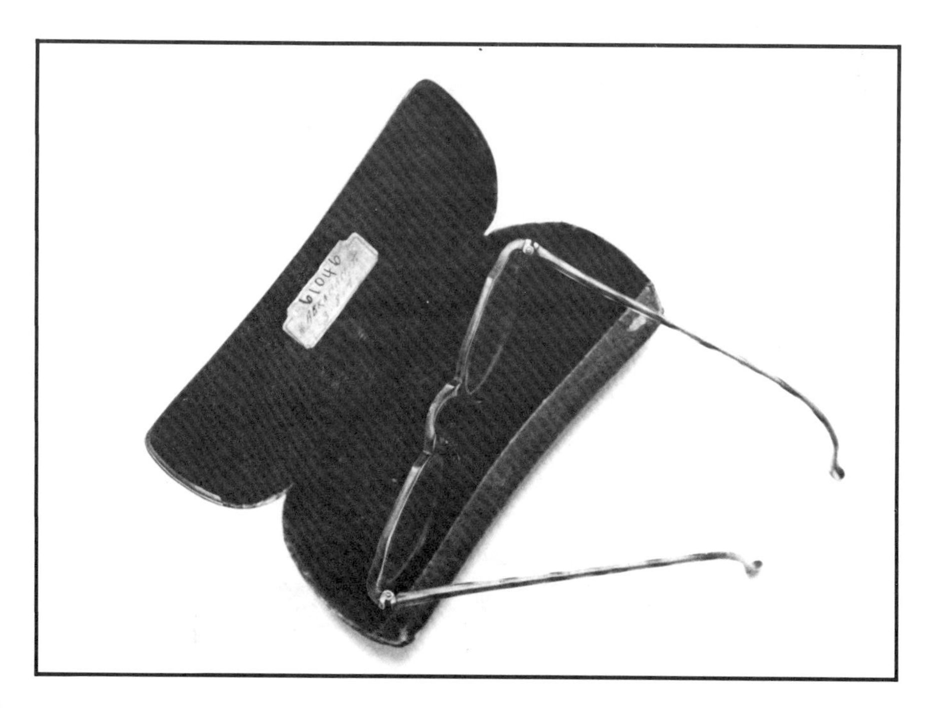

Las Piñas — Front entrance to the camp near the bridge. This area is now a housing project. The photo shows George Fox and Pat Hitchcock, both Marines, in 1967. Martin Christie (of Nichols Field), then living in Manila, furnished the transportation. (Courtesy of George Fox)

Las Piñas — The airfield at the road entrance in 1967. The road from the camp to the airfield remained unchanged and the bridge on the creek by the camp still looked like the original. (Courtesy of George Fox)

Las Piñas — An installation at the southwest corner of the airfield. The airfield has mostly reverted to rice fields. (Courtesy of George Fox)

Mining and lumber village we walked through going to work.

Below: Ishahara.

Chapter 16

The nights were usually long and cold during the winter months. One particular night, before I crawled into my bunk, I took the last four-ounce chocolate bar out of my Red Cross box and ate it. Immediately, I began to warm up. My body, having gone nearly three years without sugar, reacted quickly and noticeably — I felt a tingling sensation throughout! The gentle sound of rain beating softly on the tin roof had a soporific effect which induced sleep instantaneously.

Constant fear of Ishahara prevailed throughout the camp. He moved swiftly between the barracks and through them at irregular times of the day, looking for prisoners who should be working. However, a word of warning would be passed along from barracks to barracks whenever someone saw him coming. Sometimes he appeared in my dreams, causing me to wake up. This night was different. I had pleasant dreams of my boyhood spent with my family. The times we spent together fishing and hunting seemed very vivid and real. I dreamed of the lush green citrus trees that began in the flat lands and crept up the sides of the rolling hills, and their fragrant spring blossoms. I dreamed of Victoria Avenue with its tall, slender palm trees and huge, white-bark eucalyptus trees that dominated the two-lane avenue separated by red rose bushes and small flowering trees in the center.

At midnight the pleasant dream was ended by the loud crashing sound of the barracks door banging open. Simultaneously, Japanese guards thundered down the narrow hallway, screaming at the top of their lungs, bringing everyone to a sitting position on their bunks. Directly behind them was Ishahara and the Officer of the Day, Lieutenant Akiyama, better known to the prisoners as Tiny Tim, super sleuth. They stopped at Sloane's room and began beating on his door.

Sloane opened his door quickly and poked his head out, looking directly into the light of Tiny Tim's flashlight. Shading his eyes from the light he said, "Yes, who is it? What do you want?"

He opened the door wider as he stood in his pajamas, half asleep, his gray hair scattered wildly.

"Lieutenant Akiyama and myself are here to call a fire drill of your barracks," Ishahara explained. "Have your men get up at once and line up in front of the barracks. Do you understand, huh?"

The barracks door remained wide open as the cold, damp air poured in.

"Yes, sir," Sloane said, pulling his door shut.

The dimly lit barracks made it difficult to see the Japs, except for Tiny Tim's flashlight which illuminated some of their faces. As they stood chatting, waiting for Sloane to come out of his room, a few of the lights hanging in each section of the barracks were being turned on. A low rumble of voices expressing disappointment filled the barracks. Another bang on the door brought Sloane out, still stuffing his shirt into his pants.

"Get your men out of this barracks fast. This is a fire drill. Hurry up!" Ishahara yelled at Sloane and hurried him along with a shove.

"Yes, sir," Sloane replied, starting down the hallway, shouting at the prisoners.

Ishahara started after Sloane while Tiny Tim stood in the open doorway. Some of the prisoners were already dressed and milling around in their sections. Ishahara shouted, and Sloane stopped and turned around.

"One more thing," Ishahara said. "All your cooks must go to galley and remain there until fire drill is over. Lieutenant Akiyama and myself are going to get the fire marshal Major Duprey. So be ready when we get back."

They quickly departed through the door with two Japanese guards running ahead of them and the others trailing behind. The door remained wide open.

"Will someone shut that damn door?" a voice shouted from the other end of the barracks, and Sanborn went to the open door and stuck his hand out in the rain before shutting it.

"It's coming down pretty good out there," Sanborn informed us.

His huge frame filled the narrow doorway and partially obscured the outside light that hung over the entrance. Sloane was coming back up the hallway as men began filing out of their sections.

"Hey, Emery, what in the hell is going on?" shouted Hawkins, walking out and meeting him in the hall.

The smell of damp clothing hanging inside the barracks was present everywhere.

"They've called a fire drill."

"A fire drill! In this kind of weather, you gotta be kidding," Hawkins said.

"I wish I were," Sloane replied.

"Are we the only barracks that's having a fire drill?"

"I don't know, Willie."

"I can't see any lights on in the barracks on either side," Hawkins said, slipping on his sweater and cap and then heading for the crowded doorway.

"I can't see any lights on next door either. But that doesn't surprise me," Sloane said as he pushed his way through the crowd and out the door.

We stumbled out into complete darkness, except for the light from the small lamp that hung loosely over the doorway. A cold winter rain whipped by wind lashed us as we slipped in the mud and bumped into each other. Jammed together in front of the barracks, unable to see anyone, we stood waiting in the rain.

"How long are we supposed to stand out in this miserable weather?" someone shouted.

"I don't know. We'll just have to wait till they come back from getting Major Duprey, the fire marshal," Sloane said, standing in front of the group under the door light.

The lights in the officers' barracks had begun to turn on. They started at the front and gradually worked toward the back until the entire barracks was lit up. Shortly afterwards, they emerged from the barracks with Major Duprey and headed toward us with their single flashlight.

"Emery, where are you?" Ishahara shouted.

"Over here, sir!" Sloane yelled back, standing directly beneath the light, wiping the rain from his face with his handkerchief.

Tiny Tim walked ahead of Ishahara and Major Duprey by a few feet with flashlight tilted upwards and flanked on either side by Japanese guards. He was wearing a sun helmet dripping rain, and an oversized raincoat.

"Are all your men out here?" Ishahara shouted, shielding his face with his hand from the light and rain.

"Yes, sir. They're over there," Sloane said, pointing directly in front of him at the men several yards away.

Only the first two or three rows of prisoners were barely visible, where we stood soaking wet.

"Emery, I wish to give further instructions to your men at this time about future fire drills," Ishahara said and turned and walked a few steps toward us before stopping.

He was followed by Major Duprey and Sloane, who stood on either side of him. He was silent for a moment as he appeared to collect his thoughts before speaking.

"The Imperial Japanese authorities have called this fire drill tonight to see how quickly you prisoners could evacuate your barracks," Ishahara explained. "You must move faster. Barracks very old, will burn very fast. These barracks only shelter for you, so be careful! Also we have called out for this fire drill your fire marshal, Major Duprey. In case of fire, he will direct you prisoners in the operation of putting out the fire. So be sure to call him out. And I hope you have better luck than we did in finding him tonight. We woke up every officer before we found him."

He stopped for a moment to laugh as he seemed to find the incident very amusing.

The only means of putting out a fire was the use of the galley buckets to form a bucket brigade, which began at the galley and the wash rack. The Japanese had the prisoners dig shallow water holes between the barracks which filled up during the rainy seasons to be used in case of fire. They dried up during the long, hot summers.

As we waited for Ishahara to continue his speech, the sound of the wind-driven rain striking the tin roof grew louder. His laughter soon ceased, and he cleared his throat to speak.

"That concludes my instructions to you, except in the future you must move more swiftly from your barracks and be sincere about what you are doing. Now you may go back to your barracks," he concluded, turning to and saluting Major Duprey, who returned his salute, before they all left in the darkness.

The grumbling of the prisoners began to drown out the loud sucking noises of their shoes lifting out of the sticky mud as we slowly moved through the narrow doorway back into the barracks. The lights went out in the barracks quickly.

The early morning bugle blaring in the distance, which called for us to rise and get ready for roll call, came rather quickly after the previous night's episode. Outside the barracks, the rain and wind had stopped and the sun shone brightly; and we could feel its warmth in the cold, damp air. The area in front of the barracks where we stood the night before was a mire. Walking cautiously down to the Japanese office, I stepped over water puddles and was sliding from side to side in the mud. I could see steam rising from the barracks.

Smith had arrived at the office just ahead of me and was cramming wood into the potbelly stove when I entered.

"Nobody has showed yet?" I asked.

"No, that's why I'm trying to get this fire started before they arrive and tell us no," Smith answered. "At least we might have it warm for a little while."

He turned and struck a match across the top of the stove and proceeded to light it. I moved closer to the stove and stood next to it, waiting for it to start burning. The stove smoked a bit before the flames burst out of it, and soon the tiny room was filled with the odor of burnt wood.

The flames soon subsided inside the stove and the sides began to glow, and the room no longer was chilly. The sound of dragging boots coming up the hallway grew louder. It was Morisako. When he entered the office, he stopped, staring at the potbelly stove. He turned and glowered at us. He turned his attention back on the stove again and walked over to it. Standing with his back to the stove and hands shoved deep into his pockets, he gazed out the window. Appearing very upset, he kept making hissing noises with his mouth, the only noises in the room, which had become very quiet.

The immediate tension was broken by the entrance of the temporary Japanese Camp Commandant, Shindo, who had to stoop to get through the doorway. Shindo and Morisako greeted each other by bowing. Shindo pointed to a sheet of paper which he carried in his hand while talking to Morisako in Japanese. The two spoke for several minutes. Their conversation ended with Shindo pointing out the window in the direction of a Red Cross truck.

Morisako quickly turned and walked toward Smith telling him, "Go and bring Captain Wellington here at once. Do you know which barracks he is in?"

"He's in barracks number five that houses the Britishers, but I don't know which room for sure," Smith said, rising from his chair.

"Just ask someone. Go now and bring him here quickly," Morisako said, returning to Shindo, who was sitting at Ishahara's desk.

"Yes, sir," Smith said and left the office immediately.

While they waited for Captain Wellington, they continued to discuss the contents of the paper.

After a few minutes, Smith opened the door for Captain Wellington, who barely squeezed through the doorway. Seldom seen outside, the Britisher had a sickly complexion. He was pudgy, with a round fat face, thick lips, clear pale blue eyes, and light brown hair that lay loosely on top of his head. He moved slowly to the desk where Shindo was seated, and stopped to return Shindo's and Morisako's salute.

"Do you know why you have been called down here?" Morisako asked.

"No, sir, I don't believe I do," replied Captain Wellington, appearing puzzled at the question.

"Dr. Shindo would like to discuss the matter of the Red Cross food supplies that your people have been receiving the past year and a half," Morisako explained as Shindo was now looking directly at him.

"Yes, sir." The Captain's face remained calm and showed no signs of surprise.

Shindo glanced down at the paper before him again, then looked up and began speaking.

"Captain Wellington, I have been studying this manifest, which shows that your people are receiving food parcels twice a month from the Red Cross. Is this so?"

"Yes, sir, that is correct." Wellington's heavy arms hung limp as he stood rigid. The senior officer among a small group of British seamen, he had to be approaching fifty years of age.

"How many of your people are there who are receiving this Red Cross food?" The words came slowly to Shindo as hc chose them carefully. His face became more serious as he awaited the answer.

"There are fifty-seven, counting myself," Wellington replied quickly as Shindo cautiously prepared his next question.

"Is there any reason why this food cannot be taken to the galley and used so that all the prisoners may benefit from it," he said, closely studying Wellington's face.

"Yes, sir, there is." His answers continued to be quick and confident.

"What reasons?" asked Shindo, who lit up a cigarette and listened patiently to his explanation.

"This food that we are receiving is coming from the British Relief Society and is for British subjects only," Wellington explained authoritatively. "It is being paid for by the British solely for their benefit."

"Then you won't or can't send this food to the galley for the benefit of all prisoners," Shindo said.

"No, I won't," Wellington replied, appearing certain that he was in the right.

"But your people are benefiting from food donated by the American Red Cross, aren't you?" As he asked the question, Shindo looked at Morisako, who nodded his head in agreement.

"Well, perhaps, but I understood the food was coming from the International Red Cross," Wellington said.

Shindo turned to Morisako, who assured him that there was some food coming from both.

"Since you people are sharing in this other Red Cross food, don't you feel that it is only fair that you should share your food with the others," Shindo continued slowly and forcefully.

"No, sir. As I previously stated, this food is designated solely for the use of British subjects," Wellington said, standing firm, but turning his head from time to time to Morisako.

The questions stopped for a moment as Shindo and Morisako discussed the situation in Japanese. The Captain stood quietly studying them. He had spent many years in China as a riverboat skipper and knew the ways of the Oriental mind. He set his military cap, which he had been holding in his hand, on the desk in front of him. His dark blue uniform fit him snugly. Two gold-plated buttons were missing from one of his coat sleeves, perhaps lost during a scuffle with the Japanese while surrendering his gunboat. His pale face began to show fear as he appeared to anticipate the next question.

"What if I say to you that unless you agree to sharing this food with the rest of the prisoners that I will stop the shipment of this food to your people?" Shindo's speech continued to be slow and deliberate, and he enunciated each word carefully.

"That is your prerogative," Wellington said, unwilling to yield on his principle.

There was a short delay while Shindo asked Morisako the meaning of prerogative.

"I am asking you once more, are you willing to share this food with other prisoners?"

"No, sir, I am not." Wellington's reply was short and snappy. His face showed no sign of remorse.

"Then these food shipments will stop, and the Red Cross truck outside carrying your food supply will be returned," Shindo said.

"Very well."

Dr. Shindo turned once again and spoke briefly to Morisako.

"That will be all. You may return to your barracks," Morisako said to Wellington in almost a whisper.

There was an exchange of salutes and Wellington departed. He was soon followed by Morisako and Shindo, whom we subsequently saw talking to the driver of the Red Cross truck outside.

Smith turned to me shrugging his shoulders and shaking his head and said, "I don't believe what I just heard."

"Neither do I," I replied.

The afternoon was rather quiet in the small Japanese office without the presence of Ishahara. The thought of him being three or four miles away at Mt. Fugi was comforting. However, Ishahara arrived back in camp early in the afternoon and caught three different sections in one barracks using their stoves. The two Japanese guards that accompanied him quickly spotted the firewood which had been hidden under their bunks and reported their findings to Ishahara. Later that evening Ishahara approached Springer, who was standing next to one of the stoves, which had a teapot sitting on it.

"Where this firewood come from?" he asked, pointing his riding crop at a small pile of wood tucked under a bunk beneath the flooring.

"I don't really know for sure," Springer said, clearing his throat and trying to stay a safe distance away from him.

"What you mean, you don't know? Somebody puts wood under floor. Japanese soldiers don't put wood there," Ishahara said and walked to the stove, removed the teapot, and began pouring the hot tea onto the fire, causing it to smoke and go out.

"Well, I think the men have been collecting the wood on outside details and bringing it into camp," Springer said, continuing to distance himself from Ishahara.

"Nonsense! Wood to burn for fuel very scarce in China. Many Chinese die every winter because they don't have enough wood or coal to burn to keep them warm. Prisoners must be destroying Japanese property to get wood. They will be severely punished if caught doing this. Do you understand, huh?" Ishahara screamed, waving his riding crop violently at him.

"Yes, sir."

"The other thing that I must remind you about is that you have started these fires in the middle of the afternoon when Japanese regulations say they should not start until 5:00. Therefore, as punishment, these three stoves will be removed from this barracks for one month," Ishahara said, turning to the Japanese guards, whom he instructed to put out the other two fires and remove the stove pipes.

He proceeded to light up a cigarette and nervously moved up and down the hallway, awaiting the dismantling of the stoves. The air soon became thick with the odor of tobacco, which drove the smokers up the walls. Ishahara stopped momentarily to talk to one of the Japanese guards before leaving the barracks rather swiftly and was gone for about a half hour.

He returned, smiling, carrying a printed sign which read, "We broke floor and hid wood, stove made us guilty." He appeared in a jovial mood as he approached Springer, who was helping remove the stove pipes.

"I want you to gather enough men to carry these stoves around the camp. Also it will be necessary for your men to carry the stove pipes. So bring them outside in front of baracks," Ishahara said, pointing his riding crop.

"Yes, sir."

The stoves and pipes were soon set outside the barracks door and the men waited for his instructions. He stood quietly observing the stove and men standing next to them. He was no longer smiling, and the expression on his face grew more serious. His mood changed as quickly as the wink of an eye.

"All right, pick up the stoves and pipes and follow me," he shouted.

He headed for the muddy roadway that encircled the barracks. As he turned around to direct the parade of stoves and stove pipes carried by the prisoners, a broad smile returned to his face. He proceeded to walk alongside the group, laughing and shouting.

"Make noise by striking pipes together and raise pipes high in the air," he screamed, laughing and raising his arms straight up.

As they passed the Japanese office, those inside filed out of the run-down building to see what all the commotion was about. Some Japanese stood and merely stared while others shouted and laughed as they waved their arms.

Ishahara stopped momentarily, turning toward the rear of the column and the prisoner carrying the sign. Pointing his riding crop at him he began shouting, "Raise sign higher. Up over your head quickly!"

He quickly turned again and urged them to walk faster. The men carrying the stoves were beginning to tire as their thin bony faces became strained and their spindly legs began to buckle under the weight of the potbelly stoves.

their spindly legs began to buckle under the weight of the potbelly stoves. Halfway around the camp they stopped and set the stoves down and those who had been empty-handed took the stove pipe from those who had been carrying them. There was screaming and prodding from the Japanese guards trying to hurry them up.

As they passed by the last two barracks, Ishahara took off running between the barracks with the two Japanese guards trailing him closely. The muddy ground made it difficult for them to run very fast, and mud flew in every direction. The parade of stoves came to a halt when Ishahara spotted a prisoner cooking some beans in a can over a charcoal fire. The prisoner, who spotted Ishahara at the same time, took off running through the barracks. Ishahara walked over to the steaming can of beans and kicked it, scattering the contents everywhere. The guards then kicked the charcoal fire apart as Ishahara walked up and down the outside of the barracks looking for the prisoner before returning to the group carrying the stoves. It turned out that the prisoner had found some dried beans while on a working party cleaning some Chinese cavalry barracks. They were shaped like large lima beans and colored like pinto beans. Someone said they were fed to the horses!

The parade continued around the barracks and ended up at the Japanese warehouse, where the stoves were stored. Ishahara was no longer smiling and laughing.

Chapter 17

A gentle knock on the office door preceded the entrance of the Japanese quartermaster, Lieutenant Kabuki, who removed his cap as he quietly stepped inside, leaving the door open. After bowing briskly, his rounded figure with bowed legs, accentuated by tightly wrapped leggings, edged toward Morisako. There was a brief conversation in Japanese, and they left the tiny office in a hurry.

"What the hell was that all about?" I asked.

Mail that Morisako had been censoring lay strewn about his wooden desk, one letter left completely open.

"Who knows? Everything they do is so disorganized. How they ever get anything done is beyond me," Smith said.

"Do you think that letter they got from the Swiss Consul the other day has something to do with their behavior?" I asked.

"Maybe that's why they're hot-footing it around. Earlier I saw a truck pull away from their warehouse and stop in front of our galley. They must be preparing for Mr. English's inspection of the camp," Smith said.

We both got up cautiously and walked toward the window to have a look. Supplies were being unloaded off the back of the truck and taken into our galley as Morisako and Lieutenant Kabuki looked on.

"They want to make a good impression on Mr. English," Smith said. "Just as soon as he leaves, they'll haul everything back to their warehouse. They do it every time he comes."

"Do you think they're fooling him?" I asked.

"I doubt it," Smith said shaking his head. "I'm sure he sees through their little game."

We walked past Morisako's desk slowly, glancing at the letters, lingering only for a moment, fearful of an unexpected entrance by Ishahara.

Among other things stored in the Japanese warehouse were Red Cross food parcels for prisoners of war, which they had confiscated. One single shipment of Red Cross parcels that was distributed to us contained Old Gold cigarettes with the following printed on each package: "Our heritage has always been freedom. We cannot afford to relinquish it. Our armed forces will safeguard that heritage if we, too, do our share to preserve it."

The Japanese became very angry when they discovered this had slipped by their censors. They immediately tore open all the remaining Red Cross parcels but failed to find anymore propaganda.

The morning rains fell lightly and intermittently — never heavy enough for the Japanese to stop the outside work details but enough for the men to become wet and chilled. During the brief moments like this, when we were left alone in the office, we discussed the constant hunger and humiliation suffered by all the prisoners. We wondered whether we would ever get out of this mess we were in. The many things that we did and merely took for granted in America as free individuals in a democracy had suddenly become very precious. We decided we would live every day as if there were no tomorrow when we returned!

The familiar shuffling sound of boots coming up the wooden hallway warned us of Morisako's return. His faded olive green uniform had darkened from the rain. With both hands shoved deep in his pockets and walking in a stooped position, he quietly headed for the potbelly stove in the far corner of the room. He hovered over the stove and ignored us completely, while his dark eyes shifted quickly around the room before settling on the letters scattered across his desk.

After much shivering and squirming by the side of the stove, he finally returned to sit down at his desk and began censoring the mail reluctantly. He sat calmly studying a letter before him, when suddenly he turned to us and asked softly, "Do all American families have two cars?"

"Not all," Smith replied, apparently startled by the unexpected question. "Many wealthy American families do, however."

"This lady is telling her husband that she is putting his car in storage until he comes home," Morisako continued, referring to the letter. "That she will be driving her own car."

We stopped what we were doing and slid our chairs back to relax as Morisako appeared to be in a talking mood.

"In our country, Japanese family must be very wealthy to own only one car. Most working people must ride buses or bicycles to work. Also many Japanese cannot afford radios, motorbikes, motorboats, and many other luxury items that you Americans enjoy. Americans have too much," Morisako said.

"Well, perhaps we do have more. I don't know for sure," Smith said.

"How come Americans have so much when other countries like Japan have so little?" As he spoke he reclined in his chair, placing both hands behind his head.

"Perhaps we have better technology and can make more things for more people cheaper," I said.

Morisako stopped to think for a moment before continuing.

"Maybe part of what you say is true. But your country has more natural resources and room to expand. Our country is small and overpopulated. That is why we were forced to go to war, to obtain more land for our people." His voice was soft and his face showed a sincere concern for his people.

"In war, regardless of the outcome, both sides are losers in lives and property," I said. "If you lose the war, all the territory you are occupying will have to be returned and restitution made for all damages. It appears to me that negotiations with other countries would have been better than going to war."

He paused a moment to light up a Japanese-made cigarette. After dragging heavily and expelling clouds of the bad smelling smoke, he continued our discussion.

"Our leaders have tried peaceful means but nobody will cooperate. Even your country says we must stay on our small island, that we cannot expand our empire," he explained emotionally, moving to the edge of his chair and waving his right arm as he spoke.

Sensing his anger, Smith quickly responded that we were not familiar with our government's policy in these matters and tried to change the subject.

"Have you ever visited America?" Smith asked.

"No, but I have been to Hawaii," Morisako said.

"When?"

"Just two years before the war. I went to the University of Hawaii to take some special courses that were not available at the University of Tokyo."

"Did you like it there?" I asked.

"Yes. Very nice place and the people were also nice to me," Morisako said, appearing to be more relaxed as he continued to puff on his cigarette, sending rings of smoke toward the ceiling.

"Has Mr. Ishahara ever visited America or Hawaii?" I asked.

"I don't know about America, but he has been to Hawaii," Morisako told us. "He taught Japanese at the University of Hawaii half a day while studying English language for one summer."

I got up and put more wood in the stove because the room had begun to cool off.

"Did he enjoy his time in Hawaii?" Smith asked.

Morisako turned and looked the other way. Smith looked at me somewhat puzzled. The room suddenly became very quiet.

"Did something happen to him in Hawaii?" Smith pressed Morisako further.

"Yes, something very terrible," he replied.

"What was it?"

At first, he seemed reluctant to tell us what had happened to Ishahara, but finally after our urging the story unfolded.

"One Sunday afternoon he decided to take a taxicab to one of the nearby beaches as a sightseeing tour," Morisako explained. "Midway the taxicab was hailed down by three American sailors who grabbed him and jerked him out of the cab. They began calling him names like slant-eyed bastard, yellow heathen, Oriental creep, just to name a few. They then proceeded to beat him up. They piled into the cab and drove off laughing, leaving him at the side of the road with a broken jaw, bloody nose, and three broken teeth. He finally managed to get a ride back to town where he reported the incident to the local authorities, but nothing was ever done about it."

"So, now he hates all Americans and beats up prisoners in this camp in revenge," I said.

"I don't know about that," he said, turning back to his job of censoring the mail that lay scattered across his desk.

It was 12:00 and time for chow as we picked up and left for the barracks.

Shortly after 1:00 in the afternoon, a thunderous roar of Japanese echoed from the far corner of the camp. Someone had shorted the electric fence. A group of Marines had been working in the immediate vicinity, and a squad of Japanese guards had surrounded them. They were marched down to the Japanese office, where they were ordered to stand at attention outside. A light rain had begun to fall as dark clouds gathered.

Major Charles McGuire darted from his quarters and headed for his men. After a brief meeting with them, he hurried toward the interpreter's office. In the meantime, Ishahara had arrived at the office carrying his black briefcase. Reeking of sake, he immediately removed his army jacket, placing it over the back of his chair as he stared at the stove, half-crazed. Slowly stumbling into his chair with the upper portion of his underwear showing, he proceeded to empty the contents of this black briefcase onto his desk. His dingy white underwear, buttoned down the front, clung to his tall thin body.

There were two soft knocks on the door followed by silence and two louder knocks, which prompted Morisako to speak.

"Come in," he whispered, but there was no response so he repeated himself a little louder.

The door inched open, scraping against the floor. Major McGuire entered cautiously. He greeted us as he made his way toward Ishahara's desk. He stood waiting several minutes to be recognized as Ishahara ignored him completely while feverishly scribbling on a pad.

"Mr. Ishahara." The Major stood erect as he spoke.

He was clean-shaven, his small mustache neatly trimmed, and his uniform immaculate. His manner, which showed his diplomatic background, challenged Ishahara.

"What do you want?" Ishahara shouted, without looking.

A flash of lightning and then the sound of thunder caused him to suddenly jerk his head up and look out the window. The rain began to come down in buckets. Major McGuire's strained face showed his concern for his men standing outside in the downpour.

"Sir, your Japanese soldiers have some of my men standing at attention outside in the rain," the Major said quietly.

"What for?" Ishahara sighed.

The atmosphere of the tiny smoke-filled office became tense as the aroma of sake filtered through the room.

"The Japanese soldiers are saying that one of my men placed something on the fence causing it to short." As Major McGuire spoke, his eyes studied the slender body of Ishahara slumped over his desk.

Ishahara stopped writing and the pencil fell from his hand onto the desk as he spun around in his chair quickly, almost falling out, so he could look directly at the Major.

"If Japanese soldiers say one of your men shorted electric fence, then that is true. Japanese do not lie like you Americans." His voice grew louder and the veins in his neck began to stand out.

"Perhaps they did it for their own protection since they were working near it," McGuire said. "The point is that Colonel Burnside was told by the Camp Commandant when we arrived here that these electric fences would not be turned on during daylight hours while the prisoners were working."

McGuire stood straight as an arrow with his arms at his sides. In the meantime, Ishahara had staggered to his feet.

"Never mind what Colonel Yuse says; I will tell you what is good for prisoners. Do you understand, huh?" Ishahara retorted, swaying as he spoke. "Maybe Japanese soldier has good reason for turning on electric fence or maybe he just forgot to turn it off. No matter what the reason, you must not concern yourself."

"Very well, Mr. Ishahara, but there have been two deaths from electrocution, and three others have been severely burned. I will report these and other deaths after the war," McGuire explained, standing firmly and unflinchingly.

The Major's remarks caused Ishahara to become furious, his whole body trembling with rage. Waving a clenched fist in the Major's face he screamed, "Make your reports. I don't care. This is wartime and you are our enemy not our guest. You must expect to suffer some. Soldiers fighting at the front are dying every day!"

Ishahara then turned and sat down in his chair, propping his head in both hands, staring down at his desk.

McGuire hesitated a moment before asking, "Mr. Ishahara, may my men be excused from standing in the rain?"

"No!" Ishahara shouted. "They are being punished. They must stand at attention outside until I dismiss them."

"Yes, sir," replied the Major as he quickly turned and left the room.

Outside, the wind whipped the rain against the side of the building. Ishahara stood up to put on his jacket while staring at the smoldering fire in the stove. A sentry, carrying a large platter of steaming string beans and two small bowls of hot tea, entered the room from the main Japanese office. He appeared excited as he stopped to bow quickly before placing the tray on their desks. Then he left the room immediately.

Broad smiles appeared on the faces of Ishahara and Morisako, who went for the string beans like little children after candy. Their childish behavior was exhibited in their boisterous laughter and the way they reached for the beans with their hands. The plate of warm beans looked and smelled good, making our mouths water and stomachs growl. After they finished eating, they looked out the window and began laughing at the prisoners standing at attention in the rain. Finally, they returned to their chairs, where they sipped the tea in their small bowls and swished it around in their mouths before spitting it out onto the floor.

During the winter it got dark early, and when we could no longer see in the office, it was time to return to the barracks. We ran carefully back to ours to avoid getting too wet. On the way we saw Major McGuire standing with his men. They were eventually released and sent back to their barracks around 9:00 that night.

Chapter 18

An unusually heavy fog had delayed the Mt. Fugi workers an hour on one particular morning. Despite the muddy condition of the roadway and the likely chance of rain, Ishahara had ordered everyone out.

A short distance from camp on our march we encountered a detachment of Japanese soldiers in full pack. The Japanese officer in charge appeared drunk as he staggered from one side of the road to the other. He spotted several children coming toward him carrying baskets, and without any warning, he started running after them with his drawn saber. They scattered into the field, throwing their baskets as they ran. The officer picked one up, threw it in the air, and made a pass at it with his saber. He then proceeded to stop us and made the fellows in the front ranks button their coats. Not satisfied with their cooperation, he struck three of them in the face with his fist as our Japanese escort looked on, terrified. When a dilapidated, old Chinese truck slowly passed our column, the Japanese officer spun around to stop the truck and nearly fell to the ground. He pulled one of the passengers out of the cab, nearly scaring him to death. The Chinese civilian kept bowing and saluting simultaneously. Stumbling toward the rear of the truck, the officer thrust his saber into several gunny sacks of flour and rice, spilling the contents onto the ground.

There were several Chinese riding on the sacks, and they scattered like chickens in a henhouse being invaded by a fox. We began to move again toward Mt. Fugi as the officer followed behind us for awhile. He struck two prisoners across their backs with his saber as he reeled back and forth. Our Japanese escort, too frightened to know what to do, kept the column moving.

The Japanese officer then turned to chase an elderly Chinaman carrying a bundle of kindling wood. He quickly dropped the wood and ran into the open field with the saber-wielding officer far behind. As we left the detachment of Japanese soldiers to our rear, we saw the officer strike his own men.

Mt. Fugi loomed up in the distance, the vast stretches of flat desolate terrain surrounding it. A narrow streak of morning sunlight broke through the dark clouds, illuminating the grassy slope of the mountain. Puddles of water were scattered in front of the brick target wall that ran the entire length of the mountain. On the opposite side of Mt. Fugi, the large pond created by the removal of dirt to build the mountain had completely filled with water from the winter rains. After two-and-one-half years and much suffering, the project was nearly finished.

Ishahara quickly moved toward where we stood in front of the open mess hall. Stepping up onto a box in order to look down on us, he gazed silently over this collection of men strongly determined to survive this war. Despite the recent air attacks on Shanghai and the scuttlebut that the war was winding down, he continued to lash out at us.

"Today will be the last day of work on the mountain," Ishahara told us. "Therefore, I feel it my duty to comment on your behavior for a moment."

He hesitated before continuing as he stared at the prisoners.

"Yesterday I caught a car with a light load and I slapped each man," he said. "Every time I leave the mountain you make only half loads. You have that slave spirit. You must be sympathetic. You Americans and British are a superior race and have pride, but I cannot recognize this pride when you have that slave spirit."

He paused and leaned down to speak to one of the Japanese soldiers at his side.

"I do not like to strike you prisoners because you have no arms, but you do not follow my instructions and make it very hard for me," he said, trying to justify his behavior. "I would rather fight you on an even basis."

He immediately dismissed the prisoners except for a small group of older men who had been assigned to a light duty detail. As we slowly made our way toward Mt. Fugi, prodded along by screaming Jap guards, Ishahara began his speech to the older men.

"You men are given special consideration, but you are not doing your work," he told them. "Only two of you men have light duty slips issued by the doctor, but I do not pay any attention to the doctors. If you men do not remain on the mountain until the other men have finished, I will not favor you men, but you will have to push cars."

Ishahara had ordered the men to work placing sod on the mountain slopes, which was strenuous labor. He quickly stepped down from the box and headed toward the mountains, the older men trailing behind.

The day stayed cold and damp. The prisoners clung to their skimpy clothing, moving constantly trying to keep warm. There was very little work left to do. Everyone was working on the three smaller knolls of dirt which ran perpendicular to the mountain. They were to be windbreaks for the huge firing range.

Shortly before noon, Tiny Tim and a squad of Japanese soldiers approached the mountain. We were herded in between two of the knolls and awaited their assault of Mt. Fugi. They came upon us, crawling from all directions over the top of the knolls, waving their rifles and yelling at the top of their lungs. Sprigs of green weeds garnished their helmets, and the muddy terrain soiled their faded khaki uniforms. Leading the attack was Tiny Tim with saber drawn, waving them on as they proceeded down the knoll and up the other side helter-skelter. The siege ended quickly as Tiny Tim's battle-geared troops headed down the narrow roadway back to camp.

Gathered on the far side of the knolls, four of the prisoners were finishing their job when they spotted Ishahara coming toward them. It was mid-afternoon, and a slight breeze blew in off the China coast, chilling us to the bone as we had very little clothing. Ishahara came charging down one of the knoll slopes, nearly losing control, his arms and legs flying in every direction. Reaching the bottom, he almost fell on his face as he skidded a short distance, barely maintaining an upright position. It was very difficult for the four prisoners to keep from laughing as he approached.

"Looks like maybe you are about finished, huh?" he said, glancing at the corner of the knoll that they had just finished filling in and were shaping with their shovels.

Gates, who was one of them, straightened up and turned to Ishahara while the others continued working.

"Yes, sir, we are about finished," he replied.

His tall skinny body, haggard face, and sad eyes reflected his pessimistic attitude about ever leaving China alive.

Ishahara appeared to be in a better mood. Maybe it was because his project was about to be completed. He asked that the men put their tools down and line up in front of him. He dropped his cigarette and stepped on it with his high-top rubber boots snuffing it out in the moist soil.

"Maybe now that the mountain job is over, the war will soon be over and you will all be going home," he said, and then broke out in laughter.

The four of them stood silently and remained cautious.

"What part of the States do you people come from?" he asked.

He pointed his riding crop at each one of them, and they told him the state they were from — California, Idaho, Montana, and Texas.

Looking directly at Sanborn, he shouted, "What do you do in Texas?"

"Well, sir, I raise cotton on several hundred acres of land besides running a few head of cattle," Sanborn said.

"The state of Texas must be very large, huh?" Ishahara said, moving closer to Sanborn.

"Yes, very large. I believe we could put the entire Japanese Empire inside our state with room left over," Sanborn said, gesturing with his hands as he spoke.

"Oh, that may be so, but you have much waste land such as desert with its sagebrush and jackrabbits." He again began laughing, and he described parts of Texas, comparing them to picturesque Japan. The laughter soon ended, and he moved down the line of prisoners.

Unbuttoning his plastic raincoat, he removed a package of stateside tobacco and proceeded to give each of them two cigarettes. Concluding the distribution of their confiscated cigarettes, on a more serious note he said, "Because you are sincere workers I am awarding you so. Now please, let us pray to God."

With heads bowed, they remained quiet for about one minute, after which he told them to pick up their tools; they were dismissed for the day. Showing no emotion, he stalked off between the knolls toward the rest of us as he struck his riding crop against his rubber boots.

It was mid-afternoon when we finished work on the mountain. There was no laughter as we wearily made our way down Mt. Fugi at the completion of the long, hard project, only grumbling about the inhumane treatment administered by Ishahara. Most staggered to the mess hall, staring straight ahead, too tired to talk. After roll call, Ishahara complimented the sincere workers and gave them cigarettes, another scheme to get us to work harder.

Under partly cloudy skies we marched back to camp on the soggy roadway. Silhouetted atop Mt. Fugi against the background of the remaining sunlight was Ishahara, enjoying his triumph over this half-starved, dog-tired, pathetic-looking mass of humanity struggling down the muddy roadway. Only our strong desire to survive and our faith in God kept us going.

The hour-long hike back to camp in the mud was very tiring. We were strung out in a column three miles long, oblivious to the Japanese guards running up and down our column shouting at us. The Chinese coolies we saw working in the fields seldom bothered to look up.

A short distance from camp we passed a dead Chinaman lying in the ditch alongside the road. He had been there for three days, prompting Forrest Hill to break the long silence.

"This is a pitiful," Hill said, pausing to look at the man with much sorrow. "To think in these times a human being can be left unattended to and no one concerned about him."

"In China it is the custom that whoever picks up a dead person is responsible for him," Dawson said. "At least that is what I've been told."

Shaking his head feebly, Hill murmured softly, "It's too bad."

Carpenter by trade, preacher by preference, Hill came from a small quiet town in northern Utah called Silver Creek. In his late forties, he was short, quiet, and hard of hearing. He was called upon to preside over numerous funerals. And until a cemetery was established just outside the camp in May 1943, he accompanied several bodies that were sent into Shanghai to be cremated.

"Can you imagine something like this happening in our country?" Dawson said, turning to Hill and putting his hand on his shoulder.

"No, I can't," Hill said. "I guess life in this part of the world is very cheap. They apparently don't think more about killing a human being than they do about killing a dog. Life in our country is more precious. Hopefully, we will prevail."

As he spoke he looked squarely at Dawson, who was having a hard time walking in an upright position. Small chunks of mud, picked up by the prisoners' worn-out shoes, were scattered everywhere.

"Forrest, wouldn't you say war reduces the value of human life?" Dawson said, raising his voice for Hill, who turned his head sideways to listen with one hand cupped around his ear.

Hill thought for a moment. He dropped his hand from his ear as he cautiously walked on the muddy roadway. His face grimaced with pain as he lifted his legs out of the sticky mud. His weariness showed in his furrowed forehead, gray bushy eyebrows, and pale shallow cheeks.

"I would to a certain degree," Hill said. "Wars give an excuse to kill. For some it comes easier than for others, and the taste of killing for the first time could carry over into civilian life for some. That's the tragedy of it all."

His face looked sad as he spoke slowly and simply.

Many of us experienced the consequences of war before being interned. Now having been isolated from the fighting front for three years, there was an entirely different set of circumstances confronting us. Stripped of all means of protecting ourselves, we were placed in a situation where our enemy was our master controlling our very existence. In our case, Ishahara totally disregarded international law governing the treatment of prisoners. His burning hatred for Americans was exemplified by his unprovoked beatings and the way he constantly increased the amount of labor he required from us.

Our lengthy column was no longer straight but curved as the narrow roadway made its last gradual turn toward camp. The brisk ocean breeze was no longer at our backs but blew directly into our faces, causing our eyes to water. Each of us, I suspect, was thinking of home and our loved ones. Schultz, who had been walking behind Hill and listening to his conversation with Dawson, could hardly contain himself and rushed up to them.

"Talk about killing," Schultz exclaimed. "I don't think there is anyone in this camp who wouldn't like to kill that son-of-a-bitch Ishahara. Excuse my language, Forrest, but that is what he is!"

"I'm sure, Herman, what you say is true," Hill said. "But he isn't worth dying for. It's too bad that the Japanese have turned and looked the other way, letting Ishahara run this camp."

"That yellow bastard!" Schultz clenched his fist in anger. "He hates us Americans with a passion!"

"He's a sadist," Hill said, pausing momentarily. "We are fortunate to have someone humane like Shindo in this camp. The way he sees that we receive medical supplies and treatment is remarkable."

Unfortunately, Shindo's humane treatment of the prisoners was closely watched and restricted by his superiors.

"Yes, he is humane. I'm sure a lot of fellows in this camp can thank Shindo for their lives," Sanborn joined in, directing his remarks to Hill.

Our stride had slowed to a snail's pace by the time the outline of the camp appeared in the distance. The long hike through the sticky heavy mud was excruciating after laboring at Mt. Fugi, and we were too fatigued to heed the constant prodding by the Japanese guards to walk faster.

"Now that we have finished Mt. Fugi, I wonder what Ishahara has in store for us?" Sanborn asked.

"Who knows? Maybe we'll dig some more damn ditches or work on roads," Schultz said, adjusting his wire-rimmed glasses behind his puffy ears.

"I don't think I'll ever forget that work detail that a few of us went on the end of last January," Hill said. "We repaired a road close to a Chinese warehouse."

"Wasn't that the time that it snowed all afternoon until we got back to camp?" Sanborn asked.

"What a cold, miserable day that was." Hill said. "Do you remember those Chinese youngsters who brought us buckets of hot water to drink?"

A warm smile lit up Hill's face as he thought about the children for a moment.

"I remember them well," Schultz said. "They were full of laughter as they gathered around us. We built a fire and they stood close to it, wrapping their arms around their bodies to keep warm. The clothing they wore was tattered and torn."

"We all gave a spoonful of our rice to those kids, which they really went after like it was their last meal," Sanborn said. "And they followed us around all day, nearly tripping over our heels at times."

"Even the Japanese guards were friendly that day. Remember that guard who gave his rifle to Murphy to hold while he shoveled dirt to keep warm?" Hill said.

"Yeah, they didn't seem to hate us," Sanborn said.

When we arrived at the camp that evening, large clouds of black smoke were rising in the vicinity of our barracks. Fear gripped our group until we were close enough to see that the fire had burned the Japanese barracks next door.

Chapter 19

It was early in January 1944 when the Japanese conducted an investigation into the alleged dealings between the prisoners and the Chinese working at the firing range project. The weather at this time was bitter cold and damp from the recent rains. One day Ishahara summoned Sergeant Joe Tanner to the Japanese office where I was working.

Standing around the room waiting for him were Morisako, Lieutenant Miyasaki (Tiny Tim), and two Japanese civilians nicknamed "G-1" and "G-2." They waited silently with stony faces.

"Sit down here," Ishahara said, shoving a wooden chair toward him.

The other Japanese in the room just looked, their faces showing no emotion. For a moment the room became perfectly still, except for an occasional crackle of the wood-burning stove in the far corner of the room.

"Would you like some sugar and toast?" Ishahara asked, offering him a piece.

"No, I don't like sugar and toast," Tanner said. He sat firmly in the chair, his feet flat on the floor and his back upright.

"You are a goddamn liar!" Ishahara shouted, and struck him across the face with his leather riding crop. "Now get up and come and sit at this table over here. I have some questions to ask you."

Ishahara sat directly across the table from him as the other Japanese formed a circle around them.

"You have been brought here because of the dealings you have had with the Chinese while working outside of camp at the firing range project," Ishahara explained. "Therefore you must answer each question that I ask you honestly. Do you understand, huh?"

"Yes, sir," Tanner replied calmly.

"Well, then, did you exchange American currency for Chinese currency?"

Ishahara asked.

"No, sir, I don't recall any such. . . ."

Before he could finish, Ishahara had sprung out of his chair and struck him in the face with his fist, knocking him to the floor.

"You are lying again!" Ishahara shouted angrily.

After regaining his composure, Ishahara pulled a sheet of paper from the bottom of a stack of papers and said, "I know some of the things you have done. The Chinese have told me everything, and they have been tried by a Japanese military court and were sentenced to die because of their dealings with the prisoners. So you must tell me everything."

Ishahara seemed to have complete knowledge of all Tanner's dealings with the Chinese. He continued to question him about different transactions, but his main interest was the $1,800 in Chinese currency that he turned over to Dr. William Corey. He knew the exact date and amount of the transaction.

"Did you ever buy whiskey from the Chinese?" asked Ishahara as he leaned forward in his chair.

"No, sir. The Chinese did give me some whiskey," responded Tanner.

"What did you do with it? Did you give it to the officers?" Ishahara asked.

"No, sir, I drank it all myself."

Ishahara then struck Tanner again with his riding crop saying, "You are not supposed to bring whiskey on Japanese military reservation!"

Ishahara continued to question him about his dealings in soap, watches, rings, and other articles. But he always kept coming back to the money transaction.

"Again I ask you, did you make money exchange with the Chinese?" He asked, this time his voice cracking with rage.

"No, sir!" Tanner responded resolutely.

Then Ishahara turned to Tiny Tim and spoke to him in Japanese, which brought spontaneous laughter among the Japanese. Tiny Tim directed G-1 and G-2 to take Tanner over to a ten-foot ladder which was lying flat on the floor. They made him remove all his clothing and lie on the ladder face up, at which time they tied his arms and legs to the ladder. They opened all the windows in the room, letting in the cold air. Ishahara stepped out of the room momentarily and returned with a bucket of water. The temperature in the room had dropped rapidly to below freezing.

"So you will not talk," Ishahara said as he threw the bucket of water over him.

He stepped out of the room and returned this time with a large teapot full of water.

"You must be thirsty; you must drink lots of water," he said, and he put the spout of the teapot into Tanner's mouth. Ishahara straddled Tanner, pouring with one hand and holding Tanner's nose with the other. One of the Japanese was holding Tanner's head so that he could not turn either way. There was nothing to do but drink water. He drank so much that he began to vomit and then he passed out. When he regained consciousness, they were all standing over him watching.

Ishahara began his interrogation again. "You must tell me about the money you received for Dr. Corey. You must talk or I will kill you."

"I do not know anything about a money exchange," Tanner said. His face had become ashen as his body shivered in the cold.

Ishahara then placed a wet towel over his face and said, "I will make you talk. When you want to talk, say yes."

Someone pinched his mouth open and held his nose and his head so he could not turn it. Ishahara then poured water on the towel. He said "yes" three or four times in order to get air. But then each time he would say "no." Ishahara continued to pour water over the towel, saying, "Goddamn it! I'll make you talk!"

After Tanner passed out again and regained consciousness, Ishahara asked him if he had anything to say, and he said "no." He was then untied and told to dress. He was taken to the brig, where he spent the next twenty days.

After Tanner had been removed, Morisako went to the prisoners' barracks to get civilian Ernie Boatman.

Upon arriving at the Japanese office, Boatman was taken to see Ishahara, Tiny Tim, G-1, and G-2. The center of the room was wet with a putrid odor. Ishahara motioned for him to sit down at the table, and strutted back and forth for a few moments before approaching him.

"Do you know why you were brought down here?" Ishahara asked.

"No, sir, I don't," replied Boatman.

"Well, we have evidence that you have been exchanging gold for Chinese currency. Did you make this kind of dealing with the Chinese while working at the firing range?" he asked, moving closer to Boatman.

"No, sir, I did not," Boatman said, denying any exchanges of money with the Chinese.

This made Ishahara furious, and he began striking him about the head several times with his riding crop. Boatman fell to the floor and then Ishahara commenced kicking him all over his body, including his head.

Boatman still denied any knowledge of the money transactions. At this point they propped a bench up at a slight angle and made him lie on the bench face up with his head at the lower end. Morisako went to the next room and brought back a teapot full of cold water.

"Do you wish to talk now?" Ishahara shouted.

"No," Boatman responded.

"Then you must drink much water," Ishahara said, and he picked up the teapot and forced the spout into Boatman's mouth. Two of the other Japanese held Boatman's arms and legs as Ishahara began pouring the water.

There was nothing Boatman could do but drink the water. If he closed his mouth the water would run into his nose and choke him. After gagging and choking, he finally passed out. When he regained consciousness, he was sitting in a chair at the table in front of Ishahara. He then proceeded to list some of the things that he traded to the Chinese.

"Mr. Boatman, I ask you once again, did you not exchange some gold for forty dollars Chinese currency and also five wristwatches? If you deny this, again I must repeat the water treatment. Do you understand, huh?" exclaimed Ishahara.

"Yes, sir. I did make those two transactions with the Chinese," said Boatman, quite shaken by the torture he had received. There were several welts on his face and blood trickled from his mouth.

"Very well, you may go back to your barracks. But I must warn you not to say a word to anyone about this," Ishahara told him.

Morisako escorted Boatman back to his barracks. He was sentenced later to five days in the brig.

The second day of the interrogations commenced when Sergeant John Marlowe was summoned to the Japanese office. He was directed to sit at the table in the center of the room where a single, shaded light hung over it.

"You are Sergeant John Marlowe?" Ishahara asked, standing across the table from him.

"Yes, sir."

"Do you know why you are here?" he continued calmly.

"No, sir, I don't," Marlowe replied, looking directly at him.

"We have gathered evidence from the Chinese that you have been dealing with them at the firing range. Do you deny it?" asked Ishahara, his face showing his anger.

"I don't know anything about such dealings, sir." Marlowe's response was quick.

"You lie; all Americans lie!" Ishahara shouted, and he lashed out at Marlowe with his fist, striking him on the jaw. Ishahara immediately ordered him to stand up and strip to the waist. He then began striking him with his riding crop across the neck, shoulders, and head for several minutes until he passed out. He was revived by pouring water over his body, and helped back to the table, where Ishahara continued his interrogation.

"You could make things easy for you if you just tell the truth. I do not like to punish you but I must do these things to get the truth. Do you understand, huh?"

Ishahara looked to the other Japanese in the room and said a few words in Japanese, which made them break out in laughter.

Then he turned back to Marlowe again and said, "I ask you once again, did you make dealings with the Chinese?"

"No, sir, I did not."

This time Ishahara became furious, trembling with rage. He waved his arms and shouted at him to get up and lie down on the table face up. Two other Japanese in the room bound his arms and legs to the table. Ishahara stared momentarily at Marlowe's frail body lying secured to the table.

"Before I give the water treatment to you, I must tell you that we have information from the Chinese that you have been dealing with them at the firing range. Again I ask you, do you deny this?"

Ishahara now appeared relaxed. His ability to change temperaments quickly was remarkable!

"Yes," Marlowe respondly firmly, but his face showed that he knew the worst was to come.

Ishahara spoke to G-2 as he reached down and picked up the teapot of water. G-2 edged toward Marlowe's head and struck him suddenly with his fist, a hard blow across the bridge of his nose, causing it to bleed profusely. He then proceeded to hold his neck and forced his mouth open as Ishahara began pouring water down his throat.

He was questioned repeatedly after receiving the water treatment six times. Finally, he was taken back to the barracks. He suffered the loss of the the use of one hand for several weeks, a broken nose, and a badly burned arm. He was sentenced to ten days in the brig.

On the last day of the interrogations a light, chilly rain began to fall on the desolate barracks. Lieutenant William Corey, a medical officer, was summoned from his quarters. He was a mild-mannered man, very intelligent and had become familiar with the ways of the Orient while stationed at the Chinese Embassy in Peking. Ishahara met him at the door and politely asked him to be seated in the chair in the center of the room.

Standing beneath the light that hung down from the center of the ceiling over the wooden table were Morisako, Tiny Tim, and Fukutome. They were silent.

A slightly rancid odor permeated the large, barren room. The heat from the small wood stove was not quite enough to take the chill out. There was silence as Ishahara lit up a cigarette and offered Dr. Corey one.

"No, thank you, sir," he responded as he sat firmly in his chair, staring at Ishahara. His fair complexion showed that he hadn't spent too much time outside.

"Well, how is your health these days, Dr. Corey?" Ishahara began his questioning causally, moving about the room with cigarette in hand. He was relaxed, not angry.

"Just fine, thank you," Corey said, replying quickly, and his eyes focused on Ishahara's every movement, oblivious to the other Japanese in the room.

"And are you enjoying our winter weather? It seems to be raining a little bit outside right now I think," Ishahara said, turning to look out one of the windows streaked by the rain.

"Yes, I think so. It makes the prisoners suffer because of the dampness and bitter cold. Many have health problems, and the barracks remain unheated," Corey said, continuing to ignore the other Japanese.

"Never mind about that!" Ishahara shouted, irritated with Corey's response.

He never expressed any concern for the prisoners' health. Instead, Ishahara went out of his way to make survival more difficult. He sat down at the table and began shuffling through a stack of papers. His tightly drawn face took on a more serious look.

"Dr. Corey, have you violated any of the camp rules while performing your duties as a medical officer at the firing range project?" Ishahara asked while continuing to glance at the paper before him.

"No, sir."

"We have proof from the Chinese that several prisoners exchanged American currency for Chinese currency. Were you not involved in any of these dealings?" His voice became louder and his dark eyes fiery.

"No, sir, I know nothing about what you speak," Corey said. "However, I remind you that as a medical officer, according to International Law, I am not subject to the same rules and regulations as the other prisoners."

Enraged by this response, Ishahara shook his riding crop in Corey's frightened face. The other Japanese in the room moved back a step or two.

"Whether or not there is such a rule in International Law, as long as you are a member of this camp, you will obey the camp rules like the other prisoners. Do you understand, huh?" he shouted violently.

"Yes, sir," the doctor replied, sitting upright in his chair firmly, but shaken by Ishahara's threat.

"Now, I again must ask you, did you not receive Chinese currency that was exchanged for American dollars?" He stood directly in front of Corey, staring and holding his riding crop restlessly at his side.

"No, sir," Corey replied quickly. He had become ashen anticipating what Ishahara would do next.

"I must remind you, Dr. Corey, that we Japanese are a sincere and honest people. We do not and cannot tolerate someone who does not tell the truth and who also is not sincere in his work. Many of the prisoners act like slaves and do not perform their best work. Therefore, I find it necessary to punish the prisoners. So if you are not willing to tell the truth I will find it necessary to punish you. Do you understand, huh?"

Corey squirmed in his chair and nodded his head saying, "Yes."

At this time Morisako left the room and went to his quarters. The sparsely furnished room became very quiet as Ishahara contemplated what next to do. He paced back and forth slowly in front of Corey, who was staring down at the floor. The other Japanese in the room stood motionless with their lips tightly drawn.

"Did you receive $1,800 in Chinese currency from Sergeant Tanner?" Ishahara asked looking directly at the doctor, while grasping his riding crop firmly in his right hand.

"No. I don't know a Sergeant Tanner," Corey said after pausing to think for a moment. His attention was fixed on the riding crop in Ishahara's hand.

"You lie! All of you Americans lie!" Ishahara shouted and struck him with his riding crop across the shoulder several times and yelled at him.

Corey tried desperately to ward off the blows, which only infuriated Ishahara. Finally, Ishahara spoke to the other Japanese, who moved toward Corey.

"So you don't want to tell the truth. Well, we have ways to make you speak the truth. Now, you must go with them." Ishahara trembled as he spoke.

Fukutome helped Dr. Corey out of his chair and directed him to lie face up on the ladder on the floor. He then commenced to fasten his arms and legs to the ladder, as they had done with Tanner. Ishahara left the room and returned with a teapot of water. He proceeded to sit down on Corey's chest straddling him, while Fukutome held Corey's head.

"Now, I ask you once again. Did you receive money from Sergeant Joe Tanner?"

"I know nothing about such transactions," Corey wimpered.

The spout of the teapot was forced into Corey's mouth, knocking loose several teeth. His pale face became swollen as he swallowed the water until he passed out.

The water treatment was repeated three times, suffocating Corey on each occasion and causing him to lose consciousness. Interrogation resumed immediately each time after Corey revived.

He was finally released in a state of shock, unable to walk himself back to his quarters. The ordeal had lasting effects!

Chapter 20

The population of the camp changed from time to time as men were taken to Japan and new prisoners arrived. With the new prisoners came the latest progress of the war, which nearly always boosted our morale.

Among all the different prisoners interned in our camp, the fliers appeared to receive the most attention. There was always at least two weeks isolation followed by an interrogation by Ishahara. This took place in a private room, which required written answers to the following list of questions:

(1) How are relations, friendships, cooperation and so forth between American and Chinese air forces?

(2) What is the condition of materials and merchandise in areas in China unoccupied by Japanese forces? What are living conditions and fighting spirit of the Chinese masses?

(3) How does the American airman feel and think towards the Chinese masses and also how do they feel and think towards the Americans?

(4) How is the living condition, food supplies, all kinds of facilities, barracks, internment and so forth in your air base camp?

(5) What are the causes and what is the condition of sick men? What is the period of service on the same front and what is the length of service between reliefs on the front lines?

(6) Relate what is known about damages and casualties of American and Chinese by Japanese forces.

(7) What is your opinion and impression of the method of fighting of the Japanese air forces?

One of the more colorful fighter pilots shot down and interned in our camp was Major Sam Buckley. A Southerner from Louisiana, he had a deep drawl, a crewcut, and a medium build. He bubbled with energy when he first arrived, but then he hadn't been a prisoner as long as we had.

It was early spring when he made his first appearance at the interpreter's office. He'd hardly been in camp a month when he brought his first complaint to the office. He rapped solidly twice on the door with his fist, causing Morisako to jerk his head up quickly and shout angrily, "Come in!"

The door opened with much force as Major Buckley stepped inside and saluted briskly.

"What do you want?" Morisako shouted, still angry for being disturbed.

"I have come to complain about my quarters," Buckley said.

"What did you say? Say it again, this time a little slower so I can understand you," said Morisako, who seemed puzzled by the unfamiliar sounds of Buckley's Southern drawl.

"I said I have come to complain about my quarters," the Major said, this time speaking more slowly and loudly.

"What's wrong with them?" Morisako asked.

"It's the water basin," Buckley said.

"What's the matter with the water basin?" Morisako asked, leaning forward on the edge of his chair.

"The water from the wash basin runs onto the floor. There are no pipes connected to it to take the water outside," Buckley explained calmly, looking Morisako squarely in the eyes while he waited for his response.

Morisako thought for a moment before he answered the Major.

"I don't know if we have any pipe for such a problem," Morisako said. "Maybe you better just put bucket underneath basin to catch water."

"I have a bucket under it now," the Major said. "Would you have a piece of hose?"

He looked directly at Morisako, who had turned to look out the window. While Morisako continued staring out the window, he tried to think of a solution to the Major's problem. Buckley turned to us and smiled as he shook his head in disgust.

"What do you need the piece of hose for, Major?" Morisako asked.

"Well." Buckley hesitated momentarily before continuing. "I thought maybe I could fasten a piece of hose to the basin and run it under the floor."

"How could you do that?" Morisako asked, his face showing greater concern.

"By knocking a hole in the floor and pushing the hose through it," Buckley explained, the small room seeming to amplify his deep Southern drawl.

"No. You cannot do such a thing. You would be destroying Japanese property. This is strictly prohibited by Japanese authorities, and you would be severely punished," Morisako snapped, and he pounded his fist on the desk repeatedly.

"What do you suggest I do about this situation?" Buckley asked.

"I don't care what you do. Only don't destroy Japanese property or you will be punished. Do you understand, huh?" Morisako said and turned to some papers on his desk, ignoring the Major.

Buckley saluted and let himself out, smiling.

Many American pilots expressed bitterness about the treatment received from some of the Chinese after they had been shot down in their country. The Chinese had promised safe passage out of Japanese-occupied territory in exchange for money and jewelry. But instead, they often turned American pilots over to the Japanese forces for reward money!

In early 1945, we began to see high-flying reconnaissance planes leaving trails of white smoke, followed by B-29s bombing the nearby waterfront and airfield. These unchallenged raids created mass confusion among the Japanese, who scampered wildly about the camp screaming while their sirens blared loudly. They appeared to panic during each raid as they herded the jubilant prisoners into the barracks.

These attacks were succeeded by low-flying American fighter planes, P-40s and P-51s. They had engaged enemy aircraft a short distance from camp on several occasions with very little opposition. However, during this period, two American pilots had been shot down over Shanghai and were brought into our camp in fairly good condition. While mass confusion among the Japanese continued with each raid, our morale grew.

The Japanese authorities permitted a priest and a Japanese Protestant minister from Shanghai to come into camp to conduct Easter services in 1945. The weather was beautiful and many of us attended the morning services.

During the afternoon, most of us were outside basking in the bright, warm sunlight, watching a softball game. At the same time the air raid sirens sounded, six or seven P-51s flew directly over our camp at an elevation of about five hundred feet. They were a thrilling sight to see and brought hope that the end of the war was approaching. They roared swiftly toward the nearby Japanese airfield, bombing and strafing repeatedly as they circled the area.

The screaming Japanese soldiers quickly ordered all of us into our barracks as two P-51s thundered over our heads. They overshot a Japanese super fortress bomber that had just taken off from the airfield. Then they immediately circled around and got into position behind the bomber. With one single burst of machine-gun fire from our fighter planes, the slow-flying bomber began to smoke. As it maneuvered around to return to the airfield, we saw one of its crew members fall from the plane. It continued to smolder as it went down at the airfield, crashing with a loud explosion. Billows of black smoke were seen for hours rising from the field.

The day was no longer peaceful as the sirens screamed and the Japanese screeched, running frantically around the barracks and through them. As the P-51s passed overhead, the Jap sentries would drop to one knee and fire their rifles at them. Needless to say, they didn't shoot down any planes. For the first time our enemy showed signs of fear. Even Ishahara appeared frightened.

Much excitement prevailed throughout the barracks as we peered out the windows to see our planes in action. I was doing just that when three Japanese soldiers came running between the barracks and saw me looking out the window. The Corporal's face was full of fear and hatred as he shouted vehemently at me and motioned with his gun for me to get away from the window. As I stepped back, he growled and continued on past our barracks and into the next one.

"Do you suppose he'll be back?" I asked Hawkins as I sat down on the bench at the table.

"I wouldn't be a bit surprised if they don't come back in here looking for you," warned Hawkins, who sat in a squatting position in the center of his bunk with his arms folded together.

"They could be looking for revenge. So it probably would be smart to stay on your bunk until this air raid is over," Sanborn said.

As the air raid continued, the atmosphere in the barracks ceased to be jubilant and became tense instead. We began to fear reprisals by the Japanese. Approximately fifteen minutes passed before the three Japanese soldiers appeared in our barracks and headed toward me. I was seated at the wooden table in the center of the room when the Japanese Corporal confronted me.

"*Coorah!*" he shouted. He was heavyset and larger than the average Japanese. His round fat face quivered, and the veins in his neck stood out each time he screamed. His whole body appeared to tremble with rage as I sat helpless, not knowing what to do. Suddenly, he lashed out at me with his fist, striking me across the face. My glasses went flying across the room, landing in the hallway after bouncing off the table. Fear seemed to take the place of pain as I felt nothing more than the impact of being jolted. His anger seemed to increase because I remained seated, so I finally stood up. Incensed with hatred, the Corporal stood silently for a brief moment, looking directly into my frightened face and struck me two more times.

Terror gripped the room. No one seemed to know what to do about the situation. Finally, Sloane poked his head out of his room and slowly walked into the hallway.

"I think he wants you to get on your bunk," Sloane told me as he cautiously studied the Japanese Corporal brandishing his bayoneted rifle.

I heard Sloane, but I didn't take my eyes off the Corporal, nor did he take his off me. To get on my bunk meant turning my back to him. He seemed too anxious to use his bayonet, so I continued to stare at him while I stood at attention. My heart continued beating rapidly. Finally, the Corporal gave up on me.

Turning to leave the room, he growled at me. He shuffled out of the room, slowly searching our faces for any excuse to strike one of us. When the three Japanese soldiers slammed the front door behind them, everyone let out a sigh of relief as we stretched out on our bunks. The aroma of burning oil crept into the barracks as the roaring sound of planes faded in the distance.

I sat down for a moment on my bunk to catch my breath before I walked out into the hallway to get my glasses. Fortunately, they hadn't broken.

"You did the right thing by standing perfectly still and not saying a word," whispered Hawkins as he walked to the hallway and looked up and down it.

"I guess so," I said.

My heartbeat had finally begun to slow, and I lay down on my bunk. Flat on my back, I wiped the cold sweat from my face. With the report of four prisoners being bayoneted during the afternoon, I felt very lucky.

Outside the barracks, the constant screeching sound of terrified Japanese soldiers running wildly about the camp continued throughout the afternoon. Inside, we spoke softly to one another. Even though we were elated over the air attack, we remained fearful of further reprisals. The evening inspection by the Japanese ended with several of us being struck in the face for not having our shoes polished, shirts buttoned, and bunks properly made up.

On the walk to the Japanese office the next day, I was constantly looking up at the sky — this time not to see what the weather was going to be like, but for our aircraft.

"Do you think they'll be back today?" I asked Smith.

"They might to mop up. I didn't see any Japanese fighter planes or hear any anti-aircraft guns, did you?" Smith said.

As Smith spoke, there was a changing of the guard just ahead of us on the road. Their loud shrieks echoed throughout the camp.

"Maybe there's nothing left for them to come back for," Smith said.

As we passed the Japanese soldiers, I had the feeling that if their looks could kill, we would have been dead.

We felt uncertain about what to expect from the interpreters after the previous day's air raid. Entering the office, we found Morisako slumped over his desk asleep. Ishahara hadn't arrived yet. The scraping sound of our chairs as we pulled them away from our desks woke Morisako. He slowly raised his head up but had trouble holding it erect as it kept bobbing up and down.

"Good morning, Mr. Morisako," Smith said.

We stood looking at him, but there was no response. He deliberately avoided looking at us as he turned toward the window. He just sat there, staring out. He appeared bitter and withdrawn. We sat down at the desks and looked at one another for several minutes before Smith turned to Morisako again and spoke.

"Do you have anything special that you'd like us to do today, Mr. Morisako?" he asked, but there was still no answer.

Smith turned to me and shrugged his shoulders.

"Yes," Morisako finally mumbled.

He slowly turned to some papers scattered across his desk. Picking them up, he shuffled them together and stacked them in a neat pile.

"This camp will be vacated shortly, so it will be necessary to make certain arrangements," he said, looking down at the stack of papers in front of him.

"Will we be going to Japan?" I asked.

"Maybe, I don't know," he said, still refusing to look at us.

"Just what is it that you want us to do?" Smith asked.

There was much commotion in the main Japanese office next door. The sound of shuffling shoes and ringing telephones was constant all day.

"We need to make three separate lists of men in camp and then assign them to boxcars in groups of fifty," Morisako whispered.

He picked up the papers and thumbed through them as he took a deep breath. Suddenly, the office door opened and Ishahara entered. After sitting at his desk, he and Morisako spoke in Japanese for several minutes, their sullen faces focused on each other. Their heads kept bobbing up and down in agreement during their conversation, while both gave us the cold shoulder.

The small room became very quiet when they ended their discussion as we sat uncomfortably waiting for instructions from Morisako. Then there was a soft knock on the door.

"Come in!" shouted Morisako.

The door opened slowly, and Clay Harrison cautiously stepped inside. Middle-aged, tall, handsome, and a former business executive, he had been put in charge of a civilian group.

"What do you want?" asked Morisako.

"One of your Japanese soldiers brought this note to me which requested me to report to the interpreter's office," Harrison said, holding up the piece of paper.

"Oh, yes, I remember now. You are Mr. Harrison." Morisako said. "In the near future this camp will be abandoned, and it will be necessary to return some things to the Red Cross. Therefore, we have to make boxes and crates to ship them back in. Do you understand, huh?"

"Yes, I think I understand," Harrison replied.

"Okay, tomorrow morning you must take five or six of your carpenters to our quartermaster, Lieutenant Kabuki. He will instruct your men what he wants done. You will find him in the warehouse. Do you know where it is?" Morisako asked.

"Yes, sir," Harrison responded sharply.

"That will be all. You may go," Morisako whispered, and Harrison bowed his head gently and quietly left the room.

Ishahara had been scribbling vigorously on a long, narrow piece of paper, perhaps writing a letter to someone. Suddenly, the pen fell free from his grip, and he stared out the window. Their feelings of depression and hopelessness showed on both Morisako and Ishahara after the previous day's devastating air attack. Both appeared despondent. The silence was broken when Ishahara turned to us and said, "Maybe war will soon be over and you will be going home."

In the past he had hardly ever spoken to us, but now he seemed eager to talk.

"We hope so," Smith said, surprised by his direct conversation with us.

"You will be happy to see your families again, huh," he said.

The morning sun was bright and warmed the room as it came through the large glass window, striking the wooden desks.

"Yes," I told him.

"I suppose you are anxious to see your family, too," Smith said.

We remained guarded in our conversation, not knowing Ishahara's motive for wanting to talk with us.

"Everything is gone with the wind; everything is finished," Ishahara said, his speech being slow and his thin, narrow face showing his bitterness and disappointment. "I have nothing to go home to," he said, continuing to stare out the window.

Morisako lifted his head up slowly as he carefully glanced at Ishahara. He continued to remain silent. Sliding his desk drawer open, he removed a package of cigarettes and leisurely proceeded to light one up. He inhaled deeply and expelled huge clouds of smoke, which quickly spread across the room. He then scooted his chair backwards and turned toward us.

"What will you do when you get back to America?" he asked, looking at both of us.

Before he could take another drag on his cigarette, he began to cough violently.

After waiting several moments for him to stop coughing, I said, "Are you asking what kind of work we will be doing?"

"Yes."

"I don't really know. I'm going to have to wait and see. I probably won't do a thing for a while until I get my health back," I said.

Each time he coughed he would bend over. His face remained grim, and he turned his attention to Smith.

"What will you be doing?"

"I think I will be going back to college after I rest a while," Smith said.

"What will you study?" Morisako asked.

"Law and political science maybe." Smith said.

His reply prompted Ishahara to join the conversation.

"Maybe you should study law so that you can help your country with their problem of discrimination," Ishahara said, his eyes fixed on Smith.

"Yes, we have a problem in that area," Smith admitted.

"People with dark skins in your country are second-class citizens," Ishahara said, straightening up in his chair. "They don't have the same advantages as a white person. Why is this so?"

"I don't know for sure," I told him. "However, part of the problem could be ignorance."

"Before the war, you Americans even discriminated against us by treating us as an inferior race of people. Why?" he demanded to know, his voice becoming louder with his anger, startling Morisako, who began to squirm in his chair.

"Mr. Ishahara, I am not aware of any discrimination toward your people. I can speak only from experience in college, where several Japanese-Americans attended the same classes with me," I told Ishahara.

"Were they discriminated against?" Ishahara inquired.

"No, sir," I responded firmly. "They were treated the same as everyone else. In the state of California we have many Japanese-American citizens who have become successful businessmen."

The hatred on Ishahara's face was quite evident when he continued staring at us.

"Successful as gardeners and maids you mean, don't you?" he asked.

"No, sir," I said and continued cautiously trying to avoid a heated confrontation with him. "There are many successful farmers and independent merchants of Japanese descent. Yes, there are also many working as self-employed gardeners."

Leaning back in his chair again, he lit up a cigarette. He sat rigidly, staring straight ahead at Morisako, who kept glancing through the papers before him.

Once again the room became quiet, while the distant screeching sound of Japanese soldiers could be heard with the changing of the guard. As the room filled with cigarette smoke, Morisako began coughing again. Ishahara quickly snuffed out his cigarette and slowly walked to the window and opened it.

While standing at the window, Ishahara spoke to Morisako briefly in Japanese. Morisako kept nodding his head in approval. Clearing his throat, turning toward us, Ishahara said, "Mr. Morisako and I will be leaving you sometime before you reach your new camp. So we would like to wish you good luck and a safe journey."

Concluding his farewell speech, he nodded his head gently as Morisako stood silently studying our reaction.

"Thank you," we both replied.

As we prepared to leave the office, we didn't wish them well, but merely said goodbye, hoping to never see them again!

Chapter 21

There was mass confusion during the early morning hours on 9 May 1945 as the Japanese rousted us out of the barracks at 4:00 in the morning. We were quickly herded into an open field adjacent to the barracks, each with his possessions packed in a single cardboard carton. Outside Chinese coolies with their honey buckets dipped out the "nite soil" for the last time. As they bounced up and down, carrying their heavy loads of human fertilizer to sprinkle on their fields, they continued to chant and left in their wake a very putrid odor.

We stood in front of our possessions, which had been removed from the cardboard box and spread out on the ground. We waited patiently in partial darkness surrounded by our screaming, disorganized enemy. At the far end of the field, Ishahara could be seen, riding crop in hand, glancing at the officers' possessions. Japanese soldiers did most of the inspecting, looking for weapons.

Nearly one thousand men, with renewed hopes of the war ending after the recent air raids, watched the Japanese as they scrambled between the long lines of prisoners. The war was going badly for them, and they behaved badly as they proceeded to kick and throw our few belongings around.

A Japanese soldier bent over before me searching through my clothing for weapons. He shook each article several times before tossing it aside. He turned and started to leave, but hesitated for a moment as he stared at the clothing scattered on the ground. Suddenly, he trampled over the clothing and went over to the empty cardboard box and gently kicked it. Then he picked it up and turned it upside down and began shaking it violently.

With my eyes fixed on the box, I held my breath as he shook it. Built into the box was a false bottom, which contained three small diaries. They represented over three years of recorded prison life and unusual incidents that had occurred. I had made penciled notes in longhand on scraps of paper during the week. The bits of scratch paper originally came from the dispensary. On Sundays, I entered the notes in small Japanese notebooks in shorthand with pen and ink. I had acquired these small Japanese notebooks, the quill pen, and a bottle of ink during the early stages of captivity when I was sent on a work detail to clean up some old military barracks. I had kept my writing materials in a small wooden box, which was nailed beneath the floor next to my bunk.

The thought of losing my diaries kept running through my mind. During the years, the Japanese had confiscated many diaries, and to have them taken away now would be tragic. I would have rather had a beating than lose them this late in the confinement. Finally satisfied that there wasn't anything inside, the sentry threw the cardboard box down with much force. It bounced once and flipped over on its side with the top facing him. Bending over to retrieve it, I noticed one of the small black notebooks had fallen out of the false bottom. I quickly reached inside and tucked it back underneath the pasteboard bottom, pressing it down firmly.

Hawkins stood next to me with his few belongings scattered before him. Shaking his head in disgust he said, "Those yellow bastards are going to make it as miserable as possible for us from now on. Look at the dirt that son-of-a-bitch deliberately kicked on my clothes."

"Yeah, he sure made a mess," I said.

Hawkins began shaking the dirt out of them and folding them before he put them back into the box.

"You sure were lucky your diaries didn't fall out, as hard as he shook it," Hawkins said. "I wonder why he picked your box up like that and not the rest of ours."

He had begun to cough as a result of the dust created by the Japanese soldier.

"Who knows? They are unpredictable. I don't think they know why they do some of the things they do," I said.

A bright sun had risen, warming the early morning air and revealing a clear blue sky.

"Are you going to use those diaries to write a book?" Hawkins asked. His face had become ashen from coughing repeatedly, and his eyes were moist.

"Maybe, I don't really know, Willie," I said.

"Include me in it if you do?" he said.

Hawkins had lasted much longer than I ever believed he would. Surviving a bullet wound in his forehead, and hampered with poor health, he had a tremendous instinct for self-preservation under extremely difficult circumstances. Sometimes he faked sickness in order not to go on work details, which infuriated his barracks leader at times. This had caused friction between them, and almost ended in fights on several occasions.

Shortly after 7:00, we were hiking down a narrow dusty road toward the

Kiangwan railway station after being assigned a boxcar number. Our cardboard boxes of personal gear were left behind to be sent by truck. The native Chinese continued to show very little interest in our presence as we passed by them. On a railway siding were twenty boxcars to transport us and two or three to carry personal gear and other supplies. We were marched in groups of fifty to the front of each car.

Hawkins had proceeded to walk towards the boxcar to get a better look inside, as the central area was completely open, when a Japanese guard screeching, "*Corrah!*" ran at him with his bayonet drawn. Hawkins quickly turned and sprinted back to the group, and the guard stopped chasing him but continued to scream and glower at him angrily.

Hawkins' face had become even whiter as he gasped for breath and shouted back at the guard, "Stick it up your ass, you yellow bastard!"

The Japanese sentry stood firmly in the loose dirt, shaking his rifle and growling at Hawkins. Finally, he turned slowly and continued down along the row of boxcars.

The freight cars resembled American boxcars, except they were smaller. Soon we began to board. The Japanese yelled, "Speedo, speedo," as they pushed us forward. Our group of fifty was divided in half and shoved into either end of the boxcar after we were required to remove our shoes. Each of us carried to the railway a blanket roll and personal utensils. The car contained some rice-straw mattresses on the floor, a fifty-gallon drum of drinking water, 3 five-gallon cans, 2 teapots, 186 loaves of bread, a large box of hard tack, 50 Red Cross boxes, and 2 chow buckets.

The two sliding doors on either side of the car were opened and barbed wire barricades were set up, sealing off the center section of the car from the prisoners. This area was occupied by four Japanese sentries and their gear. The car had four small windows, two on either end. There was little more than standing room after we had crowded in, and the rear of the car soon became warm and stuffy with very little fresh air from outside. Everyone tried to jockey for position toward the front for fresh air.

The distant sound of car couplings clanging together kept getting louder and louder until our car jerked forward slowly. It was nearly 10:00 when we pulled away from the small Kiangwan station, congested with Chinese, and headed in a northerly direction.

A warm breeze filtered through the high small windows in the rear of the car as we gathered speed. The Yangtze valley was very picturesque. The terrain was flat except for a few small hills, which we saw as we neared the outskirts of Nanking. We saw several pagodas as well as water buffalo and donkeys. There were numerous graves scattered about that rose above the ground in the shape of pyramids, some with visible markings on them. The countryside was webbed with canals and small ponds with very few fence posts. We saw small children in the rice fields, without a stitch of clothing, evacuating their bowels.

We arrived on the outskirts of Nanking around noon after making several stops every hour along the way. The Japanese guards quickly hustled us out of the cars to a vacant lot. We remained there a couple of hours while the Japanese transferred the cars across the Yangtze River. We were then transported across the river by ferry and herded back into the boxcars. The river was very swift and muddy with hardly any boats plying it.

The first night in the car was very hot. I slept with only a pair of shorts on and perspired all night. In order to lie down, it was necessary for at least eight fellows to be standing all the time. This was accomplished by each prisoner standing three hours and sleeping six. However, it was difficult to get everyone to cooperate.

Early the second morning out of Nanking, five American officers jumped out of the boxcars one by one at fifteen-minute intervals. Two had been stationed in Tientsin and were familiar with the area. They took with them a little food, some iodine, and a little water. The train came to a screeching halt early the next morning when their absence was reported. The Japanese guards wildly scampered about the immediate area looking for clues and crawling under the cars. Their search was hopeless, and they proceeded to partially seal most of the windows before we traveled on.

Four Japanese guards squatted with their short legs crossed before us in the center of the car enclosed by the barbed wire barricade. Their faces showed their changing moods during the day. Something or someone caused them to break out in laughter as they pointed their fingers at one of the prisoners. The prisoner was Gates, who had gone over to the open five-gallon bucket to urinate. He stood with outstretched hand against the wall as the boxcar bounced around. Their laughter got louder the longer Gates stood. Finally, he turned around and shouted at them, "What's so damn funny? Haven't you slant-eyed yellow bastards ever seen a fellow take a leak?"

Gates stared directly at them; his thin dark face seemed to be full of hatred. Tall and slender, he moved sure-footedly, stepping over those lying down to get back to his position in the car. The constant bouncing and swaying movement made it difficult to walk through the crowded mass of prisoners. Each of us was issued a nine-pound Red Cross food parcel prior to boarding the boxcar, which added to the congestion.

Early on the fourth morning of the train trip, two civilians escaped through the windows. The train was again stopped and a fruitless investigation was made of the area. This time the Japanese guards sealed the windows completely shut by nailing boards over them. They proceeded to step on anyone who got in their way, and they jerked clothing down which was hanging on the walls, throwing the clothing recklessly about the car.

"They don't seem too happy this morning about losing two more prisoners," Hawkins said, coughing intermittently.

As he spoke, he poked his finger in a small tin of jam and spread it on a piece of hardtack, licking his finger clean.

"No, the little bastards probably got their asses chewed out," replied Gates, who stood watching them throw clothing about as they kicked and screamed at the prisoners.

Before the train continued, the prisoners were ordered outside, and all the open five-gallon cans used as toilets were emptied. It felt good to walk around and get the kinks out of my legs as well as to breathe some fresh air. We milled around in groups surrounded by our Japanese guards.

"I don't understand the reasons why these fellows want to try to escape this late in the war. I don't feel the war can last much longer," Sanborn said, gazing at the distant mountains.

"It seems foolish to me also. Hell, they could break a leg leaving the train in the dark, then what. Then there's always the danger of getting shot. Of course, our safety isn't guaranteed, but I think we have a better chance. Don't you think so?" asked Hawkins.

"I think so. Even if those fellows make it back safely, the war is likely to be over. We might even beat them home," Sanborn said smiling and tucking his shirttail in.

Some of us who rode in the forward cars began to return to our cars. A bright warm sun was nearly directly overhead as we boarded and got underway. There was a constant stream of prisoners using the fifty-gallon drum of drinking water which had been flavored with iodine to prevent diarrhea and dysentery, and we frequently stumbled over each other trying to reach the open five-gallon toilet containers at the rear of the car. This created a precarious situation, especially during the night. With the windows boarded shut, the rear of the car became stifling hot, which intensified the putrid odor coming from the containers.

After five days of traveling, we were hustled off the boxcars and marched to a large warehouse on the outskirts of Peking. Built with red bricks, it was huge, and its shabby appearance indicated that it hadn't been occupied for some time. Weeds completely surrounded the entire building, partially concealing the entrance. Small isolated Chinese villages could be seen a short distance away, each surrounded by trees. Next to the warehouse was an old, dilapidated military barracks and two smaller shacks. Down a narrow winding road about two miles away there appeared to be a vacated lumberyard. All of us were assembled in front of the warehouse, where the Japanese immediately took a roll call before deciding what next to do.

An hour passed, then two, as we stood waiting to be moved into our new living quarters. A picture of despair, we stood tired and hungry. Our clothing was damp and wrinkled, and we smelled bad. Our weary faces were heavily bearded.

"I wonder how long we'll be staying here?" Plunkett asked.

His youthful face had aged, and his copper hair covered his ears. Quiet most of the time, he came to life whenever the subject of making whiskey in the backwoods of Kentucky was mentioned.

"Who knows?" Hawkins whispered, brushing the hair out of his eyes. "I would guess we won't be here too long. I'm sure they are taking us to Japan."

"You think so?"

"Sure. They're probably getting the hell kicked out of them everywhere and have received orders to return to their homeland," Hawkins said, and waited patiently for Plunkett to respond.

"Since they're losing the war and pulling out of China, why didn't they just leave us in Shanghai for the Red Cross to look after us?" Plunkett asked. His green eyes widened at the thought of his having a solution to our problem.

"I'd go along with that, but I'm afraid our little Japanese friends have other plans for us," Hawkins said, smiling and shaking his head at the hillbilly from Kentucky.

The large double door to the warehouse had been opened for us to begin entering. It was divided into five sections, and the floor was dirt. Several porcelain lamps fastened to rafters were covered with spider webs. The smell of rotten bean curd permeated the building. Dust had collected on the walls, which had been used as blackboards for finger drawings and messages.

Schultz made his way through the crowd, holding his nose and waving his other hand at Sloane.

"What the hell is that awful smell, Emery?" he asked, spitting on the ground.

"I don't really know. But it smells like rotten beans to me," Sloane said, shielding his mouth and nose with a handkerchief from the dust caused by the movement of the prisoners inside the building.

"They should air this place out before moving us in this stinking hole," Schultz said.

"Yeah, this damn dust is making it difficult to breathe. It must be raising hell with Willie," Sloane said, and then asked, "Has anyone seen him?"

"I saw him a little while ago standing just inside the doors. He walked outside and stood until a Japanese guard ran him back in," said Dawson, who had joined Sloane and Schultz.

Ishahara and Major Charles McGuire could be seen talking outside the entrance as we were assigned our locations. There was a lot of coughing while we continued to stir about.

"Say, Emery, what are we supposed to do when we have to go to the head?" Schultz asked. "I don't see an outhouse."

"That's going to be a problem," Sloane said, shaking his head in disgust.

"Just the thought of sleeping on the ground is bad enough."

Hawkins, coughing and spitting, tears streaming down his shallow cheeks, approached Sloane and asked, "What's a fellow have to do to be able to take a crap around here?"

"I don't know what they expect us to do," Sloane said. "Ishahara is coming this way; I'll ask him."

"I shouted *benjo* at the Japanese guard at the entrance several times, but he only growled and pointed his gun at me, motioning for me to get back inside," continued Hawkins.

"Mr. Ishahara, some of the men need to use a toilet right now. Where do they go?" Sloane asked Ishahara, who had made his way over to him.

"There are some toilet facilities and water in the building next door; however, your men will be building several facilities for our stay here," Ishahara said.

"How do we get there?" asked Sloane.

"Just tell Japanese guard at the door *benjo*, and he will take you there," he said, nodding his head as he spoke.

Hawkins began poking Sloane in the back with his finger to remind him that the guard wouldn't let him go.

"But Mr. Ishahara, some of the men are saying that the Japanese guards are not cooperating," Sloane said, standing a safe distance from him.

"Never mind about that. I will speak to Japanese soldiers when I go back outside," he said.

He started to leave but stopped and turned around.

"We need a detail of men from your group to get mattresses and other supplies from train," he shouted before moving on.

The afternoon was hot and dusty as a steady stream of men carried supplies between the train and the warehouse. A narrow open trench was dug in the adjoining field to accommodate the overflow of men who had to use the head. They were watched by several Japanese guards yelling, "Speedo."

We spent several days cleaning the weeds and other debris around the warehouse and building temporary living facilities, a galley and restrooms namely. Ishahara supervised the work parties, but with much less enthusiasm than in the past. His face showed little emotion.

Bathing was permitted in an open field near the Japanese office. The facility was an artesian well, which bubbled up above the ground about three feet. The water came from a depth of nearly four hundred feet and looked beautiful. It sparkled under the late afternoon sun and tasted delicious — the first water we had that didn't have to be treated before drinking!

After we received permission, a majority of us streaked to the water hole in our handmade sandals with a towel draped around our bodies. The water proved refreshing and exciting, and some of us engaged in water fights. After three or four days passed, the Japanese issued an order that all prisoners must wear shorts to and from the water hole. It seemed that there were some Japanese girls working in the office who were enjoying the sight too much.

Two weeks had gone by and there were still no signs that we would be moving on. A twenty-one-year-old fighter pilot joined us. Shot down in April 1945, he was very skinny and was badly burned from his knees down. He told our doctor that his bandages hadn't been changed for two weeks. We were monitored by Photo Joe, our high-flying American plane, which passed over at noon this day.

The food situation had become acute. We had noodles for breakfast and dinner and watery greens for lunch, one-cupful per man. Our stomachs had shrunk many times their normal size, but it still took more than one cup of noodles to fill them. The unsanitary living conditions had caused much sickness, mainly diarrhea.

A warm sun was almost directly overhead when Tiny Tim was seen running down the road, followed by three rifle-toting guards. Shortly thereafter, the bugle sounded, which sent the Japanese running wildly in all directions. Morisako pursued Tiny Tim on his bicycle, slumped forward, pedaling rapidly. The Japanese guards were finally assembled in a group and sent down the road on the double. We were all immediately rounded up and herded back inside the warehouse. A quick inspection was made, and we were ordered to stand by.

"What's going on, Herman?" asked Gates, who kept staring outside.

"Maybe somebody is trying to escape again," Schultz said.

Three days ago the Japanese had caught a prisoner trying to escape after the evening inspection. They had found him near the galley and removed him from the camp the following day.

Dr. Corey, senior medical officer, was seen speeding off down the dirt road in the sidecar of a motorcycle operated by Dr. Shindo. They returned after an hour with the following story.

It seems that Bungie Harrison, one of the Britishers, was reported missing from one of the work parties. Harrison was better known to the prisoners as the Eskimo because he wore shorts and short-sleeved shirts and no sweaters in the dead of winter. He was found pinned under a pile of lumber. His story to the Japanese was that he had fallen asleep and some of the supports gave way, trapping him. He sustained minor facial injuries. His story must have been convincing as he received very little punishment.

After spending thirty-six miserable days in the warehouse, arrangements were finally made to move us farther north by boxcars. Our bakers were instructed to make hardtack for the trip. Rumors were that the Red Cross would furnish the food for the journey. The day before leaving, Smith and I were summoned to the Japanese office by Morisako. When we arrived, we found Ishahara and Morisako intoxicated. A large bottle of sake was sitting on their desk between them as they drank from small tea bowls. Their eyes were glassy, and their speech was slurred. The room reeked of sake and tobacco smoke.

"Mr. Ishahara and I wanted to thank you again for your work in this office and also to say goodbye. This is as far as we go," said Morisako, speaking slowly while his large head rolled back and forth.

"You won't be leaving with us tomorrow?" Smith asked.

"No. We have been ordered back to Japan where we will receive new instructions from our government," said Ishahara.

He reached out for the bottle of sake, nearly upsetting it before pouring some in his cup.

Still clinging to the bottle, he jerked his head up and said, "Would you like a drink?"

"No, thank you," we both answered simultaneously.

The thought of accepting anything from Ishahara, who had caused severe hardship and many deaths among us, was nauseating.

While watching Ishahara set the bottle back down and pick up his bowl, spilling some of the contents on his desk, I felt hatred and contempt for him. The recollection of seeing Major McGuire being escorted back to his quarters drunk at dusk the previous Christmas Eve by this vermin, Ishahara, was hard to understand.

Morisako's head continued to sway back and forth as his eyes opened and closed. Suddenly he picked up a pack of cigarettes and fumbled around for the longest time trying to remove one before he finally dumped the whole package out on his desk.

"Take care of your health," Morisako said.

"Will we be going to Japan?" I asked.

"Maybe, that I don't know for sure," he said, looking out the corner of his eye at Ishahara, whom he feared.

He lacked the courage or character to stand up to him. The room became very quiet as we stared at them, sitting there pondering their defeat and ultimate return home.

"Will that be all, sir?" Smith asked.

"Yes," Morisako replied in a stupor.

We quickly turned and left the room.

The warehouse was evacuated early the next morning on 9 June 1945. We hiked down the road to the train in three separate groups of 500, 300, and 196 men. Travel arrangements were the same as before as we continued in a northerly direction in slightly cooler weather.

The train stopped every day at different stations to pick up food and water. Our ration of food consisted of rice and a box of seaweed, fish, and pickled turnip. The food was much better on this part of the trip, which lasted four days. The train also stopped every afternoon between villages, permitting us to evacuate our bowels.

We were no longer traveling in a northerly route as we turned south and headed down the Korean peninsula. We seemed to travel between and along the edges of two mountain ranges. The rich green mountains and valleys were very picturesque, sparsely covered with small pine trees and running streams. We saw rice paddies on the flat lands as well as on terraces that extended far up the mountain sides, so very little land was wasted. Invariably, they were full of water. Men, women, and children waded with their pants rolled up, transplanting the rice from early morning till late at night.

Roads in this part of the country were few. An automobile would have been impractical. The best transportation would have been a bicycle. Nevertheless, the railroad was very good, and there were two other tracks working next to the one we were on.

Throughout the valley, we saw clusters of twenty to thirty huts built of mud and rice straw at the foot of the mountains. In the villages we saw better-looking houses built with wood and mud that had tile roofs. We saw Korean women wearing white blouses and long black skirts, carrying baskets of food on their heads. They also carried children on their backs by means of a cloth tied around their bodies with their hands folded behind them. The men dressed similar to the Chinese — white shirts with a triangle-shaped pack with a rice straw mat basket attached, which rested on their backs. The pack was used to carry many different articles, including live chickens.

Before we reached the end of the train ride in Korea, we had passed through eighty tunnels. They were rather short and cemented throughout.

Chapter 22

The train had slowed down and came to a stop in the coastal town of Pusan in southern Korea. The small depot was teeming with Korean civilians and Japanese soldiers laden with military gear waiting for passage. Outside, the ground was damp and muddy from the recent rains. The day was dark and dreary with heavy black clouds. As we waited in the boxcars, it began to thunder, and large bolts of lightning illuminated the sky. After an hour had passed, the men had become impatient and began to stir around.

"What in the hell are they waiting for now?" Hawkins asked. The air had become chilly, and he jumped up and down and rubbed his hands together to keep warm.

"They're waiting for it to rain," Schultz shouted, shaking a clenched fist. "Say, look over there at that little yellow bastard picking on that old man," he said, pointing in the direction of a Japanese soldier who had cornered a tall slender Korean man against the side of the depot.

"I wonder what the problem is," Hawkins said.

Plunkett, who had been standing near the car door opening and observed what happened, told us, "The old man walked by him and didn't salute or stop and bow to him."

The lightning and thunder continued until the rain began to fall heavily. After an hour, the downpour showed no signs of subsiding. Water ran off the roof of the depot in sheets, spilling onto the sidewalk. People crowded underneath the eaves seeking shelter. Except for the sound of the rain striking the tin roof of the depot and the occasional crackle of lightning, it had been rather calm up until now. Suddenly, loud screechings came from the forward section of the train. Japanese soldiers were stopping at each boxcar and ordering everyone outside.

"That figures; it's raining," Hawkins said, looking up from his sitting position. His frail body slumped forward and a worried look came over him. He must have been wondering how much more exposure to the weather he could endure.

Our four guards jumped out of the boxcar to meet the approaching Japanese soldiers. We were quickly removed from the cars and marched out of town in a heavy rain to a small, dilapidated military barracks about two miles away.

The wooden structure was in need of much repair as many windows had the glass broken out and the screens torn. The galvanized tin roof had been patched with assorted pieces of scrap sheet metal. Three small water spigots outside provided water for nine hundred ninety-six men to bathe in, wash their clothing and dishes in, and to use for drinking, after standing in line for an hour or two. The barracks did have a wooden floor in it and rice mats to sleep on. Outside the barracks the problem was mud; inside flies had become a problem, making it difficult to eat and generally to remain comfortable.

The next morning, the entire camp was marched about three miles toward the coast to a Japanese disinfecting station. Every one of us removed our clothing and shoes, which the Japanese took and steam-heated. Standing naked in long lines, we waited for our stool tests. This medical inspection took all day. However, after spending four days on the train in a cramped position, the hike felt good.

We spent five days at this human pigsty. The weather was very humid with frequent showers. The sanitary conditions were appalling, and cases of diarrhea became numerous. Large work details were sent out of camp to load salt onto barges.

On the eve of 28 June 1945, we assembled outside and were divided into three separate groups. The Japanese again played their usual waiting game; this time it lasted five hours, until midnight, but at least it was not raining. Following a farewell speech, we were fed a small portion of rice and broth and a delicious piece of fish.

Under the supervision of a transportation unit, we left camp about 2:00 in the morning. The hike to the boat, some three miles away, involved ascending a hill before reaching the dock in total darkness. We walked upstairs and downstairs and through the waiting room and finally onto a small ferry, where we rode third class. The boat got underway shortly after 6:00 that same morning, after we received a package of cooked rice and seaweed. The portholes were closed all the time, and it was very hot, causing us to perspire constantly. The small ferry followed a zig-zag course across the Straits of Korea for nine hours until it finally arrived at a very picturesque cove on the coast of Japan around 3:00 in the afternoon.

We spent the night on the boat and received a handful of hardtack around 10:00 that evening. The next morning, we began unloading all our belongings from the boat to a motor launch, which took them ashore. We carried them from there by foot about five hundred yards in the rain to an old barn. The area surrounding the barn was wooded and green, and the rain had cleansed the air. It was mid-afternoon when we finally received a small package of cooked rice. Immediately after eating, we were sent on with our supplies, which we carried by foot and by a small man-drawn wagon.

Dr. Corey was the senior officer in charge of our group of one hundred ninety-six men. He led the procession of men and supplies, flanked by screaming Japanese guards, through a small village along the waterfront surrounded by beautifully wooded hills. The supplies were put in a freight car two miles down the road. After a ten-minute rest, the guards moved the group on down a narrow dirt road that curved in between houses on either side. We continued to walk another three miles before stopping at a small theater, where we spent the night.

The sweet smell of incense filled the delicate room as we entered after leaving our shoes outside. The theater was clean and neat. We sprawled out on the thick mat that covered the entire floor, except for a small stage that was slightly elevated at the far end of the room. Floral paintings decorated the walls and colorful lanterns hung from the low ceiling. The theater was refreshing, and we fell asleep immediately from sheer exhaustion, only to be awakened at dusk to receive a package of cooked rice. Two large sliding doors that opened out onto the street had been shoved completely back letting the fresh cool summer air filter into the room.

As usual we attacked our meal vigorously as though it was our last. Some spooned the rice out of the small wooden boxes, while others picked it out with their fingers and licked them clean. The room began to hum with conversation.

Plunkett, the quiet copper-haired boy from the backwoods of Kentucky, set his spoon down in his box of rice and said, "I know they're not going to bring out any geisha girls or moonshine, but I wonder if we're going to get any tea or water to wash this here rice down and fill our bellies."

"I think maybe we'll be getting some tea," Hawkins said. "I heard one of the prisoners yelling, '*ocha,*' at a Japanese guard who repeated, '*ocha,*' as he shook his head and walked towards the rear of the theater."

Hawkins was chewing his fingernails for lack of a cigarette.

"Perhaps we'll get lucky tonight and get a good night's sleep," Schultz said as he stood up and brushed the rice off his shirt.

"I sure hope so, Herman," replied Gates. "Now that we're traveling through their homeland I hope we don't encounter any radical civilians. Since we're so few and there are only a few soldiers to protect us, it might be dangerous."

His deep voice got our attention, and many of us who had been relaxed, suddenly became frightened.

The sun had completely gone down, causing the small theater to become dark. As the colorful lanterns were turned on, two other groups of prisoners passed by outside on their way to new camps in Japan. Shortly afterwards the lights were turned off and everyone bedded down for the night. We were quickly awakened from our hearty sleep by the sound of air-raid sirens blaring in the early morning hours. The Japanese became very excited as they scampered around inside, making sure all doors and windows were closed and covered. We sat quietly, listening to the whining of the sirens for ten or fifteen minutes until they finally stopped. Within a half hour it was already dawn, and we were hurried out of the theater into a light rain and hiked to a railway station about a mile away.

Our leader, Dr. Corey, was able to persuade the Japanese guards to permit us to wait under the depot roof because the rains became really heavy when we arrived. We watched for about fifteen minutes as civilian men, women, and children, as well as Japanese soldiers, departed and boarded the many coaches. As the passengers crowded into the depot, we were moved out into the rain, where we remained until we boarded empty coaches at 5:00, soaking wet. As we boarded, I noted that the passenger coaches looked just like ours on the outside, black with windows to see out, except the lettering on the cars was in Japanese. Inside, there was an aisle down the center with double, full cushioned seats on either side. Small bits of paper littered the aisle and remnants of tobacco smoke gathered near the ceiling. The water-streaked windows had steamed up slightly. This was the beginning of our first train ride in Japan, which started on 30 June 1945 sometime between 5:00 and 6:00 in the morning.

The long passenger train slowly pulled away from the station, while angry Japanese civilians stared at us in a heavy downpour of rain. The train followed the coastline for a while as it wove in and out between the mountains, passing through several tunnels. The scenery was beautiful. The water-laden boughs of the trees were bent under the extra weight. The hillsides were terraced with rice paddies of various sizes and shapes. The rain didn't stop the Japanese from working in the paddies. We saw people of all ages and sizes transplanting the rice. They wore round rice hats and rice-straw mats around their shoulders and down their backs. The fronts of their bodies were exposed, and they wore no shoes. We also saw, a short distance from the coast, two sunken, small boats. We were taken off the train around noon at another depot.

Our small group gathered closely together on the depot landing as Dr. Corey prepared to speak.

"Our Japanese protective unit will be taking us through this railway station," he told us. "They say we have to go through it to get to a road on the other side that leads to an old wooden building that is our destination. They feel we have a better chance of getting through without any incident if we run four abreast. Does everyone understand what we have to do?"

The rain had subsided to a slow drizzle, and he wiped the water from his troubled face. Several of us gestured positively.

"Okay, now let's quickly line up and when I give the signal to start you run and don't stop until you are completely through the terminal and onto the road," he continued, and then he quickly turned to the Japanese guards, who began forming in front and behind as well as on either side of us.

Their faces were strained.

Dr. Corey stood at the head of the column restlessly waiting for the group to form. Spontaneously, he waved his arm and shouted, "Let's go!" The group broke quickly, stampeding through the crowded terminal like a bunch of cattle and looking only straight ahead. Before the people inside realized what was happening, we were long gone down the road.

We reached the old wooden building and found that Group A had just arrived there moments earlier. We were joined by Group B around mid-afternoon. The three groups remained there until about 7:00 after being fed twice. We left together and boarded the same train about two miles away around 9:00 that evening. While waiting to board the train, we saw three small Japanese girls standing under a lamppost, bowing in front of one of the outgoing coaches loaded with soldiers. After the train had left, they lined up one behind the other along the railroad siding and stood erect for about two minutes. They appeared to be crying, and then they bowed again and departed quietly.

This train took our three groups of prisoners in the direction of Tokyo. We rode all night and the following day, arriving at a large railway station around 7:00 the next evening. Many fires that attained great heights were visible surrounding the terminal and illuminated the area. Endless lines of Japanese soldiers stood silently in the terminal waiting to leave. Trains were coming and leaving. Hordes of Japanese civilians stood around weeping and wailing emotionally. Above the din we heard the loud shouts of young girls dispatching the trains.

Our train had hardly stopped when the Japanese guards began running up and down the coaches excitedly screaming and waving to everyone to get off. We were gripped by fear when we stepped off the coaches into a warm night filled with the odor of burnt paper and wood. As we sprinted along the sidings, some one hundred yards to another train, a large angry crowd of Japanese civilians ran toward us. Our Japanese protective unit struggled to hold back the angry mob as we filed into the coaches. Several of the civilians broke through and reached some of us while we boarded, and brief skirmishes ensued up and down the line. The enraged crowd began screaming and waving fists, striking the sides of the coaches as we pulled away from the depot. One prisoner slipped back down the steps in time to kick a civilian squarely in the face, sending him sprawling to the ground.

The train traveled swiftly through the night. Small ceiling lights lit the hot, stuffy coaches. Window shades had been drawn to prevent us from looking outside. A Japanese guard stood at either end of the coach watching as the men wiggled into sleeping positions, some of whom ended up on the floor. It was quiet during the night except for our snoring. Finally, we began straightening up in our seats and rubbing our eyes as ribbons of daylight pierced the outer edges of the drawn curtains. One prisoner pulled a window shade open with his hand to take a peek. A Japanese went running towards him screaming, "*Coorah, coorah!*" The guard stood before him glowering, and he quickly removed his hand from the window.

"What was that all about?" asked Hawkins, who had awakened, startled by the outburst.

"One of the fellows was caught peeking out the window," Schultz said, pointing his finger at the Jap guard, who growled and moved back up the aisle to the other end of the coach.

"I wonder what it is out there that they don't want us to see," Hawkins said, running his fingers through his thick crop of gray hair.

Schultz slid down in his seat until only a small part of his head was visible to the guards. Then he proceeded to open the lower portion of the curtain as Hawkins acted as his lookout. Schultz's eyes widened and his mouth dropped open in awe.

"No wonder those little yellow bastards don't want us to see out," Schultz whispered, turning to Hawkins.

"What did you see?"

Schultz stood up and shifted his damp clothing around a bit before he sat back down.

"Rubble," Schultz said. "Not a single building standing. Nothing, not even a tree — only plumbing sticking up out of the ground. No signs of a living thing as far as you can see."

Schultz shook his head in disbelief.

Hawkins quickly changed places with him so he could take a look. His face beamed with delight at what he saw. Others throughout the coach began peeking out the windows as the guards rushed around screaming. For a moment, there was an atmosphere of renewed hope and victory as we settled back in our seats.

On 2 July 1945, our small group was taken off the train. We hiked about two miles, with the sun directly overhead, to a small park, where we spent the afternoon. The brief stay in the quaint park was a welcome opportunity to use the restrooms. We were fed two small loaves of bread for supper before leaving around 6:00. Shrill shouts by the Japanese guards signaled us to begin forming columns for another hike back to the railroad depot. They seemed anxious to get us back on a train, where it was much easier for them to protect us. Some of us were slow getting up from the grass and the guards hurried us along by striking their rifle butts across our backs.

Once again we found ourselves inside a large railroad terminal. We held our breath as we walked past large crowds of Japanese soldiers waiting to be shipped out. Surprisingly, they seemed to barely notice us as we were hustled aboard three streetcars. The streetcars pulled out of the large terminal at dusk, packed with prisoners, while the guards appeared to dangle from the outside steps. The cars were powered by electricity furnished from a trolley pole mounted on the roof that made contact with an overhead line. Those of us who were crammed into the front and rear sections were blessed with plenty of fresh air while those in the enclosed central compartment nearly suffocated. The streetcars took us through the outskirts of Tokyo and the ride lasted one-half hour.

Gates stood in the front of the car waving his arm out the open window. He was pointing at a small shack which had been erected from the debris.

"Our bombers really did a job on these people," he said.

"I'd say so," Hawkins said. "I don't see how anyone could have survived it."

The evening air was cool and the wind created by the swift movement of the streetcar blew directly into Hawkins' face, causing his eyes to water. Gates nervously looked out one side of the car, then the other. He appeared to grit his teeth as his hatchet face took on a worried look.

"I sure wish the hell they'd kept us in China," Gates said. "I think our chances of getting out of this mess would have been better."

But everyone knew Gates was a pessimist, who had never thought we would ever get out of China either. Consequently, no one would have much to do with him.

The faint echo of a distant siren almost caused one of the guards to fall off the streetcar as he turned around on the steps. Small scattered fires still burned throughout the night.

The streetcars stopped at a small depot where we were rushed aboard coaches once again. The Japanese civilians stared at us as they walked by. A few stopped and chanted at us, waving clenched fists, sticks, or newspapers. Japanese guards blocked the car doors until the train began moving. We sat petrified in our seats, speechless. As the train gathered speed, we felt like we were riding on a roller coaster with the loss of speed climbing up between the mountains and the gain of speed going downhill. There was total darkness outside except for a few lights in the distance occasionally.

Our hunger and weakness was eased somewhat by the opportunity to rest. There was hardly any conversation among us as we closed our eyes for the night ride. We remained aboard the train all the next day and night as it traveled along the mountainsides stopping frequently to discharge and take on passengers. We were fed twice a box of cooked rice and seaweed.

On 4 July 1945 the train stopped at another small depot around 6:00 in the morning. We left the train and took all our personal gear off and stacked it outside the depot. When the train pulled out, only Group A remained aboard as Group B had been taken off outside of Tokyo. While we waited to be moved again, we were fed two rice balls for breakfast. The small depot was partially hidden at the base of a pine-covered mountain. Over an hour had gone by when, finally, Dr. Corey emerged from the depot with one of the Japanese guards. He approached our group and asked for our attention.

"We will be leaving shortly for our new camp which is located somewhere back up in these mountains," he said, pointing behind us.

"They informed me that we will travel from here in open mining cars pulled by small engines on a narrow-gauge track," he continued.

As he turned around toward the guard, someone shouted, "How long a ride is it?"

"They said between two and three hours," Corey said.

He was soft spoken, dignified, and respected by all the prisoners. His refined mannerisms befitted someone accustomed to high society. He handled his predicament very well.

Some of the prisoners began walking behind the depot looking for the cars we would be riding in while a Japanese guard ran after them screaming. They were quickly driven back but not before they got a glimpse of the small engines and open cars. Plunkett was all excited when he came running down the steep enbankment behind the depot where the cars were located.

"Those small wooden boxcars and little engines are just like the ones back home in Kentucky. When I was a kid, we would jump on cars like those filled with coal and ride them down the hill until we were caught and thrown off," Plunkett said, smiling.

"I'll bet you kids were black from head to foot. Didn't your folks whip you when you got home?" asked Dawson.

"Yeah, sometimes. There was a small creek nearby that we would swim in. Most of the time we could clean up enough first," Plunkett said.

The Japanese guards motioned for us to move up the bank toward the mining cars. There were sixteen cars and two engines waiting for us on the narrow-gauge track. A small detail of prisoners was ordered by the Japanese to load our supplies into the first three cars while the others began climbing into those that were open. Fifteen men squatted in the bottom of each car, packed like sardines, waiting to move out. An hour passed, then two. Finally, the two train engineers and the Japanese guard in charge of our transportation strolled out of the depot laughing boisterously. They stood for several minutes talking and laughing loudly, occasionally glancing in our direction, before approaching us. Their dragging feet stirred up the loose dirt and left a trail of dust behind them. There were two short, sharp blasts from the small engines before their wheels began to spin. Then sand was applied to the tracks, and the long string of cars began to move slowly.

The engines picked up a little speed, following a power line and a beautiful clear stream that twisted and turned up the gradual incline of the pine-covered mountain. The air was clear and clean, heavy with the odor of pine. A rich blue sky appeared through the openings of the trees. There was a dense growth of underbrush and shrubbery and a variety of ferns growing along the banks of the stream. Traveling through the forest for nearly an hour provided quiet moments to enjoy the beauty of nature. The forest represented everything that war didn't. It was peaceful, beautiful, and prolific.

The smell of tobacco smoke kept drifting back from the engineers' cabins, causing some of the prisoners to have nicotine fits as they began yelling at the Japanese guards.

"Hey, you give me tobacco!" shouted Hawkins.

Standing up in the car, his frail body swayed back and forth. As he spoke he waved at the Japanese guard in the next car, pretending he was smoking. The guard ignored him, continuing to puff on his cigarette. After shouting several times, Hawkins sat back down.

"Not very friendly, is he," he quipped.

His face was sad, but he had a strong will to see this through and return to San Francisco and its bright lights.

The small engines strained to get up the mountain, sometimes no faster than a person could walk. We stayed quiet, trying to conserve our energy; still a few of us discussed what we might expect at the new camp.

"I wonder if we're going to get another son-of-a-bitch like Ishahara in this camp," Gates said. His dark-complexioned face showed no expression as he casually chewed on a reed.

"I don't see how anyone could be any more sadistic and meaner than Ishahara. We'll soon find out. I don't imagine it's much farther. I sure hope we don't get another like him," Dawson said, his speech barely audible. It had become very difficult for him to talk during the past year.

For the most part, the trip up the mountain was quiet, and only a few of us spoke occasionally about the possibility of the war ending. The Japanese had furnished a chair for Dr. Corey to sit on in the first car. He had been enjoying the beautiful scenery when suddenly he began pointing at something ahead of us. The train had made a final curve around the mountain as it came to an opening and headed straight into a small valley completely surrounded by towering mountain peaks. We passed by wooden shacks slightly elevated above the valley floor, teeming with young children and pregnant women, who stopped to stare at us. Smoke could be seen pouring out of chimneys from the lumber mills in the distance on the banks of a large pond. The mountain air was refreshing after being subjected to the nauseating odor of "nite soil" in China for over three years.

The train squeaked to a stop as the engineers jerked their whistles once again. This time they turned around and laughed. About one-half mile straight ahead up the mountain stood our new camp with a high wooden fence surrounding it. Urged on by the screaming and prodding Japanese guards, we were soon hiking up a narrow trail to the camp, carrying our supplies.

Chapter 23

After fifty-five days on the road since leaving China, we finally arrived at our new camp in Japan shortly before noon. We were grouped in front of the barracks, which was a two-story wooden building. Our transportation unit gave us a short speech complimenting us on our good behavior before turning us over to the new camp authorities. Everyone stood patiently awaiting the arrival of the Japanese Commandant of the Camp. All heads turned toward the far end of the barracks as he slowly rounded the corner of the building and headed toward us, escorted by two guards. His walk was not steady, and he tottered noticeably. Our Camp Commandant was a very old and feeble man.

He was formally introduced to and greeted by Dr. Corey as Lieutenant Yoritomo. He stood quietly looking over the prisoners as he spoke softly to his camp officers, Sergeant Major Nakayama and interpreter Kinoshita. His address was spontaneous and brief as he reiterated the often-heard instructions to obey the Japanese regulations and not try to escape, for it was impossible. He immediately left for his quarters escorted by the two guards as Sergeant Major Nakayama took control.

A warm sun directly overhead beat down on our small, weary group as we stood assembled, once again at the mercy of a Japanese officer. Walking slowly in front of the prisoners, he stared down the irregular columns, his mouth twitching as though he had food lodged between his teeth. Stocky and bow-legged with a sword dangling from his hip, he strutted toward Dr. Corey with Kinoshita trailing behind. After receiving further instructions, we were marched into the barracks and each assigned a bunk.

When we entered the building and walked down a narrow hallway to the staircase, a huge rat emerged from an adjoining room. We were no longer quiet; we yelled and kicked at it before it ran down a hole in the floor.

"That's the first fresh meat I've seen since leaving China," Plunkett said, smiling and looking to see where it went.

"Hell, he looked big enough to put a saddle on and ride. He probably has been eating our food," shouted Hawkins.

The prisoners made their way up the wooden stairway to the second floor. The entire room had three-tier bunks built to the ceiling with narrow aisles between them. Each bunk had five thin, filthy blankets stacked on top of a thick, dirty rice mat. We were assigned four blankets, and after the Japanese gathered up one blanket from each man, they said they were still short a few. They refused to feed us until the missing blankets were found. Everyone carried their blankets outside while the Japanese sentries searched the barracks. Afterwards they counted the number of each prisoners' blankets as we returned inside. Not before several hours had elapsed did they decide there were no blankets missing and to feed us.

The loud, thunderous sound of a gong woke the entire camp the first morning at 5:00. Those that were slow in rising were quickly rousted from their bunks by rifle butts by a very noisy bunch of Japanese guards. Shortly after roll call, we received a small bowl of rice and a cup of watery beans. The beans were few and far between and had the oil removed. This was the poorest chow we had received thus far!

Plunkett was sitting on the top bunk with his legs dangling down over the side. He had just finished his breakfast and was thinking of dropping down to go and wash his dishes when Hawkins shouted at him.

"Wait a minute. I'm sitting directly underneath you and I'm still eating," Hawkins said, shielding his head with his arm.

"You're still eating. You must have got more to eat than me," Plunkett said, bending down and looking into his bowl.

"Bull shit! You just eat too fast," Hawkins replied.

Plunkett swung his legs up and stretched out on his bunk. He was quiet for a moment before he began to talk to Hawkins again.

"Say, Willie, I sure hope I don't have any of those problems I used to have when I was younger," Plunkett continued, speaking in more serious tone.

"What's that?" Hawkins asked.

"Wetting the bed," Plunkett responded casually.

Hawkins quickly jumped up from his bunk and looked Plunkett squarely in the eye as he clung to his bowl of rice.

"I sure hope you don't do it while I'm sleeping underneath you," Hawkins shouted, his face becoming red and his mouth remaining open.

Plunkett immediately broke out in laughter as did some of the other prisoners. He rose up in his bunk and dropped to the floor as he continued to laugh so hard that he got stomach cramps.

"What's so damn funny?" Willie asked.

"I haven't wet the bed for ten years," said Plunkett, continuing to laugh. He turned and walked downstairs to wash his dishes as Hawkins sat back down on his bunk to eat his rice, shaking his head.

A refreshing breeze circulated through the upstairs from several windows that had been opened. The air was scented with the odor of pine. We were informed that this barracks was built by the mining company and that our future welfare depended on how well we worked in the mines. We spent the day being examined by a Japanese doctor in a small hospital room located on the main floor next to Dr. Corey's quarters.

Dr. Corey requested that our supplies of clothing, which we brought from China, be issued to the men and the canned food be sent to the galley. The Japanese reply to his request was, "We'll release it when we receive a receipt from Tokyo." No one had a change of clothing. Later in the day our barracks leader, Sloane, announced that the next morning we would all report for work, except the old men and those confined to the hospital.

The night was long and cold. If we had still been in the Shanghai area this time of the year, we would be sweltering from the heat and fighting mosquitoes. Here we were trying to keep warm, busy picking the fleas off ourselves that had infested the rice mattresses. The ear-splitting sound of the gong announcing morning roll call on our first workday came at 4:30. We groaned that we were tired from lack of sleep. Breakfast followed at 5:00. Immediately after breakfast, the guards hurried everyone outside to go to work. A roll call was taken again before we left camp at 6:00.

That first workday the sky was overcast, and it looked like it would rain. The morning air was chilly as we clung to our shabby clothing. We marched to work quietly, in groups of two and three, down a narrow mountain trail into the mining and logging village. Passing through the village, we didn't see too many men working at the saw mill or smeltering plant. However, smoke poured out of the wood-burning sheds and the tall cement incinerators. Two heavy wire cables, which carried the ore in buckets, stretched up the mountain and across the valley to the processing plant. Leaving the small village, we turned and headed up the side of the mountain. The climb to the top was steep. Some six hundred and sixty steps had been built into the side of the mountain for the fifteen hundred foot ascent.

We finally reached the summit after leaving the camp two hours earlier. The Japanese didn't have to tell us to stop and rest because everyone dropped to the ground from complete exhaustion after becoming half sick. Despite the cold air, our pale faces were streaked with moisture from our sweat and our shirts were damp. As we lay on the ground, Nakayama and Kinoshita walked around discussing and pointing at the work to be done.

Our rest period of fifteen minutes ended abruptly when the Japanese guards began kicking and screaming at us. The strenuous hike up the mountain left me feeling numb and immobile. My legs felt like rubber. Nakayama and

Kinoshita headed toward us shouting.

"Get up! Get up!" Kinoshita yelled. "You must begin to work. So hurry over there to those cars, and Sergeant Major Nakayama will show you what must be done. Do you understand, huh?"

With his legs spread apart to keep from sliding on the steep slope where he was standing, he motioned with his arms for us to rise and walk to the cars mounted on narrow-gauge tracks.

We were chilled and shaking as we dragged ourselves toward the empty cars. Four men were assigned to a car, handed shovels, and told to remove the top soil down to the ore. Nakayama quickly demonstrated with a shovel how the dirt was to be thrown into the cars and pushed down the tracks and dumped over the bank. He remained to watch as we began to work. Immediately, he became angry and jerked a shovel away from one of us. Growling in Japanese, he began digging and shoveling the top soil swiftly into the wooden-framed car. He then thrust the shovel into the prisoner's stomach, sending him sprawling backwards, causing him to fall to the ground.

"Speedo! Speedo!" he shouted, glowering at the prisoner for a moment, his mouth twitching nervously. Suddenly, he whirled around and swaggered over toward another group. He wasted no time in shouting and striking the men.

The Japanese guards were few in number, which made it difficult for them to keep a close watch on all of us. Consequently, there were many half-full shovels of dirt thrown into the cars, and many of us were able to rest by leaning on our shovels while keeping an eye out for the Japanese. The morning air was filled with loud shouting by the Japanese, which echoed in the valley below. Their harassment resulted in making us work faster only momentarily. We were not physically capable of working at the continuous pace they required. As a result, there were many beatings.

When Kinoshita spotted a group of Chinese-Americans leaning on their shovels talking, he sprinted toward them, his small frail body stumbling forward and nearly falling. This caused some snickers among the men, which infuriated him. They had seen him coming and were working when he arrived.

"Why you rest when you should be working?" Kinoshita shouted.

It was silent for a moment as he stared into their faces.

"We were working," one of them said.

"What's your name?" he asked, looking directly at him.

"Albert."

"Albert what?" shouted Kinoshita angrily.

"Albert Lum," he said, leaning on his shovel.

"What kind of name is that?" he continued.

"Well, part Chinese and part American. I'm an American citizen but also Chinese."

Albert was born and raised in San Francisco's Chinatown.

"I think you people act more like the Americans than the Chinese because you are lazy and not industrious like the Chinese. If I catch you standing around talking again I will report you to Sergeant Major Nakayama and he will severely punish you. Do you understand, huh?" Kinoshita said and slowly walked away kicking at the grassy turf and glancing back occasionally, hoping to catch them resting.

Around mid-morning Kinoshita shouted for everyone to stop work and rest for fifteen minutes. All our shovels fell simultaneously, striking the cars, rails, and ground. Some men merely slumped to the ground where they stood, while others found a tree to sit down by and lean against. Most of us were too tired to talk, so we closed our eyes to rest. Large drops of rain began falling, waking us up as the Japanese guards screamed for us to begin working. The light rain continued until lunch time when it stopped for the sun to peek through the tops of the tall pine trees. Each man had brought his lunch with him, which consisted of a bowl of cooked rice. The lunch period lasted nearly an hour and was a welcome break.

Work continued through the afternoon until 4:00 with intermittent showers. After roll call Sergeant Major Nakayama gave a short speech, which was interpreted by Kinoshita.

"Give attention to me," he said and paused momentarily. "You are not sincere in your work. You must work faster. Do not make it necessary for me to punish you. So tomorrow you must work more honestly."

As Kinoshita interpreted his speech, Nakayama stood nervously twitching his mouth. He and Kinoshita quickly turned around to lead us back down the mountain while some of the Japanese guards trailed behind.

The afternoon rains made the walk down the mountain slippery, especially on the steep slopes where the steps had been built into the side of the mountain. Several men had picked up tree limbs and shortened them for walking sticks to help them going down the mountain. The small group of Orientals imprisoned with us always seemed to find the energy to chatter in their own language, which annoyed some of us. But not all of us were quiet on the march back; a few of us discussed Nakayama's speech.

"If he expects us to do this work faster, he's gotta be out of his mind. He acts like a maniac. I think he's going to be worse than Ishahara," Gates said.

His shallow face deepened with pain. His damp clothing clung tightly to his bony body.

Dawson had been walking alongside of him listening. Before captivity he had been robust and happy, weighing around two hundred and fifty pounds. Now, emaciated, sad, and not weighing much more than one hundred pounds, it had become difficult for him to speak.

"I think we had better get down on our knees tonight and pray that this war ends quickly, or we'll never leave this camp alive," Dawson said slowly, stopping to catch his breath before continuing. "This fellow Nakayama means to work us to death!"

"We can't possibly keep up this pace. The hike up and down this damn mountain alone every day would be enough work," Gates said, scratching himself.

Directly behind him was Plunkett, who was having a hard time standing up because his feet kept sliding out from under him on the slippery incline. He started to smile.

"A bath is good for that," he said.

Gates turned around to see if he was talking to him.

"Yeah, I mean you," Plunkett said.

"Well, a bath and clean clothes would help get rid of the fleas, but since we don't have a change of clothes or soap, I don't know how to get rid of them," Gates said, continuing to dig into his skin. "Don't you have any fleas?"

"No, not yet," Plunkett said. "But I guess I will sooner or later."

Then he slowly turned to Dawson and asked, "Have you got any fleas yet?"

At first Dawson didn't seem to hear as he kept walking cautiously down the mountain. Then Plunkett repeated his question a little louder.

"Yeah, they've started biting me, leaving red marks on my stomach. They keep me awake most of the night," Dawson said, gasping for breath.

The long string of prisoners began to bunch up as they reached the valley floor and the village road. Halfway through the village, Nakayama stopped our group and asked us to sing. Needless to say, no one sang except the Japanese guards, Nakayama, and Kinoshita. The wooden shanties that lined the rutted dirt road were crowded with pregnant women and small children watching the parade. Their faces showed no emotion and they were silent until we passed by them. Within one-half mile of the camp, the rain started again. Before we reached the camp's entrance, it became very heavy, and everyone arrived soaked to the skin. We spent another twenty minutes standing in the rain during roll call.

The weather the second day appeared to be a repeat of the previous day. So the kind Japanese provided rubber split-toe shoes to make it easier for us to climb the mountain. Those with large feet were out of luck. We were also issued a rain cap and coat. The hat was composed of two pieces of white canvas triangular in shape and sewed together. The rain coat was made of quilted rice straw and covered only our shoulders and back.

We gathered outside for roll call with our rain caps and coats on as it had already begun to sprinkle. The ground had become sloppy from the rain the day before, which made it difficult for us to stand erect. Nakayama had just given his soldiers orders to make a count of the prisoners when two fainted and fell to the ground almost simultaneously. We quickly moved back to give them air. Sloane ran into the barracks to get Dr. Corey as Nakayama and Kinoshita approached the two men lying unconscious in the mud.

Nakayama began shouting and kicking at them furiously. His mouth twitched nervously as he stood over them talking to Kinoshita.

"Get up! Get up!" shouted Kinoshita, his frail body trembling each time he screamed.

Oblivious to Nakayama and Kinoshita, Dr. Corey quickly made his way through the crowd to the two prostrate prisoners. He appeared completely involved with his two patients, as Nakayama immediately began to harass him. Finally, they began to regain consciousness and came to a sitting position as Dr. Corey continued to attend to them. Their thin faces were ashen as they were slowly lifted to their feet, their bony arms dangling limp at their sides. Dr. Corey started to move them toward the barracks to put them in the hospital when Nakayama violently intervened. He began shouting as he grabbed one of the ailing prisoners and spun him completely around. Kinoshita immediately began interpreting for Nakayama.

"Where are you taking these men?" he asked.

His faded khaki uniform fit him snugly, revealing his underdeveloped body. He stayed close to Nakayama, cowering as he spoke.

Normally quiet and soft-spoken, Dr. Corey turned promptly toward Nakayama and lashed out at him verbally.

"I'm taking these men to the hospital," he retorted, standing firmly wedged in the mud, the anger showing on his face.

"No, these men must go to work with the rest of the prisoners," Kinoshita said as he looked at Nakayama and then back at Dr. Corey.

As the confrontation continued, the sick prisoners were edged toward the barracks. Dr. Corey stood firmly as Nakayama began pushing him in the chest, yelling.

"These two men are very sick and must be hospitalized," Corey said. "They can't possibly work. It would be inhumane to work them in their present condition."

Before Dr. Corey could finish his explanation, Nakayama became furious and struck him in the chest with a clenched fist. Dr. Corey went sprawling to the ground with his arms outstretched. Quickly regaining his composure, he rose to his feet and headed toward the hospital with his two patients being carried behind him.

Nakayama stood fuming, his mouth twitching even more noticeably. He watched Corey and the two prisoners return to the barracks, but he didn't pursue the matter further. The rest of us stood frightened and speechless in our newly acquired rain apparel.

Nakayama's anger eased some, but he struck several prisoners who didn't respond fast enough to his commands. Then he bolted out the camp gate, Kinoshita running to catch up with him. The Japanese guards shouted repeatedly at the column of prisoners as they set their own pace with Nakayama several yards ahead. The low clouds clung to the mountains on either side of the valley, obscuring the peaks. The rains became heavier as we stopped in the middle of the village to add to our group several civilian Japanese men.

Gates wiped the rain from his deep-set eyes as he stood staring at the group of Japanese civilians forming at the rear of the column. His pessimistic attitude about getting out alive made him despondent and nervous.

"What are they coming along for?" he asked.

"Who knows?" Plunkett said. "Probably to stand beside us to make sure we work."

The rain was beginning to drip off Plunkett's cap and trickle down his forehead.

"They're going to be like watchdogs, you mean. Every time we stop to rest, they'll bark and Nakayama and his soldiers will come running," Gates said.

"Something like that."

Finally, after much conversation and head-nodding on the part of Nakayama and his men, we began to move again. The muddy condition of the narrow roadway made walking difficult, and we tired quickly trying to maintain an upright position. The climb up the mountain was very slow, and we fell to the ground frequently to catch our breath. The group of Japanese civilians quickly swarmed over us, shouting at us to get up. Their loud screaming brought the guards down upon us as we staggered to our feet and moved forward. The wet, slippery condition of the steep steps built into the mountain became dangerous. Some lost their footing, with nothing to grab hold of, and fell backwards down the mountain several feet, taking others with them.

Waiting for us at the top, Nakayama strutted nervously back and forth, and Kinoshita stood quietly, wiping the rain from his small baby face. Nakayama never smiled. His face appeared swollen and angry all the time, and his mouth twitched more noticeably when he became violent. He was large by Japanese standards and powerfully built. Kinoshita was the opposite of Nakayama. He was frail and intelligent and was friendly on occasion.

The rains let up for the moment when we reached the top of the mountain and began our fifteen-minute rest period. The rice-straw quilted rain coats had become saturated with water and were heavy, so everyone removed them to sit on. As the bright morning sunlight broke through the heavy dark clouds, it revealed the lush green pine trees full of moisture which sparkled in the sun's rays, making them very beautiful. We had sprawled out beneath the trees — lifeless and quiet. Our bodies were drained of strength and stripped of flesh to the bone. We were a picture of despair and ugliness!

"Get up! Get up!" shouted Kinoshita as the Japanese guards quickly surrounded us to hurry us back to work. Constant fatigue and lack of strength made it impossible for us to respond quickly to their demands. Consequently, many of us were struck across the back with rifle butts.

Throughout the morning the Japanese civilian straw bosses came down screaming at anyone who stopped for a moment to rest. They were dressed in clothing that was worn and patched in several places, and they made it very difficult to stop working because when we did, they'd signal for the guards. They appeared to enjoy catching someone resting.

Lunch passed quickly and the afternoon was unbearable until three o'clock when the rains became heavy and work stopped. Our tools were gathered together and put in the shed before we started down the mountain. The heavy rains made the descent very difficult, and many ended up sliding down most of the way on their rear ends. With clothing torn and filthy, bodies aching from falls and sudden jerks, we finally arrived at the village below to find the road a flowing river of mud. The water ran over the tops of our shoes seeping down inside, making it more difficult to walk as our feet slipped out of our shoes stuck in the heavy muck. Each step brought more pain to our leg joints as we jerked them up and out.

Approaching the camp, we saw a small group of old men and hospital patients coming down a mountain trail behind our camp. They were a herb detail, which was sent out each day to gather a green plant which resembled celery to supplement our daily diet of rice. They reached the camp gate just ahead of us with their bundles of greens tied to their backs.

Inside the camp, puddles of water covered the grounds. The rain continued to pour, running off the two-story barracks in sheets into open trenches, which carried the water down through the camp gate. After being released by the Japanese, everyone headed for the bathhouse on the other side of the barracks. Inside the bathhouse, there was a large, square wooden tank located in the center of the room. The tank was filled with warm water, which was heated electrically, and was about four feet deep. The Japanese strictly forbade anyone to enter the tank, insisting that the prisoners use the wooden ladles to dip the water out and pour it over their bodies.

Steam rose from the heated tank of water as the prisoners entered the building and began removing their muddy clothing. The room immediately appeared filled with human skeletons as opposed to fleshy bodies. Suffering from sheer exhaustion and malnutrition, many squatted on the floor while ladles of water were poured over them. Squatting eliminated having to raise the heavy water-filled ladle over one's head while standing. The warm water covered the body completely, striking the wooden floor and splashing onto the muddy clothing. After several ladles of water, our tired bodies became relaxed and were rejuvenated momentarily. The bathhouse had been very quiet until someone spotted a tattoo on Charlie Burns' chest.

"Hey, Charlie, what happened to your girlfriend? She's not as round and full as she use to be," said Emmett McCloud as he walked closer to get a better look.

His remarks brought a roar of laughter from our somber group.

"Well, I'll tell you Emmett, Marie has had to go on the same diet as I have, so she is skinny all over like me. It's too bad because she really had a nice figure." He kept looking down at her on his chest as he spoke, gently gathering up the loose skin to make her look better.

"Is she waiting for you back home?" McCloud asked.

"I hope so. I received a letter from her about five months ago when we were in China, and she was still waiting then. Wants to get married the moment I get back."

As he finished talking, he poured another ladle of warm water over his small thin body, holding his mouth open and swishing the water around in his mouth before spitting it out.

"You're lucky. A lot of fellows have received 'dear John' letters from their girlfriends. Some even from their wives," McCloud said.

"Yeah. Now if I can just get back home in one piece," sighed Burns, smoothing his long hair back in place with both hands.

Some of the prisoners had begun washing the mud off their clothes and wringing them out. After drying off with their shirts, they put the wet clothing back on and returned to the barracks. The bathhouse was luxurious in comparison to those in other camps, and the warm water was stimulating. If only the Japanese would have given us our other clothing and soap. Arriving back at our bunks, we removed our clothes and hung them on the walls and ends of the beds before climbing in.

The rains continued throughout the night and the next day, preventing outside work and allowing our clothes to dry a little as we remained in bed part of the day. The rest of the week we spent tramping through the mud to the mountain.

Chapter 24

On Sunday, 15 July 1945, the weather was foggy and damp. We were notified that the entire camp would be weighed again after working at the mine for five days. The Japanese also informed us that we could wash our clothes, knowing that we didn't have a change of clothing or soap. Some of the prisoners had begun milling around outside, hoping the sun would break through the fog, while others remained in bed, resting and keeping warm. The small herb detail was about to leave the camp in search of greens for our daily diet.

Shortly before noon, the sun had begun to burn off the thick fog that blanketed the entire valley. Dr. Corey was taking his daily morning walk around the compound when he stopped and began staring toward the sky. The faint drone of airplane engines could be heard. Everyone had stopped with heads tilted upwards, searching the fog-patched sky for planes. Suddenly, coming out of a fog bank into a clearing were seven aircraft flying directly overhead in the direction of the coast.

A smile lit up the doctor's face as he turned around and said, "They're some of ours. U.S. Navy fighter planes off a carrier nearby."

He continued his walk with more quickness as his face reflected his pride in being a part of the navy.

The Japanese guards became frightened and excited as they drove the prisoners back inside the barracks while scanning the sky. Minutes later we heard loud thunderous explosions. The camp morale was boosted; everyone felt the war was drawing to a conclusion. We heard the planes and explosions all day.

Forrest Hill sat quietly on the edge of his bunk staring out the window at the pine trees beyond. He had gathered his legs together and set his empty rice bowl on them. He religiously blessed the small amount of food he received before he ate it. He was one of the older men and prison life had taken its toll on him physically. His hair had streaks of gray and his face had wrinkled somewhat, but his alliance with God had become stronger and deeper.

"A penny for your thoughts," said Hawkins.

Hill kept staring out the window and did not hear him. Hawkins placed his hand on his shoulder and shook him gently before repeating what he had said.

"Oh, I'm sorry, I didn't hear you," Hill said as he jerked his head around toward Hawkins. "I was thinking about my family about ten thousand miles away."

He sighed and rubbed his tired eyes.

"Do you have a big family?" Hawkins asked.

"I have a wife and two girls. I had a boy but he died of cancer when he was fifteen. That's why I went to the island, so I could earn enough money to pay the doctor and hospital bills. The war kind of interrupted things. I hope and pray that they are getting along all right," he said, nodding his head and looking down sadly at the wooden floor.

"I'm sure they are getting along just fine," Hawkins tried to reassure him.

There was no immediate response as Hawkins sat studying the small man from Silver Creek. His gray bushy eyebrows and tan weather-beaten face accentuated his pale blue eyes. He continued to stare down at the floor, dragging one shoe back and forth. Finally, his foot stopped moving, and he looked up at Hawkins.

"I'm sure they are," he said, and paused momentarily. "We've always placed our trust in the Lord and things seemed to work out for the best. Willie, you know I've been a Christian for a long time as well as all my family, and He has given us strength and peace of mind."

As he spoke, he looked directly at Willie.

"Are you a Christian, Willie?" he asked.

"Well," Hawkins hesitated. "I believe there is a God who controls our destiny. But I guess I haven't lived a life that would be pleasing to Him," he said and nervously bit his lower lip, appearing reluctant to continue.

"It's never too late to repent of your sins. Willie, you only have to ask His forgiveness and He will accept you as you are. You will become born again, and your life will become peaceful and meaningful," Hill said, and a gentle smile lit up his face, and his eyes seemd to sparkle.

Unexpectedly, a loud voice came from the foot of the stairway, ordering everyone down to the hospital room to weigh in on the double. We began grumbling as we filed downstairs. We had to strip down to our shorts, and Dr. Corey stood next to the scale checking each of us carefully as we were being weighed. His face was grim. He was assessing each man's condition but unable to prescribe a remedy. He was silent. We were all skin and bones; our bodies had become like trees that hadn't been watered for some time — dying!

Sanborn stepped up on the scale and the doctor took a second look. Before captivity, Sanborn had weighed well over two hundred pounds. He was young and had been very strong. His round, boyish facial features had become drawn, and he had lost considerable weight. However, he wasn't as skinny as the rest of the prisoners.

"How come you're fatter than the others?" asked Dr. Corey, with a serious look on his face.

"I'm the cook," Sanborn replied with a smile, stepping off the scale.

The doctor smiled feebly as he turned to the next prisoner.

The results of the weighing showed that the men working at the mine for five days had lost on the average seven pounds. With the report from Dr. Corey came the news that the Japanese assured him that some of our supplies, especially clothing and soap, which the Japanese had been confiscating, would be returned to us within six or seven days.

The proximity of the camp to the coast and its altitude created an unpredictable climate that alternated between being either foggy and damp, rainy and muddy, or sunny and warm.

The Japanese were very consistent in conjuring up little surprises to keep us busy. For example, on early Monday morning beginning the second week in camp, everyone was ordered to bring a towel to roll call outside.

We began assembling in front of the barracks with our towels draped over our shoulders. The sun hadn't been up too long. We moved around rubbing our hands together, trying to stay warm. Schultz gritted his teeth and cursed the Japanese race as he usually did, when Nakayama and Kinoshita approached us.

"What in the hell do you suppose those yellow bastards want us to do with these towels?" Schultz asked.

Then he removed his wire-framed glasses, cleaned them with his towel, and carefully replaced them, adjusting the wire behind his large puffy ears and pinching them on his thick nose.

"Who knows?" Hawkins whispered, shaking his head.

The odor of firewood burning in the village below filled the air as columns of smoke rose above the scattered shanties. We stood quietly waiting for more new instructions. Nakayama towered over Kinoshita as he spoke to him.

"Give attention to me!" Kinoshita shouted, and he cleared his throat. "Starting this morning and every morning from now on you must bring towel with you for morning exercise. This is an order from Japanese authorities. Do you understand, huh?"

Kinoshita turned to Nakayama for further instructions. He was puffing on a ciagarette, creating a cloud of smoke which drifted over us. The smell of tobacco caused a furor among some of us.

"You will begin the exercise now. You must remove your shirts and place towel around your waist. You must hurry now," he shouted, his high-pitched voice cracking as he yelled.

"Now you must. . ."

Before he could continue Nakayama tossed his cigarette to the ground and broke through the crowd and headed for Burns who hadn't made an effort to remove his shirt. He struck him across the side of his face with his fist, which sent him reeling backwards, falling to the ground. Nakayama was furious as he stood over him shouting loudly in his native tongue. Burns remained on the ground, his face swollen badly. Suddenly, Nakayama stopped yelling as he stared down at him, his mouth twitching nervously and fists clenched tightly. After a swift kick to his stomach, he walked away, back to Kinoshita, who appeared frightened. Burns had to be helped to his feet in a dazed condition.

Anger and fear gripped us; all our eyes were fixed upon Nakayama. His sadistic behavior and hatred of Americans was like Ishahara's. Both never smiled and were always looking for excuses to punish us or create additional hardships.

"Does everyone have their towel around their waist?" asked Kinoshita.

There were a few nods. Kinoshita quickly ran around the group to see if everyone had their towel in position.

"Now when I say, '*Chishon,*' you must rub your body with towel," he shouted.

Again Nakayama gave him further instructions.

"*Chishon!*" Kinoshita screamed loudly, jumping up and down, his voice echoing throughout the valley below.

He and Nakayama slowly strolled in opposite directions around the prisoners, hoping to catch someone not obeying their orders. They stopped frequently to show how the upper part of the body should be rubbed down. "Rub the body harder," they would say. Kinoshita shouted, "*Chishon,*" repeatedly for ten minutes, after which the exercise stopped. While everyone put on their shirts, Kinoshita explained the reason for the exercise.

"This exercise is being done for your good health," Kinoshita yelled. "Japanese soldiers have been doing this exercise for centuries, and that is the reason they are so strong and healthy."

Kinoshita's thin frail body quivered as he strained to utter each word. His dark eyes widened and his facial skin was tightly drawn. One arm moved freely as he spoke.

The second week of work at the mine continued to peel the flesh off of us and weaken us. We didn't have too much more weight to lose. Each day the mountain got harder to climb. There was very little conversation among us. The silence was broken and our hopes raised whenever our planes passed over, which was becoming more frequent.

We were a weary bunch of prisoners, inching our way down the mountain onto the village road, when four of our naval fighter planes headed directly at us skimming the tree tops. The long column of men scattered quickly into the trees and brush as the Japanese ran screaming in all directions. The planes made one pass through the mountain village, tipping their wings gently before soaring up the side of the mountain and out of view. The roar of their engines reverberated loudly throughout the village and they were a wonderful sight.

The planes vanished as quickly as they had appeared. Fear possessed the Japanese, who hurriedly rounded us up and marched us through the village. For a moment, the Japanese seemed more frightened of us than we of them. It was no longer quiet as we began talking and shouting with excitement.

"What a beautiful sight they were," Gates said, nodding his head slowly, and smiling at long last.

"Do you still think we'll never get out of this mess?" Sanborn asked, his eyes continuing to follow the planes into the distance.

"Well, I guess our chances are looking better now. However, the war isn't over yet and these yellow bastards could still shoot us," Gates said, his face no longer showing the excitement.

Nakayama was soon several strides in front of us. Kinoshita had to run frequently to keep up with him. He seemed anxious to get back to camp in a hurry. This bully had suddenly begun to act like a frightened coward. He kept scanning the sky for more planes while shouting at us to walk faster. Only a thin trail of smoke left behind by the planes was visible now as the terrified Japanese guards ran up and down the column of prisoners yelling and prodding us to move swiftly.

"Speedo, speedo!" they screamed.

Within a matter of minutes the deadly sound of bombs exploding on the coast was heard, which compounded the fear already instilled in the Japanese. They became delirious as they began striking the prisoners at will.

This week the air attacks on the coast had increased. As we reached the entrance to the village, many Japanese women and children were seen streaming into the area from the coast carrying all their possessions on their backs.

Upon arrival in camp, Nakayama and Kinoshita moved nervously around our group, while the frightened guards sprinted back and forth in front of us, taking a fast count. We were immediately released to our barracks as the Japanese ran to their nearby quarters, continuing to look up searching the sky. The barracks became alive with conversation about the day's air raid, and the general feeling was that the war must be nearing an end.

The next day was Sunday, a day of rest. Shortly before noon the Japanese notified Dr. Corey that they would release some of our supplies that we had brought from China. They asked him if he would send a detail of men to their warehouse to pick them up. Dr. Corey accompanied a small group of us to the warehouse, where we met Nakayama and interpreter Kinoshita waiting inside. Their angry faces showed their contempt and bitter hatred for the Americans. Dr. Corey stopped directly in front of them and acknowledged them with a salute. They hesitated before returning it.

There was a brief exchange of Japanese between them before Kinoshita began speaking to Dr. Corey.

"Sergeant Major Nakayama says your people may have your luggage now," he said. "It has been inspected by the Japanese authorities for weapons and other articles that prisoners of war should not have."

Nakayama stood rigidly next to him, staring past the doctor at us. His faded khaki uniform was quite wrinkled, and it looked as though he might have slept in it. His mouth twitched continuously.

"Tell Sergeant Nakayama we appreciate his returning our luggage to us," Dr. Corey said softly. "The men desperately need a change of clothing and hand soap for bathing."

After another exchange of Japanese, Nakayama nodded his head and grunted twice.

"He says you may take your luggage now," Kinoshita said.

They turned to walk away when the doctor spoke again.

"Mr. Kinoshita, what about the canned food that we brought? Could we take it to our galley now?" Dr. Corey asked, moving closer to them.

"Never mind about that," Kinoshita said. "Japanese authorities will say when you will receive food supplies. You must remember these things belong to the Imperial Japanese. Do you understand, huh?"

His voice had gradually grown louder as he spoke, and his frail body had begun to tremble.

Our individual luggage consisted of the cardboard boxes we had packed in China containing our meager possessions. They had been neatly stacked against a wall. The Japanese had torn them open and had scattered them about the room, leaving our clothes piled on the floor or spilling out of their containers. We gathered up the clothing and placed it in different boxes, knowing there would be much bitching among us when we received our luggage with the wrong contents. All afternoon we exchanged clothing, and there were some arguments, which became heated at times. However, our weakened condition caused the disagreements to be short.

A steady stream of us headed for the bathhouse where we had our first bath with soap and change of clean clothes in over two weeks. The warm water was stimulating and refreshing. To be able to put on clean, dry clothing was very pleasant.

The Japanese surprised us by coming earlier than usual for the evening inspection and caught Wiley Emerson sleeping on his bunk. A guard jabbed him with his rifle and shouted at him, "*Coorah, coorah!*"

Emerson jumped off his flea-infested bed, scratching himself, and staggered to his feet. Nakayama was watching and waiting for him, standing erect, mouth twitching nervously, and feet spread apart. There was a moment of silence. Suddenly, without warning, Nakayama threw a punch that landed squarely on Emerson's jaw sending him reeling backwards. Another moment of silence passed after a brief conversation with the guard. Nakayama continued with the inspection, and the guard took Emerson outside the barracks.

Outside, Emerson stood with the Japanese guard under a light, their shadows reaching out toward the parade yard with one much longer than the other. An hour passed before Nakayama and Kinoshita appeared. There was more conversation in Japanese, as we watched.

"Sergeant Major Nakayama says you must be punished for not being ready for inspection. Do you understand, huh?" Kinoshita shouted, shading the bright light from his eyes with his hand as he spoke.

"Yes, sir," said a frightened Emerson.

He was tall and skinny and not too bright. While in China, he was repeatedly told to drink only water that had been boiled and treated with iodine. However, during the hot summer months he would drink the cold water directly from the outside faucets and immediately contract diarrhea.

"So now you must run around the parade yard for twenty minutes. You may begin now," Kinoshita said as he motioned with his arm for him to start.

For the next ten minutes Nakayama and Kinoshita stood watching him. Each time he passed by them, they would shout for him to run faster. His speed accelerated with each scream but then returned to a jog. The guard continued to watch him run after Kinoshita and Nakayama returned to their quarters. Before the twenty minutes had expired, Emerson collapsed in front of our barracks from sheer exhaustion and was carried inside and laid on his bunk by three prisoners. His condition was checked by Dr. Corey, who shook his head in disgust as he walked back down to his quarters.

Beginning with the third week of work at the mine, the Japanese made us carry lumber and firewood from the village to our camp on the way back from the mountain. Upon reaching camp and dropping the wood in a pile, our arms hung limp and numb at our sides. We had very little strength left. Immediately upon entering the barracks, everyone plopped on their bunks and didn't move until chow time.

The work at the mine continued at the same pace, despite the increase of the air attacks on the coast. The food remained very poor with no sign of meat until 23 July 1945, when our galley received from the Japanese the intestines of a cow and its liver and heart. They stunk! They also gave us six cans of our own butter, which they had confiscated. We stole from them a small case of our Red Cross food consisting of corned beef, salmon, and jam to be used at the first opportunity!

Our cooks mixed the extra food with the rice, making a tasty dish that lasted a couple of days. It was immediately after one of these evening meals that the Japanese ordered us to take all our personal belongings out on the parade field. As we assembled on the dimly lit field with our few possessions on the ground before us, Nakayama stood in front of us talking to Kinoshita, twirling his flashlight wildly.

"Sergeant Major Nakayama says you prisoners are permitted to have one article each of clothing," Kinoshita shouted at us. "For instance, one pair of pants, one pair of shoes, an overcoat, a hat, and so on. Everything else will be returned to the Japanese warehouse. Do you understand, huh?"

Dr. Corey stood silently, until Kinoshita finished his speech. The lights from the barracks lit up one side of his face.

"Mr. Kinoshita, my men need a change of clothing. Without that, they will become sick," Dr. Corey said.

Before he could continue Kinoshita sharply interrupted him, shouting, "Never mind about that!"

Dr. Corey continued to question Kinoshita why they were taking back some of our supplies after just returning them to us two days ago. But Kinoshita's only response was, "Never mind about that!" and he turned and walked away with Nakayama.

Most of us, however, were one step ahead of the Japanese. We had anticipated something like this or a sudden move to another camp and put on more clothing. The inspecting party had reached Hawkins and was beginning to go through his luggage. Hawkins tried to stand in the darkness, hiding a second carton of his personal belongings, when Nakayama suddenly turned his light on him. His light moved up and down Hawkins as he spoke to Kinoshita.

"Sergeant Major Nakayama wants you to step over here so he can get a closer look at you," Kinoshita said as he directed him to move forward with his hand.

Hawkins movement was slow as the quantity of clothing he wore made it difficult to walk. He appeared fat except for his thin face. Nakayama reached out and poked his body in several places before turning and speaking to Kinoshita.

"He wants you to remove your coat and coveralls," Kinoshita said.

They watched him closely as he removed his coveralls. Nakayama kept the light focused on his every movement. After some squirming and wiggling, Hawkins finally was able to take off the coveralls which exposed a pair of pants tied to the back of them. The presence of the pants attached to the coveralls brought a few snickers from the Japanese as they took both of them. Nakayama admired Hawkins' overcoat and slipped it on, walking away like a small child with a new toy.

Schultz, who had lost most of his clothing, had been standing next to Hawkins when they left.

"Well, you almost got to keep your coat and coveralls," Schultz said.

"Yeah, if Nakayama hadn't dropped his flashlight earlier he wouldn't have noticed me. His light struck the ground and shone directly on me," Hawkins said as he bent down to pick up his things and put them back into the carton.

"Well, until tonight you were the only one in camp who owned a pair of coveralls," Schultz chuckled.

"I know. Now that mean bastard has them as well as my overcoat. It was nice and warm. I still fared pretty well I think," Hawkins said, scratching his head.

"How's that?" asked Schultz.

"Well, I have some long underwear and pajamas on besides an extra pair of pants," Hawkins explained. "Also they didn't see this other carton of stuff I stood in front of."

As Hawkins spoke, he looked around to see where the inspecting party was. It was well after 1:00 in the morning before we got to bed. The thought of getting up at 4:30 to go to work was very depressing.

Upon arriving at the mountain on 29 July 1945, we were informed that this would be our last day of work at the mine. So under a dark cloudy sky that could have opened up and rained any minute, we proceeded to remove the rails and ties and stack them in piles. The cars were taken off the tracks and pushed to one side of the shed that contained all the tools. The rains came shortly after lunch, which halted the work, and we were ordered back down the mountain. The usual stop was made in the village to pick up more lumber and carry it to camp. The sight of Japanese women carrying green grass on their heads and backs had become more common. Their stone-like faces were tightly drawn and silent.

The rains continued as we reached camp and began putting the lumber into piles. Despite the rain, the Japanese made us carry firewood until 5:00. Entering the barracks, we were surprised by a strong fish odor, which permeated the entire building.

"Whew! That sure doesn't smell like any fish I ever caught back home," shouted Plunkett, grabbing his nose.

"Smells rotten to me," Dawson said and covered his nose and mouth with his handkerchief.

The barracks door shut behind the last prisoner as we stopped long enough to slip our shoes off and slowly stagger up the flight of stairs to the second floor. All shoes were left in the hallway, as we were not permitted to wear them inside the barracks. Yet the Japanese wore their muddy shoes inside anytime!

"Say, Emery, what have those yellow bastards in store for us in the way of work since we won't be working in the mine any longer?" Gates asked.

Gates had sprawled out on his bunk with his long slender arms extended outward from his body. His sadness was apparent in his dark, sunken eyes.

"I don't know," Sloane said. "Your guess is as good as mine. All I know is that we will be getting up at 4:30 as usual and going to the mountain."

Sloane ran his comb through his thin gray hair and tried to slick it down. He then turned and continued to walk down the hallway, staring out the window.

The creaking sound of heavy feet coming up the stairs with the evening chow caused a stir among us as we rose from our bunks to get ready to eat. Three men reached the second floor with the buckets of rice, fish, and hot water to drink, which on rare occasions was tea. Immediately, they began serving the food as we sat on the edge of our bunks. When they stopped in front of Schultz, he received his small ration of musty rice, and he leaned over and looked into the bucket of cooked fish and quickly jerked his head back scowling and waving Murphy away as he set his empty bowl on his bunk.

"Is that stinkin' crap supposed to be fish?" Schultz said.

"Yeah."

"It looks like shit," Schultz said. "Smells like it too. How come they cooked it so much? It looks like mush."

Schultz frowned and shook his head as he continued staring at it.

"The cooks said when they received the fish, it had some maggots in it. So they cleaned it the best they could and cooked the hell out of it to make it safe to eat," Murphy explained, stirring it and scooping some up for Schultz to take a closer look.

It had already begun to turn brown and stunk!

"You sure you don't want some, Herman?"

"No."

"You had better eat some, or you'll never make it up the mountain," Murphy said dropping the ladle back down into the bucket.

"I don't go to the mountain. I'm on the herb detail," Schultz said, turning to his rice and cup of hot water.

The evening meal was soon over, and most of us ended up eating the fish. Needless to say, its odor remained in the barracks throughout the next day. Shortly before midnight, the drone of our airplanes passing over on their way to the coast was a comforting sound. It caused much confusion among the Japanese guards, however, who locked our door to the bathroom downstairs until 4:00 in the morning.

Chapter 25

The early morning trek to the mountain on 30 July 1945 turned out to be the beginning of a new work project. Constantly hungry and bone tired after the climb up the mountain, we were completely exhausted and flopped to the ground for a ten-minute rest, before receiving our new work orders.

For a short time, the only audible sounds were those of our deep breathing and the crunching of brush under the foot of the Japanese soldiers stirring around. The leaves on the trees remained unruffled. The morning air was invigorating.

Nakayama and Kinoshita stood before the wooden shed, whose tin roof buckled in the middle and curled up at the edges. A small shiny lock, which hung at an angle on the door, was removed and the door pulled open. The Japanese guards entered and brought out several large tree saws and set them on the ground before Nakayama. We rose to a sitting position, terrified at the sight of the saws and what their presence meant in terms of work.

Kinoshita began waving and shouting at us, "Get up! Get up! You must begin to work now."

The Japanese guards moved among us yelling and prodding us to move quickly. But we had been too weak to move quickly for a long time.

Drained of any strength, we were barely able to stand to wait for our new instructions. The saws were long, straight two-man saws and curved one-man saws. They looked heavy.

"You will be divided in two groups for now," Kinoshita explained. "You must cut down trees and cut them up for firewood with those saws over there."

Kinoshita turned to point to the saws. His split-toe rubber shoes and pointed cap, which was laced in the back, made him look like a frog when he sprinted around.

We split up into two groups and walked a short distance, where, after a brief demonstration by Nakayama and the guards on how to use the saws, we began working reluctantly. Besides the regular guards, Japanese civilians who served as watchdogs surrounded us to see that we didn't stop working.

McCloud and Burns had teamed up on one of the two-man saws. They squatted down on the ground next to a tree that measured about two feet in diameter. As they pulled the saw into the base of the tree, McCloud glanced up at a Japanese civilian perched on a rock a short distance away.

"Let's see if we can't fell this tree toward that little yellow bastard sitting on that rock over there," he said, smiling at Burns.

After three or four pulls of the heavy saw, they dropped their arms to the ground. This instantly brought screams from the Jap perched on the rock. They told the Jap, "Shove it up your ass you little bastard!" and slowly began working again.

Finally, they had the tree nearly cut through when they both looked at the Jap, who kept staring at them.

"Move the saw back a bit so it doesn't cut any more," McCloud said. "And just keep pulling the saw until he turns and looks the other way. When he does I'll say now and we'll finish cutting down the tree quickly."

Several minutes passed before the Jap reached into his pocket for a package of cigarettes. As he fumbled around, McCloud blurted out, "Now!"

The tall pine tree began falling in the direction of the Jap as McCloud and Burns ran back away from it. The Jap had begun to light his cigarette when he noticed the tree coming toward him. He immediately threw his arms up over his head as he fell backwards. The tree landed squarely across the rock and the branches covered it completely.

The two prisoners stood in amazement at their accuracy.

"I wonder if that little bastard got out of the way in time," McCloud said.

They began walking toward the rock where the Jap had been sitting. There was a movement of a branch that caused them to stop and frown at each other. After he spread the branches apart, the Jap's head popped out. He was hopping mad as he kept grumbling to himself. He had lost his cap, which revealed his short-clipped hair and high forehead. His small ears extended sharply away from his round head.

His jack-in-the-box appearance brought a roar of laughter from McCloud and Burns. They stumbled backwards and fell to the ground laughing. Other prisoners working nearby stopped working long enough to laugh. Fortunately, there were no repercussions, and the civilian Jap dusted himself off as he screamed, "*Coorah!*"

The loud screeching of the civilian Japs every time a prisoner tried to rest was spontaneous. It became a game between the "watchdogs" and the prisoners to see how long a prisoner could rest before the civilians ran to the Japanese guards or Nakayama for help. The continuous pressure put on the prisoners by the Japanese to work was inhumane. The only hope for survival at this point, in the minds of most of us, was that the war might simply end that day or the next. If the Japanese thought the war might end soon, that didn't seem reason for them to ease the work load!

The first day felling and cutting of timber into firewood was long and laborious. The thought of returning the next day and the next brought looks of despair upon our faces as we slowly descended the mountain. Too tired to talk, we fell to the ground several times along the way before reaching the village road below. The screaming Japanese were quick to prod us to get up and move on.

Besides carrying lumber from the village we hauled two large iron cooking pots suspended on poles. They were placed outside the barracks to be used as fire wells. At 7:00, the Japanese ordered everyone to assemble for fire drill instructions, which required all prisoners to gather on the main floor until ordered outside by the Japanese. The drill was carried out twice before the evening inspection.

Schultz lay flat on his back on his bunk with arms folded across his chest as he awaited the evening inspection. He removed his wire-framed eyeglasses and rubbed his tired eyes, before looking at Gates in the upper bunk.

"I hear the Japs had you chopping down trees at the mountain. That must've been hard work, wasn't it?" Schultz asked, replacing his glasses.

"You better believe it. Those yellow bastards are going to kill us off, Herman. We can't do that kind of work on the diet we are receiving," Gates said, his voice getting weaker the longer he talked.

Some of us were beginning to stir, getting ready for the evening roll call. Schultz had risen to a sitting position on his bunk.

"They increased our herb detail today to thirty men. The Japs have informed the cooks that they must dry more greens for our winter food," Schultz continued as he stood up.

"They must think we will be spending the winter here, huh," Gates said as he began crawling off his bunk.

"I guess so. The cooks said they were told by the Japanese that we could get nine to fifteen feet of snow here," Schultz said.

"This war had better end before winter, or there won't be many of us going home standing up," Gates said, taking a deep breath and letting it out slowly as he turned to straighten up his bunk.

The evening roll call was soon over, and we crawled back into our bunks for the night. However, between fighting off fleas and having to go to the bathroom several times because of our poor physical condition, a night's rest was impossible. The situation was further aggravated by the Japanese guards, who kept turning on the lights in the middle of the night and taking a head count of the prisoners in their bunks. Dr. Corey protested this procedure to the camp officials but was reminded that it was being done for our protection.

The next ten days saw very little change in our daily lives. It invariably rained two or three times each week, but that had very little effect on our prison routine. Sickness was mounting. The Japanese had begun searching us before going to work and upon arriving back in camp. Also new Japanese orders demanded that we wear something around our stomachs at night to keep them warm. The guards kept waking us up all hours of the night to see that we were obeying the new regulations.

The air raid alarm sounded the morning of 10 August 1945 before work call. We were detained inside for half an hour. We saw the first planes upon arriving at the mountain around 7:00. Bombers and fighter planes were in the air constantly until 5:00 in the afternoon. We counted over one hundred planes. They seemed to fly in groups of twenty-five or thirty. Explosions and smoke were common throughout the day. From the top of the mountain we could see the planes dive on their target. They were striking an area approximately fifteen miles from us.

The Japanese were very frightened and stopped work several times to run us into the bushes. Our return through the village was interrupted by a flight of bombers escorted by fighter planes, which flew directly over us. We scrambled for the side of the mountain where we watched the planes circle around and drop two bundles by parachutes. The two parachutes floated down just over the hill on the other side of the road from us. Everyone surmised that they were dropping propaganda literature for the people in the village. The Japanese civilians ran for shelter, screaming as the planes circled around.

Work at the mountain continued uninterrupted, and each day we had to struggle to make it back to camp. On 12 August 1945 while returning through the village, we saw a large sign that had been posted. One of our Chinese boys translated it: "(1) Volunteers wanted to reconstruct the bombed areas. (2) Due to the recent bombings there will be a shortage of food and we must commence rationing same."

Near the tramway long lines of men, women, and children gathered with baskets and ration books in hand. They were dressed in filthy rags. Babies fed freely on their mothers' breasts.

Upon arriving in camp we were informed that Lieutenant Yoritomo and Sergeant Major Nakayama had left around 2:00 in the afternoon rather urgently. Also those working around the camp were stopped when it was reported that two prisoners had escaped.

There wasn't the usual silence throughout the barracks as the men discussed the escape and sudden departure of the Japanese personnel. The slightest interruption of the monotonous camp routine in the prisoners' favor elevated everyone's morale. And the sight of worried and unhappy faces on the Japanese was always encouraging.

Sitting on his bunk with his legs crossed, Plunkett puffed on a cigarette. The smoke drifted up to the ceiling and flattened out in the shape of an anvil.

Across the way Murphy had noticed that Plunkett was smoking on his bunk. He smiled slyly as he rose up from his bed and shouted, "Here comes a guard!"

Plunkett jumped down from his top bunk and fell to the floor. He picked his cigarette off the floor and looked around the room for the Japanese guard. Murphy burst out laughing as Plunkett became furious.

"Why, you son-of-a-bitch! I could have broken a leg," Plunkett yelled, brushing his hair from his eyes.

He stayed on the floor as he paced up and down the hallway puffing on his cigarette, muttering to himself.

Several prisoners had congregated at the far end of the barracks where Sloane was standing. As usual Schultz dominated the conversation.

"Say, Emery, why did those two yellow bastards Yoritomo and Nakayama leave camp in such a hurry today?" Schultz asked.

"How in the hell would I know, Herman; they don't tell me what they do," Sloane said.

"Do you know who the two prisoners were that escaped?"

"Yes, Wiley Emerson and Sidney Robinson. Both were on the herb detail," Sloane said.

"Oh, yeah, I know those two bastards. Where in the hell do they think they can escape to on the Japan mainland? Maybe they're going to swim across the China Sea to China," Schultz said, peering over the top of his wire-framed glasses.

"It was a really stupid thing to do," Sloane said, shaking his head in disgust. "The war could end any day. Hell, an angry group of civilians could kill them and nobody would know the difference. You remember how they tried to get to us when we traveled through those railway terminals. Our Jap guards had a hell of a time holding them back."

Sloane then shoved his hands deep into his pockets and walked to his room.

The fear of reprisals worried us. However, the Japanese remained unruffled and tight-mouthed through the evening inspection. The calm ended at midnight when several guards stormed the barracks and rousted all the prisoners that worked on the herb detail. They were taken to the Japanese office, where they were interrogated for two hours before being released. Eventually, the escaped prisoners were captured after two days in the cold and the rain and were placed in the guardhouse.

Dark clouds obscured the peaks of the surrounding mountains, producing heavy rains on 13 August 1945. Kinoshita, hidden under an over-sized plastic raincoat, followed the morning inspecting party around. He walked in a stooped position with his hands drawn back inside his sleeves. Following the inspection, he informed us that this day would be a holiday, and we were to remain inside the barracks. During his brief speech, I became very faint. I was perspiring and nauseous. I stepped out of line and headed for the bathroom, but I was unable to vomit. Sleeping most of the day helped bring me some relief.

The work load appeared to ease as the Japanese had declared the next three days holidays, on behalf of some ceremony, for which a shrine was erected on the mountain near our camp, they said. The rains continued and the days were dark and dreary. It was a relief being inside even though it was cold in the unheated barracks. We either walked around or stayed in bed to keep warm.

On 14 August 1945, Dr. Corey brought the news that the Commandant of our Sendai Camp, Lieutenant Yoritomo, had committed hari-kari. He was very old and feeble and had appeared before the prisoners only once when we had arrived in camp. His body was removed that night from the camp. The news was received by us as an indication that the war was over or nearly so. Our only comment was that it was too bad it wasn't that mean bastard Nakayama.

The following afternoon we were assembled outside in front of the barracks on a soggy turf. A brisk wind was clearing the dark clouds away rapidly, and we stood shivering and clinging to our scant clothing. Kinoshita stood slouched over with his hands folded tightly around his small waist. Standing next to him was the new Commandant, Lieutenant Naguchi. He was average size by Japanese standards, and his well-tailored khaki uniform fit him snugly. Middle-aged and fairly intelligent looking, he stood with his shoes anchored in the mud as Kinoshita began to speak.

"Give attention to me!" he shouted. "Lieutenant Naguchi has something very important to say to you. Please give close attention to him."

He nodded his head, whispered a word or two, and stepped aside.

Lieutenant Naguchi cleared his voice before beginning his speech. His address was brief and came in the usual Japanese style, short bursts in a high-pitched voice followed by silent pauses. There was a noticeable difference in the volume of his speech as he was much calmer than others who had addressed us. Kinoshita interpreted his address for us. The highlights of the talk were:

(1) The American people were honorable.
(2) We should take care of our health.
(3) The work we would do in the future would be for exercise.
(4) We shouldn't try to escape or do anything irrational that might be injurious to our return to our country.

At the conclusion of the speech there was a tremendous sigh of relief as we returned to our barracks. The harassment by the guards immediately stopped and the atmosphere of the camp became more relaxed. One more half day was spent at the mountain, and we spent the remainder of that afternoon resting in the barracks. The next few days we stayed inside the compound digging air-raid shelters, working some and then resting awhile. We finally received Red Cross beans and moldy hardtack. The beans had plenty of salt in them, which was something we received very seldom; the hardtack was either boiled or fried. There was no more tormenting by the Japanese guards.

Chapter 26

It was a brisk August morning, the 21st day of the month, when Sloane appeared at the top of the stairway. Instead of his usual frightened look, he appeared relaxed and even had a smile on his face. He took a few steps into the room and began shouting, "There will be no work today and everyone is to remain inside the barracks for further instructions."

"What's up, Emery?" I asked.

"I don't know. But Dr. Corey said the new Commandant has been very nice lately."

Sloane turned and started to his room when he quickly spun around and reported: "By the way, the Japanese authorities received a complaint from a Japanese woman outside our camp, who claims that someone in this camp has been stealing carrots out of her garden. Does anyone want to own up to it?"

The room became very quiet for a moment.

"Well, don't all speak at once!"

"We did," came a shout from the far corner of the room.

"Who's we?" Sloane asked.

"Willie Hawkins and Herman Schultz," was the response.

"Okay, I don't know what the repercussions will be, but I understand the Japanese woman insists upon being paid for her losses."

At 1:00 everyone was ordered outside on the parade ground for a speech from Lieutenant Naguchi. There wasn't the usual long waiting period; his appearance was prompt. Their new attitude made us suspicious and cautious.

Running in front of Lieutenant Naguchi was a guard carrying a rifle which was not fixed with a bayonet. Trailing behind the Commandant was Kinoshita and another guard. Dr. Corey stood in front of the anxious prisoners awaiting their arrival. His face was tense and his body rigid with his arms pressed against his sides.

The weather was beautiful — blue sky and a warm sun beat down on our small group of weary, half-starved prisoners. Several trails of chimney smoke rose from the village below, leaving the odor of burnt wood. The sound of airplanes and bombs exploding had ceased.

All eyes were fixed on Lieutenant Naguchi when he returned Dr. Corey's salute and positioned himself on a box squarely in front of us. His round, shiny, fat face showed no emotion as he looked out at us while waiting to be introduced by Kinoshita.

"Give attention to me!" Kinoshita shouted. "Lieutenant Naguchi has some very good news for the prisoners, so give close attention to him."

There was no longer a hateful expression in his face. He seemed to show humility. Dr. Corey stood calmly and attentively alongside Lieutenant Naguchi. Corey seemed to be smiling. The many years of service spent in the Orient had helped him to understand the Japanese mind.

Every single one of our skinny, bent-over bodies stiffened and straightened, our thin necks angling forward. Only our deep breathing could be heard when Lieutenant Naguchi cleared his throat and began his speech. He concluded with a silent smile, tipping his head before stepping down from the box. Kinoshita immediately stepped up on the box and began the interpretation.

"All nations have ceased fighting!" he shouted.

Before he could continue there was an uproar, some of us yelling while others broke down crying. Some fell to the ground; others jumped up and down flinging their arms wildly. Still others stood in silent shock. The Japanese guards were tense, their dark eyes fixed on the jubilant prisoners. Tears streamed down one guard's face as he stood motionless. No attempt was made by Dr. Corey to restrain us from expressing our feelings. This was something we had been waiting to hear for a long time, and many hadn't survived to hear it. Finally, we settled down to hear the rest of Lieutenant Naguchi's speech.

"An armistice has been reached between the nations at war, but peace negotiations have not been settled yet. Regarding the food situation, it will improve immediately, but don't expect too much because the transportation facilities are not good. The Japanese guards will remain here merely for your protection against the Japanese civilians. You will remain in this camp until arrangements can be made to move you out. How long that will be I cannot say.

"There is one other matter that I must mention before I turn the camp over to your senior officer, Dr. Corey. I appreciate the fact that two of your prisoners have admitted stealing carrots from the Japanese woman's garden near the camp. Also their willingness to give up their ration of rice as compensation. I thank them. However, that will not be necessary. I will personally see that she is reimbursed for her losses.

"In conclusion, take care of your health so that you may return to your country."

The yelling continued as Dr. Corey took control of the camp. He dismissed us immediately and went inside, where he dressed in his white uniform and saber for a meeting with Lieutenant Naguchi. The camp was no longer quiet, but filled with laughter and chatter. Even though we were still physically weak, we found the inner strength to celebrate as the yoke of slavery had been removed and we had become free men.

At 4:00 in the afternoon, Dr. Corey appeared before us on the parade field in his white naval uniform. Clean-shaven and immaculate, he proceeded quietly with his instructions.

"Effective immediately you will be under the U.S. Navy regulations and subject to their discipline. The four U.S. Army Sergeants in our group will comprise our military police. In order to prevent any more sickness in the camp and to maintain freedom among individuals, there will be a daily schedule so that you won't be spending all your time inside the barracks. Our relations with the Japanese are to be friendly."

He hesitated momentarily. Before he could continue one of the prisoners shouted, "How soon will we be leaving for home?"

"I think perhaps we could be detained here a month, so I can't stress enough the importance of keeping busy doing something while we remain here."

His pale, smooth face was calm as he spoke with concern for his fellow prisoners.

"There will be new hours for rising and going to bed," he continued. "No one is permitted to leave the camp without permission and an escort. All work will be on a voluntary basis. If you encounter any problems, I want to hear about them. That will be all for now. You are dismissed."

During the next few days our diet improved as details sent out of camp returned with potatoes, rice, beans, and cow intestines which stunk and were returned. We also received a live two-hundred-and thirty-one-pound pig, two cows, and a calf, which were all slaughtered inside the camp.

On 26 August 1945 the camp was visited by twenty U.S. Navy fighter planes around 9:00 in the morning. Several prisoners climbed up on the roof and waved at the pilots as they circled the narrow canyon. The planes first dropped messages attached to stringers informing us that within five minutes they would be dropping food parcels and that we would have to stand clear. After putting on a brief aerial show, they dropped four large canvas bags of K-rations, cigarettes, clothing, magazines, and recently dated newspapers. The drops were not sufficient to supply one hundred and ninety-six men, but each man got a taste of everything. We enjoyed most the chocolate candy and cigarettes.

Some of the Japanese guards entered our barracks to see what we received, their faces no longer scowling. Sanborn was stretched out on his bunk enjoying an American cigarette, when a guard stopped in front of him. He moved his head slowly as his dark eyes focused on an American magazine. He bent down, picked it up, and studied the colored cover for a moment before setting it back down and moving on.

"What was that all about?" asked Plunkett.

"I guess he's just curious to see what all we received from the planes. I'll tell you, Orval, it's a nice feeling not to have to jump every time one of those little yellow bastards comes around," Sanborn said.

His faded red cotton shirt was missing two buttons and the cuffs of his oversized trousers were rolled up above the tops of his unlaced shoes.

"Yeah, to be able to smoke whenever you damn please and wear your shoes inside the barracks is great. That looked like a different guard. Was he?" Plunkett asked as he kept staring at the guard who moved slowly down the hall.

"I understand that all the Japanese guards are new and that Nakayama has been removed from the camp," Sanborn continued and blew smoke rings up at the ceiling.

"Someone might have killed that mean son-of-a-bitch if he'd stayed around," Plunkett said.

The rich aroma of American tobacco filled the room and became heavy at times and increased the coughing, making it necessary to open all the windows. Many of us spent the afternoon lying on our bunks quietly, trying to realize that the war was over and that we were not just dreaming. The sudden transition from nearly four years of being humiliated and treated as slaves to freedom and dignity was hard to accept.

Shortly after breakfast the next day, four of the planes returned. The roar of their engines reverberated throughout the valley and brought everyone running outside. Dr. Corey shouted for the men to go back inside the barracks quickly before more supplies were dropped. The planes flew as close to the ground as possible before releasing twelve parcels. One struck the roof of our building and rolled off. Another went through the Japanese building, making a sizeable hole above the kitchen. Still another tore a large opening in our bathhouse roof. The remainder fell outside the compound on the mountainside. After the planes left, a detail of sixty men went out searching for the supplies. They were met outside by Murphy, who came running toward them in his shorts.

"Willie's been hit!" he screamed. "Someone get the doctor, hurry."

The men rushed to the bathhouse where Hawkins lay limp on the wet wooden floor. His mouth was bloody, his eyes glassy. Barefoot with pants on and shirt half buttoned, he appeared lifeless. Dr. Corey arrived immediately and began examining him. His face became sad as he rose to his feet.

"He's dead! He never knew what hit him. Will some of you men carry him to the hospital?" Dr. Corey asked, and he turned and walked out of the bathhouse with his head down.

"I was standing over there putting on my shorts and he was standing up buttoning up his shirt when there was this awful crashing sound. It all happened so quickly. The first thing I saw was the large hole in the roof. Then Willie sprawled out on the floor and that large canvas bag in the corner full of supplies." Murphy pointed his finger nervously about the room as he spoke with much excitement, his thin face pale and his frail body trembling.

Sloane stood shaken as he studied the crumpled body of Willie Hawkins. In the past there had been much animosity between the two men, which had nearly ended in several fist fights.

"Poor Willie. He looked forward to going home so much. It was a real struggle for him to stay alive. Now something like this has to happen," Sloane said, his bitterness toward Hawkins turning to sorrow as he followed the men carrying him to the hospital.

We were no longer rejoicing at the war's end but had become silent and remorseful about Hawkins' tragic death. He wasn't just another prisoner with a number but had been an inspiration to others who wanted to survive. Though sickly and addicted to tobacco, often trading his food ration for cigarettes, he was always optimistic about the future and managed to keep his wits and humor, challenging the rest of us to keep our chins up.

The sixty-man detail recovered all the bags of supplies that were dropped. They were again divided up equally. A note was found inside one of the bags which read, "From the boys of the USS *Bennington*. We hope this will ease your stay until you are on your way home."

The following afternoon, services were held outside for Hawkins. A plain pine box built by one of the prisoners contained his body. It was surrounded on three sides by a solemn group of men who stood quietly awaiting Forrest Hill. Standing next to Hill in full white naval uniform was Dr. Corey, whose eyes were glued on the casket. Behind them stood Lieutenant Naguchi and interpreter Kinoshita who had come to pay their respects. Directly behind them mounted on the corner of the barracks building was a small homemade American flag, which had been lowered to half-mast.

Only the distant drone of one of our airplanes on patrol could be heard above the sound of shuffling feet. The tall green pine trees that surrounded the camp stood against a background of puffy white clouds and rich blue sky. The preacher stood with his shoulders slightly slumped forward, his weather-beaten face full of sorrow for a man whom he had come to know well. Clearing his throat and taking a deep breath, he slowly began his sermon.

"We have gathered here this afternoon to pay our respects to one of our fellow countrymen," he said. "His death, like the many others, was a tragedy the way it happened. Willie was an inspiration to all of us who knew him. His courage and determination to survive was remarkable, considering his shrapnel wound and his poor health."

Hill paused momentarily to catch his breath. His tired, pale blue eyes were fixed on the pine box.

"I had gotten to know Willie rather well these past years," he continued. "Our close association day in and day out for nearly four years made it possible to know each other thoroughly. There was a point when there wasn't anything new to talk about. Everyone's personal history had been exhausted and the monotonous prison life afforded very little to discuss."

He took another deep breath, running his hand through his coarse gray hair.

"Willie came from a background of hardships, having lost his parents at the early age of ten by a car accident. His older brother raised him the best he could until Willie ran off to San Francisco to work around the docks at the age of sixteen. His only marriage ended in divorce, which caused him to drink to excess. His escape from this was Wake Island. The confinement by the Japanese had given him time to sort out his life and plan for a better future. More important, I believe he did accept the Lord as his personal Savior just recently. So he will be going home."

Hill took out his handkerchief and wiped his nose after gently drying his moist eyes.

"Let us pray. Our dear heavenly Father, bless our departed brother. We ask that You keep him and comfort him. Help us to understand the futility of war. Protect our lives as we await our journey home. Give us the strength and compassion to forgive our enemy. For we ask all these things in Thy precious name. Amen."

Hawkins' body was returned to the hospital until arrangements could be made for shipment home. Stunned by the tragedy, we milled around the camp most of that afternoon.

During the next few days some of us took short hikes outside of camp to a nearby river to swim, accompanied by two Japanese. We enjoyed our new freedom, but with it, the increase of food was beginning to create a sanitary problem as some of the men were becoming careless. Dr. Corey announced that there were several cases of diarrhea in camp and that it would be necessary for everyone to do his part in policing the grounds and killing flies. One prisoner, who refused to work, became sarcastic when Corey questioned him. He was placed in the guardhouse until the next day.

On 2 September 1945, I ate an early lunch and went with Joe Lattimore to take notes on a broadcast of the signing of the armistice. First, we stopped at one of the Japanese houses at the foot of the hill where we went inside and listened to the radio trying to get the 12:00 broadcast. The reception was so poor we heard nothing. We left with our Japanese escort at 1:00 for the mining office, where we waited near a radio for the 3:00 broadcast. While waiting inside the one-room shack, we heard the drone of an airplane around 2:00. We went outside in time to see a B-29 coming directly overhead at an altitude of about two thousand feet.

The weather was beautiful and the ship was even more beautiful! It circled around the valley two or three times, descending a little lower each time. Then it came directly over the mining village, where we were located, and opened its bomb bay, dropping its supplies, like a large whale opening its mouth. The first drop came out okay and parachutes of all colors opened up, appearing like large, colored balloons floating in the sky. Underneath the ship's wings on either side was written "POW Supplies" in large letters. The supplies landed on the side of the mountain and in the village several hundred yards away. One bundle splashed down in the center of the logging pond.

The silver B-29 glistened in the sunlight as it circled the village again. A second drop of supplies fell in the middle of the village with none of the parachutes opening. One bundle landed about twenty-five feet away from us as we ran from it, and one load of tobacco and matches landed in the stone canal and caught fire. Another hit on the edge of the canal and broke into pieces. Some bundles went through the roofs of houses, but no casualties were reported. Approximately five percent of the first supplies dropped were lost through damage, but nearly seventy-five percent of the second drop was destroyed.

At 3:00, we listened to the Japanese broadcast, which lasted about one-half hour. We waited until 4:00, hoping that we would hear an American interpretation, but that didn't happen. After we returned to camp, Kinoshita informed us that the final armistice was signed in Tokyo Bay aboard the USS *Missouri* at 9:08 that morning.

The whole camp turned out to gather the supplies and parachutes. After all the undamaged goods had been retrieved, the Japanese and Korean civilians were allowed their turn at the broken supplies. They descended on the scattered goods like vultures. They tasted everything including the toothpaste, shaving cream, and soap. The children became very excited, yelling at each new discovery.

Chapter 27

After several days of restlessness, I and three other prisoners got permission to leave camp and hike over the mountain ridge behind camp and down the back slope to the ocean on 8 September 1945. The weather was partly cloudy, but it appeared like there was a good chance it would be a clear day. Anticipating mild weather, we wore shorts and sweatshirts as we left the camp at 5:00 in the morning with a Japanese civilian guide.

Following a narrow, winding trail up the side of the mountain, we stopped frequently to rest and view the mountain valley below. Numerous trails of smoke filled the air and ponds dotted the valley cluttered with small wooden shacks scattered among the pine trees. It took us three hours to reach the summit. As we started down the back slope toward the ocean, there appeared to be two or three small farming communities stretching to the Bay of Amori. A light rain began to fall as we reached the main road which ran through one village. The dirt road took a sharp turn between the houses, and we suddenly came upon three young Japanese women with a two-wheel cart loaded with wares. They became very frightened, and they dropped everything and ran into a nearby house.

"Did you see the look on their faces when they saw us?" McCloud said. "They must think we're some kind of demons the way they left their cart full of merchandise — even that noisy chicken."

"They acted like they saw a ghost," Lattimore said, watching them disappear into a small house.

As we continued walking down the narrow road, the rain became heavier, and we encountered several Japanese. Civilian men either bowed or saluted; military personnel ignored us completely. Women and small children dressed in rags quickly moved off the road as we approached them. The fields surrounding the village were fully planted in row crops, meticulously cared for.

Walking a few strides ahead, our Japanese guide began motioning to us to walk a little faster. He was tall and slender and his loose-fitting khaki uniform was almost completely darkened from the rain. Water dripped from his small cap onto his high cheekbones that seemed to shine even under the overcast sky. Half smiling, he directed us off the main road onto a narrow path that led to a large shed near the bay. Crossing a railroad track, we ran the last hundred yards to the entrance, soaking wet.

Once inside we were greeted by an elderly Japanese gentleman, who built a small fire and gave us each a pickled cucumber and a raw egg. We all huddled around the fire, shifting from one position to another trying to get warm and dry our clothing. As soon as the chill was gone, we squatted on the dirt in front of the fire and began eating our K-rations, which we had brought from camp. Not having eaten an egg for nearly four years, my three companions quickly poked a hole in one end and started sucking. Watching them devour their eggs uncooked caused my stomach to turn, and I looked the other way. I was determined to get my egg cooked somehow as I held it carefully in my right hand. The elderly Japanese also brought us a small teapot full of hot water, which helped warm us. For an hour the heavy rains whipped against the tin roof, making thunderous crashing sounds.

Around 1:00 in the afternoon, the rains subsided. Our Japanese guide quickly conveyed to us in broken English and by waving his hands that it was time to go. We thanked the warehouse attendant for his hospitality as we departed and headed for the railroad tracks. But instead of crossing the tracks, our Japanese guide turned and began walking down them toward a small depot.

"Where in the hell is he taking us?" asked Burns, stroking his red beard, gently squeezing the rain out.

"I don't know. But we apparently are not going back the way we came," McCloud shouted, somewhat concerned.

The dark sky and the rain made it impossible to see the depot until we were almost there. The railway station was unoccupied and in complete shambles. Every window had been broken out, and glass was scattered everywhere. Once again our Japanese guide stopped long enough to give us instructions.

"You stay here," he said, pointing to a spot next to the tracks. His shiny face suddenly became serious."

While waiting for the train to arrive, eight U.S. Navy fighter planes flew by out over the bay. They looked beautiful and made us feel secure. The immediate surroundings had been bombed severely; only the plumbing remained visible in the rubble.

Lattimore had been pacing back and forth on the wet, smooth rails. After slipping off them several times, he stopped and stared down the tracks.

"I think the train must be coming," he said. "I can feel a vibration."

He moved to the center of the tracks and continued staring as we all gathered, waiting to see it. Shortly, the rails began to vibrate more as the train became visible, and we quickly moved back off the tracks. The passenger train slowly came to a stop in front of us, but no one departed. Our Japanese guide stepped aboard one of the coaches and began talking to the conductor. Following a brief conversation, he disembarked, handed us tickets, and motioned for us to go aboard. As we climbed on the coach and handed the tickets to the conductor, we noticed that our guide wasn't coming with us but stood back, waving to us.

We walked single-file down the narrow aisle looking for vacant seats as the train started moving. Staring at us from all quarters of the coach were the faces of sober Japanese officers in full uniform with sabers. They were apparently going home. Their round, fat faces showed no expression as the coach became very quiet. The interior of the car was very similar to ours. The over-stuffed seats on either side of the aisle were two across, arranged in groups of four facing each other.

Unable to find four vacant seats together, my three friends quickly sat down with one Japanese officer while I reluctantly had to sit with three others. Fear gripped me as I sat erect. The officers stared either straight ahead or out the window, their short stubby hands resting on their laps. Their lips were tightly drawn together, and the expressions on the faces of the two opposite me showed their anger and sadness. My hands were becoming moist, and I felt the mounting tension in the coach. Finally, after five minutes of complete silence, I decided to offer them an American cigarette.

"Tobacco," I whispered and cautiously extended the package of cigarettes toward them.

The two ignored me completely. The one next to me moved his eyes toward the pack of cigarettes but quickly looked the other way. However, before I took them back, he reached out and took one. He nodded his head slightly as he proceeded to look out the window, holding the cigarette loosely in his right hand. As I sat perfectly still, I wondered if our Japanese guide had deliberately put us aboard the train to frighten us. If that had been his intention, he succeeded. If there had been any conversation among the Japanese prior to our boarding, it ceased completely with our appearance.

The train began slowing down to make its first stop. My eyes were glued on the coach's exit hoping some of our passengers would get off so that we might all sit together. It wasn't until the fourth stop, however, that there were four vacant seats. The move relieved some of the tension, but we had no idea how long the train ride would be nor where it was taking us. The train followed the coastline, and we were able to see a sunken destroyer and several damaged storage tanks and buildings.

"I sure hope our Japanese guide told the conductor where to let us off,"

McCloud whispered, nervously cracking his knuckles, which drew a frantic look from Lattimore.

"I hope so, too," I said, still gently holding my raw egg in my right hand.

After each stop, we shared our coach with fewer occupants, which brought a sigh of relief. Following a very long hour-and-a-half ride, we arrived at Otoma station. The conductor waved to us to depart. You never saw four fellows so happy to get off a train!

The small station was swarming with Japanese soldiers waiting to board the train. They began moving from under the eaves of the building toward the coaches under the cover of umbrellas, newspapers, and magazines. Their stony faces showed signs of distress and bitterness. The rain had become heavy at times, and puddles surrounded the isolated depot.

The station master was expecting us. He spotted us as we stepped down out of the coach and waved us toward the rear of the depot. He had a dinky train hooked up to a small open car. We had traveled on this narrow-gauge track three months earlier when it took us to our Sendai camp. It had taken four hours for the three engines to haul approximately two hundred prisoners up the mountain, pulling several cars. So we expected at least a three-hour ride.

Climbing a slight enbankment behind the depot, we approached the small wooden boxcar.

"Look at the water in the bottom of that son-of-a-bitch," shouted Burns. "Hell, my clothes are still wet, and I'm chilled to the bone. I can't see us sitting in that water for the next three hours."

"I can't either," said McCloud, wiping the rain off his face with his handkerchief. "I wonder if we can't get something to cover us in the car."

"Yeah. Where do you suppose the engineer is?" Lattimore asked, glancing around toward the rear entrance of the station.

"He's probably inside where it's warm, drinking sake or tea," I said. I had hardly finished speaking when the rear door opened, and a short Japanese man dressed in a rain jacket and cap appeared.

He seemed to ignore us as he hurried toward the engine and stepped into the cab. We stood beside the open car and began shouting at him until we got his attention. The rain continued to pour. As he walked toward us, we indicated to him what we wanted with our hands. He shook his head and walked back to the depot. Shortly, he reappeared carrying a stick in one hand and a bucket in the other with a piece of canvas draped over his shoulder. He was smiling as he handed us these things, and we began immediately bailing out the water. We thanked him and stepped into the small wooden car. We sat down against the four sides and used the stick to prop the canvas up in the center. It kept the rain from coming down on us but didn't prevent water from dripping down the sides.

After a sharp blast from the whistle of the logging train, we were underway.

The wooden boxcar was so small that the four of us had to double up our legs to get inside. We traveled on the winding narrow-gauge track up the mountain in total darkness except for an occasional peek out from under the canvas. As the trip progressed, water accumulated in the bottom of the car and swished around constantly. The rythmic beat of the metal wheels against the narrow steel rails added to the sound of the intermittent rains that struck the canvas.

McCloud kept squirming, trying to get comfortable. Tall and slender, his head brushed against the canvas, causing the cold damp air to enter under the tarpaulin.

"If we all don't catch pneumonia it'll be a miracle. My clothes have been wet most of the day and we're sitting in water now," McCloud said, sneezing and sniffling.

"Yeah. We've got about three hours riding in this wet boxcar but after that hour-and-a-half ride with all those Japanese officers, this I can stand," Lattimore shouted as the rain whipped against the canvas, making it difficult to hear inside.

"Hell, I was so scared, I barely moved or looked around. The one time I did glance around, my eyes met a Jap officer staring at me. I held my breath for a moment," Burns said, his voice faltering as he spoke.

"I know what you mean. I sat directly across from one that stared right through me. My heart worked overtime pumping hot blood through my petrified body," I said, wrapping my arms around my knees and drawing them to me.

The long monotonous ride was partially broken up by song and laughter as we shivered in the darkness. There were the long slow uphill grades followed by bursts of downhill speed and sharp turns that caused the car to jerk from side to side. Finally, the engine began slowing down with the sound of sand under the wheels. The small engine came to a screeching halt, throwing us forward and causing the canvas to fall down upon us.

We quickly tossed the canvas to one side and stood up. Having sat in a cramped position for such a long time in the water, we had to massage our legs to get the charley horses out of them in order to get up. We slowly stepped out of the boxcar into the mud. After thanking the Japanese engineer, who nodded and smiled, we still had a good mile hike to the camp. The narrow path that led there from the end of the tracks was all uphill, and the hard rain continued. After a short time, our legs seemed to loosen up and we decided to run the rest of the way, but before too long, we tired and had to walk into camp.

It was getting late in the day as darkness started settling over the camp. All the prisoners had gone inside the two-story barracks, and some of the lights had been turned on. We headed straight for the camp bathhouse, which was located on the other side of the main building. We quietly opened the door and removed our wet clothing. The small wooden structure was comfortably warm inside. Trails of barely visible steam rose from the square wooden tank of water located in the center of the room. The water was electrically heated to somewhere between seventy-five and eighty degrees Fahrenheit. We knew that regulations had strictly forbidden anyone entering the tank, that we were required to stand on the outside of the tank and dip the water out with wooden ladles. But we were miserably cold and still shivering, and without hesitation, everyone rolled over the sides into the tank simultaneously.

The warm water immediately began removing the chills and cramps, and after soaking for about twenty minutes, we felt completely relaxed.

"I think we had better get the hell out of here before someone catches us," Lattimore said as his head popped out from under the water.

"Sounds like a good idea. What are we going to do about those wet clothes? I hate the thought of putting them on after getting nice and warm," Burns said, clinging with outstretched arms to the side of the tank.

McCloud stood up and made his way toward the side as the water struck him at his waist. He reached over the side and gathered up his clothing.

"Here's what I'm going to do about them," he shouted as he dropped them in the water. "At least they'll be warm when I put them on."

He began swishing his clothes around in the water for a while and then wrung them out. No one seemed to have a better idea, so that's what we all did.

We slipped into our warm, wet clothing and headed toward the barracks in a light, chilly rain on a slippery, muddy field.

"I don't know about you fellows, but I'm sure glad we made it back safely. Just the thought of riding in that coach with all those soldiers gives me the shakes," McCloud said and nearly fell as he lost his footing in the sticky mud.

"We will never know how lucky we really were," Lattimore said, shaking his head.

The following day was beautiful. One of the first things I did was build a small wooden fire outside and boil my egg. It was delicious!

Chapter 28

A formal flag-raising ceremony was held on 9 September 1945. We were all present as Dr. Corey led us in the pledge of allegiance to the American flag. The Marines raised the flag while the U.S. Navy prisoners stood in front near Dr. Corey, who was dressed in his white Navy uniform.

The ceremony was brief but very impressive. It brought back sad memories of when the Japanese took down the American flag on Wake Island and replaced it with theirs. That sight was like a nightmare and very difficult to adjust to. It had meant the end of any personal freedoms and the beginning of a future filled with doubt. We had immediately become the property of the Imperial Japanese who could do with us as they saw fit. They demanded more work on less food than was humanly possible, causing our physical and mental break-down. Their constant humiliation and degradation of us was accomplished with delight on their part. Ishahara on a few occasions had informed us that the Americans always made the Japanese feel like an inferior race and a secondary class of people. His bitterness turned into a personal vendetta against Americans, especially against our officers.

So standing in a distant land paying our respects to the American flag meant many things to prisoners of war, but most of all it meant that America hadn't forgotten its people. The American flag represented freedom, security, and a way of life found nowhere else in the world. We all stood taller and straighter on this day!

The sudden increase of food supplies from both the Japanese and our U.S. Navy pilots created an uncontrollable temptation to eat everything and anything until we were full. For a while our shriveled stomachs rejected most of the food, but later they stretched back to normal size. The unsuitable foods settled in our stomachs, causing them to protrude noticeably. The rest of our bodies, however, did not develop, and consequently, everyone had flat chests, thin arms, spindly legs, and bony shoulders. After such a long period on a starvation diet, with very little salt and no sugar, our sudden transition to a proper diet must have had serious effects on our bodies.

The day finally came to leave the Sendai camp on 12 September 1945, a day that brought cheers and laughter to our small isolated group of prisoners. Two meals were served that day, and rice was cooked for those who wished to take it with them on their way down the mountain. No one took any. Everyone traveled as lightly as possible.

We assembled below the camp at the narrow-gauge tracks at 5:00 in the evening. The logging trains were waiting for us with several small open boxcars. There was a large group of Japanese on hand to greet us. They had mounted a loudspeaker on a post which blared out "Auld Lang Syne." They were waving goodbye to us with big smiles.

Schultz stood in one of the cars glowering at the cheering bunch of Japanese. He was furious. A gentle breeze ruffled his thin silky hair. His beardless, fleshy face was ashen. It took him a moment to control his emotions before he could speak. His body trembled as he gritted his teeth.

"Look at those yellow bastards smiling at us. They want to be our friends now. Yesterday they were working and starving us to death. Today they want to be buddy-buddy. I can't forgive the son-of-a-bitches for the way they treated us," he stammered, spitting at them vehemently, his body swaying back and forth as he shook a clenched fist at them.

Standing in the same car next to Schultz, Plunkett firmly covered his ears with both hands. He was suffering from a hangover from the night before. The Japanese had brought several bottles of sake for the prisoners and Plunkett had acted as though he were back home in the hills of Kentucky drinking moonshine. During the course of the evening, he sang folk songs and danced until he passed out.

"What in the hell are they smiling about?" Plunkett asked as he removed his hands from his ears momentarily. The loud music caused him to flinch.

Schultz shifted his large bony body around to face Plunkett and glanced over the top of his small eyeglasses that rested halfway down his thick nose. Schultz was still trembling as the cars began slowly moving down the mountain.

"The heathen bastards want to be our friends now. Hey, look, there's that son-of-a-bitch that ran screaming to the Japs every time we stopped working," Schultz shouted as he pointed a finger toward the cheering crowd.

"Where?" asked Plunkett.

"To the right of the group, leaning up against that small pine tree. He's the one wearing a bright red shirt and waving a white straw hat. He's also got a big mouth and buckteeth," Schultz said, continuing to point his finger at him as he stammered on furiously.

"Oh, yeah, I see him now. He squealed on me and I got a hell of a beatin' at the mine one day. He also was around begging for food that we received from the planes. It's a wonder someone didn't beat the hell out of him," Plunkett said, cringing and shuddering as he spoke.

The crowd soon disappeared from view as the long string of cars picked up speed and rounded a curve that followed a swift stream. Occupying the first open car was Dr. Corey and the wooden casket containing the body of Hawkins. A small homemade American flag had been securely fastened across the top of the casket. Dr. Corey sat quietly, looking straight ahead with one hand grasping his military cap to keep the wind from blowing it off.

Gripping the sides of the wood-framed cars, we quietly contemplated our return home. Would there be any changes? For some there might be. Several had been notified by mail that their wives were leaving them; others had members of their family die. Many expressed a desire to do nothing but try to regain their health for the first few months. But just being lucky enough to get back alive was enough for most of us.

Halfway down the mountain the train came to an abrupt stop. Dr. Corey got out of his car to see what the problem was and informed us shortly that one of the engines had developed some mechanical trouble.

"How long will it take to fix it?" someone shouted.

A smile appeared on his clean-shaven face as he shouted in disgust, "They indicated to me that it wouldn't take too long. So don't wander off too far."

We all stepped out of the cars to stretch our legs, and a few slid down an embankment to the river. The river bed was surrounded with different sizes of bleached rocks and was fenced in with thick, green vegetation made lush by the frequent rains. Some stretched out on all fours to drink from the swift-moving water. Thick with pines and ferns, the mountains were beautiful and serene.

Gates stood next to the railroad tracks, throwing rocks into the river below. Tall and slender, he was beginning to develop a potbelly which hung over his trousers and showed under his loose-hanging shirttail. He casually looped rocks into the air side-arm. His pessimistic attitude about our chances to survive captivity had been a constant source of depression to us. We avoided him whenever we could.

Sanborn stood a few yards behind Gates, watching the rocks splash into the river. He began moving toward him, and the crunching sound of rocks under his heavy foot caused Gates to stop and turn around momentarily.

"How you feeling, Cleo?" asked Sanborn, but there was no response, and he moved a little closer to look into Gates' unhappy face.

"Aren't you happy about going home?" Sanborn asked.

"Yeah. But I'll feel better when I have both feet planted on American soil. Anything can happen between now and then," Gates said, continuing to pick up rocks and toss them into the river.

"I don't think anything is going to happen to us now, Cleo," Sanborn said shaking his head in disgust.

"You never know."

"I'll say one thing for you, Cleo, you've been consistently negative. I'm surprised you didn't do what Lacey Adams did," Sanborn shouted, rather upset with him.

"What do you mean by that remark?" Gates asked, dropping the rocks in his hands and appearing startled by his comment.

"Lacey apparently didn't think we would ever survive either; only he refused to eat and died of starvation after twenty-five days in camp," Sanborn said, his husky voice faltering at times, but remaining forceful.

"I would never have done that, even though I didn't think we would ever get out. But there were times when I felt like giving up," Gates snapped back.

"Who didn't?"

Plunkett had stumbled down to the river and had submerged his head into the clear, sparkling water to get some relief from his hangover. Others milled around the engine watching the Japanese work on it.

"Do you think they know what they're doing?" Dawson asked, half smiling, and he brushed his stringy red hair back away from his forehead.

"I don't know. They sure don't act like it. They've taken one part off and put it back on three times," Lattimore said.

"Yeah. I'd like to get the hell out of here and as far away from these people as possible," Dawson shouted as he turned and headed for the string of vacant cars.

Dr. William Corey stood up in his car and shouted for everyone to climb aboard after nearly two hours had passed. As the logging train traveled down the mountain there was a mixture of laughter, conversation, and silence. Some prisoners were extremely bitter and hateful toward the Japanese while others were tolerant and willing to let time heal the scars of their experience.

We finally arrived at Otoma station at 10:00 at night, where there were three third-class coaches waiting to take us on the next leg of our journey home.

Chapter 29

We were hurried aboard the waiting coaches in total darkness. The atmosphere was much more relaxed than it had been three months earlier when we had arrived at Otoma station under heavy Japanese guard. This time we traveled swiftly through the night, arriving at the port of Shiogamo Wan around 11:30 the next morning, 13 September. We left the train immediately, boarded American trucks, and were taken to a landing boat approximately one mile away from the railway station. We saw American and British sailors at this time, as well as three good-looking American servicewomen, who received loud, boisterous cheers from us. Before going aboard an LST and being taken out to the hospital ship *Rescue*, we had to discard everything except the clothing we wore and a few personal things. On the *Rescue*, after being deloused and taking a hot shower, we were given clean underwear, socks, and coveralls.

Later in the afternoon, the American sailors threw our discarded clothes overboard, and the Japanese civilians came alongside in small wooden boats to pick them up. American sailors operating small landing boats would head their craft toward them at high speeds, turning sharply in front of them, causing their small boats to almost overturn. The sailors on board the *Rescue* turned their fire hoses on them.

We were examined by a medical officer and given an identification card indicating malnutrition. We were interviewed by the U.S. Navy, at which time we were asked our name, rank, type of work we did, general health, etc. A small group of us were taken off the ship around 9:00 at night and were transferred by a small landing launch to the destroyer USS *Arunel*. The crew of the destroyer fed us our first American meal, which was delicious and included ice cream — the first that we had tasted in forty-four months. We spent the night aboard the *Arunel* and had our first real American breakfast before leaving the ship around mid-morning.

We were placed aboard a new troop transport, the USS *Sherard,* on 14 September. The ship left port at 6:00 that evening for the Bay of Yokohama and arrived there around 6:00 the next morning. Our Third Fleet was there as well as some British ships, including the battleship *George V*. This was a magnificent sight and more ships than we had ever seen at one time. We were once again transferred to another ship, the USS *Hyde,* at 8:00 in the evening. We spent two nights and one day aboard the *Hyde*, where we mingled with other prisoners who were from other camps in Japan. Besides eating regularly and increasing the size of our stomachs, we saw a musical entitled *Sing Your Troubles Away*.

On 17 September 1945, before breakfast, we left the USS *Hyde* on a LST for an airfield some four miles away. There thirty-five of us boarded a C-54 for Guam. As the plane lifted off and circled the Bay of Yokohama, I had an emotional feeling inside that made my whole body tingle. For the first time I had left their soil and their physical presence, but my recollection of my Japanese captors still remained vivid. It would take time to recover emotionally and physically from our experience. This new freedom was happening so fast that it all seemed like a dream, but each new morning made it seem more real!

The C-54 flew at an altitude of nine thousand feet and cruised at two hundred miles per hour. The flight was smooth, except for hitting an air pocket now and then. We were permitted to walk around the plane, and the crew fed us sandwiches, fruit juices, coffee, and candy. The weather was beautiful as we flew above a layer of puffy white clouds, which broke up occasionally, permitting us to view a deep blue ocean with white caps. Prior to arriving at Guam at 8:45 that night, we saw a gorgeous sunset. After enjoying the sunset for quite a while, one of the prisoners said, "We must be in heaven, 'cause we just left hell behind us."

The island of Guam sparkled with lights as we came in for the landing. Red Cross girls greeted us at the airfield with coffee and donuts. We were immediately taken by bus to the U.S. Navy hospital and checked in. The barracks beds, with clean white sheets and pillows, felt wonderful, but the excitement of being free men and getting closer to home made it very difficult to sleep.

We remained on Guam for ten days, during which time we were given a complete physical examination. One day while waiting for transportation to the States, I decided to see the island by myself. Early one morning I started off hitch-hiking down the road. The countryside was lush and green with vegetation due to an abundance of yearly rainfall. The natives that I met as I traveled around a part of the two-hundred-ten-square-mile island were very friendly. A coral reef surrounded the coastline, and a plateau ranging from two hundred to five hundred feet made up the northern half of the island, while the southern portion was mountainous. Toward the end of the day, I got lost and had to inquire at several places to get the directions back to the hospital. I arrived there at 11:00 at night somewhat tired, but satisfied by the experience.

There was much disappointment among us when we were informed that we would be leaving Guam on 27 September by boat. Everyone had hoped that the remainder of the trip home would be by plane. The vessel was a small auxiliary hospital ship carrying a few Seabees home. It left Guam crowded with prisoners and other personnel. After the nice plane ride from Yokohama Bay to Guam, this part of the trip home was miserable. I spent the first five days seasick in the hot hold of the ship in a hammock, unable to eat. I had the good fortune of running into a hometown friend, Phil Babcock, who got ice cream for me from the canteen on numerous occasions, which was great.

We arrived in Honolulu on the morning of 5 October and remained there until 4:00 in the afternoon. All of us were permitted to send cablegrams home via the Red Cross. We finally reached San Francisco on 11 October, around 7:00 in the morning.

The weather was beautiful, some wind but very little fog. A blue sky was dotted with small puffy clouds. The Golden Gate Bridge seemed cleansed by the morning sun as we passed under it. There was much emotion on the faces of the ex-prisoners of war as they gathered on the deck of the ship, searching the picturesque shoreline, which they had left four years earlier. After returning from a long period of confinement in areas of China that were dreary and desolate, seeing San Francisco with its array of colors, buildings, neon signs, cars, etc. was as if someone had taken the dirty mirror we had grown used to looking into and wiped it clean!

We were fortunate to be coming home, for there were many who had died from the lack of food and the physical hardships of slave labor. Among those of us returning, many would continue to suffer from malnutrition and other diseases. From the time we were liberated from the Japanese until we arrived home, we couldn't recall ever being restricted to the type and quantity of food we received, which seemed very strange to us considering our poor health.

A blaring band along with a huge crowd of friends and relatives greeted us at the dock. There was much confusion and excitement aboard the ship as preparations were made to discharge us. There was a constant shifting of the men on the ship as they tried to locate a family member or friend. When they did, there was an outburst of joy and spontaneous waving of the arms.

While strolling past the ship's store, a young sailor shouted at me.

"Hey, where the hell you going?"

He was tall and slender and his tight uniform fit him like a glove. He stood staring at me, waiting for a response.

"I'm looking for some of my family who might be here to meet me," I said, looking directly at him.

I turned and started to walk away when I was grabbed by the arm and swung around.

"For gosh sakes man, I'm your brother. Don't you even recognize me?" he yelled.

Still puzzled, I just stared at him for a moment.

"Oh, for heaven's sake," I finally said, regaining my composure. "You've changed a lot. You're thinner and taller. And you joined the Navy."

We shook hands and embraced. Jerry had been short and chunky at the age of twelve and thirteen when I last saw him.

"I joined the Navy right out of high school," he said.

"Did the folks come up?" I asked.

"Yes, they're all over at Roland's waiting for you," Jerry said.

We left the ship together and walked down one of San Francisco's busiest sidewalks toward his car. There were many things to talk about. We found ourselves asking each other questions faster than we could answer them. Between our own excitement upon seeing each other and the screeching sound of automobile brakes and horns, we found ourselves shouting to be heard.

The multicolored storefronts stocked with a variety of merchandise was a sight for my sore eyes. As we approached the corner drugstore Jerry stopped.

"What are we stopping for?" I asked.

"Come on, let's go in and I'll buy you lunch," Jerry said.

Suddenly a strange feeling came over me. It was a frightening sensation. I peered into the crowded drugstore.

"I don't think I could talk in there and sit at the counter and eat something," I said.

"Why not?"

"I'm still a bit nervous," I said. "I think it's going to take time before I adjust to this life again. Hell, man, I just got off the boat after coming out of nearly four years of seeing nothing but a vast, barren land of destitute people."

My hands were becoming moist as I rubbed them on my trousers.

"How about if I got a booth for us? Would that make it any easier?" Jerry said.

"Okay," I said, after hesitating a few moments and looking through the window at all those well-dressed people. I was still wearing a pair of coveralls and carrying a small satchel containing my personal effects.

We squeezed through the crowded entrance and found an empty booth. We each had hamburgers and french fries, which tasted delicious, but I found it very difficult to sit there for long. I couldn't get out of there soon enough and was quite relieved to be in Jerry's car heading for Uncle Roland's house to meet the family.

Our family was very close. When I was growing up, we did many things together. Many of my relatives lived in the same town. This was fine until someone died or went away. Then it was much harder to accept reality. Needless to say my reunion with my parents and relatives was joyful, and there was much sobbing — but it was certainly a most happy and memorable day!

The next two to three years were filled with nightmares, which persisted. They were vivid, usually ending with me waking startled in a cold sweat. They became so real that only after going to the bathroom to wash my face with cold water did I realize that it had only been a bad dream and that I no longer was a prisoner of war. Many times my wife, Jean, would wake me when I would begin to scream.

The prison camp portrayed in my dreams was not like those in China or Japan; it was located about a mile down the street from where I had lived with my parents. It was a campus for Native American children who came from out of state during the winter months to be educated and returned to their reservations during the summer months. It was called Sherman Institute and could accommodate one thousand students easily in the many old red-brick buildings. The grounds were landscaped with palm trees, and a large lawn dominated the front entrance. In my dream, the Japanese had overrun the area and gained control of the school, where they interned prisoners after enclosing the entire campus with barbed wire.

Only the passing of time diminished the intensity of these nightmares. But my memory of the experience is vivid.

Epilogue

The courtroom of the Ward Road Jail in Shanghai, China, was the setting for the trial of the *United States of America vs. Ishahara*. His arraignment was held on 7 February 1946 for the mistreatment and torture of American prisoners of war.

The trial began on 4 March 1946 at 9:20 a.m. before a five-man military commission, and two American defense officers were appointed to defend him. He was dressed in a dark suit and tie. He sat between his two attorneys calmly waiting for the trial to begin, erect and silent in his chair, listening to the seven different charges being read against him. He showed no emotion as his dark eyes focused on the gentlemen presenting them.

Afterwards he was asked how he pleaded to each of the charges and he responded to each, "Not guilty," showing no signs of remorse.

Then the prosecutor proceeded to use the thirty-nine affidavits of the prisoners of war who were familiar with the charges to build the case against Ishahara.

The defense attempted to have the affidavits thrown out on the grounds that they did not provide counsel an opportunity to cross-examine the witnesses. The commission overruled their objections. Defense pointed out that the affidavits were taken so soon after the war that the prisoners could not be objective. The defense also stated that there was a tendency on the part of some of the prisoners to exaggerate the tortures they received.

During the course of the trial, which lasted three days, the prosecution presented three witnesses who were serving at the same prisoner-of-war camps as the accused. Only Colonel Odera's testimony proved interesting enough to note.

He was the first to appear and had served as the Commander of the Camp. Neatly dressed, he, too, sat calmly and relaxed. During his tenure at the prisoner-of-war camp, he had looked like a Kentucky colonel with his handlebar mustache and polished boots. He pretty much had stayed in the background while the others ran the camp, making occasional appearances and speeches. Here is an excerpt from his testimony:

Prosecution: Did you establish a policy relative to the treatment of the prisoners of war?

Colonel Odera: Yes.

Prosecution: What was that policy?

Colonel Odera: I will relate the regulations regarding the handling of prisoners of war in prisoner of war camps. The duty of the personnel of prisoner of war camps is as follows: When a prisoner gives up his weapons and surrenders . . . he is taken to a prisoner of war camp. He is not to be considered as an enemy but an ordinary prisoner who must be protected and held and at the termination of warfare when peace is declared they are [sic] to be returned to their home country. Also it is indicated that it is important that the prisoners be treated so that they will be happy and that even in work they will have interests that they should not be made unhappy in any way. Also work and other assignments will be made to the prisoners in accordance with his ability, skill and physical stamina. This will improve the morale of the prisoners. In accordance with the law of Hirohito of Japan, the prisoner should be treated as subordinates and not as enemies or blood enemies to be treated with revengeful attitudes. That should not be violated in any manner.

The security troops or the guards were instructed at all times that they were to observe the prisoners at a distance and those that supervise the prisoners in their work and other matters were to keep a distance. They were not to lay hands on the prisoner in violence. While doing their work or exercising the guards were to hold their weapons at port arms or any direction away from the prisoners. They were not to make thrusts at the prisoners, and so forth, and thereby let the prisoner be free of fear of the guards. This instruction was given to the guards every time they changed the guards.

When a prisoner commits a crime or violates any of the regulations, the Commander of the prisoner of war camp has the authority to punish the prisoner in accordance with regulations accepted by law and also in accordance with regulations of the Japanese Army. No other person has the authority to punish the prisoner personally. Any punishment can be given to the prisoner by either the Camp Commander or he might delegate somebody else to do so.

Also at that time it was impressed upon the personnel that they were to help improve the condition of the prisoner in regard to preparations, clothing, shelter and so forth and besides the aforementioned, it is always been mentioned to the personnel and the prisoners that the prisoner will live in a prisoner of war camp without fear.

I think that looking over the record of three years it appears that the members of the prisoner of war camp, that is, the Japanese, have carried out the instructions and the regulations as set forth for the camp by the Commander.

Prosecution: Did you ever personally advise Ishahara of your policy and regulations forbidding mistreatment of prisoners of war?

Colonel Odera: I believe that Ishahara heard about it many different times and that I believe he understood my instructions.

Prosecution: Did you ever advise him personally?

Colonel Odera: Yes.

Prosecution: Did you hear that Ishahara mistreated the prisoners by making them drink water?

Colonel Odera: Yes, I heard about it so immediately I told him it was not right and I made him stop.

Prosecution: Did you take any action subsequently — disciplinary action against Ishahara?

Colonel Odera: After gathering the officers, we discussed and we considered dismissing Ishahara from the prisoner of war camp as an employee.

Prosecution: Did you take any steps to effect that dismissal?

Colonel Odera: Since we realized that after what Ishahara had done to the prisoners the relationship would be very bad and therefore we considered relieving him of his duties here. However, he being an excellent interpreter and one of the older personnel of the prisoner of war camp, it was difficult to replace him. Also he wanted to go back to Tokyo where he had a home and it was considered. However with the usual difficulty in obtaining a replacement or another interpreter, it was forgotten about later on. Ishahara resigned from work in the prisoner of war camp in January 1945.

At this time defense was permitted to cross-examine the witness.

Defense: Well, how many times did you speak to him about beating the prisoners?

Colonel Odera: I haven't seen Ishahara beat the prisoners and so forth and therefore I didn't talk to Ishahara about beating the prisoners.

Defense: But you had reports, didn't you, about him beating prisoners?

Colonel Odera: While he was there only once did I receive a report and that was concerning Ishahara's feeding of water to the prisoners and that time I stopped it.

Defense: But on the times that he came to your office before that, why did you speak to him and tell him not to beat the prisoners?

Colonel Odera: Until then I had not heard of Ishahara beating the prisoners or violating the prisoners, therefore there is no reason why I should have spoken to him about beating the prisoners or violating the prisoners.

Defense: What was the physical appearance of these men when they came before you for punishment?

Colonel Odera: There was nothing different in them.

Defense: Weren't they — didn't they appear to have been severely beaten?

Colonel Odera: No.

An affidavit was taken from Ishahara in Shanghai, China on 12 and 13 December 1945. Excerpts from his statement were the following:

I served at Woosung and Kiangwan prisons from May 6, 1942 to January 31, 1945 as a civilian interpreter. It was the official position of

Odera and Endo that there be no mistreatment of prisoner of war. I had a bad temper and did mistreat them but those acts were my own and Odera and Endo were in no way responsible for them. It came to their attention that I was mistreating prisoners and they told me not to do so and Lt. Miyasaki likewise has told me the same on one or two occasions.

I didn't want to use the water treatment because it is cruel, so first I only slapped them. Then if that didn't suffice, I used the riding crop and beat them on the body. Only if they wouldn't tell the truth after such beating did I use the water. Lt. Miyasaki was there that third night and I think he was there one other night. He had the power and authority to order me to stop but he was new and young and he knew I hated Japanese officers, so he was afraid to order me to stop.

After Ishahara's statement was read to the court the prosecution and the defense proceeded to examine him on all the charges brought against him. He admitted committing them but denied the extent and manner described in each charge.

At this time Ishahara was cross-examined by the Commission.

The Commission: What was the reason for your leaving the camp in 1945?

Ishahara: I'd like to thank you for the question because I'd like to explain that. Yesterday Colonel Odera explained I will not except anything. What he said it is all true, but one thing, the reason of my resignation. I tried in my camp to resign three times. It was right after I came to the camp and I understand my treatment from the Japanese Army. I tried to resign, then to Colonel Odera I tried two times. The first time is connected with the general affair of the war prisoners. One of the sergeants was taking care of the Red Cross supplies from Shanghai International Red Cross and also from the American Red Cross. But this man was wounded in battle, in the head, and he thought so easily and continued to do his duties properly so there were many supplies from the prisoners to me. Better change this man in camp. Not only that, this sergeant was a pet of Endo because both belonged to the same regiment so Captain Endo never changed him. But one day I found out that this sergeant traded himself with the prisoners of war and he brought two golden watches from the prisoners of war and he paid for that with money and with cigarettes. So I thought this is absolutely spoil the discipline among the Japanese soldiers and how he can control the prisoners of war when we ourselves do breaking the regulations. So if I tell to Captain Endo, the camp manager, I know I can do nothing so I write a letter of resignation to Colonel Odera and I went to his room and this time I succeeded. I got scolded by the officer but I succeeded to change the sergeant and Sergeant Matsawa changed with him and he speaks English and he understands English so after that the distribution of Red Cross parcels went perfectly and never a bit of complaint from the prisoners of war.

The second time Ishahara tried to resign was over his dispute with the Japanese engineers on how the rifle range should be constructed and its use by the Japanese 13th Army.

The Commission: And did Colonel Odera accept your resignation at his time?

Ishahara: He accepted it. This point I am very glad you questioned me. I wanted to correct it, for my honor.

On 7 March 1946 at three o'clock in the afternoon Ishahara appeared before the Commission to receive his sentence. He stood with arms extended the length of his slender body, slightly stoop-shouldered, showing no emotion as he awaited the verdict.

The sentence of hard labor for life was read to him. Unflinchingly, he casually remarked, "I accept my fate. However, I think the sentence is too severe."

He died after serving five years.

Index

Compiled by Lori L. Daniel